Acclaim for Radclyffe's Fiction

Lammy winner "...*Stolen Moments* is a collection of steamy stories about women who just couldn't wait. It's sex when desire overrides reason, and it's incredibly hot!" – *On Our Backs*

Lammy winner "...*Distant Shores, Silent Thunder* weaves an intricate tapestry about passion and commitment between lovers. The story explores the fragile nature of trust and the sanctuary provided by loving relationships." – *Sapphic Reader*

Shield of Justice is a "...well-plotted...lovely romance...I couldn't turn the pages fast enough!" – Ann Bannon, author of *The Beebo Brinker Chronicles*

A Matter of Trust is a "...sexy, powerful love story filled with angst, discovery and passion that captures the uncertainty of first love and its discovery." – *Just About Write*

"The author's brisk mix of political intrigue, fast-paced action, and frequent interludes of lesbian sex and love...in *Honor Reclaimed*...sure does make for great escapist reading." – *Q Syndicate*

Lammy Finalist *Justice Served* delivers a "...crisply written, fast-paced story with twists and turns and keeps us guessing until the final explosive ending." – *Independent Gay Writer*

By the Author

Romances

Innocent Hearts

Love's Melody Lost

Love's Tender Warriors

Tomorrow's Promise

Passion's Bright Fury

Love's Masquerade

shadowland

Fated Love

Turn Back Time

Promising Hearts

When Dreams Tremble

The Lonely Hearts Club

Night Call

The Provincetown Tales

Safe Harbor

Beyond the Breakwater

Distant Shores, Silent Thunder

Storms of Change

Winds of Fortune

Honor Series

Above All, Honor

Honor Bound

Love & Honor

Honor Guards

Honor Reclaimed

Honor Under Siege

Word of Honor

Justice Series

A Matter of Trust (prequel)

Shield of Justice

In Pursuit of Justice

Justice in the Shadows

Justice Served

Justice for All

Erotic Interludes: *Change Of Pace*
(A Short Story Collection)
Radical Encounters
(An Erotic Short Story Collection)

Stacia Seaman and Radclyffe, eds.:
Erotic Interludes 2: *Stolen Moments*
Erotic Interludes 3: *Lessons in Love*
Erotic Interludes 4: *Extreme Passions*
Erotic Interludes 5: *Road Games*
Romantic Interludes 1: *Discovery*

Visit us at www.boldstrokesbooks.com

JUSTICE
FOR ALL

by

RADCLYffE

2009

JUSTICE FOR ALL
© 2009 By Radclyffe. All Rights Reserved.

ISBN 10: 1-60282-074-0
ISBN 13: 978-1-60282-074-6

This Trade Paperback Original Is Published By
Bold Strokes Books, Inc.
P.O. Box 249
Valley Falls, NY 12185

First Edition: April 2009

Credits
Editors: Jennifer Knight, Ruth Sternglantz, and Stacia Seaman
Production Design: Stacia Seaman
Cover Design By Sheri (graphicartist2020@hotmail.com)

Acknowledgments

This book belongs to all the readers who asked for this series to continue and who have supported and encouraged me in its creation. My deepest gratitude.

Many thanks to first readers Connie, Diane, Eva, Paula, RB, and Tina, and to Jennifer Knight, Ruth Sternglantz, and Stacia Seaman for outstanding editorial guidance. Congratulations to Sheri for reading my mind on cover design yet again.

And to Lee, for always wanting another story. *Amo te.*

Radclyffe 2009

Dedication

For Lee
All Ways

PROLOGUE

Tell me again, Vincent, how it is that in six months I've lost a third of my income."

Before the visibly sweating man standing in front of his desk could reply, Kratos Zamora swiveled his leather desk chair to face the floor-to-ceiling plate glass windows. His office on the twenty-fifth floor of the high-rise he owned in Center City commanded a view from downtown Philadelphia across the Delaware River into southern New Jersey. The panorama was book-ended by the Benjamin Franklin Bridge to the north and the Walt Whitman to the south. The Port of Philadelphia stretched off to his right and, as the silent seconds passed, he contemplated a cargo ship lumbering up to the pier loaded with twenty-by-forty-foot containers stacked ten high. Some of those carried his legitimate products, and others should have carried his far more lucrative merchandise. And there was his problem.

Squinting slightly in the late afternoon sun, he continued in a conversational tone as if reading from a grocery list. "Seventy-five percent of the online entertainment revenues and over half of the escort service's have dried up. And now," he paused to spin back around, "you're telling me our direct line to City Hall has disappeared. Did I hear that right?"

"Not exactly disappeared," the big man in the ill-fitting suit answered diffidently. "More like…dead."

Kratos winced inwardly, because even though his offices were routinely swept for surveillance devices at the start of every eight-hour shift, he still avoided discussing business indoors. He'd rather take his chances outside where traffic noise and physical obstacles made long-range audio surveillance problematic. However, most of his men had grown up in a different era and were slow to retrain. He had inherited the business from his father only five years before, at the age of thirty-two, even though his older brother Gregor was the first son. Gregor had his talents, but they tended to be of the physical variety. Kratos had earned his MBA at Wharton and their father, in a break with tradition, had named him heir to Zamora Enterprises. Surprisingly, Gregor hadn't objected and now served as Kratos's security chief. Many people assumed Gregor headed the family and Kratos was content to let the fallacy go unchallenged. There were advantages to being seen as a legitimate businessman. In fact, he considered himself a modern entrepreneur, even if on occasion he employed methods that were never covered in his curriculum at the University of Pennsylvania. A flexible approach was necessary in order to secure his goals.

"You didn't answer my original question," he prodded gently. He knew the answer, of course, but in lieu of killing the messenger, he would merely make him suffer. Crossing his knees and casually flicking a nonexistent wrinkle out of the leg of his charcoal gray blended-silk trousers, he regarded Vincent Costa with a bland expression.

Vincent, one of his more trusted captains, folded his hands over his crotch and stared into space. "There's this new unit...the High Profile—"

"Yes, I'm aware of it." Kratos glanced at the single sheet of paper in the center of his desk.

A list of names and nothing else was typed down the left-hand side: Detective Lieut. Rebecca Frye, Detective First William Watts, Detective Third Dellon Mitchell, JT Sloan, and Jason McBride. The High Profile Crimes Unit. An odd assortment of local law enforcement and civilian consultants first formed to break an Internet pornography ring that used underage models. That online entertainment operation just happened to be neatly folded into one of Zamora Enterprise's subsidiary corporations, and its loss had been costly. Only days ago, this crime unit had intercepted a delivery of young girls destined to become stars in high-demand pornography films as well as call girls for an exclusive escort service also run by Zamora Enterprises.

"What I don't understand is how they've managed to do in a few months what an entire police force hasn't been capable of in two decades."

"I don't know, boss."

"Guess, Vincent." Kratos needed men like Vincent, men who were close to the street, far closer to the blood and the grime than he had ever been. While he was welcome at $10,000-a-plate benefit dinners and luncheoned frequently with the mayor, he had never personally pulled the trigger on an enemy. He'd never walked the mean streets except as a boy under his father's protection. He wasn't bothered by the fact there were things his men could do better than he, as long as he was certain that they never knew it.

"It's the computers," Vincent said, blinking as a trickle of sweat settled in the corner of his eye.

Interested, Kratos sat forward and clasped his hands in the center of his desk on top of the offending list. The sunlight glinted off the heavy gold signet ring he wore on the small finger of his right hand. The edge of his pristine white cuff covered a portion of the list, so all he could see was the name Rebecca. "What do you mean?"

"It's not like the old days, you know? Used to be cops were out on the streets, listening to the chatter and squeezing their snitches to find out what was going on. Hell, now they can follow you with that little chip thing in your cell phone. They don't even have to get out of their car."

"Are you saying our electronic security is a problem?"

Vincent lowered his gaze to meet Kratos's. "Couldn't hurt beefing it up, but that's not gonna stop them. They fingered our inside man at City Hall pretty fast, and they pulled in all the midlevel porn distributors by tracking them through their computers. They're good, boss."

"We've got some muscle in that area too," Kratos said, thinking of the leggy redhead who had set up the spyware that had ultimately given him access to confidential records at City Hall and One Police Plaza. She was good, very good. But one of the first things he'd learned from his father was never to go into a fight with only one plan of attack. "What happens if we break up this unit?"

"Buys us time. Maybe permanently." Vincent's eyes glinted. "You want me to arrange some accidents?"

Kratos sighed, bothered less by the indiscreet question than the option itself. Assassination was not his preferred approach, not because it concerned him to neutralize his adversaries, but because murder was usually sloppy and always drew unwanted attention. He'd been opposed to eliminating the undercover officers who'd gotten close to exposing the kiddie porn operation but had finally consented in order to assuage his new Russian business partners. The compromise seemed necessary to gain a greater percentage of the profits, but as a result, he and *his* businesses were coming under far more scrutiny than the Russians. He didn't want to invite even more.

"Perhaps there's another way," he said, recalling another of his father's lessons. Where there was an obstacle, there was usually an opportunity also. "After all, we need a new representative at One Police Plaza."

"Turn one of those cops?" Vincent laughed, then quickly smothered his smile. "From what I hear, they're all a bunch of Boy Scouts."

Kratos leaned back and tapped the list with one finger. Five people—three women, two men. "Find me the weak link."

"I heard some of them are queers."

"If you heard it, then it's common knowledge and blackmail would be pointless. No," Kratos mused. "It won't be greed that provides the lever we need, and it won't be power. It won't even be fear of death." He smiled, enjoying the challenge. "It will be love."

"Boss?" Vincent frowned.

"Bring me everything you can find about their families."

CHAPTER ONE

Rebecca Frye studied her face in the mirror over the tiny sink in her hospital room's bathroom. The harsh institutional light mercilessly highlighted the purple-and-green bruise that extended from her left temple down her cheek to the angle of her jaw. Her upper eyelid was so swollen she could barely make out the ice blue rim of her iris. At least the blood in her hair was gone. She'd finally gotten a shower after two days of insisting to the nurses that she was perfectly capable of standing upright. Actually, the first time she'd tried to get out of bed, the room or her head—or possibly both—had spun so badly she'd nearly vomited. Thank Christ Catherine hadn't been there to witness the episode.

Rebecca wasn't bothered by the mess the gunshot had made of her face. To her way of thinking, if she was standing up and able to see the damage, she was way ahead of the game. What bothered her was that every time her lover, Dr. Catherine Rawlings, looked at her, she would be reminded how close Rebecca had come to being a casualty. Catherine tried to hide her worry and her fear, but the shadows flickering just below the surface of her green eyes gave her away. For Rebecca, the pain of being shot was nothing compared to the pain of knowing Catherine was suffering because of her.

She opened and closed her jaw carefully. Stiff and sore, but in working order. For a few seconds she contemplated trying to cover the bruises with makeup, but that would only call more attention to the injury. And no attempt at camouflage was going to diminish the reality of what had happened. She turned away from the mirror, flicked off the overhead lights, and padded barefoot back into her room.

Catherine stood by the windows, her arms folded beneath her breasts, her back to Rebecca. She wore a sage green silk suit, the slim skirt coming to just above her knees, the jacket cinched at the waist. Her auburn hair fell in waves to her shoulders, and for the first time, Rebecca noticed the silver at her temples. She was elegant and beautiful and tender and wise. She was also strong and intuitive. She was all the things that Rebecca was not, and Rebecca could still not understand what it was Catherine needed from her.

She stopped by the end of the bed, feeling disadvantaged in nothing more than a hospital gown and a pair of gym shorts. "Aren't you supposed to be in clinic?"

"I'm playing hooky." Catherine turned from the window, her gaze going immediately to the bruise. She quickly smiled, but not fast enough to cover her flinch of distress. "It's good to see you out of bed."

"I'm clean, too."

"Even better." Catherine crossed to Rebecca and kissed her on the cheek. "How are you feeling?"

"Not bad. I don't suppose you know when I'm getting out of here?"

"As a matter of fact, I do." Catherine tried to keep her tone light. "Since I expected that would be your first question, I made some calls on my way over."

She appraised the damage to Rebecca's face. Even though she knew, rationally, that Rebecca would heal, she couldn't prevent the sinking feeling she got in the pit of her stomach at the sight of the injury. The bullet had glanced off Rebecca's skull just above her temple. The impact had been enough to flay open her scalp and give her a hairline fracture, but the neurosurgeons assured Catherine once the concussion resolved there would be no permanent damage. Still, it was impossible to erase the image of Rebecca lying so still and pale on a stretcher, her blond hair matted with congealing blood. Catherine tried to tell herself it was because Rebecca was so skilled, so good at what she did, that she'd managed to avoid serious injury. If she pondered the possibility that it was only luck that had kept the bullet from striking Rebecca a half-inch lower or a half an inch farther to the right and killing her instantly, she'd never be able to sleep again when Rebecca was out on the streets. Luck was far too fickle a lady to be the guardian of her lover's life.

"Ali said she'll stop by as soon as she's finished in the OR, and if you promise to behave, she'll let you go."

"I'll promise her anything she wants," Rebecca said.

Catherine raised an eyebrow. "It's a good thing I trust Ali Torveau, then."

"You can trust me." Rebecca slipped her arm around Catherine's waist and kissed her. When she felt Catherine's resistance, she loosened her hold and eased back. She looked away, fearing what she might see in Catherine's eyes. "I should get dressed."

"Let me get your clothes."

"I can do it." Rebecca walked to the tall narrow closet next to the door. "I know you have patients waiting."

"I want to drive you home."

"That's okay," Rebecca said briskly. "I'll call one of the team."

She opened the closet. A shirt and clean pair of jeans hung on hooks where Catherine had placed them when she'd brought them from home. They weren't officially living together, but they might as well be. Rebecca still had her small, spare apartment above a mom-and-pop grocery store in South Philadelphia, but she spent almost every night in Catherine's Victorian near University Hospital where Catherine was the assistant chief of psychiatry. They'd been talking about living together, but that was before the shooting—the second time Rebecca had been shot in the line of duty since she and Catherine had been together. She wouldn't be surprised if Catherine wanted to reconsider. Every other woman Rebecca had ever been with had eventually decided that the demands and risks of her job were too much to deal with.

"You should get back to work," she told Catherine without turning around.

A pair of hands slid over her shoulders and Catherine leaned ever so gently against her back. With her mouth very close to Rebecca's ear, she whispered, "I'm not going anywhere and you can't chase me away."

"Is that what you think I'm doing?" Rebecca stared into the closet. She hadn't realized she was cold until the heat of Catherine's body warmed her. She never realized what she needed until Catherine gave it to her without being asked. She covered one of Catherine's hands. "I'm sorry."

"Turn around."

Slowly, Rebecca turned.

Catherine's heart clenched at the fear she glimpsed on her lover's face. Rebecca was the bravest, strongest woman she'd ever known, and she couldn't bear to think that anything she had said or done might have put that look in Rebecca's eyes. "Do you love me?"

"More than my life," Rebecca whispered.

Catherine laced her arms around Rebecca's neck. "As long as that's true, I'll be right here."

Rebecca clasped Catherine's waist and kissed her again, and this time nothing stood between them. Immediately, her heart felt lighter. Catherine was a few inches shorter than her own six feet, and she loved the way Catherine's body fit against hers. Holding her, knowing Catherine was hers, was like shining a light in the dark places in her soul. "I love you."

"That's all I need, Rebecca." Catherine feathered her fingers through Rebecca's sleek, fair hair. "It's really so simple."

Rebecca leaned her forehead against Catherine's. "Why can't I understand that?"

"You will, darling. You—"

The hall door swung open at the same time as a sharp rap sounded, and a brunette in surgical scrubs breezed into the room. Ali Torveau, Rebecca's trauma surgeon and a good friend to them both, planted her fists on her slim hips and regarded them quizzically.

"Why is it every time I have a cop for a patient I end up finding her in a clinch with some good-looking woman before I even have a chance to sign the discharge papers?"

Catherine slipped out of Rebecca's arms. "This is not a clinch. Clinching is for teenagers. What you witnessed is an embrace."

"Uh-huh. Looked a lot like a clinch to me." Ali pointed toward the bed. "Rebecca—in bed."

"I feel fine," Rebecca protested.

"Down," Ali repeated with just a hint of a growl.

"Okay. Okay." Rebecca stretched out on the narrow bed. As soon as she did she noticed that her headache dialed down a notch or two. She decided to keep that information to herself.

"Any double vision?" Ali flicked the beam of a penlight back and forth between Rebecca's eyes.

"No."

"Headache?"

"No."

"Let's try that one again. Headache?"

Out of the corner of her eye, Rebecca could see Catherine's concerned expression. "Mild. Nothing worse than a bad hangover."

Ali swung her stethoscope from around her neck, hooked it in her ears, and pressed the bell to Rebecca's chest. "Take a deep breath. Again. One more time." Then she straightened and slung the stethoscope over her shoulder. "Fortunately the x-rays don't show any evidence of sternal or rib fractures. I don't expect you'll have the same kind of pulmonary problems you had after the chest wound."

The last thing Rebecca wanted was Ali reminding Catherine of another brush with death. "Look, this was nothing. I was wearing a vest and it did its job. I got caught with a glancing round. The ER guys should've sent me home with a couple of stitches."

"We all know what happened, darling," Catherine said quietly. "And we all know what could have happened. Let's just—"

Another knock sounded and a slightly overweight, gray-haired man in a brown suit that was shiny at the knees lumbered in. He took in the group and quickly looked at the ceiling. "Is everything covered? I hope not."

"You should be so lucky." Rebecca had never been so happy to see her partner, William Watts. She hadn't wanted to work with the sometimes crude, reputedly over-the-hill detective after her longtime partner had been executed along with another undercover cop just less than a year before. But her captain had insisted and it hadn't taken her long to realize that Watts was no burned-out cop putting in time until his pension. He was astute, hardworking in his own laid-back way, and most importantly to Rebecca, completely trustworthy.

Watts grinned, his blue eyes twinkling in his heavyset, ruddy face. "I always thought those little hospital johnnies were a turn-on. Better view from the back, though."

"Jesus," Rebecca muttered. "Get out of here so I can get dressed."

"Getting sprung, huh, Loo?"

"Yes, and you're my ride."

"Sure thing. I'll be outside." He nodded to Catherine and Ali as he headed out the door. "Ladies."

"I can drive you home, darling." Catherine glanced at Ali. "If you're going to let her go?"

Ali stood back from the bed. "Your CT scan shows a small hematoma just below that hairline fracture in the left temporal area. Ninety-nine point nine percent of the time it resolves over the course of a few weeks. Every once in a blue moon we see delayed bleeding, usually from a vein tearing during excessive exercise or something else popping because of severe hypertension. What that means is you need to take it easy. No driving for two weeks. No workouts, no jogging, and no vigorous sex."

"Got it," Rebecca said through gritted teeth.

"There's an even smaller chance, maybe one in five thousand, that this hematoma could resolve with a small area of scarring. Scarring in the brain equals a focus of irritation, and we sometimes see seizures. If you notice weakness, numbness, olfactory disturbances, memory loss, tremors, I need to know about it immediately."

"What about prophylactic Dilantin?" Catherine asked.

Rebecca's stomach tightened at the slight quiver in Catherine's voice. She hated this—she just wanted it over, fast.

Ali shook her head. "The risk is smaller that she'll have problems than the potential complications of taking the drug. I'd rather just wait and watch." She fixed Rebecca with a piercing stare. "If I have your word that you'll follow instructions."

Rebecca reached for Catherine's hand. "You have it."

"Good enough. I'll leave prescriptions for you at the nurses' station. You can pick them up on your way out. I want to see you next week in clinic." Ali started toward the door, then looked over her shoulder. "I'm glad you're okay. Keep the rest of your people that way too."

"I plan to," Rebecca said.

❖

Watts was slouched against the wall next to the door when Rebecca and Catherine walked out.

"You really should go downstairs in a wheelchair," Catherine murmured.

Watts grinned and Rebecca shot him a look. "By the time someone finds one, I could be relaxing in the car. You did park out front in the fire lane, didn't you, Watts?"

"Right at the curb, Loo."

"Good enough. Let's go."

Catherine sighed. "I can't fight you both." Then she stepped closer to the big detective. "I'm counting on you to look after her, William."

The smirk disappeared from Watts's face and he straightened, warmth replacing the usual sarcastic gleam in his eyes. "Yes ma'am. I'll do that."

"Move it, Watts," Rebecca grumbled. The last thing she needed was babysitting. She kissed Catherine's cheek. "I'll see you later. Don't worry."

Catherine brushed her fingertips over Rebecca's uninjured cheek. "Get some rest."

"I won't do anything strenuous. Promise."

The three rode down in the elevator together and then parted in front of the hospital as Catherine hurried off to the medical arts building down the block. Rebecca eased into the front seat of the department-issue Crown Vic and was instantly at home. The interior smelled of smoke from Watts's cigarettes, grease from the McDonald's containers on the floor in the backseat, and the unmistakable scent of dozens of bodies. For the first time in days she felt like herself.

Watts settled his belly behind the wheel and pulled out into traffic. "Your place or the doc's?"

"Neither. Let's head to the office."

"I don't want to get my balls in a vise here, Loo. You're supposed to be taking it easy."

"No one said I couldn't sit in a chair and talk." Rebecca leaned her head back and closed her eyes. "Assemble the troops."

"I ought to be wearing a cup," Watts muttered. "My balls are aching already."

"Shut up, Watts." Rebecca smiled to herself when she heard his happy chuckle.

❖

JT Sloan took the call at just after 2:00 p.m. Watts's message to meet at the unofficial headquarters of the HPCU in her private office building was a welcome reprieve to a life prison sentence. She'd just spent the last five hours working with two detectives who, along with her, made up the fledgling Electronic Surveillance Unit at the Philadelphia Police Department. In a moment of pure insanity, she'd signed on as the civilian consultant to help set up the unit and train the newly assigned detectives whose knowledge of cybersleuthing began with being able to turn on a computer and ended with signing on to the Internet for their e-mail. Fortunately, they made up for their lack of knowledge with eagerness. Still, there was a limit to how long she could rein in her temper, not one of her talents.

"Gotta run, fellas," she said, clipping her phone back to her belt. "Go ahead and start the downloads from the archives."

Lloyd Elliott, a sandy-haired, boyish-looking detective who was the reverse of Sloan's black haired, blue-eyed good looks, straightened up in his chair in alarm. "Without you? What if—"

Sloan waved a hand and headed for the door. "There's nothing you can do I can't fix. Have fun."

Hearing their grumbles as she made her escape, she laughed. There was a lot to be said for being her own boss. On her way to her Porsche, she made another call.

"Michael Lassiter's office," a smooth, sophisticated voice answered.

"It's Sloan. Is she around?"

"Of course, Ms. Sloan. I'll get her."

"Just Sloan," Sloan said automatically. She wasn't sure why her partner's executive assistant couldn't get that straight.

While she waited, she put the top down on the Carrera and took a deep breath of the cool autumn air. The sun was bright, but it lacked heat. She should probably get her leather jacket out of the trunk, because she'd feel the chill in just her usual white T-shirt and blue jeans, but she didn't bother. She wasn't going far and she liked the freedom of the air blowing against her skin. She'd spent three days behind bars once and that was enough to make her hate any kind of confinement for the rest of her life. She pushed the thought away. All that was behind her.

"Sloan?"

"Hi, baby."

"This is a nice surprise," Michael Lassiter said.

Sloan got a little rush just hearing her speak. Michael not only had a kind of Lauren Bacall beauty, she had the voice to go with it. "I'm headed back to the office. Rebecca is out of the hospital."

"That's wonderful news."

"How are you feeling?" Sloan asked. Michael had been injured herself not long before and was still only working half days at Innova, the design corporation she headed.

"I'm fine."

"No migraines?" Sloan started the engine and let it idle while she talked.

"Really, sweetheart. A little tired, maybe, but I'm all right."

"Don't overdo, okay?"

"I promise. I'll see you at home in a little while."

"I might still be in the office when you arrive," Sloan said. The cyberinvestigation company she'd founded with another ex-federal agent, Jason McBride, after she'd been falsely arrested and dismissed from her Justice position, occupied the third floor of a renovated warehouse in Old City. She'd been sharing her loft apartment on the floor above with Michael for the last two years. "Call me when you get home."

"Sloan," Michael chided softly. "You know very well if you're involved in something I won't be able to drag you upstairs."

Laughing, Sloan gunned the Porsche across the lot and out onto the Benjamin Franklin Parkway heading east. "Baby, I want to see you. And being dragged away sounds like fun."

"Oh, I'm sure I can think of other fun things too."

"Can't wait. See you soon."

Michael said good-bye and Sloan hung up, just barely managing not to ask again if Michael was sure she was all right. She had argued against her going back to her job so soon, but she understood the need to work. Until she'd fallen in love with Michael, all she'd had was work. Even now, when the hunt was on, the chase consumed her. Sometimes she couldn't tell the difference between being the hunter and the hunted and all she could do was keep running through the complex labyrinth of cyberspace until she won or dropped. Only Michael had ever been able to call her back.

❖

"Tell them no," Sandy Sullivan mumbled, wrapping her slim arm around Dellon Mitchell's narrow waist and tethering her with a leg across the thighs.

"Work, babe," Dell whispered, trying unsuccessfully to extricate herself from Sandy's grip. Not that she really wanted to go anywhere. Sandy might be half her size, but she was curvy in all the right places and her skin was so smooth Dell could lose herself for hours just running her fingertips over every inch. Not that she could really last for hours without doing more than just touch her, but it *felt* that way sometimes. The only thing in the world that could get her out of bed with Sandy was a call to arms. The only thing she loved as much as Sandy was being a cop. She was the youngest member of the High Profile Crimes Unit and awakened daily hardly able to believe she was part of the team. She'd do anything to prove herself. "I gotta go, babe."

"Screw that, Dell. It's your day off." Sandy propped her head on her elbow, her short blond hair spiky and her eyes even sharper. "Even cops and whores get a day off."

"You're not a whore. You were never a whore."

Sandy rolled her eyes. "Okay. Even classy streetwalkers like myself get a break once in a while."

"I had a day off. Well, most of the day. And you kept me busy." Dell pushed up against the pillows, brushing strands of dark hair back from her face. Sandy automatically curled up against her chest and Dell stroked her hair. "The lieutenant's out of the hospital."

Sandy stopped playing with Dell's nipple, thank God, and sat up facing Dell. "Frye's okay?"

"I guess so, or they wouldn't have let her out. I told you I would have taken you to visit her." Dell wasn't crazy about the fact that Sandy was her lieutenant's confidential informant. In fact, she hated the risk Sandy took every time she went out on the street to gather intel. It only bugged her some that Sandy was a little bit in love with Rebecca Frye.

She trusted the lieutenant. She trusted Sandy. It's just that she couldn't imagine measuring up to the lieutenant in anybody's eyes. Frye was not only good-looking, she was an awesome cop. Dell thought if she turned out to be half as brave and smart at her job as the lieutenant, she'd be satisfied.

"She had enough people hanging around her," Sandy said dismissively. She ran her finger down the center of Dell's thigh, smiling when Dell twitched as if an electric current had shot through her. "Sure you have to go?"

Dell grabbed Sandy's hand. "You know I gotta. And yeah, I'm gonna be thinking about what I'm missing the whole time."

Sandy kissed her, rubbing her breasts lightly over Dell's. "Yeah?"

"Yeah." Dell grabbed her and flipped her onto her back. Then she settled her hips between Sandy's legs and gently bit down on her neck. She could spare ten minutes.

Chapter Two

R ebecca shook Watts's hand off her elbow as they climbed the few stairs to the alcove at the entrance to Sloan's building. "Will you cut that out. I'm fine." She glared up at the palm-sized surveillance camera tucked into the corner. "Rebecca Frye and William Watts."

Watts leaned forward so the camera could pick up his face. "You look like shit," he muttered without moving his lips.

"Thank you. Now that you've registered your opinion, stop hovering."

When the door didn't automatically click open, she knew they were the first to arrive. A few seconds later a faint beep sounded and she quickly keyed in her security code. The door opened and she stalked into the cavernous ground level with Watts on her heels.

"I was just saying, you—"

"Unless you want to walk up to the third floor," Rebecca said, punching the button to the elevator, "you should put a sock in it."

Her voice echoed around the unfinished brick walls. Wood beams extended twenty feet overhead, enclosing the space that housed Sloan's vehicles and the sophisticated mechanics controlling the building. Sloan's security was beyond state of the art and her company's electronic surveillance center made the NSA look antiquated. With its hi-tech equipment and privacy, her building was the perfect place from which to run the HPCU.

"Man," Watts muttered, hastily sliding into the elevator, "it was so nice and peaceful the last couple of days. Nobody bitchin' at me. Nothing more strenuous to do than fill out a few forms."

"I'll bet it was great," Rebecca said as the elevator whisked soundlessly upward. "Bored yet?"

"It was enough to make a man cry."

Rebecca smiled as she stepped off into Sloan and Jason's domain. Two huge U-shaped workstations holding more than a dozen computers faced each other around an open central area. No one was currently at work but data streamed across many of the oversized plasma monitors. "I'll be in the conference room. You think you can rustle up some stuff to make coffee?"

Watts frowned. "Is it okay, do you think? I mean, coffee's like a stimulant, right? Makes your blood pressure go up?"

"Don't tell me you were listening at the door." Having Catherine worry about her was bad enough. Appearing weak in front of her colleagues, especially those she commanded, was just adding insult to injury.

Watts held up both hands. "I'm not saying a word."

"Coffee. Black. Strong. Now, Watts."

As soon as he headed off to the small kitchen tucked into one corner, Rebecca made her way to the only other enclosed area in the expansive space. The conference room held a massive antique library table surrounded by ten chairs, a counter in the back where a never-empty coffeepot usually sat on a warmer, and one entire wall of monitors. The screens provided views of the streets in front and rear of the building in both directions, the entry alcove, the elevator, and everywhere else in and around the building except Sloan and Michael's living quarters one floor up. A laptop rested on the table in front of Sloan and Jason's customary seats. Rebecca eased into a chair in her spot on Sloan's right, happy to be off her feet. She needed to be able to think, and the less she moved around, the less her head bothered her.

It felt good to be back at work. She'd been part of the special sex crimes unit until her previous partner, Jeff Cruz, was murdered. She'd been in the middle of an intense manhunt for a serial rapist, and between the stress of the case and Jeff's death, she'd almost come unglued. But she'd met Catherine, and her life had changed in ways she'd never dreamed. Then her captain had assigned her to head the HPCU. She had worked in multijurisdictional task forces before, but not with civilian consultants. She'd resisted at first, even though both Sloan and Jason were highly skilled ex-federal agents. Now she couldn't envision her team without them, any more than she could envision her life without Catherine.

"Here you go, Loo." Watts slid a mug of coffee in front of her and put the pot on the warmer at the back of the room. Then he dropped into a chair across from her and sighed. "Home sweet home."

Rebecca was about to answer when she caught movement out of the corner of her eye.

"It's about time you two showed up," she said when Sloan charged in.

Sloan's sleek dark hair was windblown, her face flushed from the fast ride in the cold air. Jason McBride, a svelte handsome blond with piercing blue eyes, followed her in. As usual, he was impeccably attired in an open-collared pale blue shirt and dark trousers. He looked every inch the successful young businessman, which he was. What everyone on the team knew, but few others did, was that he was also a breathtakingly beautiful transvestite named Jasmine.

"How you feeling, Frye?" Sloan asked as she and Jason took their seats.

"Good."

The sounds of running footsteps heralded the arrival of the last team member, newly minted Detective Dellon Mitchell. Five-eight, black hair, blue eyes, slim and muscular, she wore low-slung black jeans, a black T-shirt molded to her slender torso, scuffed black motorcycle boots, and an equally well-worn leather motorcycle jacket. At first glance she might be thought either a strikingly handsome young woman or a beautiful boy. At times, she was both.

"Lieutenant!" Mitchell's eyes sparkled with welcome. "Hey. Great to see you."

"Detective." Despite her headache and fatigue, Rebecca put some force into her voice. The team *would* function without her, but just as much as she needed to be here, they needed to believe she was fit and ready to lead. "Sorry to interrupt your day off."

"No problem." Mitchell slouched into a chair, her legs spread casually. "It's just so good to see you…" She colored. "I mean—"

"So," Rebecca interrupted, saving both Mitchell and herself further embarrassment, "somebody fill me in on what the hell we accomplished the other night."

She'd been shot in the middle of a raid and, despite her demands, none of her team was given access to brief her. Consequently, she had no idea where things stood with their ongoing investigation into a web of human trafficking and sex slavery that extended from the Port of Philadelphia deep into the heart of the city.

"We blew away the scumbag who shot you, for starters," Watts said, his eyes hard and flat.

Rebecca hated to let on that she couldn't remember exactly what had happened, but she knew who'd been backing her up. "Thanks, Sloan."

Sloan nodded. At the instant she'd pulled the trigger, she hadn't been thinking of anything except that if she didn't shoot the guy, he was going to shoot her and finish off Rebecca too. Afterward, she hoped the dead man was the one who had nearly killed Michael during a thwarted attempt on Sloan's life. She wanted retribution for Michael's injuries even more than she wanted to put a stop to the abuse of young girls and dismantle the organization behind the prostitution, pornography, and drugs.

"Anything on the ballistics yet?" Rebecca doubted they'd hit the one house where the man who'd assassinated her partner just happened to be guarding a group of smuggled Russian girls, but stranger things had occurred. Sometimes police work was just a lot of sweat, drudgery, and occasional luck.

"No match to anything in the system," Watts said. "He was using a semiautomatic. These guys probably import them by the case."

"So the weapon used to kill Jeff and Jimmy is still out there. And presumably the shooter is too," Rebecca summarized. Initially they'd theorized that her partner Jeff and an undercover fed, Jimmy Hogan, had been executed by a contract killer who was long gone. However, an assistant district attorney, George Beecher, was murdered more recently, only days before the HPCU raid. He was shot with the same weapon used to kill the detectives.

Mitchell piped up. "So what are we thinking? That the shooter is local? A mob guy, maybe?"

"Pretty ballsy for anyone local to kill a cop," Watts said.

"Yes, if we're talking about the usual suspects," Rebecca said. Organized crime bosses preferred not to bring down heat in their own backyards. The killings were an escalation that suggested direct involvement from outside players, most likely foreign interests, since the girls were being smuggled in on ships from Eastern Europe. "Mitchell," she said, "grab the whiteboard and let's put down what we know and what we better find out."

Several hours passed as the team shared information and speculated. Finally, Mitchell put the marker down and they all stared at the names and arrows and tried to complete the picture.

"What do we know?" Rebecca looked around the table. "Who's bringing these girls in and how?"

"They have to have local contacts to work the container switches on the docks and to put them to work in the sex clubs," Sloan said. "That's the Zamoras' territory."

"Probably," Rebecca agreed. "But the Zamoras are not in it alone. Are we getting any information from Irina?"

Dell Mitchell turned bright red. She had gone undercover as Mitch, a drag king, to establish contact with a young Russian woman, Irina, who appeared to supervise a group of smuggled girls when they were dancing in local strip clubs. Mitch had needed to seduce Irina to discover the address where the girls were held at night under armed guard. Some of the surveillance team had listened in during the seduction, a fact that still embarrassed the young detective.

After a minute, Mitchell said, "I tried to get information on the girls who were in the house, including Irina, down at headquarters. The story is as soon as our people brought them in, Immigration claimed jurisdiction and moved them to a federal facility. No one's heard anything since then."

Rebecca pinched the bridge of her nose, trying unsuccessfully to back off the headache that was accelerating by the moment. "It's not Immigration. It's probably Justice, and it's probably Avery Clark. Immigration doesn't have the pull to get in the middle of an operation like this. But Clark and the Justice Department do. God damn it. Every time we get close to inside information, he shuts us out." She leaned her head back and closed her eyes. "Watts and I will track him down and see what we can squeeze out of him."

As if tuned into her fatigue and frustration, Watts picked up the ball. "We know a lot more than we did a week ago. We know the Russians are bringing young girls in through the port in containers and we know where some of them were working. What we need is to connect the Zamoras to these girls, because if we can, that's a federal crime and they're going down for a long long time."

"We need eyes and ears back in the clubs." Rebecca straightened and looked at Mitchell. "Is your cover good?"

"Yes ma'am," Mitchell said. "As far as anyone knows, including Irina, I was just at the wrong place at the wrong time. I'm pretty sure she saw me get cuffed."

"Good. Then I want Mitch to reconnect with his drag king buddies and get back into the clubs. Jasmine too, for backup. There'll be a lot of talk on the streets, and we'll need our CIs working their sources hard."

"Oh goodie," Jason breathed in a husky whisper that was pure Jasmine.

"Yes ma'am," Mitchell said stiffly. Sandy was one of Rebecca's CIs. A friend of hers had been murdered just a few days before, when she'd gotten too close to some major players in the porn film business, and Mitchell wanted Sandy off the streets, but it wasn't her call to make. If she pushed her, Sandy would get pissed and be less likely to tell Mitchell if she ran into trouble.

Jason leaned forward. "Somebody has to be doing fancy work with the computers at the port to reroute the containers with the girls in them and bury the shipping manifests. I don't see anyone down there having the know-how for that."

"Plus," Sloan added, "someone injected a very smart Trojan horse into the City Hall system to hack into confidential files."

"What are you saying?" Rebecca asked. "There's a high-level hacker at work for the opposite side?"

"Undoubtedly," Sloan said.

"Can you find them?"

Sloan grinned, her eyes darkening to indigo with the scent of the hunt. "Oh yeah. Now we've got two intrusion sites—at the port and City Hall. Even the best hacker leaves fingerprints."

"Do it," Rebecca said. "Watts, I need you to pave the way at the port for our people. And check in with the organized crime team and see if they've got any intel on Zamora's activities that might help us." She took a deep breath. "Our target is the Zamoras. The feds will chase the Russians. If we happen to trip over them, all the better. But we need to clean up our own house first."

"The OC guys aren't going to like us poking around on their turf," Watts pointed out mildly.

Rebecca shrugged. "The HPCU has cross-divisional jurisdiction. We'll be polite, but we'll go where the trail leads."

Watts chuckled again. The day just got better and better.

❖

Michael turned the corner for home with a mental sigh of relief. She'd gotten caught up in a project meeting that afternoon and hadn't realized how very tired she was until it was close to six. Just the short drive across town seemed endless. Her eyeballs pounded as if she hadn't slept in weeks, when all she seemed to do *was* sleep. As she slowed to pull into the garage, she noted a familiar figure leaning against a lamppost a few yards ahead. Sandy looked even younger than her eighteen years in the muted glow of the streetlight. She also looked like she must be cold in her very short skirt and her thin red faux-leather jacket. Hugging herself, Sandy strolled up as soon as Michael got out of the car.

"You can't be waiting for a bus," Michael said, "since none of them can get down these streets."

Sandy smiled shyly, as if caught out doing something untoward. "I might as well be waiting for some bus that will never come. Waiting for Dell when she's in a cop meeting isn't much different."

"Ah." Michael shifted her briefcase to her other shoulder. God, she ached all over. "Still at it, are they?"

"Either that or they're up there sitting around drinking beer and watching television."

Michael laughed. "I sincerely doubt it. You know they'd rather talk shop than anything else." She touched Sandy's shoulder. "Come on upstairs. I'll make some tea."

"Oh," Sandy said quickly, "that's okay. I'm good here."

"I'd like the company, and this is perfect timing. I was going to call you tomorrow." Michael knew that Sandy was sensitive about her history on the streets, despite being proud and self-sufficient and incredibly brave. Michael was fond of the young woman and admired her. The last thing she wanted to do was make her uncomfortable. "There's something I wanted to talk to you about."

Sandy looked concerned. "Is something wrong?"

"No," Michael said, gently grasping Sandy's hand. "Come upstairs. I'll tell you."

"Okay, sure." Sandy fell into step with her, nervously smiling, her hand still in Michael's.

❖

Across the street and six floors up, Angelo DeVito stood at the darkened window, his video camera trained on the building he was supposed to be watching. He absently reached down and rearranged his crotch while he filmed the two blonde babes as they cozied up together. The one he'd first taken for a hot little whore seemed to know the tall leggy one with the shoulder-length hair and movie star face. Man, he'd love to see them get it on for real. From what he understood about the targets, he just might get the chance. He flicked off the camera when the women disappeared inside hand in hand, and noted the time to mark the spot on the tape and the license number of the car. Then he settled in the chair in front of the window to wait.

CHAPTER THREE

"Excuse me," Sandy said to Michael when her phone rang out the melody to "I Kissed a Girl." She fished it out of her jacket pocket and swiveled away from the breakfast bar where they'd been drinking tea and talking.

"Hi, babe," Dell said. "I'm at Sloan's. We're just wrapping up, but I'll be a little while yet. You anywhere nearby?"

"Like upstairs?"

"Oh hey, that's good." Dell didn't sound all that glad.

"What's up?"

"The lieutenant is here. She wants to talk to you."

"In person? Now?"

"Yeah."

"I'll be down in a few." Sandy disconnected and shrugged at Michael. "Sorry. Frye wants me."

"Of course. I understand. Are you still...helping out?" Michael hesitated. "You don't have to tell me, if you can't."

"I don't think it's a secret. I mean, Sloan probably tells you everything, right?"

Michael smiled, but said nothing.

"Dell tells me stuff. Not much. She's really all about the rules when it comes to the cop stuff." Sandy grinned. "She's loosened up some since she's been hanging out with Jasmine, though."

"Sloan doesn't like to talk about her work very much either," Michael said. "In fact, when she's involved in a case, she pretty much forgets to eat, sleep, or do much of anything else except work."

"That worries you, huh?"

"Oh," Michael said quickly. "I didn't mean… She's intense. I fell in love with her because of how focused she is, how driven. How…" She blushed. "Passionate."

"I get that part all right." Sandy laughed. "Any girl with a beating heart gets that part about Sloan."

"Apparently." Michael laughed. "I had to get used to that pretty quickly. Fortunately I'm not really the jealous type."

"I am."

"I don't think you have much to worry about from what I can see," Michael said softly.

"I didn't know I was—jealous that way. Until her." Sandy shrugged. "Dell is the first one who ever mattered, you know."

Michael nodded. "I do know. Exactly."

Sandy grinned. She had girlfriends, sort of. Girls she hung with on the street. Girls she looked out for and who looked out for her. But mostly they talked about what they needed to know to get by—which johns to avoid and which pimps were quick with their hands and which cops wanted favors. And the rare ones, like Frye, who didn't. But she'd never talked to any of them about Dell. About being with her. About having someone of her own. "I should go. Frye gets cranky if you keep her waiting."

"Does she now." Michael chuckled. "She's never been anything except completely chivalrous with me."

They eyed one another for a few seconds, and then burst out laughing together. Michael draped her arm around Sandy's shoulder and walked her toward the door.

"You'll think about what I said?"

"I will. I should talk to Dell, you know?"

"Absolutely. Take all the time you need."

"Thanks," Sandy said, feeling so much more than gratitude but not quite knowing what to say.

"You don't need to thank me," Michael said gently. "We're friends."

"Yeah," Sandy said with a sense of wonder as she stepped into the elevator. "We are."

❖

"Hiya, Frye," Sandy said as she plopped into a chair across the table from Rebecca in the conference room. On her way through the main room she'd seen Dell bent over a computer with Jason and Sloan, but Frye was alone. Frye never talked to her about street stuff in front of others, especially not Dell. "You look like crap."

"I've heard that two times too many today."

"You okay or just playing macho cop?" Sandy didn't add that she'd been scared just about brainless when she'd heard that a cop had been shot in a raid, because Dell had been in on the bust, and she'd felt only a little less terrified when she'd learned it was Frye. Frye was special in a crazy kind of way she couldn't explain. Frye was a hard-ass and pain in the ass, but she'd never lied to Sandy about what she wanted from her. Even back in the early days when Sandy was working the streets for real and Frye squeezed her for information, she never took advantage like some cops. Frye always paid and treated her like she mattered. She was the first person who ever had.

"I'm okay enough," Rebecca said. "Everything quiet?"

"As far as I know." Sandy picked at a chip on the red polish on her thumbnail. "I haven't been out since things went down the other night. I wasn't sure—" She glanced through the open door in Dell's direction, but Dell was busy tapping away at a computer. Dell always got hinky when she was working for Frye. She liked that Dell worried about her, but she didn't want her to worry too much. She liked that Dell got a little jealous. Okay, sometimes a lot jealous. She liked that feeling of being special and cared about. But she would never make her jealous on purpose. She'd played games to survive her whole life, and she would never do it with Dell.

Rebecca stood. "Let's go for a walk."

"Are you kidding me? You look like—"

"You said that already. Come on. We won't go far."

Sandy shook her head, but followed Frye to the elevator. Dell looked over once as they walked through the room, then quickly back to her keyboard. Sandy kept her distance while they rode down, aware of the cameras everywhere. But once outside on the street, she looped her arm through Frye's without being invited.

When Frye gave her a raised eyebrow, she snapped, "You don't look that steady. I don't want you falling into the street and getting run over. I'll never get any dinner, which is what I came here for to begin with."

"Let's go to the deli around the corner," Rebecca said, moving her arm out of Sandy's grasp to curl it around her shoulder. "Why the hell don't you ever dress for the weather? You're shivering."

"I'm used to it."

"That's not what your body is saying."

"I'm in charge of my body," Sandy said flatly.

Rebecca said nothing. A few minutes later they slipped into a greasy spoon on the corner of Market and Fourth that smelled like fried onions, strong coffee, and tomato sauce. They claimed a booth at the back and a waitress asked them what they wanted, not bothering to offer them menus. Rebecca ordered a sandwich and coffee, then thought better of the coffee and switched to water. She still had a headache and maybe the caffeine wasn't such a good idea.

"Just a Bud," Sandy said.

The waitress cocked her head at Rebecca and Rebecca nodded. Sandy was legal in all the ways that counted. She'd proved herself enough times to deserve a beer.

"So, what's the deal," Sandy asked.

"Things have changed," Rebecca said. "We've put a crimp in the supply line by exposing the trafficking operation down at the port. I'm sure there's plenty of those foreign girls still around, but my guess is whoever is running them is going to be very cautious for a little while. That means a lot more action is going to come to your friends."

Sandy sipped the beer the waitress brought her. "Don't you mean *me* and my friends?"

"Not if you're not hooking, which you aren't. Right?"

"Jeez, don't start sounding like Dell."

Rebecca frowned. "Are you and Mitchell having problems about that?"

"No," Sandy said quickly, afraid that she might get Dell in trouble somehow. "She's just, you know...overprotective. Must be a cop thing."

"Must be." Rebecca waited until the waitress slapped a heavy white plate with a thick sandwich down on the table. She wasn't really hungry, but she couldn't remember the last time she ate. She knew she needed the food, so she forced herself to take a bite. "I want you to find me a replacement."

"For Dell?" Sandy said, her heart rising in her throat. Man, Dell would lose her mind if Frye let her go.

"No," Rebecca said in exasperation, trying not to shake her head and make the pounding any worse. "For you."

"Why? I've got the contacts, I like the money, and besides—you know you can trust me."

"Like I said, the situation is different now."

Rebecca had thought long and hard about this while she'd been lying in a hospital bed. Any reliable confidential informant was invaluable, and Sandy was not only trustworthy, she was smart and street savvy. She was as much a member of the team as any of them. But she was also the least trained and probably the least capable of taking care of herself. Rebecca had intentionally used her, put her at risk, more than once. It was necessary because she needed Sandy to get the job done, and the job was everything. The job had always been everything, more important than her lovers, more important than her life. But something had changed, and she wasn't quite sure how or what.

Six months ago, if Sandy had been hurt while gathering information for her, she would've been angry. If Sandy had been killed, she would've been saddened, hurt. And she would've hunted down whoever had done it no matter how long it took. Because that was her job, and Sandy was hers to protect. Now if Sandy got into trouble some night, if she was hurt, Rebecca wasn't sure she could live with it. She knew Mitchell wouldn't be able to. She closed her eyes and pinched the bridge of her nose again. How the hell had she gotten this attached to one of her CIs? And how did she end up with a cop on her team involved with her CI, a prostitute no less? It was a recipe for disaster, completely against protocol. Why hadn't she put a stop to it? At times like this, she thought maybe she still should.

"Look," Sandy said, gripping Rebecca's arm. "I'm careful. I'm smart. And I've got friends out there. People I care about, just like you care about Dell and Jason and Sloan. Hell. Even Lard Ass."

"That's Detective Watts to you," Rebecca said, smothering a smile. "I'll look after your friends. That's my job."

"Yeah yeah. You'll look after everyone. Sure. Look at you. You are as gray as this floor." Sandy pulled her phone out of her jacket again. "I'm calling your lady to come and get you."

Rebecca jerked upright and winced. "No! I'm heading home soon." She looked at her wrist and for the tenth time that afternoon remembered she didn't have her watch. Catherine must have taken it home from the hospital when she'd been admitted, because it hadn't been with her personal effects. "What time is it?"

Sandy looked over her shoulder at a round-faced wall clock with a faded Hershey's ice cream logo hanging on the wall behind the counter. "Almost six thirty."

"Oh, Christ," Rebecca whispered. Catherine would be home any minute. She pulled money from her pocket and dropped it on the counter. Thankfully, Catherine had made sure she had cash when she left the hospital. "I've got to go. We'll talk about this tomorrow."

"You're not driving, are you?"

"No, Watts is my ride. He went back to headquarters to finish up some paperwork. I'll call him to pick me up outside of Sloan's."

Sandy jumped up and wrapped her arm around Rebecca's waist when Rebecca swayed. "Gimme your frickin' phone and tell me his number."

"It's number two on speed dial." Rebecca didn't resist the help. She really did feel like crap.

❖

"So," Vincent asked when Angelo picked up the phone. "You doing anything over there besides pulling your crank?"

"Hell, yeah." Angelo raised his left shoulder to hold the phone against his ear while he handled the video camera. "Are you sure you don't have me watching some kind of whorehouse? There's more action going on in that building than in some of our joints."

"Yeah? Like what?"

"Like girls coming and going. Real lookers and real friendly-like. Some of them are dykes for sure."

"Heard that. You getting ID?"

"They're not wearing name tags, but I've shot some great footage. Real boner material."

"Just keep it in your pants. The boss wants to know who's shacked up with who."

"There's some little blonde who looks like she's servicing the whole team. She has to know plenty. We ought to put one of the boys on her."

"Don't worry. The boys are gonna be plenty busy soon. See you in the morning, and you better have more than tits and ass on film."

"Believe me, I've got plenty." Angelo dropped the cell phone on the windowsill and zoomed in on the face of a tall, chiseled blonde in casual clothing who climbed into the passenger side of a Crown Vic. Had to be a cop. When the car pulled away, the skinny little whore in the red leather jacket went back into the building. Man, she was a busy little beaver. He settled back into his chair and laughed at his own joke.

❖

"Hey, babe," Dell said as Sandy leaned against her back and wrapped her arms around her from behind. She shivered when Sandy kissed the side of her neck. Technically, she wasn't on duty, but she *was* scanning shipping manifests for Jason, looking for discrepancies that might indicate other deliveries of girls from Eastern Europe. "I'm sort of working here."

"And I'm sort of hungry. Maybe a few other things too."

Dell grinned, closed the file she was working on, and swirled her chair around. "Yeah? Already?"

Sandy let out an uncharacteristic squeal as Dell pulled her down into her lap and nuzzled her neck. "Jesus, Dell," she snapped, pushing her away. "What if Sloan walks in?"

"She won't care."

"Well, Frye would kick your ass."

Dell stiffened. "She's still here?"

"No. Watts is taking her home. She shouldn't have been here at all this afternoon. What's wrong with the bunch of you?"

"She's the boss. She calls the shots."

Sandy snorted. "Are you gonna take me somewhere for dinner or do I have to go by myself?"

"I'm done here for now. Take off your jacket."

Sandy punched her. "I said not here. Geez, rookie. What's wrong with you?"

Dell rose, pulled her leather jacket off the back of a nearby chair, and held it out.

"I don't want your jacket," Sandy said.

"You do if you want a ride. You'll freeze in what you're wearing." Dell waited. "Besides, it turns me on when you wear my clothes."

Sandy rolled her eyes, but she took off her skimpy vinyl number and accepted the black leather jacket Dell slung around her shoulders. "What about you?"

"You'll figure out some way to keep me warm."

"If you're lucky." Sandy slowly ran the tip of her tongue over her bottom lip.

"I'm always lucky." Dell kissed her quickly and held up five fingers as she started away. "See you downstairs."

When Dell pulled up in front of the building on her Ducati, Sandy climbed on behind her, leaving the heavy leather jacket unzipped. It enclosed them like a tent as she wrapped her arms around Dell's waist. The only thing between her breasts and Dell's back was her thin bra and Dell's T-shirt. Sandy's nipples got hard.

"I'm not so hungry anymore," she breathed, licking the rim of Dell's ear. "Maybe we should just go home."

Dell grabbed one of Sandy's hands and cupped it in her crotch. "We'll pick up some takeout and eat it in bed. Later."

Sandy laughed and squeezed until Dell yanked her hand away. "Much later."

❖

Angelo craned his neck to watch as the motorcycle roared down the street. Then he shut off his video camera. "Gotcha."

CHAPTER FOUR

Catherine slowed as she turned the corner onto her block, a five-minute walk from the hospital. Streetlights in her West Philadelphia neighborhood of Victorian twins were few and far between, making visibility a challenge, but she thought she recognized the dingy gray Crown Victoria idling at the curb in front of her house. She told herself she was imagining things. It couldn't possibly be a departmental vehicle, and the hulking form behind the wheel couldn't possibly be William Watts. It was almost 7:00 p.m. and Rebecca must have been home hours ago. William wouldn't be coming by to discuss business at this hour. He knew Rebecca needed more recovery time.

Catherine took a few steps, chiding herself for her overactive imagination. She'd barely slept in the last few days and had been stressed and apprehensive in the weeks leading up to the raid. It didn't matter that she knew Rebecca was superb at her job, or that the odds of a mortal injury were low. She didn't believe in statistics, not where the woman she loved was concerned. So she'd worried and tried to keep her fear from distracting Rebecca. Because Rebecca would do what Rebecca would do, and she needed all of her mind on the job to do it safely. Then Catherine had opened the door in the middle of the night to find Sloan on the porch, and for one terrifying second the rest of her life gaped empty and barren before her. Rational thought or even the reality of Rebecca beside her could not mitigate the agony of that moment. It would haunt her forever.

Let it go, she thought, although she suspected that was one battle she wouldn't win.

Then Rebecca climbed out of the passenger side of the sedan.

She didn't notice Catherine but walked slowly up to the house, obviously exhausted. For a few seconds, Catherine hovered on the verge of turning and walking away, she was that angry. Not only angry. Hurt. At times like these, being a psychiatrist was not the least bit helpful. It didn't matter that she knew what she *should* do, what she should say, what might help defuse the emotional situation. It didn't matter that she understood some of the things that drove Rebecca to drive herself. At this moment, she didn't care about all the things she knew or sympathized with. She was hurt and disappointed and frightened, and thinking her way through this was not going to be easy.

She waited until the Crown Victoria pulled away because she didn't want Watts to witness anything personal between her and Rebecca. Rebecca would hate for a colleague to get a glimpse of their private life, and Catherine was far too personally reserved to allow it either. Rebecca, moving at only a fraction of her normal pace, had just reached the landing in front of the door when Catherine fished her house keys from her briefcase and climbed the four broad marble stairs to reach around her.

"Are you just coming home?" Catherine fitted her key into the lock.

"Yes, I—"

"Don't," Catherine said softly. "I'm not quite ready to hear it just yet."

Rebecca hesitated on the threshold. "I can call Watts. Have him come back and take me to my apartment."

Catherine looked back at her for a second. "Rebecca, I'm upset." She deposited her briefcase on the parson's bench in the foyer and shrugged out of her coat. "You look exhausted."

"I didn't do—"

Catherine shook her head. "Now is not the right time to talk about this, but what's happening is part of being together. Come inside."

"I hate this," Rebecca said.

"I know. So do I. Are you hungry or do you want to go straight to bed?"

"I'm not hungry, but you must be. I'd like to sit in the kitchen with you while you have something to eat."

Catherine took her hand. "Come on, then."

❖

Kratos Zamora poured another glass of Bollinger Blanc de Noirs and leaned across the table in the private dining alcove to light the redhead's cigarette. He enjoyed watching her slowly exhale a thin stream of fragrant smoke. Even in the candlelight he could make out the emerald tones of her eyes. Her shoulder-length curls were the color of a summer sunset over the ocean, the same blood-red that often heralded a storm. She regarded him with a hint of amusement, but rather than be annoyed, he was intrigued. Women usually fawned or primped or seduced, but they never laughed at him. Or challenged.

"You think very highly of my talents," she said.

"You've never disappointed me." Kratos never ate at the same restaurant twice in a row, and there were half a dozen private dining areas like this one in the restaurant. The likelihood that a listening device had been planted was slim, but his men had swept the space earlier, and he felt secure discussing business here.

Talia raised an eyebrow. A smile played over her perfect lips.

Kratos shrugged. "Where business is concerned." He'd tried to seduce her once, and she'd refused. He'd been surprised and that was rare. He wasn't deluded enough to believe women were drawn to him rather than his power and wealth, but he was used to getting what he wanted. This woman had merely said no, but when she refused she'd held his eyes in a way few men dared, and he understood that persisting would be to no avail.

"Five years ago almost no one had the skill to detect electronic intrusion. That's no longer the case." Talia tapped the delicate ash against the edge of a crystal ashtray and it shattered into powdery shards. "What you ask is difficult."

"But not impossible." Kratos watched her maroon-tinted lips close deliberately around the end of the cigarette. Her mouth tightened slightly as she inhaled and her flawless high-boned cheeks hollowed. His erection throbbed, and he enjoyed the sensation, but didn't let the pleasure distract him. "Disrupt the communications and you create chaos. Chaos leads to inefficiency and distrust."

"What about the new investigative division at One Police Plaza?" she asked. "How much of a threat are they?"

"My friends there tell me that the unit is barely functional. I doubt there is any danger from that direction."

"And yet you said our plant inside City Hall was identified. That took a sophisticated cyberinvestigation."

Kratos waved a hand. "He was careless."

He was not about to admit his concern that the HPCU might be able to trace the man they'd had inside back to him. Besides, he was always careful to keep several layers of people between himself and culpability. If by some miracle the authorities were able to determine who had placed the spyware in the PPD computer systems, they would not come up with his name. But he doubted that was a possibility.

Talia regarded him through narrowed eyes as the smoke curled in the air between them. "Tapping into computer files is different than actively sabotaging a police communications network. The government no longer takes cyberterrorism lightly."

"Of course," Kratos said. "And your payment will reflect the risk."

"Three hundred thousand," Talia said evenly. "Fifty percent to be wired immediately to my account."

Kratos nodded.

"I need everything you can tell me about the principals. Can you be certain of your sources?"

"My family came to this city almost a hundred years ago. Politicians and lawmen have always been our friends. Nothing has changed, it's only more subtle." Kratos handed her a piece of paper folded lengthwise and covered in single-spaced typing. "The names and background briefs."

Talia took the paper and slipped it into her purse. "Which one is my target?"

"Her name is JT Sloan."

❖

The first thing Sloan saw when she stepped off the elevator into the loft was Michael curled up on the sofa in front of the fireplace, a book on her lap and the firelight casting her face in a soft, warm glow. She wore a loose white shirt and silky black slacks, and she was barefoot, her legs drawn up beneath her. When she turned in Sloan's direction and smiled, Sloan's heart stutter-stepped in her chest. Michael was the calm center of her universe, solid ground in the surging seas of her unrest and barely contained anger. She didn't deserve her, and she knew it.

"Hi, baby," Sloan said, her throat tight.

Michael patted the couch beside her. "Come sit down and tell me about your day."

"Sorry I'm so late."

"You don't have a curfew. Did you eat?"

Sloan shook her head as she dropped onto the sofa next to Michael. When Michael put her book aside and shifted to lean against her, Sloan drew her close and kissed her. "Do potato chips count?"

"I'm not answering that." Michael stroked Sloan's face. "There's a plate with chicken and pasta in the kitchen. It should still be warm."

"How was your day?"

"I asked you first," Michael teased.

"Routine." Sloan rested her chin against the top of Michael's head. Michael's hair was fragrant, her body supple, her breath warm against Sloan's throat. Sloan saw herself stretched out in a green glade in the warm sunshine, a breeze ruffling the leaves overhead and teasing over her sweat-damp skin. She caught her breath as Michael eased her T-shirt from her jeans and slid a hand underneath. The breeze carried a hint of distant thunder now and Sloan tensed.

"Your days are never routine," Michael murmured.

"How was yours?"

"Tiring but good." Michael kissed the hollow of Sloan's throat, then the side of her neck, then just below her ear. She laughed softly when Sloan shivered. "I had a nice talk with Sandy, and then I took a nap while I was waiting for you."

"That sounds...nice." Sloan's voice was strained. Michael, for all her sophisticated elegance, could seduce her with the barest touch of her fingers, a mere brush of her lips. Sloan bent to her will as a seedling bends to the sun, trembling and needy. She knew with absolute certainty that all her strength was a ruse, a handful of sand that would slip through her fingers and disappear on the wind without Michael by her side. "How are you feeling?"

"I'm not tired now." Michael pressed more tightly against Sloan, continuing to kiss the side of her jaw and her neck. She let her fingertips dance over Sloan's breasts and up and down her abdomen before skating lower and streaking beneath the top of her jeans. "What, darling?" she asked, hearing a groan.

"I'm not hungry either." Sloan clasped the back of her neck, tilting Michael's head so she could slant her mouth across Michael's. Michael opened to her, and as they kissed, Sloan groaned again, lost in the seductive warmth of Michael's mouth, a steady pulse of desire unfurling in her depths.

"You're going to be busy with another case soon, aren't you?" Michael pushed Sloan down on the couch and stretched out on top of her, fitting one leg between Sloan's thighs. She slid her hand up to cup Sloan's breast. "With Rebecca back?"

"Work?" Sloan gasped, opening the buttons on Michael's shirt with one hand while she caressed her ass with the other. Michael made it impossible for her to think. She was the only one who could do that. "You want to talk about work?"

Michael kissed the tip of Sloan's chin, then her mouth. "No. I want you all to myself for as long as I can have you."

"I'm all yours," Sloan whispered, never meaning anything more in her life.

❖

"Babe? You want that last French fry?" Dell reached over Sandy's prone body and scooped the fry in question from the Styrofoam container on top of the bedside table.

Beneath her, Sandy pushed her butt up firmly into Dell's crotch. Dell paused, her arm extended and the French fry forgotten. Sandy had nearly made her come on the ride home on her Ducati, and once they reached the apartment they shared south of Bainbridge, Sandy had finished the job. Twice. In between orgasms and takeout, Dell had reciprocated, plus an extra just because it made her feel ten feet tall to hear Sandy cry out her name when she climaxed. Now her clit was swollen and satisfyingly sore and she'd thought they were done. Or maybe not.

She dropped the French fry back in the box, let her weight settle on Sandy's back, and then bit and sucked a spot in the curve of her shoulder until Sandy squirmed under her. "Still horny?"

"Maybe," Sandy murmured, her face burrowed in the pillow. "What time is it?"

"About midnight." Dell eased off to one side and stroked the inside of Sandy's thigh. She cupped her sex from behind and squeezed gently, slowly circling Sandy's clitoris with the tip of one finger. Sandy was hot and wet. For her. Lust shot through Dell like a fever and she struggled not to slide inside her right away. Sandy liked it hard and fast, but slow and teasing was good sometimes too. It's just that Dell had a hard time keeping her head when she was excited, and Sandy always excited her. She rubbed the hard prominence at the apex of Sandy's center and Sandy made a little sound, halfway between a whimper and a purr. Dell thought her head might explode, but she kept the pressure light and languid. Sandy's hand clutched the pillow, and just that little movement made Dell's clit pound. She kissed Sandy's cheek, then the corner of her mouth. "I love you."

"Don't make me come," Sandy whispered. She groped behind her, grabbing Dell's hand when she found it. "I don't want to come until you fuck me."

Dell groaned, pressing her forehead to the back of Sandy's shoulder as she ground against Sandy's ass. She kept up the slow steady massage, careful not to push Sandy over the edge, but she couldn't control her own runaway clit. "Fuck, babe. I'm gonna come again."

Sandy laughed, her voice shaking. "Let it go, baby."

"Oh man," Dell moaned, her stomach turning somersaults as a cannon went off inside her. She panted against Sandy's back, openmouthed and trembling like a first-timer. Beneath her, Sandy twisted, pushing Dell away until she could roll onto her back. Then she grabbed Dell's hand and pushed it between her legs.

"You're up, rookie," she breathed into Dell's ear. "Now fuck me until I come."

And just like that, Dell felt the power surge through her. She braced herself on one arm and filled Sandy with her fingers. Then she kissed her, stroking inside her mouth to the rhythm of her thrusts between her legs. She used her thumb to work Sandy's clit because she knew Sandy came harder that way. Distantly she felt Sandy's hands dig into her shoulders, her nails scratching in anxious circles. Sandy tightened around her fingers, body arching into a tight bow. Dell broke their kiss so Sandy could breathe.

"Oh God, Dell," Sandy cried. "Baby, baby, I'm coming so hard."

Her eyes slammed shut as her face twisted in pleasure, but Dell kept her eyes open, drinking her in, filling her mind and body with the sights and sound and sensation. Sandy was so beautiful, so open and vulnerable and trusting in that moment that Dell wanted to cry. She kept going until Sandy collapsed bonelessly onto the bed, her arms flopping out to her sides, her breath fluttering out on a long, contented moan. Dell stopped thrusting and lightly caressed Sandy's still turgid clitoris.

"Get your hands away from me," Sandy muttered.

Dell laughed and kissed her nipple.

Sandy swatted at her head. "I mean it. Off. No mouth either."

"You said you wanted—"

"Shut up, Dell." Sandy stroked the back of Dell's head, then yanked on her hair. "Who said you could get off by yourself like that?"

Dell leaned on her elbow and pulled the sheet up to their waists. "I can't help it if you get me so excited I practically pop."

"Geez, what are you? Fourteen?"

"Only where you're concerned."

"Better remember that," Sandy said, her expression suddenly serious.

"I remember, babe," Dell said just as seriously. As part of her cover, she had to hang out in strip clubs and get friendly with the working girls. Sometimes acting friendly meant getting a little physical. She'd had a hard time at first not responding to the foreplay, and Sandy knew it. It wasn't that she wanted to get turned on by anyone except Sandy, but the adrenaline rush of being undercover coupled with the physical stimulation was arousing. "I've got a handle on it now."

"Uh-huh." Sandy wrapped one leg around the back of Dell's thigh and curled more tightly into her embrace. "You're not going out tonight, are you?"

"Not tonight. I have to call the guys tomorrow to set something up. Probably tomorrow night."

"Me too," Sandy said sleepily.

Dell wanted to argue about that, but not now. Now she just wanted to hold her. She settled against the pillow, Sandy in her arms, and closed her eyes. "Love you."

"Yeah, me too, rookie." Sandy sighed. "Michael offered me a job."

"Yeah?" Dell asked carefully, suddenly wide-awake. "What did you say?"

"That I'd think about it."

"That's good." Dell's heart did a little dance at the thought of Sandy being off the streets and tucked away somewhere safe. But the decision was Sandy's, and Dell vowed not to push.

"Yeah, I guess." Sandy sighed again. "I'm not so sure."

"Go to sleep, baby. We'll figure it out."

"Yeah?"

Dell kissed her. "Promise."

Chapter Five

I didn't know Rebecca was planning on going to work," Catherine said to Watts.

The doorbell had chimed at seven forty-five just as she was pouring the morning coffee. She'd rearranged her early-morning patient hours so that she could be home with Rebecca on her first day out of the hospital. Apparently, she was the only one who thought her lover needed a few days to recuperate.

"Sorry, Doc." Watts quickly found something fascinating to study on the ceiling. "The Loo isn't answering her pager or cell phone, so I figured I'd just swing by."

"Her cell phone is missing. I think her pager's in a drawer somewhere. They gave it to me at the hospital with the rest of her things." Except her weapon. They hadn't given her Rebecca's shoulder harness and gun. She imagined those were somewhere at police headquarters and, seeing Watts at the door, she was sure Rebecca would be wearing them before the day was out.

"Right. I would've used a landline, but I thought maybe you'd be sleeping."

Catherine laughed wryly. "Usually I'm gone by now." She held the door wide, glad that she was wearing a loose long-sleeved pullover and cotton pants rather than her normal sleepwear. "Come in, William. Have some coffee. I'll tell Rebecca you're here."

"I can wait in the car." Watts halted just inside the door. "Uh... maybe I'll just come back—" He broke off, his attention riveted across the room.

Rebecca came downstairs into the living room, wearing faded

chinos and an open-collared shirt, toweling her hair as she walked. She slowed when she saw Watts. "Problem?"

"Sorry, Loo. I got my signals crossed. The captain wants us in his office, and I thought…" He glanced at Catherine and started to back out onto the porch. "I'll fill you in later."

Catherine turned to Rebecca. "Are you going in?"

"I thought this afternoon." Rebecca glanced at Watts. "Is it urgent?"

He held up his hands and shrugged. "Henry called me. Said he wanted us in his office first thing. I'm just the messenger, Loo. I'll tell him I couldn't reach you."

"William," Catherine said, "go get that coffee. Rebecca and I just need a few minutes."

Watts glanced at Rebecca, who nodded, and he hurried toward the kitchen.

"It didn't occur to me you were planning on going back to work today," Catherine said as she walked to the far side of the living room.

She stopped in front of the French doors that opened onto the small, stone-walled backyard. Rebecca came up beside her. Catherine could smell the woodsy tang of her cologne and thought of all the nights she had gone to sleep alone with only a hint of Rebecca's fragrance for company. She pushed the thought away. She needed to deal with now.

"I meant to talk to you about it last night," Rebecca said, "but I fell asleep. I'm sorry."

"No, it's not your fault. You needed to sleep." Catherine watched the fallen leaves, only shriveled brown ghosts of their former gloriously colored selves, swirl across the gray flagstones on the small patio. Winter was right around the corner.

"I didn't realize you'd taken the morning off." Rebecca brushed her fingertips across Catherine's shoulder.

"I forgot to tell you." Catherine shook her head. "It seems we're both guilty of assumptions."

Rebecca shoved a hand through her hair and made an exasperated sound. "Could we be any more civil?" She grasped Catherine's shoulders and gently pulled her around until they were face-to-face. "I should have come straight home yesterday. Or at least I should've told you where I was going. It was thoughtless of me. I'm sorry."

"Why didn't you?" Catherine waved a hand. "Not the call me part, but why didn't you come home? What was so important that you had to go straight from the hospital to work?"

"I'd been out of the loop for a couple of days and I had no idea what was going on with the operation," Rebecca said, searching for the right words. "It felt like part of my life had dropped into a black hole. I just wanted to get reconnected."

"Reconnected." Catherine tried not to be hurt at Rebecca choosing her work over their relationship. She tried to imagine how she would feel if she were suddenly unable to go to the hospital and keep her patient appointments. She'd be concerned over not taking care of her responsibilities, and she'd be anxious until she had arranged for someone else to cover for her. But she wouldn't feel as if a piece of her life were missing. But then, she was not Rebecca.

"You're wrong about that," Rebecca whispered.

"What?" Catherine asked, startled from her internal analysis.

"The job isn't more important to me than being with you."

And there it was—what she feared most, even though she was embarrassed to admit it. That she would never be first in anyone's life. That just as the child she'd been—of two people who loved her, but had loved each other more—she would always be waiting to be seen. Catherine sighed. Rebecca's words reminded her of why she had fallen in love with her, despite how hard some parts of being with her could be—moments just like this, when Rebecca saw her so clearly, even more clearly than she could see herself, and gave her the very thing she needed most. The certainty that she was loved. She believed in Rebecca's love even when Rebecca's life, *Rebecca's* needs, hurt and frightened her.

"I'm terribly in love with you," Catherine whispered. "And I need you so much."

Shifting her hands from Catherine's shoulders into her hair, Rebecca cradled Catherine's head tenderly as she kissed her. "I'm an idiot. When I hurt you like this I want to shoot myself."

Catherine pressed her fingers to Rebecca's mouth. "Don't even joke."

"I'm not joking. You're the best thing in my life. The best thing that's ever happened to me, or ever will. I don't mean to make you unhappy. I don't mean to frighten you."

"I know that. In my heart, I know that. And that truly is what's most important to me." Catherine wrapped her arms around Rebecca's waist and kissed the side of her neck. "But you must promise me that you'll stop and think. And remember that you're not indestructible."

"When I went in yesterday, I was only planning to sit at a desk," Rebecca said. "That's what I'm still planning on doing."

Catherine fixed her with an intense stare. "Are you going to tell me the only thing you did yesterday was sit with your feet propped up somewhere?"

Rebecca looked away. "I went for a very short walk with Sandy."

"Sandy?" Catherine shook her head. "Sandy is a remarkable young woman, but I would rather have William or Sloan or Dellon protecting you."

"I don't need them protecting me. I'm their boss."

"Yes, darling, you are. And when you're a hundred percent, there's no one better qualified. But you're not a hundred percent. Not quite."

Begrudgingly, Rebecca nodded. "And that's why I'm going to sit my ass at a desk. All right?"

"Can I ask William to be sure that you do?"

Rebecca's eyes shifted from their ordinary icy cool to blue flame. "Hell, no."

Catherine laughed softly. "I had to try."

"Are you also trying to make my blood pressure go up?" Rebecca teased, tightening her grip and skating her lips along the edge of Catherine's jaw. "Because if that's your goal, I can think of more pleasurable ways to achieve it."

"Don't play with me, darling," Catherine whispered. "Because we don't have time and we have instructions not to make love, remember?"

Rebecca growled. "Like that's happening."

"No." Catherine eased away. "We're not. Not until Ali says we can."

"You can't be serious. I feel fine." Rebecca had the sudden urge to drag Catherine upstairs and show her just how fine she really felt. She was willing to take a backseat at work for a while, but she'd be damned if she'd keep from touching Catherine. Not when she needed to be sure Catherine understood just how essential she was. Maybe, Rebecca thought, she didn't always have the right words, and maybe she was selfish most of the time, but when they made love, she came as close as she ever could to showing Catherine how much she loved her. "And I want you."

"Go talk to William." Catherine caressed Rebecca's face. "No coffee."

"Jesus," Rebecca muttered under her breath. "No coffee, no work, no sex. I might as well have stayed in the hospital."

"I'm not going to say I agree, but I do." Catherine clasped Rebecca's hand and kissed the back of her fingers. "So stop grumbling. Call me later?"

"I will."

"Go then, Detective," Catherine murmured, because she had to let her go. Rebecca was many things, but first and always a cop.

❖

Rebecca buckled her seat belt as Watts pulled away from the curb.

After a few seconds of silence, he said, "So I guess you got your balls busted for going back to work, huh?"

Rebecca slowly turned her head. "Sorry?"

"Nothing, Loo," Watts said, the corner of his mouth twitching. "Didn't say a thing."

"That's what I thought."

Despite rush-hour traffic, Watts made it across town in record time and pulled into the parking lot at One Police Plaza at a little past 8:30. They walked across the parking lot to a side door, avoiding the main lobby that serviced the administrative offices. A back elevator took them to the third floor. Since the formation of the HPCU, Rebecca reported directly to Captain John Henry, one of the few administrators she liked and respected. A former street cop who had worked his way up through the ranks, he gave her as much room as he could to run her unit the way she wanted. As she and Watts wended their way through a jumble of desks assigned to detectives from homicide, vice, and special crimes, Rebecca nodded and muttered her thanks to the colleagues who congratulated her on the recent successful raid or asked after her health. At that hour of the morning, most of the desks were occupied with men and women reviewing reports, organizing case files for court, and planning the day's work. She disliked fanfare for just doing her job, and she definitely didn't want to dwell on almost taking a bullet in the face.

Henry's door was open a few inches. With a sigh of relief, she rapped and a deep voice inquired, "Yes?"

"Frye and Watts, Captain."

"Come in and close the door."

Rebecca and Watts entered and remained standing until Captain Henry waved them to a couple of straight-backed chairs in front of his desk. As usual, he wore a crisp white shirt, subdued tie, and dark jacket, and sat ramrod straight, his smooth mahogany features giving no clue as to his thoughts. Only the sharp glint in his dark chocolate eyes revealed his irritation. That and the early-morning summons confirmed Rebecca's suspicions that she was about to hear bad news.

"I got a wake-up call from Agent Clark this morning," Henry said.

Watts uttered an insult directed at Clark's parentage just low enough so that Henry wouldn't be able to hear. Rebecca managed to contain her own oath. Avery Clark was a federal Justice Department agent who managed to show up just in time to claim jurisdiction every time she and her team made an arrest. They'd been ordered from the brass on high to cooperate with him. Unfortunately, no one had told Avery that teamwork was a two-way street.

"What does he want now?" Rebecca asked.

"He wants us to know he appreciates the HPCU's expertise, and he knew there were things we could accomplish that he couldn't."

Beside her, Watts snorted. Rebecca shook her head. "He doesn't pay compliments without a price."

Henry nodded. "My guess is his resources are stretched thin, and he needs to ride our coattails as long as he can. He figures that we have the best chance of tying the sex slavery business to the local crime syndicate. If we can prove that they're taking these girls across state lines for purposes of prostitution, the federal case gets a lot stronger."

"He wants us to make his case for him," Watts grumbled. "Just like old times."

"Clark has a point," Henry said. "The best shot at finding the people behind the trafficking operation is to uncover the link to the local crime organization."

"That means we have to get someone deep inside," Rebecca said. "That kind of undercover operation takes a lot of time to set up. And the Zamoras are going to be looking for a plant, especially after Jimmy."

Running an operative undercover was one of the most frustrating jobs someone in Rebecca's position could have. She had to put her people in danger and could do very little to protect them. She didn't like it. Jimmy Hogan had managed to infiltrate the Zamora organization and he'd turned up dead. Undercover cops knew the risks, and often thrived on the constant stress and adrenaline high, but Zamora knew he was a target. The timing was all wrong.

"We've already got someone inside his organization," Captain Henry said. "Courtesy of Avery Clark."

"Uh-oh," Watts said. "I'm starting to feel like there's a dick up my ass."

Henry pursed his lips. "Thank you for that personal revelation, Detective Watts."

Watts grunted. "Fucking Clark."

"If the organzied crime unit has an undercover agent inside the Zamora family, why are we just hearing about it?" Rebecca asked. Interdepartmental communications weren't always seamless and cops could get territorial, but her team had been poking around the edges of the Zamora organization for long enough that someone in OCU would have either waved them off or filled them in by now. Something wasn't adding up. And that something had to be Avery Clark's doing. When she'd woken up that morning, her headache had receded to a low-level throbbing. Just thinking about Clark interfering in her investigation, yet again, made her eyes ache.

"What aren't I seeing here, Captain?" Rebecca asked.

Henry rose and carried a file folder with him around to the front of his desk. Opening it toward Watts and Rebecca, he displayed several typed pages and a glossy photograph clipped to the inside cover. Rebecca leaned forward, recognizing the woman in the photograph at the same time as Watts.

"Hey," Watts said. "That's our boy Mitch's new squeeze."

"Irina Guterov," Henry elaborated. Anyone else would've leaned against the edge of the desk, but he didn't.

"She was picked up in the raid the other night," Rebecca pointed out. Irina had unknowingly led them to one of the houses where the Russian girls were being held under armed guard. Mitch and Irina had been about to have sex when Rebecca's team burst in.

"Clark has convinced her to work for us," the captain said. "*She's our way inside.*"

Rebecca replayed the details of the raid earlier that week. Mitch and Irina had been in the back bedroom, and all the working girls had been upstairs. The only other occupant of the house, the girls' armed captor, was dead. The girls had immediately been sequestered by Immigration and would probably be deported, so no one in the crime ring knew Mitch's true identity.

"Does Irina know Mitchell is one of ours?" Rebecca asked.

"Clark says no, but she'll have to be briefed since the whole plan hinges on Mitchell being her contact."

"That might fly," Rebecca conceded. "Irina has worked with the handlers who send these girls out on jobs. It's one step further up the ladder." She took the folder from Henry and studied the photograph. Even the stark black-and-white police photo couldn't diminish Irina's haunting beauty. "The problem is, Zamora's people have to know she was in that house when we raided it."

Henry nodded. "Her story is going to be that she and Mitch went out the back window and they've been hiding until the heat died down. No one knows we've had her under wraps."

"Then she has to get back into circulation quickly. With Detective Mitchell."

"That's why you're here," Henry said. "You need to get your boy back on the streets with her. Tonight."

"And we're going to trust her, why?" Watts asked, his voice laced with suspicion and anger. "Mitch is gonna be hanging out there by himself. You can bet Clark isn't going to lose any sleep over him."

"According to Irina, her little sister is in a house just like the one you took down the other night," Henry said. "That's part of the reason Irina has been willing to work for these people to begin with. She's been trying to find her."

"She says," Watts snorted.

Henry lifted a shoulder. "Clark believes her."

"And I've got a ten-inch pecker."

"If her story's true, she's got motivation to play along. At least until she finds her sister. Do we have an ID on the sister?"

"Not yet. The feds are searching the international databases, but she's probably not in any of them. Irina says she has a picture of her at the club where she works," Henry said.

"Ziggie's," Watts said.

"Right. Another reason we need her and Mitchell back there."

"Where's Irina now?" Rebecca asked.

"Clark's got her stashed somewhere." Henry's face showed a flicker of anger. "He doesn't trust our security and won't tell me where. He'll deliver her when we arrange a meet between her and Mitchell."

Rebecca rubbed her forehead. "Do we have any room to negotiate here? I'd like to talk to her before I put Mitchell in the middle of this."

"Clark already took the plan to the top, and the brass like it. It's an election year, and it looks good whenever we take a bite out of organized crime."

"Let's hope they don't take a bite out of us first," Watts muttered.

"They won't," Rebecca said flatly. It was her job to make sure that didn't happen.

Chapter Six

Dell clenched her fists under the table, trying like hell not to let anything she was feeling show on her face. Lieutenant Frye was still talking, but she was having a hard time concentrating. Her mind was going in a million directions at once. The lieutenant had called them all together to brief them on a new operation, an undercover operation targeting one of the biggest crime families in the country. And she was the point man. Never mind that it was a career-making assignment. What mattered to her was making the lieutenant proud. Making her team proud. But hell—Irina. Jesus. She hadn't figured to see her again, although she'd tried to find her after the raid, just to be sure she was all right. Now they'd be working together, pretending to be a couple. Irina and Mitch, that is.

"Are you with us, Detective?" Rebecca asked.

"Yes ma'am," Dell snapped, straightening in her seat.

Rebecca stared at her hard for a few seconds, then turned back to the whiteboard. As she talked, she blocked out the highlights of the operation. "Mitch will continue with his cover as a friend of the Kings. He's been seen with them a couple of times in Ziggie's and at the Troc. He's known to have a girlfriend, but he plays around. It helps that he's already been seen with Irina."

"The boy gets more action than most guys with real dicks," Watts groused.

Ordinarily Dell would have shot back that it wasn't what you had in your pants, but what you did with it, but her stomach was in knots and she couldn't muster up any levity. Since she'd started working undercover in drag, she'd discovered that Mitch wasn't just an assignment. She'd connected with a part of herself that felt natural and necessary. Lucky for her, Sandy liked Mitch too. And so did Irina.

"Maybe Mitch scores so well because he knows how to treat a lady," Jason said with just enough of a lilt in his voice to remind everyone he knew what he was talking about.

"Mitch needs tighter backup than we can provide with ordinary surveillance," Rebecca said. "We can't wire him routinely because we're *hoping* Irina will be taking him places where he's going to get patted down." Rebecca focused on Jason. "I can't order you to do street work, but—"

"I hope you're not going to suggest that a lady can't be trusted with Mitch's ass," Jason said, his tone still light but his eyes serious.

"You're a civilian, Jason. And it won't be just Mitch's ass on the line."

"I'm in," Jason said. "Jasmine has a show Saturday night before the Kings go on. Mitch can bring Irina. She'll figure Jasmine is just part of the group."

Rebecca nodded. "I like it."

Dell was glad Irina would know she was a cop because she didn't want to lie to her anymore, but she started to sweat when she imagined taking Irina to the Troc like it was some kind of date. They'd just be acting, she reminded herself. Both of them.

"This might be our only chance to find out who took out your cops," Sloan said to Rebecca. "We're not going to quit with the middlemen, are we?"

"A few token arrests might be enough to make City Hall happy," Rebecca said, "but we're going after the top dogs."

"Fucking A," Watts muttered.

Sloan nodded. "I still want to continue the forensic analysis of the computers at the port. We might find a tie-in there."

"Agreed. Stay on it." Rebecca looked at Watts. "Talk to the captain down there today so Sloan can get started." She wrote "midnight" on the board and circled it. "Mitch and Irina are due to show up at Ziggie's tonight at midnight. Watts and I will take surveillance."

Watts's eyebrows rose as if he were going to object, but a look from the lieutenant shut him down.

Dell cleared her throat and hoped her voice didn't crack. "Where's Irina going to stay? She can't go back to the house where she was living with those girls, not alone."

"Her cover story," Rebecca said, "is that the two of you went out a back window and hid out in Mitch's apartment. For now, that's where she'll be staying."

"Mitch's apartment." Dell's stomach rolled. The studio she'd rented when she went undercover was down the hall from Sandy's apartment and its only furnishings were a mattress and a ratty sofa. Her mind shut down before she could think about taking Irina there. "Okay. Right."

Rebecca sighed. "Unfortunately, there's more."

"There always is when the feds are involved," Sloan said grimly.

"Clark wants more information on the Zamoras' political connections, and he thinks we're in a better position to get it than his people." Rebecca pulled out a chair and dropped into it. "He's probably right. Kratos Zamora is a big supporter of the mayor's campaign."

"Pretty dicey association for the mayor," Sloan said.

"Kratos Zamora is a legitimate businessman, and he donates big bucks to the local political machine." Rebecca shrugged. "And for all intents and purposes, he's squeaky clean."

"So what's the brilliant plan?" Sloan asked.

"There's an upcoming fund-raiser for the mayor, and Clark wants us there."

"Us?" Sloan narrowed her eyes. "Why would we be there?"

"I'll be there representing the force, to show the department's support for the mayor. Normal politicking." Rebecca stared at Sloan. "Clark thinks you'd have a chance at getting close to Zamora if you were with Michael, because she's one of the wealthiest businesswomen—"

Sloan shot to her feet. "Clark can go fuck himself. Michael's not going anywhere near Zamora."

"All right," Rebecca said. "I understand."

"Are you planning on taking Catherine?" Sloan asked angrily.

"Catherine's already going." Rebecca would have preferred Catherine stay far away from anything even remotely connected to the case, but she couldn't ask her to skip the event. "She's on the board of the city's AIDS/HIV commission. She attends a lot of fund-raisers."

"Michael is out of it." Sloan sat back down, her eyes stormy. "I'll go stag. Sloan Security does business with all the big firms in the city. We're not without resources, so I'd have a reason to be there."

"What about the rest of us?" Dell asked.

Rebecca shook her head. "You need to stay away from Zamora for the time being."

"Sandy's going to be pissed she missed it."

"No doubt." Rebecca grinned fleetingly.

Dell would have laughed, except she was thinking that Sandy was going to be pissed about a lot of things.

❖

"Talk to you a minute, Loo?" Watts said as the others filed out of the room.

Rebecca nodded, mentally reviewing her hastily thrown together operation. Mitchell might end up chasing a dead lead. With the girls Irina had been supervising out of the picture, Irina's conduit to the crime organization might have closed. If that was the case, they'd waste a few weeks of surveillance time. But if Mitchell actually did get inside, she'd be there on her own. Because there was no way backup was going to be able to follow her where she needed to go. Rebecca had lost one partner. She wasn't losing a member of her team.

"...my ass."

"What?" Rebecca said sharply. "Nobody likes surveillance, Watts, but it's necessary—"

"I'm not saying I don't want to freeze my ass off out in the cold while Mitch is inside a titty bar getting his crank pulled," Watts shot back. "Hell, what guy wouldn't want to be the one freezing his nuts off in the car? All I'm saying is, you can't go."

"*What?*" Rebecca straightened. "I don't think I heard you right, Detective."

"Excuse me, Loo, but you're supposed to be on desk duty. And excuse me again, but I don't feel like having my ass chewed out by your...woman. Whatever."

"My woman?" Rebecca raised her eyebrows.

Watts shrugged. "The doc. I sort of promised her."

Rebecca turned around and strode to the opposite end of the room. She braced both hands on the counter and closed her eyes. She'd promised her too. Except that she hadn't known at the time that Henry planned to put the team back out on the street so fast. Units like hers typically spent months building cases through surveillance and wiretaps and gathering street intel. They tapped their confidential informants, they followed midlevel drug dealers, they rousted street pushers and pimps. They toiled at their desks and spent endless hours cruising the streets, until maybe they got lucky and could put a case together. But this was different. They were going hunting, and they were sending their youngest, their least experienced, into the jungle alone.

"God damn it," Rebecca said quietly.

"Yeah, it blows," Watts said from behind her.

"Don't you have somewhere to be?" Rebecca said without turning around.

"Sure thing, Loo."

Rebecca listened to Watts's fading footsteps, then went to find Sloan. She needed a car.

❖

Kratos Zamora ended his conference call with his European business associates, finished his coffee in a single swallow, and pushed the ceramic mug to the front of his desk where his secretary would pick it up and refill it upon his return. Then he stood, donned his silk and wool blended double-breasted charcoal suit jacket, checked the knot in his tie, and walked to the double mahogany doors separating his office from the adjoining conference room. When he stepped through, his brother Gregor was already seated near Vincent. On the opposite side of the room, a matching pair of double doors led to Gregor's office. Kratos sat down at the head of the polished walnut table. Another cup of coffee awaited him. He sipped it and regarded the other two men steadily.

"Well? What have we learned?"

Gregor clicked a remote to lower the room lights, then activated an LCD projector. "JT Sloan's business address is a matter of record, and Angelo has been shooting everyone going in and out. Mostly women, one guy who is definitely a cop, and another young guy who we figure is Sloan's partner. There's a Jason McBride listed on their corporate holdings."

"Let's see them," Kratos said.

Angelo had done a good job, shooting multiple photos of people coming and going. Two were clearly cops—a beefy middle-aged man and a tall, thin blonde who looked to be all business. Probably the detective lieutenant in charge. She looked like she could be a lesbian.

Kratos leaned forward. "Stop right there."

Angelo had caught a full-face view of another blonde, this one elegant and sleekly beautiful. In her thirties, smooth-skinned and slender. The face of an artist's model.

"Who is that?" Kratos asked.

"No name yet, but she's a looker," Vincent said.

Kratos shot him a steely glare and Vincent averted his gaze. Another shot came up, this one showing the beautiful woman holding hands with a thin, wild-looking girl. A friend, maybe, because a woman as sensual and feminine as that one couldn't possibly be a lesbian.

"I want her name," Kratos said.

"Sure thing, boss," Vincent said.

Gregor clicked off the slides. "Angelo has a straight sight line right down to their front door. He could take one out, probably two or three, and still get away clean."

"And we'd have police in our lobby before the bodies hit the ground," Kratos murmured, still thinking about the beautiful blonde. "For now, we watch."

"Papa would never have let *puttanas* like that interfere with our business," Gregor grumbled.

"Papa was a great man," Kratos said softly as he stood, turning his back on his brother to address Vincent. "Have Angelo print out head shots of all of them. And I want names to go with them."

❖

"Sorry to keep you waiting," Ali Torveau greeted Rebecca as she stepped into the examining room and closed the door.

"No need to apologize," Rebecca said, already regretting her unscheduled visit. Ali's wrinkled, faded green surgical scrubs looked about as worn out as she did. The shadows under her eyes, which already seemed a permanent fixture, were darker today than Rebecca remembered them. "I'm the one interrupting your day when you're probably due to go home. Sorry."

"Not a problem. I'll be here awhile." Ali pulled the stainless steel stool out from under the tiny shelf that served as a writing table and instrument stand and sat down, leaning her back against the shelf. "Just finished a fifteen-hour marathoner. A couple of rival gangs went to war last night. Three dead. Two others may be joining them soon. Just kids."

"Rough."

"Stupid waste." Ali shook her head, then focused on Rebecca, her fatigue appearing to vanish. "So what's wrong?"

Rebecca hadn't bothered to undress even though the nurse had instructed her to when she ushered her into the room. She sat on the examining table, the white paper covering crinkling beneath her. She detested being in a position where she had to ask someone else to empower her to do her job, even when that someone was a friend. "I need you to clear me for active duty. Today."

Ali was silent for a long moment. "And how is today different than yesterday morning when I said two weeks of desk duty?"

"Yesterday morning I didn't have a new street operation about to kick off."

"What's so important that someone else can't pinch-hit for you?"

Despite Ali's conversational tone, Rebecca felt her temper rising. If it hadn't been for her promise to Catherine, she wouldn't be here at all. She didn't need medical clearance because she'd only been admitted to the hospital for observation. Her discharge sufficed to clear her for duty. No one actually knew about the restrictions that Ali had imposed. Except Catherine. And Watts, who couldn't keep his nose out of her goddamn business all of a sudden. She bit back a sharp reply because Ali looked like hell and it wasn't her fault that Rebecca hadn't been fast enough to dive out of the line of fire. If Sloan hadn't been so quick to back her up, she'd be dead and Catherine's pain would be on her head. The wave of remorse was enough to cool her frustration.

"This isn't something I would ordinarily tell anyone." Rebecca hesitated. This was not something she wanted Catherine to hear, and

Ali's quick nod confirmed that their discussion was confidential. "I've got a young detective going undercover tonight. It's dangerous. Anything could happen, and I need to be there. Me. No one else. But I'm just going to be sitting in a car to coordinate."

Ali made a face. "Don't give me that, Rebecca. You just told me anything could happen."

"I won't be alone. Watts will be with me." Rebecca took a breath. "I don't expect anything to happen, at least not right away. But that doesn't mean I can sit at home with my feet up."

"What happens if I don't clear you?" When Rebecca said nothing, Ali stood up. "If I wanted to play hardball, I could call your captain. Get you sidelined for as long as I wanted. The city is very antsy about lawsuits, and an impaired cop on the streets is a liability."

"You won't do that," Rebecca said with confidence.

"You're right. I won't. I could call Catherine."

Rebecca stiffened. "Catherine has enough to worry about."

"No, Catherine worries about *you*, and she's not going to worry any less if I give my blessing for you to head straight back out into the same jungle that almost got you killed."

"I'm a cop. That's what I do."

"I know that. If I didn't, I wouldn't be standing here." Ali pulled an ophthalmoscope out of the charger next to the examining table. "Look over my left shoulder."

Rebecca complied while Ali shone a bright light into first one eye, then the other. She felt like an ice pick was piercing her brain, and her eyes watered. "Jesus."

"Sorry," Ali said, not sounding particularly remorseful. "You understand that there's a small but definite risk that you could have an intracranial bleed?"

"That could happen if I were sitting at my desk, too, right?"

"It could, that's true. But every day that passes without an incident makes the risk less likely. The first seven to ten days after the injury are the high risk period." Ali put the ophthalmoscope away, and then took Rebecca's blood pressure.

"I'm not going to do anything crazy," Rebecca said. "If it weren't for Catherine, I'd never say that. But I'm not going to do anything else to hurt her."

"You're cutting that line pretty thin just by going back on duty," Ali said.

"I know. But it's the best I can do."

Ali removed the cuff from Rebecca's arm. "All right, Detective, I'm taking you at your word. Be careful."

"I'll try." Rebecca shook Ali's hand, thanked her, and headed out the door. She had one more stop to make.

❖

"Rebecca?" Catherine dropped the file she was reviewing onto her desk and stood. "What's wrong?"

"Nothing," Rebecca said hurriedly. "I'm sorry. Joyce said you were free."

"I am. I don't have another patient for almost an hour. What are you doing here?" Catherine came around the front of her desk and met Rebecca in the center of the Oriental rug that covered most of her office floor.

"I'm not allowed to visit you?"

"You're welcome here anytime, darling, but you generally only drop by if you're worried, upset, or have something serious to tell me."

Rebecca tossed her blazer onto one of the two leather club chairs in front of Catherine's desk. She'd sat in one of those chairs the first night she'd come to interview Catherine, six months ago. She'd been sure that Catherine would not help her. Certain, too, that Catherine would never be able to understand how badly she needed to catch the man who was violating the city's women, because no one had ever understood what drove her to put an end to violence and abuse no matter the cost. She'd been wrong about Catherine's willingness to help, wrong about pretty much everything where Catherine was concerned. She winced, trying to remember the last time she'd sent Catherine flowers or just called her to ask after her day. "I'm a crappy lover, aren't I?"

"No." Catherine clasped Rebecca's waist but resisted embracing her, which she would have done on any other day. Lightly tracing the sharp line of Rebecca's jaw with her fingertips, she said, "You're a wonderful lover. This is about whatever Captain Henry wanted to see you for this morning, isn't it?"

"You're starting to sound like a cop's wife."

"That must be because I am." Catherine kissed Rebecca's cheek and led her to the moss green upholstered sofa opposite the windows. A small coffee table stood in front of it. They'd eaten takeout off that table more than once. They'd made love on that sofa one night when they'd been barely more than strangers, desperate to banish the terrors of the night with the heat of passion. Thinking about it now made Catherine flush, not with embarrassment at something so out of character for her, but with desire.

"What is it?" Rebecca asked quietly.

"Not anything I want to talk about just now."

Rebecca laughed as she settled onto the sofa. "Later, then?"

"Most definitely later." Catherine angled away from Rebecca so she could see her face and not be tempted to touch her. "Tell me what Henry wanted."

"He laid out a new operation for us this morning. Starting tonight."

Catherine drew a sharp breath. "What kind of operation?"

"Pretty much what we're planning to do anyway, although on an accelerated schedule." Rebecca hesitated.

"Don't censor it, Rebecca."

"The plan is a little more aggressive than I might like."

"Define aggressive," Catherine said carefully, locking down her emotional responses. Rebecca was here, sharing the kinds of things that were difficult for her to share, and Catherine needed to hear them, no matter how hard.

"Clark wants someone undercover. Mitchell."

"Isn't that what she's been doing all along?" Catherine had the clearance to be informed of procedural details, because in her capacity as a consultant to the police department, she often spoke with officers and their supervisors about classified information. She'd participated in some of Rebecca's recent investigations. She knew Dellon's role.

"This time she's going undercover with one of the Russian women who helped hold the girls captive."

"Why?"

"We're supposed to get a line on the local organized crime syndicate, and Mitchell is the one going inside."

JUSTICE FOR ALL

"Well." Catherine gave a pensive sigh. "That's definitely aggressive."

"I can't sit on the sidelines, Catherine. I'm sorry."

"No, I don't suppose you can."

"I just came from Ali's office. She said—"

"What happened?" Catherine's heart raced. "Why didn't you tell me you weren't feeling well?"

"No, no. I'm fine. I just wanted Ali to take a look at me so she could clear me."

Catherine blinked. "You voluntarily went to see Ali for an examination?"

"Sounds crazy, doesn't it?" Rebecca shook her head. "Felt that way too."

"What did she say?"

"She said I could work. And to be careful."

Catherine moved closer on the sofa and laid her hand in the center of Rebecca's chest. "I know you didn't do it because you wanted permission."

Rebecca laughed.

"Thank you," Catherine whispered. She leaned closer and kissed Rebecca. "I know you must have hated that."

"Not as much as I hate upsetting you." Rebecca cradled Catherine's head and kissed her back. "I'm sorry about all of this."

"Don't apologize. Just keep your promise to Ali and to me." Catherine closed her eyes. "Would you mind just staying here for a few more minutes?"

Rebecca rested her cheek against Catherine's hair and held her tightly. "I'll stay just as long as you want me to."

❖

"Hi, baby," Sandy said as she breezed through the door of the two-room apartment. She dropped a shopping bag on the single chair, shed her jacket, and climbed onto the couch, pulling up her short skirt so she could straddle Dell's lap. Then she wrapped her arms around Dell's neck and kissed her, giving her a little bit of a lap dance while she dueled with her tongue. "Mmm, you taste good."

Dell clasped Sandy's ass in both hands. A little bit of something covered an inch or so of the space between Sandy's legs, but Dell didn't think a scrap of satin that small could really be called panties. Otherwise, despite the cold, Sandy's legs were bare. Dell got a mental picture of the wet spot she bet Sandy was leaving on her fly and was instantly totally stoked. She skimmed the cleft between Sandy's legs with her fingertips and Sandy moaned, tilting her hips just enough so Dell could tease her from behind. Dell flicked one finger over the firm knot poking up against the soft satin and Sandy bit down on her tongue.

"Ow!" Dell jerked her head back and laughed despite the fact she'd been worrying about seeing Sandy all afternoon. "Jesus, what have you been doing? You're so hot you're going to shoot off like a rocket."

"I met Michael for lunch and we went shopping," Sandy whispered, licking her way around Dell's ear. "It was so much fun."

Dell dropped her head back, her mind going fuzzy for a second. "Shopping turned you on?"

Sandy bit her earlobe. "No, blockhead. I kept thinking about dressing up for you, and then I imagined you taking everything off me. Then I got horny."

"So you want to give me a show?"

"Uh-uh." Sandy dived in for another kiss. "Later. Now I want you to make me come."

Dell massaged Sandy's ass some more, encouraging her to keep circling in her lap. She wished to hell she'd known Sandy was gonna come home like this, because she would've been more prepared for her. "If you give me a minute, I can give you something to really ride on."

"Just play with me like you were doing. All I need is a little bit." Sandy nibbled on Dell's lower lip and rubbed her breasts back and forth over Dell's chest. "Come on, baby."

"Okay, babe." Dell cupped one of Sandy's small firm breasts and rubbed the tight peak through the thin cotton tank with her thumb. She watched Sandy's eyes until they clouded and her lips parted in a soft, surprised *oh*, and then she edged two fingers between Sandy's legs from behind and circled her clit. Sandy shuddered and gripped Dell's shoulders. Dell tried to make it last, because she loved to watch Sandy's face get all dreamy and the little frown line form between her eyes when she was getting ready to come, but Sandy was already there. She gave one sharp cry and collapsed in Dell's arms, her flesh pulsing sweetly beneath Dell's palm.

"You're so hot," Dell whispered as she kissed Sandy's neck.

"Mmm." Sandy stretched and pulled one leg over Dell's lap so she could curl up in her arms. She rested her head on Dell's shoulder and rubbed Dell's chest lazily. "You do me so nice."

"Shopping, huh? We're going to need bigger closets."

Sandy circled Dell's nipple with her fingernails, scratching lightly at the tight black T-shirt covering it. Dell took a sharp breath and Sandy smiled with satisfaction. "So I went to Michael's office today. She said I could try the job for a little while. If I didn't like it…" Sandy shrugged. "No big deal."

"Yeah?" The lump in Dell's throat made her sound hoarse. Sandy's teasing had her nerves jangling, but she wanted to talk. They needed to talk. "When are you going to start?"

"Monday, probably." Sandy nibbled on the side of Dell's neck. "She said I don't have to come in until ten in the morning."

Dell's brain was a little slow because most of her blood was hammering between her legs, but she finally put it together. She grasped Sandy's hand and moved it away from her breast. "You're going to try to do this job *and* still work for Frye? Why?" She couldn't keep the edge out of her voice, and felt Sandy stiffen. "There's no reason for you to be out on the streets anymore."

"What did you expect?" Sandy sat up straight, her chin thrust out. "Do you think I'm going to all of a sudden become someone else? Just because I've got some new clothes and a day job?"

"No, Jesus." Dell clenched her hands by her sides as Sandy hopped off her lap and stalked across the room. "That's not what I meant."

Sandy picked up the bag of clothes, tossed it inside the tiny closet next to the door, and slammed it closed. Then she spun around, her arms folded beneath her breasts. "If you wanted a girlfriend you could take home to meet your family, you should have picked someone else."

Dell jumped up. "I never said that, San."

"Then why do you want me to take this job so much?"

"Because I want you to be safe," Dell yelled. "Is that so hard to figure out?"

"Hey!" Sandy yelled back. "Get over yourself, rookie. I never asked you to worry about me. And I sure as hell never asked you to look out for me."

Before Dell could say anything else, Sandy yanked open the door and stormed out. The walls rattled as the door crashed shut.

Dell yanked her hand through her hair. "What the fuck was that?"

❖

Sloan ignored the muted whir of the hydraulics as the elevator ascended. A few seconds later, a faint whoosh indicated the doors had opened, but she kept on scanning the data scrolling on three screens. The click of heels on hardwood floors pierced her concentration and she spun on her chair. Michael was smiling as she wound her way through the labyrinth of desks and equipment.

"Hey," Sloan rose, "what are you doing here?"

"Looking for a dinner partner."

"Really? A little early, isn't it?"

Laughing, Michael propped her briefcase in front of the bank of computer monitors and laced her arms around Sloan's neck. Then she kissed her. "It's after seven, love."

Sloan frowned. "It is?" She checked the room, realized she was alone, and vaguely remembered Jason saying he was leaving. Dell was gone too. Hours ago, now that she thought of it. "Am I late for something?"

"No, but we could be if you're not all that hungry." Michael traced the muscles in Sloan's shoulders through the cotton shirt she wore. "I was going to suggest that we walk over to Old City and grab something for dinner, but if you have something else in mind…"

"I do now," Sloan muttered, nipping at Michael's lower lip before she kissed her more thoroughly. She was always ready for Michael. "The team is going to get pretty busy pretty soon. Maybe we should have dinner. You can tell me what's happening at the office."

Michael leaned back in Sloan's arms, smiling softly. "Now *you* want to talk about work?"

"I want to talk about you. What do you say?"

"I say I love you." Michael grasped Sloan's hand. "Let me take you to dinner, and then we'll come home and you can do unspeakably wonderful things to me."

"I think I can handle that. I'll just grab my jacket." Sloan slid from Michael's grip and started toward the conference room.

"Don't forget the benefit this weekend," Michael said casually. "If you're not too busy, I'm counting on you to be my date."

Sloan spun around. "What?"

Michael started, her expression confused. "I'm sure we talked about it. The Women's Business Association is one of the sponsors for the mayor's outreach program. There's a fund-raiser this weekend?" She frowned. "I know my memory's still a little patchy, but—"

"You can't go," Sloan said flatly.

"I don't understand." Michael searched her face. "What's wrong?"

"Nothing." Sloan turned her back and started for the conference room again.

"Sloan," Michael called after her. "What are you saying?"

"I'm saying you can't go." Sloan shoved open the conference room door and stormed inside. The room was dark and she didn't bother to turn on the light. She grabbed the nearest chair, lifting it a few inches as she thought about throwing it somewhere. Anywhere. A red haze of anger blurred her vision and her ears rang as if someone had fired a round right next to her head.

"Darling," Michael said from behind her.

"Don't turn on the light," Sloan said, afraid for Michael to see what was in her face. Fury and fear and foreboding. And a terrifying sense of impotence, as if things were spinning out of control and she was helpless to stop them.

"You're starting to scare me." Michael rested both hands gently on Sloan's back. "You're shaking."

"I'm fine."

"No, you're not." Michael wrapped her arms around Sloan from behind, rubbing her palms over Sloan's chest. Sloan's body was so tight it felt as if she might snap like a high-tension wire breaking in the wind, lashing anything in its path. Michael might have been frightened if she hadn't known with every fiber of her being that Sloan would never hurt her. She leaned her cheek against Sloan's back. "I love you."

"Then just trust me on this, Michael."

RADCLY*f*FE

"I do trust you. But that doesn't mean I don't need to understand you." Michael kissed the side of Sloan's neck. "I have to go to this, darling. I'm giving one of the introductory speeches."

"Get someone else to do it."

"I can't. I have a job, too, Sloan."

"God damn it, Michael," Sloan barked, spinning around, breaking Michael's grip. "It's just a job."

Michael backed up, the light from the main room falling across her face, etching her shock in stark chiaroscuro. "Where is this coming from?"

Sloan knifed around her, not letting their bodies touch, and stalked out of the room. She picked up speed as she hit the elevator button. What could she tell her? That she had an irrational fear that Michael would be drawn into the evil that was a daily part of her life, that the deadly depravity would find her, would take her. The roaring in her head made it impossible for her to think. Or to explain.

"Sloan," Michael called, but the elevator doors had already closed behind her. Michael sagged against the table, trying desperately to understand what had just happened. Trying to dispel the cold, distant expression in Sloan's eyes. Sloan had looked at her as if they were strangers.

Michael waited in the dark, praying for Sloan's return. As the night and the aching silence stretched on, she finally went upstairs alone.

CHAPTER SEVEN

M itch sat alone at a table in the back of the darkened room, nursing a beer and watching the performance onstage at the Troc with only half a mind. Sandy hadn't come home before he'd had to leave. He kept thinking of the new clothes abandoned on the floor of the closet, and wishing he'd had a chance to see Sandy model them. Wishing he hadn't pushed so hard, because he knew Sandy hated to be pushed. Sandy didn't talk much about her life before the streets, but it didn't take much imagination to figure out she'd been pushed around a lot when she was a kid. Why else would any teenager leave home to sleep in a flophouse and sell the only thing that belonged to them just to survive another day. Sandy was tough, she was smart, and she could take care of herself. Mitch knew it. He loved that about her.

"Fucking coward," he muttered. Him, not Sandy. He was afraid he'd lose Sandy, just like he'd lost Robin. But he lost Robin because Robin had walked out. Robin had been ashamed of them. Mitch dropped his head back and closed his eyes. Yep, he'd blown it. One thing Sandy was not, was ashamed. Sandy had more pride than just about anybody Mitch knew. "Asshole."

A firm hand clamped Mitch's shoulder and a deep raspy voice said, "Talking to yourself, guy?"

"Not anymore." Mitch rolled his head to the side and squinted up at the wiry figure looming over him. Even in the semi-gloom he recognized the sharply cut profile of Phil E. Pride, one of the members of the Front Street Kings drag troupe. Mitch checked the stage and realized the show was over. Man, he'd been drifting, which was not a good idea while he was working. He straightened in his seat and kicked out a chair. "Sit down. I'll grab us a couple of fresh beers."

"Thanks," Phil said.

Mitch hustled to the bar tucked into one corner and snagged two drafts from the bartender just ahead of the crowd. Holding them high so they didn't spill as he jostled his way back to the table, he reviewed his cover story in his head. Then he set the beers down and reclaimed his chair. While he'd been gone, Ken Dewar, the leader of the Kings, had joined Phil.

"Sorry, Kenny," Mitch said to the flat-topped blond with the construction worker's build. "I didn't get you a brew."

"No problem." Ken swiped Phil's glass and took a long pull.

"Solo tonight, Mitch?" Phil asked conversationally as he reached across the table and retrieved his beer from Ken.

"Yeah. I'm kind of in between girls, if you know what I mean. So I needed a little peace and quiet." Mitch sipped his beer and cupped himself for a second to settle his dick more comfortably in his tight black jeans. Somehow the fullness in his palm and the pressure against his crotch felt reassuring. He knew these guys and he liked them, and they seemed to like him too. They never probed into what he did for a living, and he suspected they knew he was more than the bar back and occasional bouncer he let on. The deception bothered him, but he reminded himself that his secrecy was as much for their safety as for the success of his assignment. He knew nothing of their other lives either.

"In between?" Ken laughed. "You mean you've got two girls pissed at you instead of one?"

"Something like that," Mitch said.

"So, uh, Sandy break up with you?" Phil asked.

Mitch tamped down the swift surge of jealousy, but it wasn't easy. Phil had made his appreciation of Sandy pretty clear when Mitch had introduced them. Since Mitch had been trying to get close to Irina, he'd been forced to let on he wasn't super serious about Sandy. Considering new developments, he could hardly get territorial now. But Phil was a good-looking guy. Strong shoulders, trim waist, and a nice healthy bulge in his jeans. He was also way confident around women. A lot more confident than Mitch. "Sandy didn't dump me yet. I'm hoping she'll cool off and cut me some slack."

"Well, good luck on that." Phil slapped Mitch's back. "But if you need a little help keeping her entertained, you know who to call."

"Sure, right," Mitch said, forcing a grin. "Listen, I'm meeting Irina at Ziggie's later, so in case anyone's asking, you haven't seen me."

Ken let out a long whistle. "Man, you really do like to live dangerously."

"What's the point, otherwise?" Mitch drained his beer. "I thought I'd bring her around to the show on Saturday. Introduce her properly to you guys."

"Sure. Always happy to meet a lady." Phil eyed Mitch speculatively. "If you need us for anything, just give us a call."

"Sure, but everything's cool." Mitch rose. "I've got it all under control."

As he headed for the door and his meeting with Irina, Mitch hoped to hell he was right.

❖

Through the swirling haze of anger, Sloan recognized the dark expanse of water to her left and the twisting road in front of her. West River Drive. The road peeled away beneath her and she took the tight turns fast, leaning hard into the curves, her body knifing through the wind. She was on her motorcycle because Rebecca had borrowed her car earlier and hadn't returned it yet. Sloan hadn't given any thought to where she was going when she walked out on Michael. All she'd wanted was to outrun her rage before it spilled over on Michael and contaminated the only good thing in her life.

As the white lines flashed beneath her, the cold wind off the water bit at her face below the visor of her helmet and her mind started to clear. Her focus shifted once more to Avery Clark. It all came down to the feds, the same group that had turned on her. They'd put her in jail and years later, they were still manipulating her life. Only this time, Avery wanted her to risk something far more important than her life. Michael.

She pulled into a turnoff that was empty save for one pickup truck at the far opposite end. Cutting the engine, she settled her feet on either side of her Harley and unzipped her jacket. Her body was hot and the cold air blowing off the water chilled the sweat against her skin. She wasn't afraid for herself. She *wanted* to get close to the men at the top. She wanted the man who had ordered the execution of two cops, and who had sent someone to run her down in the street outside her own home. Except she hadn't been the victim, Michael had.

The man responsible for that attack had to be out there, and there was no reason to think he wouldn't try again. Nothing had changed. In fact, the closer the team got to exposing the criminal conspiracies, the more likely the men pulling the strings were to take drastic action. She wasn't afraid on her own account. She'd spent enough time doing covert work in Southeast Asia to know how to protect herself. Professional assassins in that part of the world put American wiseguys to shame. But Michael didn't have that kind of skill, and Sloan didn't know how to protect her.

Her options were few. She could quit the team—she wasn't a cop or a federal agent anymore. But if she did, there was no guarantee the threat would disappear. She could find whoever had tried to kill her and force them to tell her who gave the order. She'd never been an assassin, but she would kill to protect Michael, and she knew it wouldn't bother her.

❖

When the buzzer rang, Michael jumped up from the sofa, excitement overriding her worry. Then disappointment struck her hard. It wouldn't be Sloan. Taking a steadying breath, she checked the small monitor set into the wall beside the elevator. Then she flicked the intercom. Sandy's voice greeted her.

"Hi. Sorry to bother you. I know it's late. Is Dell there?"

"No. No one's here. Want to come up?"

Sandy looked up and down the street, her uncertainty and unhappiness clear even in the small black-and-white image.

"I'm not having a very good night either," Michael said. "You don't have to talk about anything."

"Okay. Sure. Why not."

Michael disengaged the lock on the front door and watched the monitor until Sandy was inside. Then she went into the kitchen to make tea. A moment later, the tall double doors enclosing the elevator slid back almost soundlessly. She called over her shoulder, "Come on out to the kitchen. Are you hungry?"

"No," Sandy said, climbing up onto one of the stools. "Mind if I have a beer instead of tea?"

"One of those nights, huh?"

Sandy snorted. "For sure."

"So," Michael said, joining her at the breakfast bar. She handed her a bottle of one of Sloan's microbrews and set her own tea aside to cool. "Dell wasn't happy about the job offer?"

"Oh, she was. She can't wait to stick me behind a desk."

Michael couldn't help but smile, considering that was how she spent almost all her time. But she understood what Sandy meant. "A little overprotective?"

Sandy rolled her eyes. "Like working in an office is going to erase the last two years of my life."

"Is that what you think she wants?" Michael asked quietly.

"Don't you? After all, would you want a whore for a girlfriend?"

Michael cradled the steaming teacup while she give that some thought. "I would absolutely hate anyone to use someone I loved, physically or in any other way. I think I'd be jealous too. Of someone touching her, even though I know that's not what it's about. And of course, I'd be afraid of her being hurt."

Sandy leaned her elbow on the smooth granite surface, cupped her chin in her hand, and stared at Michael. "What about being ashamed or grossed out. You left that part out."

"If I loved someone the way I know Dell loves you, I wouldn't feel that way about what she needed to do."

"You know she went to West Point, right? That she's really smart? I mean, they're all smart—even Watts." Sandy sighed. "You didn't meet her sister, Erica. She's an uptight version of Dell, and she definitely didn't think I was good enough for her."

"I can't see Dell caring."

"She says she doesn't. Now."

"You know," Michael said carefully, "you could get your GED if you wanted."

"Maybe. Someday." Sandy picked at the corner of the label on her beer bottle with her thumb. "I want to take the job you offered. I don't want Dell to support me, so I need to be able to make money without doing guys for it. Besides, I'm sick of faking it."

"Good."

"But I'm doing something important already. With Frye." Sandy met Michael's gaze. "What I do for Frye makes a difference, just like what Sloan and Dell and the rest of them are doing. I don't want to stop, and Dell wants me to."

"Aha."

"Yeah." Sandy looked around the loft. "Where is everybody?"

"I don't know. Something's happening, but I'm not sure what it is." Michael sighed. "Sloan didn't tell me, but from the way she's wound up already, it's something big."

"Oh boy," Sandy said.

"Yes." Michael squeezed Sandy's hand. "So, Monday at ten?"

Sandy finished her beer, slid down from the stool, and placed the empty bottle on the counter next to the sink. "Okay. You'll be there, right?"

"I will. You're welcome to stay here. I have a feeling Sloan won't be back for a while."

"Thanks, but I think I'll hit a few places before I head home. Look up some friends."

Michael slid her arm around Sandy's shoulder and walked her to the elevator. "You will be careful, won't you?"

"Sure. I know what I'm doing." Sandy kissed her on the cheek. "No worries."

For the second time that night, Michael listened to the elevator descend before turning back to her empty apartment.

❖

"Yeah," one of Gregor Zamora's men said as he answered his cell, turning his wrist to check his watch at the same time. 11:15. He'd been sitting in the same position behind the wheel in the cramped front seat of the Dodge sedan for so long his ass was numb.

"See the skinny little blonde headed away down the street?"

"The one that just came out of the building? Yeah, I see her."

"Follow her."

"You sure? I can't see her being any kind of trouble."

"I didn't ask for your opinion."

The line went dead.

"Prick," the man muttered as he pocketed his keys and slid out of the car. Fucking footwork. At least she had a nice ass, which he kept in his sights as he started after her.

❖

"Funny how a slicked-back haircut and getting rid of the tits makes such a big difference," Watts held forth between slurps of coffee. "Hell, he even walks different than Mitchell. Must be the package he's carrying between his legs."

"Sure. That must be it." Rebecca checked her rearview mirror, then scanned the street in front of them.

Ziggie's was a strip joint in the middle of a block of abandoned factories, a darkened Mobil station on the corner, and very little in the way of foot traffic. They'd been in position for two hours, and during that time a dozen cars had parked, disgorging passengers, all men, who straggled alone or in groups into the club. The girls who danced in the dank, cavernous space or performed sexual favors in the airless rooms in the back would use the rear entrance. They hadn't seen Irina.

"The boy better keep his head on straight," Watts said.

"Mitch can handle it." Rebecca knew Watts was partly concerned that Mitch would run into trouble and they'd be too far away to help, and partly jealous that Mitch was point man even though he was still green. But they couldn't do anything to change either thing, so she focused on something they could affect. "If Clark's people are here somewhere, I can't see them."

"Bet your ass they're around somewhere," Watts grunted, crushing the paper cup and dropping it on the floor between his legs. "Clark can pretend he doesn't have enough manpower to run his own operation, but you can bet he's got enough to fuck things up for us."

Rebecca tended to agree. Clark's modus operandi was to let her people do the dangerous or the boring work while he watched from a distance until something shook loose. Then all of a sudden he and his agents were right in the middle of it. She often wondered whether, if she had the power of his position, she would do the same. She didn't like to think so.

"Let's hope Irina shows, and that Clark is right about her," Rebecca said.

"She could be playing him, you know," Watts said. "Hell, if my choice was being shipped back to some gulag or pretending to work for the feds, I'd volunteer to rat out my fellow sleazeballs too. Doesn't mean that once she's out from under Clark's thumb, she's really going to do it."

"I know." Running a double agent was always a risk, because if they were informing on their one-time friends, they could just as easily turn the tables and betray you. If Irina was double-crossing them, she'd need information to convince the Zamoras and the Russians that she was still on their side. And she'd need to get that information from Mitch. Rebecca didn't see that they had any choice except to go forward and hope that Mitch would be able to tell if Irina was stringing him along.

As if reading Rebecca's mind, Watts said, "I don't mean to put the boy down, but you heard the two of them over the wire. She can seriously twist Mitch around." He shifted his bulk and sighed. "She could definitely give me a little wood, and once that happens—"

"Not everyone's brains are smaller than their dicks, Watts."

Watts laughed. "Probably a good thing Mitch's rod isn't hardwired."

Rebecca didn't bother to explain how wrong he was about the way things really worked.

❖

"Beer?" the bartender asked as Mitch slid onto a stool and dropped his motorcycle jacket onto the one next to him.

"Sounds good." Mitch swiveled around to face the stage, putting his back to the bar and the husky blond bartender with muscles bulging beneath his tight white T-shirt. Like every other time he'd been here, a mostly naked girl gyrated in the center of the raised platform, one arm draped around a gleaming pole, her legs spread and her hips cocked, her pelvis an open invitation to the hulking figures lurking in the shadows. He didn't recognize her, but then the faces changed frequently in places like this. Women were used up quickly when they were bought and sold like commodities. This one, though, seemed too old to be one of the Russian girls smuggled in through the port. Mitch felt a flash of disappointment. Maybe the Russians had moved on.

"Here you go," the bartender said, sliding a bottle in Mitch's direction.

Mitch caught it and took a swallow. The cold rich flavor felt good in his parched throat. Nerves, he thought. As he took another deep slug, arms came around his waist from behind. He felt the pressure of full breasts against his back and warm breath wafted across his ear. Fingernails played down his chest and over his abdomen.

"Hello, new boy," Irina whispered, dropping her hand onto the inside of his thigh.

Swinging back around, Mitch parted his legs and pulled her in tight to his body. He kissed her, taking his time. She pressed slowly into his cock.

Mitch cupped her ass and leaned back with an easy smile. "Hello, baby."

CHAPTER EIGHT

S andy walked east on Market Street, then cut over to Front Street and the footbridge that arched over the four lanes of Delaware Avenue. Once she reached the other side, there was nothing between her and the river except empty parking lots, darkened buildings, and the occasional attempt at a park meant to tempt tourists. At night, those isolated patches of grass served as sleeping grounds for the homeless. She walked fast, her shoulders back, her eyes vigilant. The silent, shapeless forms of men and women huddled on the benches and in doorways did not frighten her. The men in cars who slowed to track alongside her as she walked did not frighten her either, but they were far more dangerous to her than the drunk and the disenfranchised. Their whispered calls formed a familiar litany.

"Hey baby, need a ride?"

"I've got something special for you, sweet thing. Come take a look."

"Fifty bucks to suck my cock."

Fifty dollars for ten minutes' work, maybe less. Food money for a week. She could blank her mind for ten minutes, hell, she could be somewhere else in her head for a whole night if the price was right.

"Suck my cock. You know you want it."

Sandy almost laughed as the car kept pace with her, the passenger window rolled down. Out of the corner of her eye, she could see him leaning across the space between the front seats, steering with one hand while the other most likely worked his cock. *You know you want it.* She so didn't want it. She didn't have anything against cocks. She loved

Mitch's. She loved to watch his eyes get all fierce and hot when she rode it, and she loved the way she felt connected to him all the way through when he was inside her. Yep. She liked cock just fine, as long as it was Mitch's.

"You got to see my man about that," Sandy called back, never breaking stride. The car zoomed off. Married guys from the suburbs always panicked at the mention of a pimp. An anonymous blow job in an alley was okay, but they didn't want to be reminded of exactly what it was they were doing. Paying another man for a piece of a woman's body.

Sandy angled across a parking lot lit sporadically by the few remaining lights that hadn't been knocked out. The Blue Diamond was another strip club in a long line of sex clubs, and just as popular with women as men. In a lot of ways it was safer than some of the other clubs because men didn't hit on the women in the audience as much. A girl like her could still turn a trick, but nobody would expect her to. And that was good. Because fifty bucks wasn't worth getting on her knees for. Five hundred wasn't even enough. She wasn't foolish enough to think she might never have to do it again, but tonight she had a choice.

"Hey, hot stuff," the Mini Cooper–sized bouncer at the door said, treating her to a thrust of his bulging crotch. "Look me up later and I'll give you a present."

"It's not my birthday, but thanks," Sandy said, breezing by him. He always had a come-on line, but unlike some of the bouncers and bartenders, he didn't bother the girls if they didn't put out. She was pretty sure he was gay.

Inside, the place was indistinguishable from a dozen others like it—dark, crowded with tables, smelling of beer and smoke and sex. The namesake recessed blue lights shrouded everyone except the dancers in a ghostlike pallor. Three gleaming poles jutted from a stage set against the far wall, and a woman in white cowboy boots, a suede vest, and red tassels on her nipples slithered up and down the center one.

On her way to the bar, Sandy scanned the crowd. One of her friends, Lily Chou, was giving some guy a hand job under the table. Sandy caught her eye and tilted her chin toward the far end of the bar. Lily nodded, never slowing the steady up and down of her arm. Sandy hopped onto a stool, stretched a leg out across the stool next to her to save Lily a place, and waited for the bartender to make his way down.

The African-American's head was huge, completely bald, and gleamed like polished wood beneath the blue lights. The massive muscles in his shoulders and arms strained his black T-shirt.

"What can I get you, honey," he asked in a bored voice.

"Beer." Sandy didn't want it, but she needed the prop. After all, she was supposed to be working. When it came, she sipped at the tepid foam. God, the beer in these places sucked. She shifted her leg aside as Lily stepped in beside her. "How's it going?"

"The same. You know." Lily made a subtle jerk-off motion and dropped onto the adjacent stool.

Sandy smiled wryly. "Yeah, I know."

"I heard you've got some new kind of action going on."

Sandy's pulse jumped. Frye was always careful not to be seen with her unless she made it look like she was rousting Sandy. Fuck, maybe someone had seen them in the diner the other night. She'd had her arm around Frye's waist while they were walking down the street. Hell, Frye had had her arm around *her* shoulders. Being cozy with a cop was not a good way to make friends around here. "What would that be?"

"Some pretty boy who rides a big bike?" Lily cocked her head. "Maybe a boy with something a little different in his pants."

Sandy shrugged. Not Frye, then. Mitch. "He's fun to play with. And he knows what to do with it, you know what I mean?"

"Hey, if it works, why not." Lily laughed. "Does he have a friend?"

Sandy bumped Lily's shoulder. "Three of them."

"Maybe someday."

"Let me know."

"So what do you hear?" Lily asked.

That was just the question Sandy was hoping for. The fewer times *she* had to ask for news, the better. She looked around to be sure they wouldn't be overheard, then leaned closer. "I heard some guys are looking for new talent. The party circuit, maybe films. You get anybody asking, I want in."

"Funny," Lily said. "That kind of action dried up earlier this year, but Julie told me last night a couple of guys were asking around for models. Stills, and maybe some videos. Said there might be other work soon too. Parties and like that."

"Damn, I could have used a little something extra." Sandy signaled the bartender to get Lily a drink. "Did she say who the guys were?"

Lily shook her head. "Uh-uh. None of the regulars. They were talking up the girls at the Zodiac."

"Oh well," Sandy sighed, pretending to check out the room. "I ought to be able to score something here."

"Don't go in the back," Lily said. "There's a cop hanging around there somewhere. Getting a blow job, I think."

Taking the easy excuse, Sandy stood up. "I don't need any of that. I'll catch you later." She started away, then turned back. "Listen. Tell the others to call me if those guys come around again."

"Gotcha. Thanks for the beer," Lily called after her.

Once outside, Sandy headed back the way she had come to catch the subway home. She heard footsteps keeping pace behind her, but she neither sped up nor slowed. At one in the morning the streets were nearly deserted. An occasional cab zoomed by, and now and then someone staggered out of a bar, but she was on her own.

She was used to that, but for the first time she realized she had someone who would care if she didn't come home. She liked the feeling. A lot.

❖

Talia sipped her pinot noir and watched numerals scroll on her computer screen. A fire burned in the marble fireplace across from her antique carved walnut desk. Floor-to-ceiling bookcases lined her study walls, the uppermost shelves accessible by a brass ladder rail that ran around three walls. Behind the double glass doors, first editions mingled with contemporary works. Opposite her desk, a matching 1930s art deco sofa and chair bordered the edge of a Persian wool rug. The understated elegance of the room and the rich, warm atmosphere afforded by the rare books and furniture filled her with pleasure.

Taking another mouthful of wine, she let the velvety liquid play over her tongue, then tapped a few keys. She always worked better when her senses were sated, and the wine was very smooth, its fruitiness underpinned with just a hint of earth and wood. She studied the screen intently. Reconnaissance was one of her favorite parts of hacking into a remote system. Sending out probes and enumerating the OS parameters, generating port maps, looking for the forgotten opening—the chink in the armor, the way in. Cracking was very much like seducing a woman—teasing out her desires and her weaknesses and playing to them, until *she* invited you beyond her defenses. Those early encounters were so exciting that Talia rarely stayed beyond the moment of capitulation. Bedding a woman was certainly pleasurable, but far less rewarding than that explosive moment when the object of her campaign surrendered.

She smiled, thinking about Kratos Zamora and his persistent probing, his subtle forays into seducing her. He was an attractive man, a powerful one, and she enjoyed dominating powerful men almost as much as powerful women. But she didn't trust him not to take a sexual encounter as a sign of weakness, and in her line of work, it was important never to appear weak. The weak were ultimately culled, and she had no intention of making herself vulnerable.

She sent another probe, not expecting instant results. She knew within moments of scanning the system that she wasn't going to find something as simple as an open port or a weak password, so she didn't even bother to try cracking JT Sloan's authentication process by brute force. If she tried, the system log would undoubtedly trigger the activity, and for now, she preferred to remain anonymous. No system was unassailable, and eventually she'd find an insecure program to exploit or a way to write one to gain superuser status. Until then, she had other avenues to explore.

Leaning back in her Victorian leather desk chair, she regarded the image on the computer screen adjacent to the one still scrolling data. She'd found the photograph in the archives of a tabloid newspaper and the picture was slightly out of focus, but the poor quality did nothing to detract from JT Sloan's incredible charisma. Talia appreciated the jet black hair, slightly hooded deep-set eyes, and etched-in-marble features, but what ignited the excitement in the pit of her stomach was the wild ferocity in Sloan's gaze. She'd been caught by a photographer as she climbed out of an ambulance, her hand clasping that of a woman on a stretcher. Captioned "Center City businesswoman victim of hit-and-run," the brief article gave few details, but Talia didn't need to see any more. It might take her some time to find the weakness in Sloan

Security's computer network, but she'd already found the woman's personal Achilles' heel. She wondered how much the information would be worth to Kratos.

❖

Mitch couldn't tell if anyone in Ziggie's was watching them, but he had to assume they'd attracted the attention of the men who controlled Irina and her girls. Possibly the Russian handlers, possibly Zamora's men. The Zamoras would never have let outsiders set up competition in their territory unless they had a piece of the action, and Mitch had to trace that connection. But for now, he just needed to convince anyone checking them out that he and Irina were an item.

Irina wasn't as small as Sandy, but her hips fit easily between his thighs. He rolled her tight round ass beneath his palms, molding her pelvis to his. She wore satiny slacks that fit her like skin and he could almost feel her sex gliding over his cock as if there were nothing between them. She pressed her breasts into his chest and her mouth against his ear.

"You promised to fuck me, new boy. But you lied."

For a second, Mitch wasn't certain Irina understood that he was a cop and had been acting last time. Then she reached between them, gripped his cock, and worked it around hard between his legs. Caught off guard, he groaned at the firestorm she started in his belly.

"I won't forget," she whispered.

"Sorry," Mitch gasped.

She leaned back, relaxing her grip, and kissed him again. When she sucked his lower lip into her mouth, she bit down hard enough to make him wince. The pain quickly morphed into another jolt of pleasure and he struggled not to jerk back. Her kiss was brutal and arousing. Through half-closed lids, he saw the bartender watching them. He skimmed his fingers over the outer curve of Irina's breast. Her blouse vee'd deeply between her unfettered breasts and his thumb brushed her nipple. It was hard.

"Mmm," Irina murmured, finally drawing away. Still firmly wedged between Mitch's legs, she looked over Mitch's shoulder with a seductive smile.

"Hello, Max."

"Not working tonight?" the bartender asked, leaning on his outstretched arms as he stared.

Irina caressed Mitch's cheek. "A little of both."

"Huh," the bartender grunted. "Where's Olik?"

"I don't know," Irina answered, "I thought he would be here."

"Haven't seen him for a couple of days."

His tone was as flat and unreadable as his smooth, solid features. The conversation quickly put out the tension blazing in Mitch's hard-on, and he was grateful for that. He didn't need the distraction. He needed to get a handle on Irina's game. He didn't know the players, and he had to find out fast. The bartender seemed to be probing for information. Obviously, no one trusted anyone else, and neither Irina nor the bartender was giving anything away.

"Tell him to call me." Irina stepped back from Mitch and gripped his hand. "Come on, new boy. You promised me a good time."

"What's your number," the bartender called after her. "If he comes in."

Irina looked back. "Olik knows."

"So what if he forgot?"

"Then I'll be here tomorrow night."

Mitch dug a five out of his pocket and tossed it on the bar. His knuckles brushed along the length of his cock, and the feeling was both foreign and grounding. Irina was either a natural-born actress, or completely fearless. His stomach roiled, but he'd be damned if he'd let on how nervous he was. He slung his arm around Irina's shoulders. "My bike's out back."

As she led him down the narrow hall toward the rear exit, he heard the sounds of frantic sex in the shadowed alcoves along the way. He and Irina had come close to having sex back here one night. She'd done things to him that he didn't mean to let happen and that had twisted his head around until Sandy straightened him out as only Sandy could. His thoughts cleared as he thought about her. Sandy kept him steady.

Irina pushed through the fire door and he followed her quickly out into the alley. He'd left his Ducati against the wall at the far end. Otherwise, the area was deserted save for a few rats scurrying from the shaft of light that had cut through the shadows from the open door.

He glanced at Irina. "Are you—"

She slapped him across the face so hard his head rocked back and his lip tore open against the edge of a tooth. He tasted blood and braced himself for the next blow. It wouldn't be the first time he'd been beaten in an alley. The last time he'd been trying to prevent a john from roughing up Sandy. He'd won the fight then, but he wasn't about to hit Irina.

"That's for making me want you," Irina snapped.

"Like I said," Mitch replied evenly. "Sorry."

"Let's go," Irina said. "This place stinks almost as bad as the jail."

"Where are we going?"

"My place. I want clothes."

Mitch rubbed his jaw and felt a bruise rising. He couldn't think of a reason not to go back to Irina's house. If the Russians were watching, they'd see them together, which was just what he wanted. He didn't have a way to signal Frye and Watts about the plan, but in this kind of job, he was going to be on his own a lot. He was okay with that.

"Did anyone come with you?" he asked.

"No," Irina said sharply. "Some men dropped me off and said you would be here." She stopped by the side of his bike. The light from the street highlighted her face. Her expression was hard and cold. "They explained to me what would happen if I didn't do as they say."

"What did they tell you to do?"

"Anything I had to do to find out what they wanted to know." She looked him up and down. "Including fucking you."

"You're not going to have to do that."

Mitch straddled the bike and handed her a helmet. She put it on and climbed on behind him. Then she wrapped her arms around his waist and slid her fingers underneath the waistband of his jeans.

"Maybe I will anyhow."

❖

"Aw, for fuck's sake." Watts jerked upright in his seat as the Ducati roared around the corner and headed in the opposite direction toward North Philadelphia. "There he goes."

Rebecca didn't bother answering. She cranked the starter and made a quick U-turn to follow Mitch. Since this part of town was fairly deserted midweek in the middle of the night, she had to hang back without other traffic to use as cover.

"Keep an eye out for anyone else following him," she said.

Watts divided his attention between the side mirror and squinting into the distance at the single red taillight. "You think Clark has a tail on them too?"

Rebecca grunted. "Don't you?"

"Christ almighty, it's a fucking daisy chain. With this many people trailing along after him, the boy's cover's gonna get blown."

"Maybe Clark really is stretched thin," Rebecca said. "Maybe the feds really don't have the manpower for street-level surveillance."

"Maybe. And maybe my dick's got two heads too."

"That is not an image I want stuck in my brain, Watts." Rebecca cut over one block and turned left. Then she sped up, running parallel to the street Mitch and Irina had taken.

"Jesus, Loo! We're going to lose him if he jumps onto 95."

"Your concern for Mitch is starting to worry me, Watts. Something you want to tell me?"

"Yeah, I've suddenly developed the urge to suck salami. He's still green, that's all."

Rebecca cut back toward Mitch's street and as they crossed the intersection, she caught a glimpse of Mitch's taillights two blocks north of them. She kept going another block, turned right, and paralleled him again. "I know he's green, but he's good. And I know where he's going."

CHAPTER NINE

Sloan pulled into the garage, cut the engine, and sat astride her bike, wondering how she had come to be sitting alone in the dark while the woman she loved waited four floors above, feeling four thousand miles away. She'd moved from the clandestine streets of Southeast Asia to the pristine corridors of DC, and when forced from government service had convinced herself that work in the private sector was satisfying. At times, it was. And in addition to being very lucrative, private contracts had brought her Michael. But she never felt the thrill of hunting a white-collar criminal the way she did when she knew her work would rid the world of someone truly evil. She had felt that way since working with Frye and her team, but Michael had paid the price for her ego gratification.

Sloan figured she'd been selfish long enough. She swung her leg over her bike and strode to the elevator. After punching in the code, she let her mind go blank. She had nothing left to think about. A few moments later, the elevator opened and she stepped into the loft. A fire had burned down to embers, and in the dying glow she saw Michael curled in a corner of the large sofa. She wore dark, loose cotton pants and a long-sleeved scoopneck top. Her legs were drawn beneath her and her arms wrapped around her slim torso. She looked cold, and Sloan felt a surge of self-loathing. She stripped off her leather jacket and tossed it onto a heavy wood frame chair on her way into the sitting area.

"Did you have dinner?" Michael asked.

"No." Sloan detoured to add more logs to the fire before settling onto the sofa next to Michael. The six inches of space between their bodies felt like miles. "I'm okay."

"Well, that makes one of us."

Michael's tone was not accusatory, but Sloan ached at the undeniable sadness. She took Michael's hand. "I'm sorry."

"For what, exactly?"

Sloan tried to find an answer that would be the truth. "I lost my temper and I took it out on you. That's unforgivable, but I hope you'll forgive me anyhow."

Michael laughed softly, but the sadness was still there. "You have always been so charming. I've never been able to resist you."

"Bad thing? Good thing?"

"Our thing." Michael traced the tight tendons in the back of Sloan's hand with her fingertips. "I know I'm not capable of doing a lot of the things that you do. I wouldn't really want to. I'm not interested in learning to shoot a gun. I'm probably a coward at heart—" When Sloan started to object, Michael shushed her. "I don't enjoy physical confrontation. I live inside my head, and you—God, one of the things I love about you is how physical you are. I love how I know what you're feeling, what you're thinking, when you touch me." Michael's voice trembled. "So when you leave me like you did tonight, I feel lost."

Sloan pulled Michael into her arms. "I'm sorry. I'm so sorry, baby."

"Why don't you want me to go to this fund-raiser? Catherine and Rebecca are going."

"Rebecca and I will be working," Sloan said.

Michael settled her head on Sloan's shoulder and looped an arm around her waist, trying to decipher the message. Sloan didn't want to tell her something, and whatever that was, she seemed tormented by it. "You think there's danger, and you don't want me there."

"I don't know. Possibly. Probably." Sloan stroked Michael's shoulder. She didn't know her enemy's face, she didn't know how to stand between Michael and harm, and that was driving her crazy.

"It's a public function," Michael pointed out gently. "I'll be arriving with you and leaving with you. And the entire time I'm there, I'll be surrounded by police officers and businessmen and women. What could happen?"

"I don't know," Sloan whispered.

"I'm all right now, Sloan. I feel better every day. I'm not going to get hurt again. I'm fine." Michael straightened and took both of Sloan's hands in hers. "What I need is you by my side, loving me. If you do that, that will be enough."

"Okay," Sloan said softly, rising to walk with Michael to the bedroom, all the while knowing she had lied.

Sandy didn't see Dell's bike in front of their apartment building. She pulled the front door key from one of the many zippered pockets on her fake red leather jacket as she climbed the stoop, her stomach sinking. She'd stormed out in a huff and now Dell wasn't home. Crap. Dell was probably mad. Well, so was she. Sort of. A little bit. And she hated the disappointment that choked her when she let herself into the dark apartment. She already knew Dell wasn't there, so why did that make her feel bad, anyhow? It's not like she needed her around all the time. They both had their own stuff to do. Just because they slept together most every night, it wasn't like they were really living together. Dell still had her expensive fancy condo in Center City, although come to think of it, Sandy couldn't remember the last time Dell had been there.

After switching on the light, she stripped on her way to the bathroom. She showered and washed the smoke out of her hair, then fished a ratty T-shirt of Dell's she slept in out of the laundry basket. She couldn't find a clean pair of sweatpants so she checked in Dell's half of the dresser. The first drawer she pulled open was empty. She stared at it for a long moment, the sick feeling in her stomach growing. She'd finally pissed Dell off so much she'd left. Got sick of her running the streets, mouthing off, going her own way. *What did you think? That she was going to stay forever? Grow up.*

Sandy's hands shook when she pulled open the next drawer. Her knees almost gave out when she saw Dell's T-shirts and underwear neatly folded and stacked. Turning quickly, she raced to the single narrow closet and pulled it open. A few hangers were empty, but most of the stuff Dell had brought over from her condo was still there.

Relief left her shakier than the terror had. Tears filled her eyes and she headed for the kitchen to find a beer. A folded piece of paper sat beneath the salt shaker on the counter next to the refrigerator. Sandy stared at it as if it were a dead mouse. No way. She wasn't touching it. Instead, she opened the refrigerator and pulled out a can of Black and Tan. She popped the top and took a long swallow while eyeing the paper. *Get a grip. Geez, what a coward.*

After another deep swallow, she plonked the can on the counter, knocked the plastic shaker aside, and snatched up the note. The message was short, but after reading it three times, she still couldn't figure out what it meant.

> *Babe. I'm working and I might not be back tonight. I might not be back for a couple of nights. Don't worry. If you see me anywhere, especially in the building, pretend you don't know me. I love you, babe. D.*

"Pretend you don't know me?" Sandy shook her head angrily. "What the fuck, Dell."

Pissed again, but finally feeling like she might not throw up, she settled onto the sofa bed to wait.

❖

Mitch pulled his motorcycle along a wooden fence behind a block of row houses in North Philadelphia. It wasn't the kind of area where anyone, even the inhabitants, walked around unarmed after dark. Many of the houses were boarded up or had been claimed by crack addicts, drug pushers, and squatters. The Russians had kept Irina and her charges in a house in the middle of the block. No lights shone from the building now, and as Mitch and Irina crossed the cracked cement patio toward the back door, he could see that most of the windows on the first floor were broken out. Those along with the door had been hastily boarded up.

"Let me go first." Mitch leaned down and pulled a Beretta .25 from his ankle holster. "A place like this is a blinking red sign for vandals and looters. We might find company inside."

"Wait," Irina whispered.

Mitch watched wordlessly as she ran deftly across the debris-strewn yard. Then he couldn't see her, but he heard stones scraping. A minute later she was back at his side, a Glock in her hand.

"Christ," he muttered. Whoever had searched the place after the raid hadn't done a very good job. "Any more surprises inside?"

"If I told you," Irina said, "they wouldn't be surprises."

Mitch grabbed her arm. "You can't shoot anyone. If you do, you'll end up back behind bars again."

"I'm not going back," Irina said with finality. "Come on."

By unspoken agreement they avoided the door. If anyone was inside, they'd probably be smart enough to rig the door with some kind of alarm, even if it was just a row of cans strategically placed on the floor. Keeping to the shadows, Mitch skirted around to the left side of the house, keeping Irina in sight, just ahead of him. Her bedroom window was still intact.

"Let's forget this," Mitch said. "We can get you some more clothes tomorrow."

"Give me a boost up. The latch is loose on purpose."

Mitch cupped his hands and sure enough, after a minute, he heard the window slide up and Irina shimmied inside. He jumped to grasp the lower windowsill, dug his toes into the soft wood wall, and clawed his way after her. Inside, the air smelled like cordite and blood. He remembered how his own blood had smelled pooling beneath his body not that long ago. With his body too weak to move and the knife jutting from his thigh, he'd wondered if he was about to die. And then Frye had leaned over him. She'd been the one to take the knife out, to stop the bleeding, to tell him he would be all right. He'd believed her.

"Bastards," Irina cursed. The closet door was standing open—hangers in a jumble on the floor, and the single dresser was upended. The drawers had been tossed into a corner and their contents strewn around the room. The mattress lay half off the bed, its stuffing erupting from a long rent down the center. Police, probably.

"Let's make it fast." Mitch moved to stand by the left side of the door.

If anyone tried to come in, he would be able to swing into the open doorway and take them out by cracking them on the head with his gun. He didn't want to have to shoot anyone. If anyone *was* inside, it wouldn't be cops. Not enough manpower to continue a stakeout. Still, he didn't want to shoot a drugged-out teenager or a drunken prostitute.

He glanced over his shoulder and saw Irina pawing through the mess on the floor. She quickly jammed items into a small bag she'd dug out from underneath the corner of the mattress. Then she hurried to the closet and stepped inside. A thud sounded on the ceiling upstairs, and Mitch tensed. They weren't alone. When he heard footsteps shuffle over his head, he abandoned the door and jumped across the small room to the closet.

"We have to go," he whispered urgently, wondering what she was so eager to find. He reached inside, grabbed her arm, and yanked her out. "Now."

She jerked her arm free. "One minute." She fumbled around the floor and came up with what looked like a knee-high leather boot.

"You've got be kidding me," Mitch cursed. "What is it with girls and their shoes. Jesus."

"Here." Irina thrust the bottom of the boot toward him. "Hold the heel."

Deciding that agreeing with her was likely to get them out of the room faster than anything else, Mitch grabbed the four-inch stiletto and held on tight as Irina clutched the shoe and yanked hard. The heel broke off in his hand. Irina tugged at the sole and it stripped away from the bottom of the shoe. She pulled several items from inside, shoved them into her bag, and ran to the window. She looked back, her face framed in moonlight. "Are you coming, new boy?"

Then she disappeared.

Mitch dropped through the window and onto the ground, half expecting her to be gone. But she was crouched by the gate, waiting, and in another minute they were racing down the alley to his motorcycle. Mitch straddled the big bike and Irina jumped on behind him. They jammed helmets on and he wheeled the bike out into the street before starting the motor. If anyone in the house heard them, it would be too late to catch up with them now.

He drove fast through the empty streets until the lights of Center City appeared, and then he pulled over. He yanked off his helmet and angled around in his seat so he could see Irina. "What was that all about? And don't tell me just clothes."

Irina smiled, her eyes gleaming in the lights from a nearby gas station. "Why should I trust you?"

"Because…" Mitch hesitated. He was about to say because he was a cop. One of the good guys. But he realized that would be a tough sell to Irina. He didn't think she was innocent in the prostitution and porn operation. Maybe Clark was right and she hadn't had a lot of choices, but she'd still kept those girls practically prisoners, and had sold them to the men who used their bodies like so much merchandise. "Because if you don't work with me, you're not going to find your sister."

"What do you know about my sister?"

"Not enough, unless you tell me. But I've got a lot better chance of finding her than you do on your own."

"They promised us a new life," Irina said bitterly. "We would be models and hotel managers and hostesses in fancy restaurants. We would have clothes and a house with heat in the winter and running water all year round." She shook her head. "Instead they made us slaves. Worse than slaves."

"Who, Irina? Who?"

"I don't know. Men from our village drove us all night to the seaport. They kept us in rooms, brought us food, told us we must stay inside or we would not be able to leave when the boat came. Then there were other men who took us from the docks here and brought us to these houses. These prisons. I don't know who they are."

"Okay," Mitch said softly. "We'll find out. And we'll find your sister."

"You think your American police care about women like me?" Irina scoffed.

Mitch thought of her lieutenant and the others on her team, and the blood they'd already shed. "Yes. I do."

"You are a fool, new boy."

"Come on, it's time to get some sleep. Then we'll talk about your sister."

When Mitch pulled back into the street, Irina put her arms around his waist and nestled her face between his shoulder blades. Sandy did that when she rode behind him. He missed her. He missed her a lot.

CHAPTER TEN

S eeing as how you're still on the sick list," Watts said, his words sounding as if he were pushing them through a meat grinder, "I'll be the one to kick his ass."

Two blocks ahead, Mitch turned onto Bainbridge.

Rebecca pulled the car over abruptly. "He's taking her to his apartment. At least *that's* according to plan."

There hadn't been any way to stop him from taking Irina back to the stash house in North Philadelphia, and once he pulled his motorcycle into the alley, they couldn't get closer than a full block away or their vehicle would have been immediately visible to anyone watching. If anything had gone wrong they couldn't have provided backup, and the frustration of being unable to protect one of her team ate at her.

"You think the Russians got someone watching that house?" Watts asked.

"If they're not sure whether any girls got out during the raid," Rebecca said, "then it makes sense to watch the house. Where would girls like that go except back to the only place where they had shelter? They don't speak the language, they don't know the city, they'd have no way of making money. They wouldn't even be able to sell their bodies."

"So the Russians have probably seen Mitch with her."

Rebecca nodded, rolling forward again until they cruised through the intersection at the end of Mitch's block. "That could turn out to be a good thing. It definitely helps establish their connection."

"Unless they've decided Irina is a liability, or they think she got out of the building because she was the one who fingered them. Then they just might dispose of her, and anyone who might miss her."

Rebecca parked and turned off the engine. Mitch's motorcycle was pulled up onto the sidewalk in front of the building where he and Sandy lived. Settling into surveillance mode, Watts pulled a crumpled pack of Camels out of the inside pocket of his equally crumpled suit jacket and shook one out.

"There's too much we don't know," he said. "The whole setup blows."

"For once we agree." Rebecca glanced over at him. "Not in the car."

"Jesus, Loo, I've been in this sardine can half the night."

"And just think how much cleaner your lungs are already."

He snorted and stuck the pack back in his pocket. "You really think we'll get close to the guys at the top using a bottom-level whore like Irina?"

"Irina isn't a prostitute—and even if she was, that doesn't make her unimportant." Rebecca struggled not to jump down his throat, because she knew his crude disregard for just about everyone was often a substitute for concern. Of course, sometimes he really just didn't give a damn. "How many women do you think there are like Irina? With enough English to deal with clientele and enough strength and smarts to handle a house full of girls and keep them from panicking or running away? My guess is they're going to want her to set up housekeeping with a new bunch of girls as soon as possible."

"It'll be sweet if it works that way."

"Yes," Rebecca said, thinking of the million ways it could all go wrong. "Sweet all right."

❖

Irina turned in a half circle, surveying the room. "You live here?"

"I flop here sometimes." That was stretching the truth by a lot. Mitch kept the room as part of his cover but he'd never actually spent a night in it. He slept with Sandy, three doors down the hall. "There's milk and bread in the refrigerator. And peanut butter in the cabinet. That's all I had time to get, but—"

Irina laughed. "I know how to shop, unless you're going to lock me in here."

Mitch flushed. "I'm not your jailer. I know you probably don't want to be doing this, and if you want to walk away, that's between you and Clark."

"And you won't try to stop me?" Irina's tone was incredulous.

"No." Mitch indicated the mattress pushed into one corner of the small studio apartment. "I'm sorry. I don't have any sheets, but there's a blanket and the mattress is new."

Irina sank down on the mattress and dragged the blue blanket around her shoulders.

Guiltily, Mitch said, "Why didn't you tell me you were freezing?"

"Because I wasn't. This…" Irina waved her hand toward the window. "This is not cold for me."

Mitch shook his head. He wasn't thinking the way he should be. "I should have given you my jacket while we were on the bike."

"No matter. The cold will pass. But I *am* tired. I couldn't sleep where your friends put me."

"They didn't hurt you, did they?" Mitch had no idea how far the feds would go to convince someone to flip on their associates. Probably pretty damn far since 9/11, especially when foreign nationals were involved.

"They tried to frighten me." Irina shrugged. "I have known men who were better at it."

Mitch didn't doubt her. Why else would she have fled her country on just the word of strangers? "I'm going out. I won't be back tonight, but I'll bring coffee and something to eat in the morning. Then we can get this place into some kind of shape for you to stay here."

Irina regarded him steadily. "You have someone."

Mitch knew he probably shouldn't talk about his personal life. He definitely didn't want Irina to know anything about Sandy. But he needed her to trust him, and trust meant taking a few risks. He nodded. "Yes."

"And this…girl? You like girls, yes?"

He nodded again.

"This girl, she doesn't complain when you fuck other women?"

Irina draped the blanket around her like a shawl and leaned back on her arms. Her breasts thrust forward, straining the buttons on her blouse.

Mitch sensed he was being tested, and he wasn't certain what answers he should be giving. He remembered Frye saying once that the truth, or at least part of the truth, was often the best answer in a tough undercover situation. "She minds."

Irina pulled the blanket closed over her breasts and curled on her side, resting her hand beneath her head as she pulled her knees up close to her body. "Were you going to fuck me, before the police came?"

"No," Mitch said, sliding his hands into his pockets. His jeans tightened over his cock, and he felt the pressure through to his spine. "But I wasn't pretending, either. You're...very hot."

Irina's eyes drifted down his body, lingering on his crotch. Mitch didn't move, but he twitched in his jeans. "Go, new boy," she said softly. "For tonight."

"I'll see you in the morning." Mitch walked to the door, then looked back. "Do you have a picture of your sister?"

"Why?"

"Because it will help us find her if we know what she looks like."

Irina shook her head. "No. The police will lock her away. Then I will never see her again."

"I won't let that happen."

"Even if I believed you, you are just one." Irina folded her arms and pillowed her head, then closed her eyes.

Mitch returned, crouching down by the side of the mattress. "I'll talk to some people. About protecting your sister, okay? Then will you let me see the picture?"

"Do you keep your promises, new boy?"

"Yes," Mitch said.

Irina opened her eyes, searching his face. "Come back in the morning. Maybe we'll talk."

❖

Sandy heard footsteps in the hallway and a shadow blocked out the sliver of light beneath the apartment door. She wrapped her arms around her bent legs and rested her chin on her knees, holding her breath until a key rasped in the lock. Mitch was backlit briefly in the square of light as the door opened, then his blade-like figure disappeared into darkness again.

"You can turn on the light," Sandy said when she heard him bump into something.

"Jesus," Mitch gasped. "It's three in the morning. I thought you'd be asleep."

"Not without you."

"Didn't you get my note?" Mitch fumbled on the dresser a few feet from the door and pulled the chain on the small lamp. He removed his jacket and hung it on a hook on the wall.

"Yeah, I got your message. What's this shit about not coming back for a while? And where are your clothes?"

Mitch sprawled on the couch beside her and kicked off his boots. "I'm going to be working a lot at night, so sometimes I might not make it home."

"I get that. That happens sometimes. But something else is going on this time, isn't it?"

Mitch stared at the ceiling. Frye hadn't said not to tell her. "I've got this assignment. We're going after the mob who are hooked up with the Russians."

"I know that. Frye thinks with foreign girls out of the picture, all the action is going to swing back to the local girls again. I've been asking around. I think she's right." Sandy turned sideways on the couch and poked Mitch's shoulder. "What's your part?"

"One of the Russian girls flipped after she was arrested. I'm working with her."

Sandy jumped to her feet and strode across the room, then spun around. "Working. Working as in what? Following her? What?"

Mitch sat forward, trying to stay calm. "We're supposed to be a couple. So she can get me close to some of the guys in charge."

"Perfect. It's Irina, isn't it?"

"Yeah." Mitch didn't see any point in denying it. Sandy knew Irina, or at least what she looked like. She'd seen Irina's picture when she was screening porn videos for Frye, trying to identify the models. She also knew that Mitch had had to get physical with Irina before.

Sandy stalked back to him, her eyes narrowed. "Where is she?"

"In my apartment down the hall."

"Which is where you moved your clothes."

"I thought I better have a change of clothes there, just in case." Mitch waited, expecting an explosion. When it didn't come, he really started to worry. "Look, I know you're pissed off."

"Is she there right now?"

Mitch nodded. "She's going to be staying there for a while."

"Why aren't you there?"

"Because I'm here." Mitch stood up suddenly and pulled Sandy into his arms. He couldn't stand the distance between them any longer. She felt stiff in his embrace, but she didn't push away, and she would have if she'd been really, really pissed off. He rubbed his cheek against her hair. "I'm sorry. I wanted to tell you earlier, but then we had a fight, and I didn't have a chance."

"I'm going to kill Frye," Sandy whispered.

Mitch laughed. "Good. Better her than me."

Sandy wrapped her arms around his waist, pressing tight to his body. "This is crazy, baby. She could get you hurt."

"You're worried about me?"

"Duh." Sandy bounced her forehead against his shoulder. "She flipped on these guys, and she has to know they'll kill her if they find out. So if it comes down to her or you, you think she's going to stand by you? She'll turn you over to them to save her ass."

"How do you know that?"

Sandy was still for a long time. "Because that's what I would do, if I were in her place."

Mitch cupped Sandy's chin and lifted her face. He kissed her and kept kissing her until she softened and molded into his body. "No, you wouldn't."

"You don't know what I'd do," Sandy said, pulling his T-shirt from his pants. "I don't want to talk about her. I don't want to talk about Frye. I don't want to talk about anything." She unbuttoned the top of his jeans and yanked down the zipper. Then she reached inside and pulled out his cock. She dropped to her knees, her fist around him. She looked up. "I just want you."

"Babe," Mitch whispered, bracing his hands on her shoulders as his legs got suddenly weak. Her fist covered half the length of his cock, and as she took the head into her mouth, she pressed the shaft into his clit. He groaned, watching her through hooded eyes. She swallowed him, and while his head spun, his world steadied. Sandy owned him. "I need you, babe."

"I know." Sandy rubbed her face against his cock, then kissed the base of his belly. "Me too. Take off your shirt and the wrap. I want to touch you. I want to feel your heart beat while you fuck me."

Dell ripped her T-shirt off over her head, then unstrapped her breasts. She dropped on her back on the sofa, her cock standing straight up between the vee of her jeans. She palmed it, circling the base slowly over her clit while she watched Sandy undress. She was already hard enough to come, and Sandy knew it. Sandy took her time undressing, her smile flickering as she watched Dell's hand move.

"Ready, baby?" Sandy knelt on the edge of the sofa and Dell's hips started to twist.

"Totally." As Sandy climbed up over her, naked, vulnerable, her face filled with need, Dell felt humbled and unworthy. "I love you. I love you so damn much."

"You better." Sandy pushed Dell's hand away and fisted her cock, seating the head between the folds of her sex. She hissed as she braced her other hand in the center of Dell's chest. "You like being inside of me?"

"God, yes."

Sandy gasped as she took an inch. "How much?"

"More than anything ever."

"You like"—Sandy closed her eyes and shivered, tilting her pelvis to take the thick wide shaft. Her voice came out breathy and slow—"coming in me?"

Dell gripped Sandy's narrow hips, steadying her while she thrust carefully, stretching and filling her. She grunted sharply when Sandy's weight abruptly settled on the full length of her, crushing her clit beneath the cock. "So much I'm going to explode any second."

Sandy slapped Dell's tense stomach sharply. "You better not, rookie. You've got work to do first."

"Aw, babe—"

"Forget it," Sandy gasped. "You're lucky you're getting any. Now shut up and fuck me."

Laughing, Dell focused on Sandy's face, sliding in and out a fraction of an inch at a time as Sandy set the pace. She loved making

Sandy come even more than having her own mind-blowing orgasms, and concentrating on pleasing Sandy helped her last longer. She knew if she thought about how sweet it felt for even a few seconds she wouldn't be able to hold back, so she just put everything she had into making Sandy feel good.

"Like it, babe?"

Sandy nodded, her eyes glassy. "Oh yeah." She hugged her lower lip between her teeth and sagged forward, catching herself with both hands on Dell's chest. She gripped Dell's breasts, her fingers closing convulsively around Dell's nipples as she pumped her hips harder and faster along Dell's length.

"Oh, fuck." Dell's clit pulsed as Sandy tugged on her nipples. She felt the orgasm building, curling through her stomach and down her thighs. She clutched Sandy tighter and jerked up hard into her.

"Oh," Sandy whimpered. "I'm gonna come on your cock. Okay? Okay, baby?"

"Do it," Dell panted, "do it…with me."

Sandy's head snapped back and she let out a long, keening wail and Dell exploded. She came so hard she thought her head would burst open. Maybe it did, because she was pretty sure she was blind, maybe paralyzed too.

Sandy lay like a dead weight across her chest, with Dell still inside her. All Dell could move was one hand, so she stroked the damp hair off Sandy's face.

"Good, babe?"

"Awful," Sandy mumbled. "Worst sex I ever had."

Dell laughed. "Still mad?"

"Shut up, Dell. I'm thinking about coming again."

"Okay," Dell said quickly. "Okay, sure."

Sandy pushed herself up on one elbow, looking soft and satisfied as she circled her pelvis lazily. "Tired?"

Dell shook her head vigorously.

"Liar." Sandy nipped at Dell's lip again, then sucked on her tongue, still slow pumping on her cock. "You're going to see her in the morning, aren't you?"

"Sandy." Dell brushed her fingertips over Sandy's breasts. "I love you."

"I got scared," Sandy said breathlessly, "when I came home and you weren't here."

Dell wrapped her arms around Sandy's waist and turned her gently onto her back, careful to stay inside her. She supported her body on her forearms and kissed Sandy, flexing her ass rhythmically, pumping in and out. When she sensed Sandy getting ready to come, she whispered, "Look at me, babe."

Sandy's lids fluttered and she struggled to focus. "You're making me come."

"I'm always coming home," Dell promised as Sandy clamped her heels tight around the backs of her thighs and bowed beneath her. "Always."

CHAPTER ELEVEN

After Watts dropped her off, Rebecca let herself quietly into the house and clicked off the porch light that Catherine had left burning. Another light shone dimly in the hallway and got brighter as she approached the bedroom. Frowning, she eased open the bedroom door and stepped inside. Catherine was propped up on the pillows, asleep with a book on her chest. Rebecca smiled when she recognized the name of a top-selling thriller. Six months ago, she wouldn't have had any idea what that author wrote, but then a lot of things had changed in six months. She would still have been out on the streets at this time of night back then, roaming around in her personal vehicle on her own time, searching for something to fill the void in her life, in her heart. Now, for a few hours, she could leave all the death and depravity behind. In Catherine's arms, she found not only peace, but completion. Moving silently, she crossed to the bed and eased the book from between Catherine's fingers.

"It's late," she said when Catherine opened her eyes and smiled up at her. "Go back to sleep."

She reached over to turn out the light, but Catherine grasped her wrist. "Leave it on until you come to bed. I like to watch you get undressed."

"If you expect me to follow Ali's instructions, you shouldn't say things like that." Rebecca sat on the side of the bed and leaned down to kiss Catherine on the mouth. When Catherine's arms came around her neck, she pushed the sheets down and slipped her hand beneath Catherine's silk top.

Catherine murmured, her nipple hardening as Rebecca's fingertips brushed over it. "My God," she said, pulling back breathlessly. "Ambush. You just ambushed me."

Rebecca grinned. "That wasn't an ambush, it was just a greeting."

Catherine placed her palm against Rebecca's chest and held her away. "No more. I'm weak at the moment." Her smile twisted fleetingly. "I've missed you."

"I feel fine. Never better." Rebecca quickly undressed, all the while watching Catherine watching her. Then she hurried around to the other side of the bed and climbed under the sheets. Catherine rolled toward her, and Rebecca took her into her arms. Still, Catherine kept one hand braced against Rebecca's chest, preventing their bodies from completely touching. Rebecca grumbled in frustration. "At least let me kiss you."

"I can't. I have no willpower where you're concerned. If we start, I won't be able to stop."

"Good."

Catherine brushed her fingers through Rebecca's hair. "Darling, you look tired. It's too soon for you to be working this many hours."

"I was sitting in the car the entire time. It was deadly boring and Watts was enough to drive me crazy, but it wasn't strenuous. I promise."

"What were you doing?"

"Following Mitch. He met Irina tonight. First contact since the raid."

"Did it go all right?"

"I don't know. We're stuck with visual surveillance only." Rebecca almost snarled in frustration. "I can't hear them, so I don't know how well Mitch's doing."

"Is Dellon ready for this?"

"She's got a knack for the work." Rebecca rested her forehead against Catherine's, slowly caressing her shoulders and her back. She hadn't felt as relaxed all day, and miraculously, her fatigue seemed to drop away. "I think she's solid."

"But something is off, isn't it?"

"I don't know. Maybe. I've only got Clark's report that Irina is really willing to go along with the double cross. And Clark probably doesn't care about risking my people with a shaky informant."

"This young woman—Irina—she can't have had much experience with this. She must be terrified."

"She may never have done this before, but to have survived this long…" Rebecca shrugged. "To have even made it as far as this country means she's strong and resourceful and smart. I just wish I had a better sense of whether we can trust her. I can't even question her, because I don't want her to know who Mitch's backup is. That could compromise him down the road."

"What if I talked to her?"

"No," Rebecca said immediately. "I don't want you involved."

"I have an official position with the department," Catherine said gently. "It would probably make sense to her that someone like me interviewed her. Besides, I don't care how strong and resourceful she is, she's got to be frightened. That can't possibly be good for her and Mitch if they get into a difficult situation."

"You're using my weaknesses against me," Rebecca muttered.

Catherine laughed softly. "How is that?"

"You know I'll do anything I have to do to protect my people." Rebecca rolled Catherine onto her back and settled on top of her, one thigh between her legs. Leaning on a forearm, she brushed her thumb over Catherine's chin. "I'd do anything except put you in danger."

"I can hardly be in danger talking to someone in my office."

"I'd rather you didn't get anywhere near this operation." Rebecca frowned. "I'm pretty much working in the dark."

"Let me help shed some light."

Rebecca kissed her. "You always do."

Catherine's eyes softened and she pushed her fingers into Rebecca's hair, pulling her down for a kiss. When she released her, she murmured, "I love you. I want to help you, but it's more than that. It's my job too."

"Maybe." Rebecca sighed. "I'll think about it."

"Good. Now you need some sleep."

"What I really need is you." Rebecca eased onto her side and Catherine curled into her body after switching out the light.

"You have me. And when Ali gives us the okay, I'll show you just how much."

"Promise?" Rebecca murmured as she felt herself slipping away.

"With all my heart."

❖

Sloan didn't remember falling asleep. She remembered undressing Michael by the side of the bed. She remembered sitting on the edge, still fully clothed, and Michael, nude, standing between her thighs. She'd caressed Michael's breasts, her abdomen, her hips, the insides of her thighs while watching her face in the moonlight. After a while Michael had braced her hands on Sloan's shoulders because her legs trembled. Sloan hadn't wanted to stop. She wanted to touch her everywhere, inside and out. She wanted to affirm that Michael was hers, and always would be. She slid her fingers between Michael's thighs, stroking through her wetness, refusing to stop even when Michael warned her of what would happen, teasing relentlessly until Michael climaxed in her hand. She caught Michael as she collapsed and guided her into bed, cradling her until she fell asleep.

She hadn't meant to sleep, but she must have, because now she was waking up. And Michael was touching her. Sloan sucked in a breath and opened her eyes. Michael was leaning over her, her blue eyes bright, her lips parted in an expression of anticipation. Groaning at the surge of pressure in the pit of her stomach, Sloan raised her head enough to see Michael's hand moving between her legs. She had a grip on her clitoris and was slowly massaging her.

"Uh…Jesus." Sloan collapsed back on the bed.

"Good morning," Michael said, her voice silky and deep. She slid her fingers up and down a little faster.

Sloan made an unintelligible sound, and her eyes rolled back in her head.

Michael laughed softly. "I was going to tease you until you got all excited and woke up, but you were already hard when I touched you."

Sloan panted, feeling the orgasm swirl along her spine and coalesce beneath Michael's fingers.

"You didn't finish last night, did you?" Michael squeezed and pulled until Sloan's shoulders came off the bed again, and then she abruptly released her.

"Baby." Sloan stared at Michael, her gaze pleading. "I need—"

Michael kissed her, plunging her tongue into Sloan's mouth while she caressed her breasts and stomach. When Sloan's hips bucked into empty air, Michael quickly pushed down on the bed between her legs. "Watch me."

Sloan braced herself on her elbows and watched Michael lick her. The first warm, wet caress brought her right to the edge. It was so good, and she needed to come so much. "Suck it?"

"Mmm," Michael murmured, circling with her tongue. "I will. In a little while."

"Feels so good."

"You taste so good." Michael sucked light and fast, a flutter of teeth and tongue.

"I'm going to come," Sloan blurted.

Michael backed off and went back to licking. Every now and then, in no particular pattern, she drew Sloan completely into her mouth. Each time she did, Sloan felt herself starting to come. And each time Michael would relax and let her slip out again.

Sloan tugged at the sheets, pulling them loose until they were bunched up around her body. The muscles in her legs clenched so tightly they started to go numb. She felt the faint scrape of teeth and then Michael was sucking her again, faster now. She clamped one hand on the back of Michael's head and pushed herself deeper between Michael's lips.

"Harder," she gasped. "I'm close, baby."

Michael's eyes, brilliant with power and pleasure, found hers as she worked her just the way she needed to finish.

"Coming," Sloan shouted hoarsely, bending forward to cradle Michael's shoulders, climaxing wildly in her mouth. Michael didn't let up and the pressure doubled, tripled, until Sloan was writhing and sweating and coming again. She fell onto her side, shuddering, struggling for breath, tears leaking from her eyes.

Michael quickly rose up beside her and pulled her into her arms. "It's okay, it's okay," she murmured, wiping the moisture from Sloan's face. She cradled her head and kissed her forehead, her eyes, her mouth. "I love you. I love you completely."

Sloan turned her face to Michael's breasts, clinging to the sound of her voice and the strong steady beat of her heart. "I'd do anything to keep you safe."

"I know. But the only thing that could ever hurt me is losing you."

"I love you," Sloan whispered, wishing that were really enough.

❖

Sandy, in one of Dell's T-shirts and nothing else, curled up in the corner of the disheveled sofa bed with a cup of coffee and watched Dell get dressed. She loved the way Dell did everything with precision and care, smoothing out the wrinkles in her T-shirt as she tucked the bottom tightly into her jeans, placing her wallet squarely in her back pocket, clipping her holster in just the right position on her hip. She could picture Dell in a uniform like her sister Erica had worn, all bright and shiny and flawless. Dell was like one of those poster soldiers, representing everything that was good and brave and true. Except she was real.

"You're not going to do anything stupid, are you?"

Dell looked over, frowning. "Huh?"

"You know, like trying to save Irina and all those other girls and getting yourself killed?"

"Jesus, babe. Where is this coming from?"

"You," Sandy said softly, staring into the empty cup. "You forget you're not indestructible."

Dell knelt down in front of Sandy, put the cup on the coffee table behind her, and took both of Sandy's hands. "I don't forget. I'm a good cop, San, and I'm not going to do anything reckless. I promise." She leaned forward and kissed Sandy on the mouth. "And look who's talking. Where did you go last night?"

Sandy shrugged. "Around."

"Around where?"

"A couple places to meet up with some friends."

"Uh-huh. Strip clubs down on the avenue, right?"

Sandy shrugged again.

"I carry a gun, babe. I've got backup. I know how to fight." Dell rested her forehead on Sandy's knee, sliding her arms around Sandy's waist. "Jesus Christ. You're out there all alone."

Sandy grabbed a fistful of Dell's hair and pulled her head up. She stared fiercely into her face. "I'm not stupid, either. I carry a phone, I watch where I'm going. I have friends out there who watch out for me. I want to come home to you too."

"I wish you weren't doing what you're doing for Frye."

Sandy blinked. Dell hadn't said to stop, she'd just said she wished she wouldn't. Dell was scared. Her brave, steady cop was scared. "I know, baby. And I'll be careful."

"Fuck, this is hard," Dell muttered.

"Yeah." Sandy tugged on Dell's hair. "I want to know what happens with Irina."

"Aw, babe—"

"I mean it, rookie. Because if you don't tell me, I'm just going to make things up in my head. And they'll probably be a lot worse."

"Hell."

"Uh-huh." Sandy smoothed Dell's hair back and kissed her. She played with Dell's tongue and nudged her knee into Dell's crotch until Dell made a hungry sound. Then she pulled back. "I guess we're just going to have to trust each other."

Dell smiled crookedly. "I guess so."

"Call me later?"

"I will. Go back to bed. I've got to meet with the team." Dell took a long breath. "After I get some coffee and stuff for Irina."

Sandy's eyes flashed, but she just nodded. "Okay." She brushed her hand over Dell's chest. "Just remember where you belong."

Dell grinned. "I got it. No problem."

Sandy curled up on the couch and willed herself back to sleep. She didn't want to hear Dell's footsteps going down the hall toward Irina.

❖

Dell unlocked the apartment door, knocked softly, and let herself in—holding her breath until she saw Irina perched on the front windowsill, watching the street. Her wavy dark hair was wet and she wore a pair of Dell's jeans and a button-down-collar cotton shirt that was tight across her breasts.

"I guess you found the shower." Dell handed her a cup of coffee and a muffin from Dunkin' Donuts.

"Yes. And the clothes." Irina nodded toward the bag she'd taken from her house the night before. "I borrowed yours. I need to wash mine. They have footprints on them."

"There's a place around the corner." Dell took her wallet out and handed Irina a twenty. "It takes quarters, so you'll have to stop at one of the bodegas to get change."

Irina stared at the money.

"You know how to make change, and everything, right?"

"I know the money." She looked at Dell. "But no one has ever given me any before."

"What about—" Dell flushed, about to ask her about the johns. Jesus, could she be any more of an ass?

"None of us got to keep anything we...earned. The enforcers... they gave us everything. Food. Clothes. Medicine."

"They kept you dependent," Dell said. "It's hard to run away, to fight back, when you have nothing and nowhere to go."

Irina turned quickly to the window.

Dell put her hands in her pockets, feeling more like a fool. "I'm sorry."

"No. I...the coffee is good. Thank you."

"I have to go out for a while," Dell said to Irina's back. "Like I said, you're not a prisoner, but you should be careful if you go anywhere. People are probably looking for you."

Irina turned around. "What is your real name?"

Dell tried not to fidget when Irina's stare drifted from her breasts to her crotch and lingered. She wondered if Irina liked women, then wondered why she cared. "Dell."

"Do you mind if I just call you Mitch?"

"No, I don't mind at all."

Irina nodded. "I will wait here. After the clothes washing, I will wait here."

"Good. Thanks." Dell walked to the door. "I'll be back."

When Irina said nothing, she slipped out and closed the door.

CHAPTER TWELVE

"S he's got a picture of her sister," Dell said to the others gathered around the conference table at Sloan's. "But she won't let me see it. She doesn't trust me, and I guess I don't blame her."

"If she won't give it to you," Watts said, slurping his coffee, "then take it. She doesn't have a lot of choice in this game."

Dell shook her head, biting back a retort. "I'm not going to force her to do anything. That's not the way to get her to cooperate." When Watts raised his eyebrows, she hastily added, "Detective."

"So what are you gonna do, big man," Watts goaded. "Fuck her until she's brainless and begs to give you anything you want?"

"Watts," Rebecca said in a steely voice.

"Well, for Christ's sakes, Loo," Watts snapped. "The girl's a criminal, but instead of getting her sweet little ass shipped back to Mother Russia, she's walking around here free as a bird. Telling us what she'll do and what she won't."

"She's scared," Dell said.

Watts muttered something about bleeding hearts.

"What do you suggest, Detective," Rebecca said, giving Mitchell her head. Mitchell was the one closest to Irina, and it was her ass on the line. They had to trust Mitchell's take on the situation. Rebecca didn't like it, not because she didn't trust Mitchell, but because she was never comfortable being forced to make decisions based on other people's judgments.

"If we're going to get her to cooperate, I think we have to help her find her sister. And the only way we're going to do that is to promise her sister will be safe."

"Promise her Witsec, for both of them." Sloan stood, coffee cup in hand. "Anybody need a refill?"

"I'll get it," Jason said, rising as well. "And I agree. Offer her protection—for both of them. Offer them a new life. It might buy Mitch a safety net."

Dell looked at Frye. "Can we?"

"I don't know. Technically, she belongs to Clark."

"Fucking Clark," Watts muttered. "I say we do it."

Rebecca swiveled on her chair and regarded him sharply. "Why the sudden change?"

Watts shrugged. "Because it will burn Clark's ass." He shot a look at Jason and Sloan. "And because it's more likely to put Irina firmly on our side, and that's good for Mitch."

"She might not be an easy sell," Sloan said. "I've seen plenty of girls sold into the sex trade in Southeast Asia. All they know is lies and abuse. How much do you think she trusts you, Dell?"

"I don't know. Some."

"Are you banging her?" Watts asked.

Rebecca said, "Jesus, Watts."

"No, I'm not," Dell said stiffly.

"Well maybe you should. Then, when she's all softened up, you can—"

Dell shot to her feet and strode out of the room.

Rebecca rubbed her eyes. She'd slept soundly, but only for a few hours. Her head throbbed dully. Better than the day before, but still there. She pushed away from the table and stood. "Watts, go down to the port with Jason. Then see if you can get a line on the Zamoras' lieutenants from OC. They're probably the ones playing messenger with the Russians. Somebody get me some names."

Watts looked in the direction Mitchell had gone, his expression confused. "I was just saying—"

"Dell likes her," Jason said softly to Watts. "And when Dell likes a woman, she wants her treated right."

"Oh. Well hell, that complicates things."

Jason laughed. "So what else is new?"

❖

"Sloan. Talk to you a minute?" Rebecca said as the conference room began to clear.

"Sure." Sloan hiked a hip onto the edge of the conference table. When they were alone, she asked, "How are you feeling?"

"A little rough around the edges, but I'm getting there."

"You and Watts can't cover Mitch every night. I can take some shifts. I've got a badge again, remember?" Sloan still couldn't believe Clark had given her official agent status when she began working with Rebecca's team. She wasn't exactly a fed again, because she answered to Rebecca, which suited her just fine. Rebecca she trusted.

"I can't get departmental authorization for the manpower to cover him twenty-four/seven," Rebecca said. "No undercover agent gets that kind of backup."

"I'm not asking to get paid," Sloan said.

"I appreciate your volunteering. I can use you." Rebecca shrugged into her wool blazer, as close as she ever came to a winter coat. "I want to cover the two of them as tightly as we can for the first week or so, until we get a feel for how things are working out with Irina. Then, other than critical meets, we'll have to rely on Mitch to call for backup if he gets in a tight position.

"I'm good for it any time."

"Thanks." Rebecca considered the more pressing matter they needed to square away. "About this fund-raiser—"

"Michael is going," Sloan cut in. "She already had it scheduled—a business thing. I forgot she told me. I'm still hoping to talk her out of it."

"She doesn't have to get anywhere near Zamora," Rebecca said evenly. "If it comes to that."

Sloan hesitated, then looked out into the main room, checking that no one was around. "Something doesn't feel right about this, Rebecca. Not any of it. I don't trust Clark. He's always working the angles for himself, and he doesn't care who pays the price."

"I've got the same feeling, but I can't put my finger on the reason. I'm going to talk to Clark today about Witsec, and I'll see if I can get a better feel for what he's not telling us."

"Call me. I'm heading over to Police Plaza for a while and check on my boys. Make sure they haven't fried the system while I've been gone."

"Thanks for lending me your car yesterday." Rebecca grinned. "Nice ride."

Sloan sketched a salute. "Just don't let Watts drive."

Rebecca watched her walk away. Sloan was volatile at the best of times and she'd been wrapped tight since Michael was injured. Still, Rebecca trusted her. Whatever it was Sloan had done for the Justice Department, she'd been good at it or Clark wouldn't have pulled her back in. And Rebecca needed someone with that kind of experience. Sloan would keep her head, as long as Michael didn't get drawn in.

Scanning the work area, Rebecca headed for the huge bank of windows at the far end. As she expected, Mitchell was waiting there, slouched with her hands in the pockets of her black jeans, rocking back and forth in her heavy motorcycle boots.

"You want to finish your report?" Rebecca asked.

Dell continued to stare down at the choppy gray surface of the river. "I'm sorry I lost it. I know he doesn't mean half the things he says."

"He probably means the other half. But I promise you he'll always have your back."

"I know." Dell faced Rebecca. "Irina is used to protecting herself. She handled the bartender at Ziggie's last night really well. I think she can get me inside."

"You think the Russians will contact her again?"

"Once the word gets out that she's been spotted at Ziggie's, yeah, I think so. Especially since she's reaching out, like she wants to get back to work."

"You're going back tonight, right?"

Dell nodded. "I'm taking her to the Troc first to meet the guys. And Jasmine."

"Good." Rebecca studied the young detective. She looked calm, despite the enormity of the operation and her position on point. She looked solid. "How's Sandy doing?"

"She's good." Dell took a breath. "I don't think she should stay at her apartment if Irina's going to be down the hall."

"I don't imagine Sandy's too happy about that."

"She's okay. But if trouble follows us home, I don't want her around. Besides, with Sandy working the streets for you, I think it would be better to put some distance between us."

"You're right, but she's not going to like it."

"I can put her up in my condo for a while."

Rebecca shook her head. "I don't think so. Too isolated. I know their security is tight, but none of us are close enough if there's trouble." She watched a tugboat push a huge oil barge up to one of the refinery docks. "She can probably stay here with Michael and Sloan."

"Oh, man, you think so? This place is like a fortress. And Sandy really likes Michael."

"I'll check it out. In the meantime, how are you doing with Irina?"

"Okay, no problem," Dell said, flushing.

"You need to keep some objectivity there," Rebecca said. "You can't let yourself get attached."

"I know."

Rebecca had run cops undercover before, but usually sting operations on porn dealers or pimps. Nothing this long term or at such a distance. She needed to know what might shake Mitchell up. She needed to know what might get Mitchell killed. "Are you going to be all right with her and the physical situation?"

"I don't feel that way about her. I mean, she's attractive and..." Dell looked away, then squared her shoulders and met Rebecca's gaze. "I can't help getting turned on sometimes. It's not like I mean to, or even want to. I...I'm keeping my focus, though."

"I think it would be tough getting up close to her and not feeling anything at all." Rebecca was proud of Mitchell for admitting something that a lot of cops wouldn't. Whether it was drugs or girls or easy money, temptation was everywhere, and no one wanted to admit to being tempted, even when they managed to resist. "But you need to keep your head clear. And that includes not feeling bad about reactions out of your control."

"I'm trying. I'm good."

"I want you to talk to Catherine about it."

Dell stiffened. "I don't—"

"Not a request, Detective." Rebecca gripped Mitchell's shoulder. "I trust you, okay? But you've got to be completely on top of things. For your own safety. For Irina's. And for Sandy's. You read me?"

"Yes ma'am, Lieutenant."

"Good. I'll tell her you'll be by today." Rebecca touched her knuckles briefly to the edge of Mitchell's jaw. "You're doing a good job."

"Thank you," Dell whispered as Rebecca walked away, the praise running through her like a warm caress. "Thank you, Lieutenant."

❖

"Of course I'll make time to see her," Catherine said when Rebecca phoned her. "I'll tell Joyce to fit her in whenever she calls. What about Irina?"

"I'm on my way to see Clark right now," Rebecca said. "Hopefully we'll be able to put her with you in the next day or so."

"All right, darling. Are you driving?"

"Yes, but not very far. Just—"

"How's your vision?"

"Perfect. A little headache," Rebecca volunteered, "but otherwise no problems at all."

"Will you do me a favor?"

"Yes."

"Go home for a few hours this afternoon. Take a nap."

Rebecca did some quick mental calculations. She wanted to shadow Mitchell when she took Irina to the Troc and Ziggie's, and that meant being out on surveillance most of the night. In fact, almost everything that was going on in the operation was going to happen at night. She could take a few hours' downtime during the day. She wouldn't ordinarily, but Catherine asked so little of her. "All right. I will. I'll call you when I get home."

"Thank you, darling. I love you. I've got to go. Patients."

"I'll call you later. Love you." Rebecca disconnected and pulled into the underground parking lot below the federal building at Sixth and Market. With any luck, she'd be able to track Clark down.

❖

Kratos Zamora touched the edge of the linen napkin to his mouth, then deposited it next to the china plate in front of him. He placed the heavy silver knife and fork engraved with the crest of the Union Club together on the plate and smiled at Talia. Seated across from him, she wore a red dress in a style appropriate for a business meeting, but even the subdued lines and conservative cut couldn't hide her inherent sensuality. He enjoyed the persistent arousal her presence always instilled. He always found the unattainable exciting.

"How was the lamb?" he asked.

"Delicious." Talia sipped her wine, aware of the glances from the mostly male diners. Only a few years ago, women had not been welcome as members of the elite business club, and she wagered that Kratos had not been welcome either. At one time his lineage would have been enough to deny him entry, but now, money was the main requirement. Money legitimized everyone and abolished social divides, at least on the surface.

"Might I hope that the reason for your lunch invitation was simply that you wanted my company?" Kratos inquired, reaching across the table to stroke Talia's hand.

Carefully, she shifted her hand to her wineglass, not wanting to make the movement appear as a rejection to him or anyone who might be watching. Swirling the claret before sipping, she allowed the wine to linger on her tongue, inhaling slowly, savoring the bouquet. She knew he was watching. His eyes were hungry. "I'll need some time to breach Sloan's system."

"But you can do it."

Talia smiled. "Of course."

"Good."

Talia was silent as the waiter glided up to the table. When he inquired if there was anything else she needed, she replied, "Espresso, please."

"Very good, madam. And for you, sir?"

"Just coffee."

When he disappeared as soundlessly as he had arrived, Talia said, "Someone like her could be very valuable."

"What do you mean?" Kratos asked.

"She could do anything she wanted and no one would have the expertise to detect it. And she has direct access." Talia shrugged. "Interviews, files, evidence—all of it."

"Can't you do the same thing?"

"I'm touched by your faith," Talia said with a faintly mocking lilt. "Yes, given enough time. But I can guarantee that Sloan's primary agenda right now is to make the central files as impregnable as possible. It would be so much nicer if she were helping us get in rather than working to keep us out."

"What kind of leverage do we have?"

"This." Talia reached into her purse and withdrew the photograph of Sloan and the blonde in the ambulance. She'd added another clipping after searching newspaper archives that morning.

Kratos took the two photographs and stared at the woman who had caught his attention in the surveillance videos. The caption said her name was Michael Lassiter. *Michael.* She was wholly feminine, and the androgyny of her name only heightened her allure. Enjoying his instantaneous erection, he brushed his thumb along the outline of her body. "Sloan's lover?"

"It would appear so."

"We can't touch her." He shook his head. "Not after all the attention our Russian friends stirred up recently."

Talia laughed softly. "You can't honestly think I was suggesting something as crude as that, can you?"

Kratos frowned. "What then?"

"How would you like to get to know Ms. Lassiter personally?"

"I'd like nothing better," he said, his gaze drifting to her mouth. "*Almost* nothing."

❖

Avery Clark didn't keep Rebecca waiting long, once she'd found his office in the warren of hallways lined with nondescript wooden doors and frosted glass windows. She announced herself to the lone secretary in the tiny waiting room and had just settled into an uncomfortable, thinly upholstered chair against the wall when Clark himself opened another unadorned door at the rear of the room and gestured her inside with a surprisingly friendly smile.

Rebecca followed him into the inner office and closed the door, waiting for him to walk around behind his plain gray metal desk before she sat in yet another uncomfortable chair in front of it. With his jacket off and his white shirt sleeves rolled up, Clark was standard government issue—somewhere between thirty-five and forty, brown hair, dark steel-framed glasses, conservative haircut, conventional suit, dark tie, plain shirt. Wedding ring, hip holster, sharp eyes.

"Lieutenant," he said, settling into the fake black leather desk chair. He tilted back slightly and swiveled a few degrees from side to side. "Back to work already? Glad to see that injury isn't slowing you down."

"Thanks," Rebecca replied, wondering just how glad Clark really was to see her back on the job. Her headache had ratcheted up the moment she'd walked into the federal building. She doubted the dull throbbing behind her eyes had anything to do with her injury. She'd never liked the politics of law enforcement, but now that she'd been promoted, she had no choice but to navigate the murky waters populated by self-interested elected officials, federal agents, and local police. Power and control were the sought-after prizes, and public perception often more important than results. It wasn't a game she liked, but she had to play.

"I appreciate you all helping us out," Clark said.

"We didn't exactly have a choice on that, since you went over our heads with the plan."

Clark shrugged, his smile still in place, his expression a mixture of false innocence and self-satisfaction. "Time was of the essence, so I just wanted to avoid getting bogged down in red tape. I'm sure you can appreciate that."

"What I'd appreciate," Rebecca said, holding his gaze, "is a look at the statements from Irina Guterov and the other girls in that house, along with whatever you have on the Russian connection to local crime. You want us to do your legwork and the brass agrees. I don't intend to do it blind."

"Well," Clark said as if he were thinking, "the girls didn't really give us much. They don't know very much. Most of them don't even speak English."

"Irina does."

"True, which is why we can use her." Clark's eyes narrowed. "Girls like Irina are not that easy to replace. The Russians need women like her to indoctrinate the new girls into the system. The fresh ones have to be taught how to behave at private parties, what to expect when they go to a video shoot, how to handle johns at the clubs. They're going to want her back, and soon."

"I agree." Rebecca crossed her legs, letting her arms drape casually along the wooden armrests. His casual dismissal of the plight of the girls, all victims, even Irina, grated on her. But she hadn't come to fight a battle she couldn't win. "What makes you think we can trust her?"

"She doesn't want to go back to Russia." Clark shrugged. "And then there's the matter of her sister. She wants to find her. She wants to protect her. All things considered, we've got serious leverage."

"Where is her sister?"

Clark shook his head. "No idea. The sister arrived here after Guterov. Not that long ago, apparently, as some sort of reward for Guterov's cooperation in running the other girls. Except the Russians didn't put them together the way they promised."

"Using a little leverage of their own," Rebecca mused. Keeping Irina obligated to them—first with promises to bring her sister to this country, then by stringing her along and keeping them apart.

"Yes. Threats against families are one of the traditional means of controlling these girls."

"So the sister might not even be in the city."

"Possibly, although she probably is. They don't cycle them out of here that quickly, and I suspect they'd keep her close in case Guterov threatened to stop working if they didn't produce her."

"I don't want Irina trading my officer for her sister," Rebecca said. "Now that she's back on the streets, she might be tempted to do that."

Clark looked unconcerned. "She knows we can pick her up and deport her."

"Not good enough. I want incentive for her to stay on our side. I want Witsec for her and her sister."

Clark pursed his lips. "Witsec is expensive. It's getting pretty selective these days, too, especially when we're trying to persuade people to testify against terrorists."

"Get them to make an exception. My undercover officer has to be protected."

"I'll look into it."

"I want an answer soon or I'll pull my people out."

"Your captain won't be happy about that. Neither will the commissioner."

"I'll take my chances."

Clark studied Rebecca and whatever he saw in her face must have convinced him she wasn't bluffing. He nodded. "I'll get back to you."

"So tell me about Kratos Zamora."

"He's a businessman. A very wealthy one." Clark spread his hands. "And a staunch supporter of the present administration."

"What's your interest?"

"His family may be doing business with persons of interest to us."

"His family? Or him?"

"That's what I was hoping you could help us with."

Rebecca's internal temperature soared to just below boiling, but she didn't move an inch. She reminded herself that just because she and Clark were supposed to be on the same side didn't make them teammates. "Help how?"

"You can tell a lot about a person by the company they keep. And the people they do business with."

"His business interests should be a matter of record. One thing you federal types are good at is chasing paper trails." Clark's expression shuttered closed, but Rebecca didn't care if he was insulted. He wanted to use her and give nothing in return. "Besides, his brother heads the family."

"That's what Kratos would like us to believe," Clark said. "We're not so sure. That's why we want a more personal look at him. Business gets discussed at events like this fund-raiser tomorrow night. Alliances are forged. We want to know who's in his inner circle."

"Why don't you put your people on him?"

"Because he's smart and he's careful," Clark said, frustration evident in his voice. "All we need is an initial legitimate business connection. Then we can insert our people and run with it."

"I can't help you. Sloan has plenty of connections in the private sector, but if the Zamoras don't know about her working with us, they would soon enough."

"I wasn't thinking of Sloan."

Rebecca shook her head. "Who then?"

"Innova Design is one of the biggest companies on the East Coast. And Michael Lassiter—"

"She's a civilian," Rebecca snapped. "She nearly died already and she's completely untrained."

"I don't expect her to do undercover work," Clark shot back. "All we need is the initial overture and then we'll put our people inside her firm."

"No."

"Think about it."

"I already have." Rebecca rose. "And the answer is still no."

Chapter Thirteen

S ince Joyce, Catherine's secretary, had gone to lunch, Catherine checked the waiting area herself a few minutes after one. As she expected, her special appointment was waiting. "Dellon. Hello, come on in."

"Thanks for seeing me." Dell followed her into the office, removed her windbreaker, and took her customary chair in front of Catherine's desk. "The lieutenant thought we should talk."

"What do you think?" Catherine settled into a chair facing Dellon. The first time they'd met, Dellon had sat nearly at attention in her seat, feet firmly on the floor, eyes straight ahead. Today, she was a little more relaxed, her back still not touching the chair, but her shoulders no longer rigid. In her black street clothes, with her black hair and dark eyes, she was wildly attractive. Catherine could imagine her capturing the eye of any number of females, of any age. That kind of sexual magnetism could pose a problem, especially in the kind of work she was doing.

"I think if the lieutenant thinks it's a good idea, it is," Dell said.

"That is a very diplomatic answer." Catherine laughed softly. "So how are you?"

Dell grinned and interlaced her fingers, resting her hands between her thighs. "I think I'm doing okay, but...there's a lot going on, you know?"

"I know some of the details of the operation. Why don't you tell me how you see it."

"The assignment's great," Dell said enthusiastically, filling Catherine in on the basic details. "It's good. It's what I want to do. I feel like..."

"Like what?" Catherine asked after a minute of silence.

"Like I'm doing something that no one else can do. 'Cause I'm really good at this undercover thing." Dell smiled. "Well, Mitch is, anyhow."

"Is Mitch a police officer too?" Catherine leaned closer as Dell stared. "By that, I mean does Mitch make decisions from the same set of rules and regulations that a police officer would?"

Dell frowned. "Um."

"You know this is private, don't you?" Catherine said gently. Dellon had matured since their first meeting. She'd filled out, metaphorically, from a heartbreakingly innocent young officer into a confident detective. Catherine was glad to see the changes, because she knew Dellon would be safer on the streets, but growth spurts like that could leave someone off balance. And that could be dangerous."Even though your lieutenant thinks it's a good idea that we talk, what we discuss here is between us."

"Yes ma'am. I know that. It's just…I never thought about it before. Mitch…yeah, Mitch is a cop. I mean, when I'm Mitch, I still think like a cop, even if I have to do things I might not do when I'm not undercover."

"What kind of things?"

Dell stared at her hands. "The things I do with Irina. I wouldn't do them with her, with anyone."

"When you're intimate."

"Yes."

"Do you feel guilty about it?"

Dell searched Catherine's eyes. "Should I?"

Catherine smiled and waited.

"I don't feel guilty about Mitch acting like Irina's boyfriend. I mean, when you're undercover, you have to be into it. It's gotta be real. If it isn't, it won't work."

"That makes sense," Catherine said. "So when Mitch and Irina act like lovers—when they're physically intimate, that feels okay."

Dell nodded. Then after a second, she shook her head.

"Yes and no? A little of both?"

"It's okay we kiss and fool around." Dell slowly met Catherine's gaze. "It's not okay that I…want to."

"You want to be intimate with Irina." Catherine waited until Dell nodded again. "Do you want to make love with her?"

"Sometimes. I mean, I get turned on and part of me wants to keep going."

"What about when you're not actually being physically intimate with her? Do you think about making love with her when you're not with her? Do you look forward to seeing her and hope you have a chance to have sex?"

"No." Dell straightened her shoulders and set her feet squarely on the floor. "No, I don't."

"Why not?"

"Because I don't love her."

Catherine wanted to smile, but she kept her expression neutral. Oh, she could see this one breaking hearts everywhere she went. "So let me see if I understand. You find her physically attractive, but you're not in love with her and you aren't interested in having a sexual relationship with her."

"Right," Dell said when Catherine paused.

"But when you have to be physical with her because of the roles you're both playing, you become aroused."

"Yes."

"What is there about your body's response in that situation that makes you worry?"

"I bet the lieutenant wouldn't get turned on. I bet she'd be cool. She's always in control."

"Everyone is different, Dellon," Catherine said, carefully not thinking about her lover becoming aroused with another woman. She'd have to think about it later, especially the quick surge of jealous anger the idea provoked. "Our bodies are different, our physical triggers are different. That's neither good nor bad. It's just a fact."

"So you don't think I should feel guilty about it?"

"I think when you're working, the most important thing is that you keep your mind clear. It's important for your safety and Irina's that you be totally focused on the situation. If you're worried about what you're feeling, put that aside temporarily." Catherine squeezed Dellon's arm. "You can talk to me about it later, if you want to."

"Sandy says she never got turned on when she was working," Dell said in a low voice. "That always made me glad. I hate thinking about her touching anyone else. Having them touch her."

"Sandy isn't you, Dell. And what she was doing is very different than what you're doing. There are some similarities, yes. The physical interaction with someone you don't love—that's the same. But there are so many differences, you can't compare them."

"I can tell she doesn't like Mitch and Irina spending time together, but she's trying to deal."

"Are the two of you able to talk about it?"

"Some." Dell sighed. "We're working on it."

"Good. That's exactly what you need to do." Catherine hesitated, wondering if she should talk to Rebecca, then pushed on. "If the two of you want to talk with me, you can call me."

"Yeah?" Dell's eyes brightened.

"Yes. There are no rules for what you're doing, Dellon, and I think you're doing a terrific job. Both you and Sandy."

"Could you tell my lieutenant that?"

"Oh, I most definitely will." Catherine stood. "Come see me next week, all right?"

"Okay, yeah. That would be good." Dell rose and slid her hands in her pockets. Rocking back on her heels, she grinned. "I guess the lieutenant was right about me coming to see you. She's pretty much always right."

Catherine laughed. "Let's not remind her of that."

Watts rapped on the partially open door of the large utilitarian room with one wall of windows overlooking the docks at the Packer Avenue terminal of the Port of Philadelphia. A robust African-American woman in a spit-and-polish uniform looked up from behind a desk when he pushed the door open a few more inches.

Captain Carla Reiser smiled, her smooth mocha features relaxing, taking ten years off her already youthful face, and dropped the sheaf of papers she was studying onto the center of her desk. "Bill. Good to see you."

"Yeah. You too." Watts ambled a few feet into the room. "Busy?"

"Half a dozen of my dock supervisors have been arrested and I've got feds crawling all over my port." Carla shrugged. "Normal day."

Watts laughed. "Yeah, I know what you mean."

"Social visit?" Carla's voice held just a hint of playfulness and Watts tried not to grin like an idiot. Carla headed security for the whole port, and she'd helped orchestrate the interception of the last shipment of girls from Eastern Europe. She was sharp and savvy and smart, and he couldn't believe his luck that a woman like her even noticed he was alive.

"You remember Jason?" Watts asked.

"The blond computer cop, right?"

"Yeah, that's him." Watts was foolishly pleased that she hadn't commented on how good-looking Jason was. Everyone always referred to him as too handsome to be a man. Geez, it could give a guy a complex. "He's up at the IT center, poking around in your computers, trying to figure out who did what and how."

"If he finds anything, I hope he lets me know."

"What about the feds? Are they turning up anything?"

"Who knows. If they talk to you, then you're doing a lot better than me."

"That's a no, then," Watts grunted.

Carla gestured to the worn plaid sofa pushed against one wall. "Sit down. Coffee?"

"I'll get it. I'm up." Watts poured coffee from the Pyrex carafe into two oversized Styrofoam cups, added powdered creamer, stirred both with one of the wooden sticks from a nearby tray, and carried the cups back to the couch. Carla had settled into one corner, and he handed her the coffee. "Light, no sugar, right?"

"Very good."

He felt himself coloring and hastily sat down on the opposite end of the sofa. "So are you catching any heat from the arrests, or shouldn't I ask?"

"I'm the ranking officer in charge on-site. All my superiors man desks downtown." Carla sipped her coffee, her eyes contemplative. "They're looking at me, but they haven't put me on administrative leave. Yet."

"That blows."

Carla laughed. "It surely does." She shifted until her knee touched his and leaned forward. "I don't believe for a minute that those six supervisors were anywhere near the top of the food chain. Whoever was running this operation had to have international connections and some way of moving human beings and God knows what else out of this port. I want them."

"You're gonna have to get in line," Watts said softly. "These guys almost killed my lieutenant."

"I heard you had casualties. Is she okay?"

"Back on the job," Watts said.

"Tough."

Watts nodded. "Oh yeah."

"What can I do to help?"

"Just clear Jason to look at anything he wants to, should anybody ask. If anyone balks at that, let us know, and we'll look extra hard at them." Watson set his cup on the scarred coffee table in front of the sofa. "Got any ideas where we ought to look?"

"I've got four warehouses and a hundred thirty loading docks at this terminal alone. We have thousands of containers offloading every month. Do we lose one for a few hours or a day because bills of lading were filled out incorrectly by someone who doesn't even speak English ten thousand miles away? Yes. Does contraband come through inside the cars or barrels of cocoa beans or tons of clothing merchandise? Undoubtedly." She shook her head angrily. "But people? Human beings transported across the ocean in pitch-black unvented metal coffins? If I had any idea which of my officers helped, I'd drag their sorry carcasses to you myself."

"I guess that's why they call those girls slaves," Watts said. Then he thought of what he had said, and to whom. "Well fuck. Sorry, I didn't mean—"

"No need to apologize, Bill." Carla collected their cups and threw them into the trash. Back at her desk, she scribbled something on the back of a business card and held it out to him. "Give this to Jason. It's my direct number. Anything he needs, tell him to call me."

"Thanks," Watts said, pocketing the card. "Well, I have to get back to headquarters."

Watts was almost to the door when Carla said, "Bill."

He turned, aware he was holding his breath.

Carla's eyes sparkled as if she were about to laugh, and the lighthearted expression made her look welcoming and sexy at the same time. "How about dinner some night?"

"How about tomorrow?"

"For how long, Dell?" Sandy exclaimed, standing across the small room, her arms folded tightly beneath her breasts.

Dell could almost see her quiver. She hoped with anger, not hurt. "I don't know, babe. A few days, a week maybe."

"Or two weeks? Or three? Maybe a month?" Sandy's voice shook. "You want me to stay at Michael's, in a strange bed, alone, while you're here with Irina? Going out with her every night. Coming home with her?"

Sandy looked around the room, her eyes wild. For a second, Dell thought she might be looking for something to throw. She took a cautious step forward. Then another. When Sandy wouldn't even look at her, she kept going until she was right in front of her. Inches away. Then she very gently rested her hands on Sandy's shoulders. Sandy still wouldn't look at her, so she tilted her head down until their eyes could meet. "I'll come over there whenever I can. You think I want to sleep without you?"

When Sandy didn't answer, Dell tucked two fingers under her chin and turned her head until she was sure Sandy had focused on her. "When are you going to believe me? I love you. Like crazy. Like so much all I think about is you."

She kissed her, letting her lips linger on Sandy's mouth even though Sandy did not return her kiss. She brushed her lips back and forth until Sandy's breath fluttered out on a sigh, then danced her tongue over Sandy's lower lip until Sandy's arms slipped around her neck. The tightness in Dell's chest eased and she moved them backward to the sofa. Then she pulled Sandy down beside her, keeping Sandy in the curve of her arm, tight against her body.

"Why don't you trust me?" Dell asked.

Sandy thumped her arm. "It's not about that."

"Then what is it about?"

"It's about me missing you."

"You think I won't miss you?"

"You'll be working," Sandy said softly, her voice muffled against Dell's T-shirt.

Dell shifted the short soft strands of Sandy's hair through her fingers. "I'll always be working. That doesn't mean I won't be thinking about you. Jesus, San, I love you."

Sandy sat back, her eyes searching Dell's face. She remembered a conversation she'd had with Frye, one of those up close and personal ones she'd rather not have. Frye had said if she loved Dell she couldn't make her crazy, because then Dell wouldn't be thinking about work. Instead she'd be thinking about her, and she'd get hurt.

"I love you too," Sandy told her. "I like knowing you're coming home to me. I like coming home to you. I like it a lot."

"Fuck." Dell pushed her fingers through her hair. "I thought I was doing a good thing, moving you out of here. I don't like Mitch and Irina being so close to you. I don't know what the guys Irina has been working with will do when she hooks up with them again."

"You think they'll hurt her?"

"I don't know. Probably not. But just the same—"

"You're gonna be with her, Dell. What about you getting hurt?" Sandy slapped Dell's chest. "And don't give me that crap about you being a cop. You don't wear a vest when you're with her. Anything could happen."

"Maybe," Dell admitted. She wasn't going to insult Sandy by blowing smoke at her. "But I'll have backup. The lieutenant and Watts are following me."

"Yeah, just like they were following you when you went into that house with her the last time. Frye almost ended up dead." Sandy grabbed Dell's face between her hands. "If something happens to you, rookie, I don't know what I'll do."

Dell covered Sandy's hands with hers. "That's how I feel about you, don't you get it? I'm totally soft for you, babe."

Sandy laughed, her eyes flickering down to Dell's crotch. "Since when?"

"Up here," Dell said, tapping her forehead.

Sandy straddled Dell's lap. "What are you doing tonight?"

"Uh…it's hard for me to think right now."

"Try." Sandy leaned forward and kissed Dell fleetingly before leaning back.

"Working." Dell could tell from Sandy's stare that she wasn't going to get away with anything short of details. "At the Troc. Then Ziggie's. Then I don't know."

"Jesus, Dell," Sandy whispered. "You gotta be careful."

"I will. I promise."

Sandy kissed her again, but it wasn't a *fuck me* kiss. It was an *I love you more than anything* kiss. Then she climbed off Dell's lap, walked to the small closet, and pulled out a worn floral fabric suitcase.

"What are you doing?" Dell asked, her voice hoarse.

"Packing some stuff to go to Michael's."

"You sure?"

Sandy looked over her shoulder and made herself smile. "Yeah, Michael is cool. No problem."

"I'll be there later tonight."

"Okay. That's good."

Sandy carried the bag to the dresser just inside the door and started pulling items from the drawers. Dell went up behind her and put her arms around her, tugging Sandy back against her chest. She nuzzled Sandy's neck. "I know you don't want to."

"I said it's okay."

"I know. But it sucks. And I'm sorry."

Sandy turned in Dell's arms and pressed into the curve of Dell's body until not even a whisper stood between them. "I want to do this for you."

"Thank you," Dell murmured, amazed when her eyes filled with tears. She probably should have been embarrassed, but she wasn't. She just held on more tightly. "Thank you."

Chapter Fourteen

Michael had just finished changing from her work clothes into loose cotton slacks and a pullover when Sandy buzzed from downstairs. Tugging the clasp from her hair, she shook out the shoulder-length waves on the way to the elevator.

"I hope you didn't eat," she said when Sandy emerged. "I just ordered Chinese."

"That sounds great. Thanks for letting me crash here again." Sandy followed Michael to the spare bedroom and dropped her suitcase by the closet. She plopped down on the bed and stared at her hands.

"You're always welcome." Michael sat next to Sandy. "We can go into the office together on Monday."

"Geez. That seems like such a normal thing to do."

"It does, doesn't it?" Michael took Sandy's hand. "So what's the deal?"

"Dell wants to stash me somewhere so she can shack up with Irina."

"That's handy. And you went along with it? Big of you." Michael's tone was teasing.

Sandy cut her a look. "Yeah right. As if."

"Uh-huh. That's what I thought."

"But she does want me out of the way for a while. In case things get hinky."

"Will you hate me if I say I think that makes sense?"

Sandy picked at the seam on the inside of her pale pink pants. "No. I get why she wants to do it this way. But I don't like it."

"I don't blame you. Needing to leave your house is really upsetting."

"Yeah well," Sandy muttered, "when Dell got the apartment down the hall from me, we didn't know she was going to end up with a girlfriend. *Another* girlfriend."

"You're not worried about Irina, are you?"

"Oh, no. She's only practically gotten Mitch to fuck her two or three times already." Sandy shifted further onto the bed and folded her legs beneath her. She glared at Michael. "And trust me. When a girl grabs a guy's dick, he stops thinking about anything. Including his girlfriend."

"Ah, I won't argue." Michael smiled. "Although I don't think it's completely a guy thing."

Sandy snorted. "Okay. I suppose when Dell starts in on me I'm not thinking about much of anything either."

"Mmm-hmm."

"Sloan too?"

"She can be persuasive." Michael gave Sandy's hand a shake. "I've got a really good idea."

"What?"

"Let's open a bottle of wine, eat Chinese, and watch a movie."

"Can I still bitch about Irina?"

"Oh, absolutely."

Sandy glanced around. "Sloan still at work?"

"She's in a meeting with Rebecca. I think she'll be there for a while."

Sandy smiled. "In that case…what about sharing the inside scoop on her when she's being persuasive."

"I don't like to brag."

Laughing, Sandy bumped Michael's hip with hers. "Yeah yeah. I'll just stick to my fantasies."

❖

"So what've we got?" Rebecca asked when she found Sloan working at a computer in HPCU headquarters.

"Pull up a chair," Sloan said, hitting a few more keystrokes before swiveling to face her. "Someone's trying to get into our network."

"And that's unusual?"

Sloan shook her head. "Not really. Random intrusions are very common. Usually they're probes launched en masse looking for susceptible computers to access."

"I take it this isn't random?"

"No. This is a very subtle and very smart assault. They hit the computers at Police Plaza too. Had more success there because the network's not fully shielded yet."

"All right," Rebecca said. "Run this down for me. What are we looking at here?"

"Since I don't believe in coincidences," Sloan said, "I have to believe this is the same person who infiltrated Police Plaza before."

"I thought we tracked that back to Beecher, and he's dead."

Sloan shook her head. "No. Beecher was the entry point. But he didn't set it up himself. He was a middleman. A cyberbagman."

Rebecca smiled grimly. "I get it. And now that the bagman is out of the equation, we're moving up the ladder."

"Oh yeah. Way up the ladder." Sloan glanced at the monitor, then back at Rebecca. "There's probably only a handful of people in the country that could do this. If you take out Jason and me, maybe three or four."

"Do you know who they are?"

Sloan's eyes narrowed. "Ten years ago I would have. When I was still with Justice."

"Son of a bitch. Clark knows, doesn't he?"

"I'd bet money on it. I bet he's known all along." Sloan leaned back in her chair and shoved her hands into the pockets of her jeans. "He's playing us."

"What do you he think he wants?"

"What every fed wants. A high-level informant inside the organized crime family."

"And this thing with Irina and Mitch?"

"He's hedging his bets. Irina might pay off for them, but she's a long shot." Sloan thought about Clark and Kratos Zamora and Michael. There were no coincidences. Avery Clark would use anyone, risk anyone, to get what he wanted. "There are no good guys anymore."

"Wrong," Rebecca said softly. "There's us."

Sloan swung back to her monitor, not wanting Rebecca to read the truth in her eyes. She hadn't been one of the good guys for a long time, and with every day that passed, and every time she faced the evidence of another betrayal, she knew she moved further away from the light. Rebecca might believe that their leaders weren't corrupted, but she didn't any longer. "I don't want Clark to know we suspect. I want to let this guy try to get in, and every time he does, I'll chase him back to his hole. I'll find him."

"I want to know when you do." Rebecca waited in the silence, letting Sloan make her choices.

"Right," Sloan said quietly.

Rebecca rested her hand on Sloan's back. The muscles beneath her fingers were tight as steel. "You're wrong, you know."

"How's that," Sloan said hoarsely.

"There are still people you can trust."

When Sloan turned around, Rebecca was gone. She wanted to believe her, needed to believe her. She needed not to feel so alone.

❖

Mitch was a lot better at dressing than he used to be, but he really missed having Sandy around to approve the details. He smoothed his hand over his chest to be sure the Ace wrap lay smooth beneath his black T-shirt. Lucky for him, he didn't have a lot to hide up top and his naturally rangy build meant he didn't have much in the hip department either. He opened a drawer on his side of the dresser and selected a new item he'd never used before, a semi-rigid cock that let him pack comfortably, show a little more in his jeans than a softy would, and have a pretty functional dick if he needed it. Not that he planned on using it with Irina, but if he was taking her out and about, he wanted to come off to anyone checking them out like a guy who planned on treating his girl right.

As he checked his hair and the little bit of makeup he used to darken the angle of his jaw, he thought back to the first time Jasmine had shown up in his apartment with an array of dicks. He'd been embarrassed and excited. Jasmine had helped him get ready, but it had been Sandy, who had looked at him and immediately seen Mitch, that had made everything work. That still made everything work. He didn't think he could do this job without her. He checked his watch. He had two minutes. He called her.

"Hi, babe," he said when Sandy answered.

"Mitch?"

"Uh-huh."

After a moment, Sandy said, "Ready to head out?"

Mitch knew she was trying to sound casual. "Soon. Whatcha doing?"

"Watching an old movie with Michael and getting buzzed. I think I like red wine."

"What movie," Mitch asked, smiling at the thought of Sandy getting into wine.

"*St. Elmo's Fire*. There's this guy who kinda reminds me of you. Except he's an asshole."

"Who?" Mitch heard Sandy say something to Michael, but couldn't quite make it out.

"Rob Lowe."

"We'll have to watch it together."

"So I'll see you later?"

"Yeah," Mitch said. "It'll be late."

"I don't care about that." More silence. "So be careful, rookie. See you."

"See you, babe."

Mitch disconnected, patted his pockets to be sure his wallet was in place, double-checked that his jeans didn't bunch up around his ankle holster, and grabbed his jacket on the way out the door. When he got to Irina's—his—apartment, he knocked. When she didn't answer after a few minutes, he knocked again. Swearing, he used his key and let himself in. The efficiency was empty. The blanket was folded neatly on one corner of the mattress. He checked the refrigerator. A container of milk, a carton of eggs, butter, an apple. A pot rested upside down on the drain board next to the sink. So she'd shopped. She probably wouldn't have done that if she were skipping out on him.

He walked to the closet and pulled it open. A stack of clothes sat on the top shelf. A few blouses hung from hangers. He sniffed them. They were clean. She'd done laundry. But where had she gone? Maybe she had a contact in the city they didn't know about. Maybe she'd been free to move about between safe houses the whole time, and she was already back with the Russians. Maybe she had a secret boyfriend, or girlfriend.

He'd been up most of the night before, so he stretched out on the mattress to wait and closed his eyes. The Army had taught him to sleep lightly, and he was instantly alert at the first scratch of metal on metal. He sat up in the dark room.

"Come in and shut the door," Mitch said when he saw Irina backlit by the hall light. He didn't want her standing there like a target.

Irina closed the door and flipped on the wall switch. She stared at him from across the room, her gaze traveling slowly over his body. "Hello, new boy."

"Hi."

"Aren't you going to ask me where I've been?"

Irina removed a thin quilted jacket and hung it in the closet. Beneath it, she wore formfitting black slacks with narrow tapered legs and a red wrap-around top. She couldn't be too much older than Mitch, but her body was lush and womanly and Mitch had the sudden image of rich fertile fields bursting with life. He unexpectedly had the urge to plant some part of himself in her, and he quickly forced the thought away.

"I told you I wasn't your keeper." He didn't add that she could easily lie to him, so what was the point of asking.

"So you didn't follow me today?" Irina asked.

"Jesus. No." Mitch jumped up. "Was there someone?"

Irina shrugged. "Sometimes I thought yes. Sometimes no."

"You'd be able to tell?"

She smiled grimly. "I am used to making myself invisible. And I know when eyes are on me."

Mitch spun around to the window. The sidewalks below were deserted. In the patchy light filtering through the neighboring rowhouse windows, the cars lining the street all appeared empty. For one brief second he was so happy Sandy wasn't here. Then he concentrated on Irina.

"Did you actually see anyone?"

Irina shook her head. "Many someones. No one I recognized."

"All right. If you see anyone suspicious, or even think you see anyone, tell me."

"Where are we going?"

"We need to let people know we're a couple, so your...associates... believe us. I'm taking you to a club. Then we'll go to Ziggie's."

"Like a date," Irina said.

"Like work," Mitch replied. "We need to get you a warmer coat. We'll be riding my motorcycle again."

"I'm all right."

"No, you're not. We'll stop on Market Street and get you something."

"It's nighttime, Mitch."

"Those places are always open." Mitch held out his leather jacket. "Wear this for now."

Irina studied him curiously. "Why do you care? I am...an enemy. No?"

"No." Mitch couldn't say that she reminded him of Sandy. She was very proud and in her own way, very brave. He couldn't say that he wished someone had given Sandy a warmer coat, or that she would take his more often.

"What will you do with these men you want me to help you find?"

"They'll be arrested, and they'll probably go to prison."

"They will be killed?"

Mitch shrugged. "I don't know. It depends on what they've done and what can be proved."

"I will be sent to prison?"

"What did Clark tell you?" When Mitch saw her blank expression, he said, "The federal agent who said you had to help us?"

Irina laughed bitterly. "He told me I would go free."

"You don't believe him."

"Would you?"

"No, probably not." Mitch held his jacket open and after a few seconds Irina slid her arms into it. When she turned to face him, he gently tugged it closed. "We're going to try to help you."

"You should not be a cop, new boy."

"Why?"

Irina kissed him. "You are not hard enough." She put her hand over his heart. "In here."

Mitch hadn't anticipated the kiss, not here and not like this, but he hadn't felt anything other than an odd sadness. He put his hand on her back and guided her toward the door. "Let's go."

"Do your friends believe we are together?" she asked him as they walked down the hall.

"Yes."

Irina smiled. "Good."

❖

Talia sipped her wine, stretched her stockinged feet out onto a silk brocade hassock, and launched another probe. She didn't really expect the bot to strike pay dirt. Thus far, she hadn't found any easily accessible back doors in JT Sloan's corporate system. No admin shortcuts, config errors, easily deciphered passwords, or unsecured remote access ports. Sloan's system was completely unlike the one she'd encountered at Police Plaza when she'd done a quick scan a few hours earlier. After only moderate effort, she'd gotten in deep there. Granted, the average hacker would not have had such an easy time, but then she wasn't average. She hadn't launched a serious assault because she didn't want to risk leaving a trail back to her home base—she'd only created her own back doors for access at some future time. With luck, a few would remain hidden long enough to be useful.

She chuckled as she encountered yet another roadblock. JT Sloan was very good. She thought back to the grainy newspaper images and the dark good looks that even the poor photographs couldn't hide. Intelligent, handsome, and something of a cipher herself, Sloan had stood among the players whose names Kratos had provided. Talia had run background checks on all of them, and while several were notable locally, Sloan and her partner McBride were ex-federal agents, and both their dossiers had more blacked-out sections than available information. Sloan's in particular had been thoroughly cleansed. Whatever she had done for the U.S. government, it had been cloaked under deep cover and high security.

"You're going to be fun," Talia murmured, sending a Trojan horse she doubted would get past Sloan's firewalls. But even experts made mistakes sometimes, and she had no doubt she would eventually find this woman's weakness.

Being able to envision Sloan's face while battling her mind, on a field where few could compete with her as an equal, excited her. She was looking forward to meeting her in person. Bedding her, knowing that Sloan was unaware of her identity, would make the climax all the sweeter. Talia let her fingers drift over her nipples. They were hard and tingling beneath her sheer blouse. The wine warming her depths, the arousal that always accompanied a hunt, and the persistent image of her quarry made her want sex. The brief caress had created an answering echo between her legs, and she was aware of her clitoris throbbing. No one had captured her attention, mind *and* body, so completely in a very long time.

Finishing her wine, she called up another program and continued with her campaign to best JT Sloan. As she watched the screen, she reached for the phone beside her and punched in a number from memory.

A woman answered, her voice eager, as if she had been waiting for Talia's call despite the late hour. "Yes?"

"Hello," Talia said throatily. "I have been thinking of you."

"I'll be right there."

"Good." Talia disconnected.

As she refilled her wine, she wasn't thinking of the woman whose mouth would soon bring her to climax. She was envisioning a far more challenging and intriguing seduction.

CHAPTER FIFTEEN

T his place," Irina said as Mitch guided her toward the entrance of the Troc. "It is like Ziggie's?"

"Not really." Mitch grabbed the door and held it open. "No dancers here. Different kind of performers."

Irina hesitated for a second, giving him an odd look. At first glance, the place did look like Ziggie's. A large, dark, rectangular room that smelled faintly of old whiskey and spent desire. But the Troc wasn't a strip club, and although customers might be getting it on in the shadows, sex wasn't the main course. Entertainment was the chief offering, and at the moment, the Front Street Kings were on the stage.

"Mitch!" Jasmine glided out of the gloom like an exotic bird. Her coppery lamé dress was formfitting and cut low, accentuating the slender length of her elegant neck and a tease of cleavage. Her lustrous, artfully tangled blond tresses danced over milky shoulders. Taller than Mitch, she moved with a sinuous sensuality more innate than impersonated, wholly female. She draped her arms around Mitch's neck and kissed him on the mouth. "I've missed you."

Even prepared for Jasmine's entrance, Mitch was caught off guard, especially when Jasmine stroked her tongue ever so lightly along the edge of his lip and snugged her pelvis into his. He clasped her waist automatically and pressed a little closer, and she responded with an audible purr. As if to remind him where he belonged, Irina gripped the back of his neck. Her possessive gesture was so much like something Sandy would do he experienced a few seconds of dizzying disorientation.

Jasmine finally took pity on him and eased away, trailing her fingers over his chest before turning to take in Irina. "And who do we have here?"

"Jasmine, this is Irina." Mitch slid his arm around Irina's waist and tugged her against his side. "Jasmine is a friend of mine, Irina."

"I see that," Irina said, appraising Jasmine coolly. "You dance?"

"I sing," Jasmine replied, her throaty voice carrying an edge.

"You like to play with boys like Mitch?"

Jasmine threw back her head and laughed. "Oh, I do. But I can see he's going to be busy with you."

Irina undulated against Mitch's body and ran her hand slowly over his chest and down his stomach, then brushed her fingers along the swelling adjacent to his fly. "Yes. He is."

Mitch caught the sparkle in Jasmine's eyes and knew she was having fun jousting with Irina, but he didn't need the two of them using his body as their combat zone. Jasmine *was* his friend, as well as his backup, and even though she was gorgeous and sexy and an outrageous tease, he'd never been attracted to her. His absence of desire had nothing to do with the fact that all that blinding sensuality was equal parts Jasmine and Jason McBride. Mitch just didn't sexualize his friends. Irina, though, was different. She wasn't his friend, and she wasn't just teasing. Her hand was still on his cock, and he didn't need a hard-on distracting him tonight.

"Let's get a table, baby." He shifted away from the questing fingers.

Jasmine smiled briefly at Irina and stroked Mitch's cheek. "And I've got to get ready for my show. See you later?"

"Sure," Mitch said and led Irina to a table as Jasmine disappeared. "Want a beer or something?"

"Vodka." Irina smiled. "It is the best liquor."

"Ice?"

"Yes."

He leaned down and kissed her. "I'll be right back."

At the bar, he gave his order and turned toward the stage to watch Phil and his other buddies perform. They were great. In between numbers, they changed clothes, effortlessly appearing first as hard rockers, then country-western stars, then suave crooners. They were handsome and rugged and sexy.

When an arm snaked around his waist, he expected Irina, but it was Jasmine. "Ooh," she crooned, "hello again." She flicked a perfect nail over the fold of his fly. "Nice."

"Are you trying to get my balls busted?" Mitch asked loud enough for anyone watching them to hear.

"Would I do that, lover?" Jasmine leaned closer, traced the edge of his ear with the tip of her tongue, and lowered her voice. "Everything okay?"

"Irina thinks she might have been followed today."

Jasmine swayed against him to the beat pulsing from the speakers. An observer would conclude she was into some serious cock-teasing. "Frye know?"

"Not yet."

"Are you still up for Ziggie's?"

"Got to. Irina left a message we need to follow up on."

"Don't disappear until after my number. I want to stick close." She kissed his cheek. "And try to keep your dick in your pants."

"Right." Mitch grabbed the drinks and returned to Irina. As she sipped the vodka, he asked, "How do you like the guys?"

"I know them from Ziggie's. Nice boys, and they are good, what they do."

"Yeah."

"Jasmine." Irina's lips pursed. "She is very beautiful."

"Like I said, she's—"

"I'm your girlfriend, no?"

"Yes."

"So I let her know you are not hers to touch." Irina shrugged. "No woman would let another one kiss her man like that."

Mitch didn't want Irina to suspect that Jasmine was working with him, so he played along. "I think she got the message."

Irina slowly stroked the inside of Mitch's thigh. The back of her hand rubbed over his cock. "Good."

❖

"Hey, Mitch, my man!" Phil said exuberantly, crossing to the table and clapping Mitch on the back. He caught Irina's hand and lifted it to his lips, bowing slightly as he kissed the back of her fingers. "And hello, beautiful lady. I'm Phil."

"Hello, Phil," Irina said, drawing out his name as if it were a delicacy.

Phil raised his eyes, his mouth still hovering over her hand. Something glinted in their dark depths and his mouth quirked into a suggestive smile. "You're far too fine to waste yourself on Mitch here."

Irina laughed.

"Hey, that's my date you're drooling over," Mitch complained good-naturedly. He kicked out the chair next to him. "Park it."

"I didn't get your name," Phil said as he straightened, his gaze still on Irina.

She looked him over, taking her time. "Irina."

Mitch could almost see Phil's chest puffing up under the scrutiny. Jesus, he looked like he wanted to take a bite out of her. Phil flirted with every woman, even Michael, but Mitch had never seen him look at a woman quite so intently before. Irina didn't seem to mind. Mitch supposed he should act jealous, like Irina had acted with Jasmine. But Phil knew he had another girlfriend. Plus he and Irina weren't a serious couple. They were just supposed to be dating. He cleared his throat. "Want a beer, Phil?"

"Yeah," Phil said, only taking his eyes off Irina's face long enough to stare at the breasts molded by her tight red top. "That'd be great. Thanks."

By the time Mitch got back from his second drink run, the other Kings had arrived and were clustered around Irina at the table. She seemed to be enjoying the attention. He shuffled bottles around the table and reclaimed his seat. Jasmine was onstage, partway through her first number. Unlike many female impersonators, she didn't lip-synch when performing. Her voice was sultry and rich, and as naturally feminine as the rest of her. Most of the men in the audience were riveted by her, their collective lust palpable. Mitch wondered how they dealt with the knowledge that this beautiful woman was also a man, but maybe that was part of the attraction.

Irina leaned close. "She is good."

"Yeah," Mitch agreed.

"She is not your girlfriend?"

"No way." Laughing a little, Mitch kissed her neck. "You are, remember?"

"Hey, Mitch," Ken called. "Give the rest of us a break, huh? We're all out here in the cold."

"We're going to Ziggie's later," Phil said to Irina. "The night would be perfect if you would come with us."

Irina smiled lazily at him while rubbing slow circles on Mitch's stomach. "Mitch and I have plans for later." At Phil's crestfallen expression, she laughed softly. "But maybe for a little while. If Mitch wants."

Phil cut his eyes to Mitch. "What do you say, buddy?"

What Mitch wanted to say was that Phil needed to get stuck on some other woman, because Irina was off-limits, for real. He didn't want to see Phil get hurt. But he had a part to play, that of a good-time guy who didn't mind sharing the wealth with his friends. Plus, he and Irina were headed to Ziggie's, and going with the Kings just helped his cover. "Sure."

"Good," Irina said, standing. "I am going to freshen up. I will be back in a minute, Mitch."

As soon as she was out of earshot Phil pulled his chair close to Mitch. "So just how serious are you about her?"

"What do you think?" Mitch said, trying to work out an answer.

"I think you've already got a hot girlfriend who's going to fry your ass if she finds out you're fooling around." Phil grinned, although his eyes were unsmiling. "So I think you should let me take care of this one."

"I told you, I'm not married." Mitch took another sip of his first beer. "And the thing with Irina is intense, you know? For right now."

Phil regarded him fixedly for a few seconds, then nodded. "Okay. If things change, let me know."

By the time Irina returned, Jasmine was on her last number. The Kings regaled Irina with stories of shows they had done, flirting and posturing for her. She was a natural-born actress, indulging them with smiles and laughter and carrying on as if she and Mitch were really on a date and this was just a fun night out.

A short while later, Jasmine joined them, having changed into a clingy sweater, tight black slacks, and heels. She settled into Phil's lap, crossing her legs and demanding breathily, "So where's the party?"

"We are all going to Ziggie's." Irina's fingers were curled around Mitch's thigh, but her eyes were on Phil. "Yes?"

"Yes," all of the Kings, including Mitch, responded enthusiastically.

Jasmine raised a sculpted brow at Mitch. "Oh, goodie."

❖

Mitch checked the road in his rearview mirror as he headed up Broad Street toward Ziggie's. Irina hugged him tightly from behind, warming herself against his back, but he was still glad he'd stopped earlier to get her a hip-length leather coat. He could see his breath in the dark night air. Jasmine was with Phil and the guys in a car a few blocks ahead. If the lieutenant was behind him, he couldn't see her.

After he pulled into the mouth of the alley and cut his engine, he pulled off his helmet and swiveled on the seat to face Irina. "If anyone in there wants you to leave with them, try to put them off. If that doesn't work, say you're not going anywhere without me. Say you're scared because of what happened at the house. Tell them I took care of you, protected you. You feel safe with me along."

"These men. They are much stronger than you," Irina said, her hands now resting lightly on the outside of his hips. "You cannot fight them if they force me to go with them."

Mitch shook his head. "I'm not letting them take you. Don't worry about that."

"You could let me go. You could say you couldn't stop them."

"They're not going to let you find your sister," Mitch said. He believed that to be true, but it didn't make him feel any better about preying on her fears. Manipulating her. "We can help you find her. But you have to help us."

She didn't say anything for a long moment, her eyes probing into his. "They will not be so easy to convince as your friends that we are together."

"Whatever it takes."

Irina reached between his legs and squeezed his cock, pressing it into the apex of his thighs. "And if they want proof?"

Mitch laughed hoarsely. "Like what? Unlike flesh-and-blood cocks, mine doesn't shoot—so what exactly would they see?"

"You would fuck me if they say?"

"Jesus." Mitch slid his fingers between his cock and Irina's hand, and clasped her fingers gently. "I'm not going to let them force me to treat you like that. I'll convince them some other way. Don't worry."

"I am not the one to worry." Irina stroked his face. "It is you they will hurt."

❖

"What the hell were you doing out there, spawning?" Jasmine hissed when Mitch slid into the booth with her and the Kings. An assortment of beers and a vodka on ice sat in the middle of the table already. "Where's Irina?"

"She went to talk to the bartender."

"And you let her? What if she slips out the back?"

"She won't." At Jasmine's frown, Mitch said impatiently, "I can see her from here. Besides, if she wanted to ditch me she could have done it anytime today." He lowered his voice. "What about the backup?"

"I called Frye from my dressing room at the club. They should've picked you up on your way here."

"Okay." Mitch felt a little steadier knowing that the lieutenant and Watts were outside. Working undercover was lonely and scary, even though it was a rush, too. He glanced past Jasmine and saw Phil craning his neck, watching Irina. He hoped Phil believed him that Irina and he were an item, and that he would keep his word to stay away from her. He especially hoped he was becoming more adept at lying. Sandy always said he sucked at it.

"Uh-oh," Jasmine whispered. "She's heading toward the back."

Mitch pushed out of the booth. "There's a rear door. If I'm not back in fifteen minutes, check the alley for my bike. If it's still there but we're not, it will probably mean we had to go somewhere to keep our cover. Hopefully the lieutenant will pick us up."

"Just don't let them take Irina."

"I'm not planning on it." Mitch hurried after Irina, knowing events didn't always turn out as planned.

❖

"Hey! What's going on?" Mitch demanded when he discovered Irina with her back against the wall, pinned by a hulking guy with fair hair cut so close to his head he appeared at first glance to be bald. His arm muscles bunched beneath a tight white T-shirt, and his tree trunk–sized thighs bracketed Irina's lower body. He turned his head and gave Mitch a flat, cold stare.

Acting on instinct, heart thumping in his chest, Mitch ignored the guy and caressed Irina's shoulder. "You okay, baby?"

"Who is this?" the man growled in accented English.

"I am with him," Irina said, a note of defiance in her voice.

The Russian looked Mitch up and down and made a dismissive sound. "You need a man? I can take care of that."

Irina sneered. "Like Yuri did?"

She pushed against her captor's chest, and he moved back as if surprised. She had just enough room to slither out from beneath his arm. Mitch immediately pulled her close and angled his body so he was standing between her and the man he presumed was one of the Russian enforcers.

"Yuri did nothing to protect us when the police came," Irina spat. "Mitch helped me get away. All the others at the house…" She made an angry gesture. "Gone."

"You come with me," the Russian said, grabbing her arm.

"Back off," Mitch warned, hoping he'd be able to get off at least one punch before the guy planted one of his huge fists in his face.

"She comes with me," the Russian said.

Mitch shook his head. "No way."

Just when he was sure the guy was going to swing, Jasmine appeared out of nowhere. "There you are!" she exclaimed, rushing up. "We're ready for the next stop." She looped her arm through Irina's, dragging her a few feet down the hall. "I just love club hopping." Over her shoulder she called to Mitch, "Are you coming or are you going to let the other boys have all the fun?"

The Russian's eyes flamed. "You are making a mistake, Irina."

She slowed until Mitch reached her side, then said, "Tell Olik if he wants me, he has to come himself. Not send his lapdog."

When the Russian's face suffused with fury, Mitch hurried both Irina and Jasmine back into the main part of the bar.

"Jealous boyfriend?" Jasmine said archly.

Irina gave her a feral smile. "I would not let him fuck my shoe."

"Oh, poor Mitch." Jasmine laughed. "You're going to run him ragged."

"He does not wear out easily." Irina whispered in Mitch's ear, "We should go before he calls someone."

"I guess that's my cue to get started," Mitch said with a grin. "We'll catch you all another night."

When the Kings called good night, Mitch noticed that Phil didn't look up from the table.

"What about this guy Olik?" Mitch asked Irina as they headed for the door. "How do we get to him?"

She flicked a long, dark strand of hair away from her face. "He will come for me."

CHAPTER SIXTEEN

R ebecca slipped into bed just before dawn. When Catherine turned toward her, she said, "You don't need to wake up just yet."

"Mmm." Catherine ran her hands up and down Rebecca's back. "You're warm. Feels nice." She burrowed into Rebecca's neck. "Smells nice."

Rebecca chuckled. "I took a shower in the guest room. I was trying not to wake you up."

Catherine slipped a firm thigh between Rebecca's. "I thought you promised you would."

Rebecca sucked in a breath. The silky glide of Catherine's flesh between her legs teased her into full arousal in seconds. "I didn't think I'd be so late."

"Is everything all right?"

"Yes." Rebecca couldn't manage more than short sentences as Catherine rocked her leg steadily, insistently, into her. "Stayed to watch Mitch. All quiet."

"You're making my leg wet," Catherine whispered. "So hot, so slick."

Rebecca groaned. Her vision grew dark at the edges as she stroked her hand along the curve of Catherine's hip, to the dip at her waist, and up to cradle the full oval of her breast. She rubbed the pad of her thumb over the tight ball of Catherine's nipple. Catherine surged in her arms, her thigh driving high between Rebecca's legs—opening her, cleaving her. Rebecca arched her hips and thrust, tormenting her already tortured clitoris, forcing it back and forth over Catherine's leg. Her mouth was on Catherine's, and she matched the pulsations between her legs with deep, probing sweeps of her tongue. When Catherine gripped her hips to increase the force of her thrusting thigh, Rebecca broke away, panting for breath.

"You're going to make me come," she warned.

"That's right. I love it when you come," Catherine said fervently. "I love to feel you shatter in my arms, so beautiful." *I love it when you need me,* she didn't say. *I love to protect you.* "Oh God, touch me. I can't stand it. I've needed to come for hours."

Rebecca pushed her hand between their bodies and cupped Catherine's sex, her fingers sliding up and down the smooth, hot valley, her thumb sweeping back and forth across the rigid clitoris. Catherine jerked in her arms, and Rebecca felt her control unravel. She concentrated, bearing down with her thumb.

"Oh, darling," Catherine murmured, burying her face in Rebecca's neck. "So good. You're so good. Stay on it, darling, stay—oh God, just like that."

"Catherine," Rebecca moaned, her clitoris threatening to release. The pressure was agonizing, her mind incapable of thought. Her hips pumped, and the burning spread outward from the apex of her thighs. "It's coming. I can't...oh, *fuck*, here I come."

"Don't stop, I'm close," Catherine gasped, her teeth setting into the muscle stretched taut along Rebecca's neck. "I'm so so clo...oh!"

Catherine's cry ignited Rebecca, and she shuddered as heat raced through her. She fired fast, peaked hard, and came down quickly, but Catherine kept pulsing in her hand, undulating waves of pleasure filling her palm.

"Oh God, oh God, oh God," Catherine whimpered breathlessly.

Rebecca massaged her until the last spasms quieted, then wrapped her tightly in her arms. "I love you."

"Oh, I love you." Catherine rested her face against Rebecca's chest. "Don't leave me."

"I won't," Rebecca promised, her heart twisting. She knew Catherine would never have asked if all her defenses hadn't just been shattered, and she might not even remember it later. But Rebecca would not forget the helpless plea in her voice. She kissed her, slowly, as she stroked her hair and her back, calming her. "I won't."

Catherine smoothed trembling fingers lightly over Rebecca's mouth, as if to stop her from making promises impossible to keep. "Hold me. Just hold me."

Rebecca could give her that, and she did.

❖

"Hey," Michael whispered, resting both hands on Sloan's shoulders. "Any chance I could talk you into coming to bed? It's late, and you didn't get much sleep last night."

Sloan tilted her head back against Michael's midsection and closed her eyes. When Michael's fingers threaded through her hair and massaged her scalp, she groaned.

Laughing softly, Michael leaned down and kissed the angle of her jaw. Circling her fingertips over Sloan's temples, she said, "You're tired, darling. And this case is just getting started."

"Someone's trying to crack my system," Sloan murmured, her eyes still closed. "But they're playing games."

"What does that mean?" Michael asked with a frown.

"They're not really trying to hide what they're doing. They're letting me see them, like a game of hide and seek." Sloan grasped Michael's hand and pressed a kiss to her palm. "Or chess."

"Really? Why would a hacker do that?"

Sloan shook her head. "Arrogance. Boredom. Maybe he hasn't had anyone at his level to compete with. Because he's good. Very good. I can't find his trail." She took a deep breath and let it out with a frustrated sigh. "He knows how to bait the hook."

"Playing with you." Michael caressed Sloan's neck, then slid a hand under the top of her T-shirt and rubbed her chest. "Not very smart."

Sloan arched in the chair, her hand drifting away from the keyboard for the first time in hours. "Michael. You're cheating."

"I never cheat," Michael whispered softly in her ear. "I just play to win. Are you coming to bed?" She caught her breath as Sloan's eyes opened and sought hers, unguarded arousal shimmering through the blue depths. "God, darling. Say yes."

Sloan stood, shoved the desk chair away with her foot, and caught Michael against her chest. She kissed her, filling her hands with

Michael's hair and her senses with Michael's scent. "Yes. Definitely, yes."

❖

Sandy sat up, instantly alert, at the quiet snick of the door lock catching. Dell looked even paler than usual in the gray early-morning light, her eyes shadowed and wary. The bedside clock said 6:30 a.m. She'd been out all night. With Irina. Dell stood statue still as if awaiting judgment until Sandy flicked back the sheet, indicating the bed beside her.

Wordlessly, Dell stripped, then climbed into bed and lay on her back.

"Are you all right?" Sandy asked.

"Yeah."

"Did something happen?"

"Not really."

"How come you're so late?"

Dell sighed. She'd wanted to come earlier, but she didn't want to leave Irina until she was certain no one had followed them. She couldn't leave her unprotected.

"Sorry."

"I didn't ask you to be sorry." Sandy rolled onto her side and put her hand on Dell's stomach. The muscles were hard as wood. Dell's stomach felt that way when she was getting ready to come, or when she was really upset. Sandy rubbed up and down, slow steady sweeps, and Dell shivered. "You're really wired, baby."

"Things got a little tense for a few minutes. They sent muscle to collect Irina."

"Did they take her?"

"No," Dell said hoarsely.

"Did things get physical?"

"Almost."

Sandy sucked in a breath. What Dell was doing was dangerous. Dell knew it, and she knew it. Telling her to be careful wouldn't do any good. Asking her not to do what she needed to do wasn't an option. She shifted on top of Dell and wiggled her hips between Dell's legs, forcing her to open. As soon as Dell parted her thighs, Sandy pushed her way down on the bed and pressed her cheek in the delta at the base of Dell's belly. Dell's clitoris was erect, a firm bulge against her face. She shifted and brushed her lips over it.

Dell dragged in a shaky breath.

"I'm going to take care of this so you can sleep," Sandy whispered, her lips moving over the distended shaft. "You want?"

"Oh yeah."

"Will you come for me, baby?"

"Will you do me really slow?" Dell's voice broke. "So I can feel everything?"

"As slow as you want, for as long as you need." Sandy dropped feather-light kisses over Dell's clitoris, her inner lips, the insides of her thighs. She teased under the hood with just the tip of her tongue, sweeping round and round, until Dell's hips bucked and twisted. She licked, she sucked, she stroked the flat of her tongue the length of Dell's sex. When Dell's legs trembled, Sandy held her down, closing her hands over Dell's lean, taut thighs. When Dell gasped for breath, Sandy stilled, keeping her just on the edge of exploding, knowing the buildup would make the release all the sweeter. She knew what Dell needed. She needed to go beyond thought, beyond fear, beyond uncertainty. She needed to drown in pleasure, to be held in safety.

"Sandy," Dell groaned.

"You need to come now, baby?" Sandy crooned, sliding first one finger, then two, inside. With her other hand she pressed on the base of Dell's stomach, forcing her clitoris to stand up straight. "Want to come in my mouth?"

"Please." Dell's voice was unsteady and low.

Sandy pulled on Dell's length with long strokes of her pursed lips. She kept it up, stroke after stroke, as Dell arched and mumbled incoherent pleas, then looked up to see Dell propped on her elbows, staring down at her with a dazed, delirious expression. She felt Dell's clitoris expand, saw her face twist in an agony of pleasure, and curled her fingers forward to massage the spot that made Dell's clitoris leap between her lips.

"Uh." Dell jerked. Once. Twice. Then her arms gave way and she fell back with a cry, writhing as her muscles tightened and convulsed. "Keep sucking. Just suck. Jesus!"

Sandy lost count of how many times she coaxed Dell's clitoris to stiffen and explode, but she kept working it until Dell whimpered for her to stop. She was so high on the power she couldn't. She wanted to make Dell come again. She wanted Dell to be hers, and only hers, forever. She teased the swollen head with her tongue and Dell twisted away.

"Babe, please," Dell whispered weakly. "Hold me. San?"

"I'm here, baby," Sandy said instantly, clambering up to pull Dell into her arms. Dell was nearly twice her size, but it didn't matter. Right now, she felt like a giant. She tightened her grip on Dell's shoulders and rocked her. "I love you, baby."

"I need you, San."

"Shh." Sandy kissed Dell's sweaty brow and stroked her face. "You go to sleep now, baby."

"Play with your clit," Dell murmured, cradled in Sandy's arms. "Know you need to."

"I'm okay, baby."

Dell nuzzled Sandy's breast and drew her nipple into her mouth. When she bit down, Sandy felt as if she'd been electrocuted. Her legs jerked and her clit twitched like crazy. She reached for it, moaning when she discovered how wet and hard she was. She hadn't been aware of her own excitement until then. All she'd known was Dell. Fingers squeezing, she closed her eyes and rested her cheek against the top of Dell's head.

"Good?" Dell muttered.

"Uh-huh," Sandy whispered, twisting and tugging her aching clit. A huge balloon filled her insides until she couldn't breathe. She squeezed and pulled until the balloon burst open and she was coming. "God, baby. God!"

Dell sighed with pleasure and relaxed in her arms. Sandy stroked her until she heard her breathing slow and knew she was falling asleep. She knew that if anyone came through that door wanting to hurt Dell, she would kill them. She only wished she could always be there to protect her.

Chapter Seventeen

K ratos folded the *Wall Street Journal* and set it aside as his driver
pulled the Town Car to a stop in a parking lot in the shadows
of the Benjamin Franklin Bridge. A blustery wind was coming off the
Delaware River, but he did not button his topcoat when his bodyguard
opened the door. Bareheaded, he stepped out and approached a black
Mercedes SUV with darkened windows, his bodyguard and Vincent
on either side of him. The two Russians standing next to the vehicle
watched him, their broad, heavy features expressionless. He stopped a
few yards away and waited. The rear door opened and a thin, blond man
in a cashmere coat similar to his own stepped out.

"Stay here," Kratos said to his companions.

"Boss," Vincent muttered, clearly unhappy.

"I shouldn't be too long."

Kratos walked to the edge of the pier, ignoring the two Russian
bodyguards, deliberately giving them his back as if they were of no
consequence to him at all. He wanted to reinforce that they were on
his turf, where he held the power, and that he did not fear them. Mind
games. The kind he loved.

A few seconds later, the Russian boss stepped up beside him.

Kratos did not turn his head to acknowledge the other man. "Winter
is coming," he said, staring out at the muddy river.

"Good," the Russian said. "Cold weather is good for business.
Men want to be inside with a warm woman."

Kratos laughed briefly. "Are you going to be able to supply what
we need?"

"There are always girls."

"Yes, but not ones as beautiful and easy to manage as yours." Kratos disliked discussing the specifics of business with anyone because the only thing he was certain of was that no one could be trusted. Still, a discussion outdoors in the wind in an open parking lot was as safe as any could be, unless the Russian was wired. To counter the possibility, Vincent carried a radio frequency jammer in his pocket that would distort audio transmissions enough to make the recording inadmissible in court. "I understand that you have lost a substantial amount of your inventory."

The Russian shrugged. "When your authorities lose interest in us, I will bring more. Until then, the American product will do."

"My clients are used to quality," Kratos said.

He provided women to some of the most powerful men in the state, in several states, and they expected beauty, compliance, and skill. They also expected anonymity. He couldn't send common prostitutes or even high-class escorts who might recognize the men or who might be under surveillance themselves. The only reason he had allowed the Russians to move in on a corner of his prostitution business was because they could provide him with young, attractive, healthy girls who were no threat to his high-powered clients. The Russian girls wouldn't recognize the men, and even if they did, they didn't speak enough English to be able to betray anyone. Many of his clients preferred the young Russians for another reason, even if their expertise was sometimes lacking. For these men, power was more erotic than flesh, and the combination of fear and innocence was more appealing in a woman than a talented mouth.

"Do not concern yourself," the Russian boss said. "Your clients will have everything they want." He looked at Kratos for the first time. "How is it that your police interfere with my business, but not yours?"

Kratos shook his head. "I am sorry for your misfortune. I'll do what I can to interest them elsewhere." He didn't add *for a price*, but it was understood. If he used his influence to divert the investigation, the Russian would be in his debt. It was also understood that when he called in the debt, he would collect many-fold. He waited.

The Russian nodded. "I would be grateful."

"Think nothing of it, my friend." Satisfied, Kratos turned to go.

"I will need another house. Two would be better."

"Someone will call you with the addresses," Kratos said without looking back. He nodded to Vincent, who stepped behind him to protect his back until he slid inside the car once more. As they moved off, he called Talia. With his supply lines secured, he could accelerate his plans to disrupt the investigation.

❖

"You know, we could just skip this thing," Sloan said, wiping water from her eyes and groping at a nearby counter.

"Looking for this?" Michael teased, holding up a large white terry-cloth towel. She wore a pale blue silk robe tied at the waist.

At the sight of her breasts moving gently beneath the thin material, Sloan cared even less about the benefit they were supposed to attend. She was also tired. And frustrated. After being lured to bed the night before, she'd actually fallen asleep for a few hours, then worked all day trying to discover who was attempting to breach her system. She'd made little progress tracing the source of the cyberattacks and was increasingly worried that Michael would be drawn into danger because of the new investigation.

"Couldn't you find anything to wear?" she asked. Michael had been choosing a dress for the benefit when Sloan got home.

"I got distracted." At Sloan's look of confusion, Michael laughed. In slow, succinct bites, she explained, "You. Naked. Taking a shower."

"Sorry."

"Oh, I don't think so."

Sloan heard the words, but it was the invitation in Michael's voice that held her attention. "How are you feeling?"

"Wonderful." Michael hooked a finger around the top of the towel and pulled it loose. When it dropped to the floor, she wrapped her arms around Sloan's neck and kissed her, moving from her mouth over her jaw, and then down her neck.

"I'm going to get you all wet," Sloan murmured.

"Done," Michael whispered. She licked a bead of water from the hollow at the base of Sloan's throat as she caressed the muscles in Sloan's shoulders and back. "You snuck out of bed this morning before I had a chance to say good morning."

Sloan reached back and grasped the edge of the counter on either side of her body. She let her head fall back as Michael cupped her breasts and squeezed gently. "I'm sorry. Again."

"Really?" Michael murmured, drawing a nipple between her lips.

"Not so much right now." Sloan closed her eyes. "Michael. The time."

"Don't worry." Michael dropped to her knees and slid both hands around to Sloan's ass. "We have plenty."

Sloan looked down, mesmerized as Michael kissed her belly, then the angle of her thighs, then the sensitive cleft between. She hissed between her teeth. "If you're just teasing…"

Michael glanced up, her lids heavy, her mouth curved into a hungry smile. "Oh, I'm teasing. In fact, I think you should see just how much." She dragged her nails lightly over the crest of Sloan's hipbones and down her stomach. Then she used both thumbs to part Sloan's swollen flesh. She held Sloan's eyes for another few seconds before extending her tongue and flicking at Sloan's clitoris.

Sloan tightened her thighs, which suddenly felt like jelly, and leaned forward to watch Michael play with her. Her clit had already plumped up to its full size at the first touch of Michael's tongue, and now it twitched with each lick. "Do you want me to come in your mouth?"

"Try not to right away," Michael murmured, sucking Sloan's clitoris delicately between her lips.

"I really really want to," Sloan warned, her voice catching in her throat.

Laughing softly, Michael released her clitoris and stroked her tongue deeper into Sloan's center. When Sloan groaned, Michael traced Sloan's inner lips with a fingertip down to the muscled ring between her buttocks. She massaged the tight opening and took Sloan's clitoris into her mouth again.

"That's going to make me come," Sloan said desperately. "Oh, baby, really soon." She felt her clitoris rise and stiffen as heat poured into her stomach. The pressure took her breath away.

Michael's fingertip entered her and the reflex muscle spasm made her clit jerk. Michael murmured appreciatively and repeated the motion.

Sloan twitched. "You make me want to come so bad." She watched Michael's tongue swirl over her clit. "Can you fuck me, baby? I'm right there."

With a sharp cry of pleasure, Michael pulled on Sloan's clitoris with her mouth and pumped her finger in and out of the smooth tight ring of muscle. Sloan's orgasm crashed through her with such force she shouted, and she doubled over, clutching Michael's shoulders to keep from falling.

Then Michael was in her arms, her mouth against Sloan's ear. "In me, Sloan. Hurry, darling. Hurry."

Sloan kissed her, plunging her tongue into Michael's mouth as she filled her with her fingers. Michael trembled in her arms as her hips rocked, demanding satisfaction. Sloan caught her rhythm and thrust, her tongue and her hand moving together, forcing Michael to feel all of her, everywhere inside.

"Oh yes," Michael cried, tossing her head back, eyes slammed shut as she tightened on Sloan's fingers. "Yes, darling. Yes."

When Michael slumped in her arms, Sloan caressed her hair and gently kissed her. "We're going to need another shower."

Michael laughed. "I've missed that so much."

"I love you."

"I'll hold you to that." Michael nipped at Sloan's chin. "Come on. Let's get this event done with so I can have you again."

❖

Talia held the door open for Kratos.

"I hope I'm not interrupting," he said, his eyes taking her in.

"Not at all." Talia had almost changed her mind about meeting him at the door in a dressing gown because she did not want to be too obvious about wielding her body as a weapon. His attraction to her blunted his usually intense focus and gave her a slight advantage in their business dealings, but she did not delude herself into thinking she was safe with him.

Men like Kratos Zamora were wholly without sentimentality for anyone other than their wives and children. She had no doubt he would dispatch her without a second's thought if he felt she had become a liability. Or a threat. He was a powerful man who wielded his power as much for the pleasure of it as anything else. She wasn't entirely convinced that he cared about the police investigation or the fact that his dealings with his Russian colleagues might be disrupted. She thought he might simply want to prove that he was beyond the reach of the authorities by beating them at their own game.

"Come into the sitting room," she said. "The maid will bring coffee in a few minutes."

Talia led him into the adjoining parlor, where a fire burned in the fireplace. She sat in one of the upholstered English armchairs and Kratos took the other. She could tell from the way his eyes lingered on her breasts that her choice of the burgundy satin robe was as distracting as she intended. She willed her nipples not to rise. She wasn't aroused by his desire, but rather by the game between them. The danger inherent in any encounter with him always aroused her, and she enjoyed the edgy anticipation in the pit of her stomach.

"I took your advice," he said, finally meeting her eyes. He slipped a small envelope from inside his jacket and placed it on the Queen Anne table between their chairs. "I had an interesting business meeting yesterday."

Intrigued, Talia picked up the envelope and lifted the flap. A memory card was the only thing inside. She laughed softly. "Let me guess. Photos?"

Kratos nodded.

"We're very much alike, you and I," she mused.

"How is that?"

"Easy victories are far from satisfying," Talia observed. She was talking about Kratos's campaign against the authorities who had the audacity to challenge his power, but she might just as well have been talking about his interest in her.

"Sometimes," Kratos said, his voice smooth and seductive, "playing can be almost as pleasurable as winning."

"Then by all means," Talia said. "Let's make the game a challenge."

❖

Whistling softly, Sloan threaded the gold and platinum cufflinks through her French cuffs as she walked into the kitchen. She thought a glass of wine with Michael before they left would be nice because once they arrived at the benefit, Michael would be busy networking and they would spend the rest of the evening in their separate spheres. Between the recent investigations and Michael's injury, they'd had very little time to enjoy one another, and she realized how unbalanced her life had become without the simple joy of being with Michael.

Sloan stopped in the doorway when she saw Dell Mitchell standing in front of the refrigerator with two bottles of beer in her hand. She wore threadbare gray sweats hanging low on her hips and a black sleeveless T-shirt with the PPD emblem.

"Hey," Sloan said. "How are you doing?"

"I'm solid. You look slick."

Sloan glanced down at her tux shirt and pants and shrugged. "Gotta play the game."

"Yeah," Dell said, twisting the cap off one of the bottles before taking a long swallow. She still had dark circles under her eyes, but she looked a little more rested than the last time Sloan had seen her. "I know what you mean."

Sloan reached for a bottle of wine and fished a corkscrew out of the drawer. She lowered her voice. "Things going okay with Irina?"

"I think we're getting somewhere. At least we're attracting some attention from the Russians."

"Frye know?"

Dell nodded. "Yeah. I filled her in on the phone a while ago."

"We're all tied up tonight, so you need to stay off the streets. No backup."

"I'm just going to check on Irina in a while. I don't know how hard anyone is looking for her, and she's alone."

Sloan frowned and pulled the cork from the bottle. "Keep your eyes open."

"Will do."

"Jasmine with you last night?"

Dell smiled. "Oh yeah. She's amazing. Hot too."

"Hot." Sloan chuckled. "That she is. And then some."

"Out here talking about other women?" Michael said as she came around the corner. She held out her hand for the glass of wine Sloan had filled. "Is that for me?"

Wordlessly, Sloan handed it to her, taking in Michael's midnight blue evening dress. The color made her eyes even more vivid, and the form-hugging cut accentuated her slender body and full breasts. In heels, she was taller than Sloan, close to six feet, and she looked as if she had just stepped off a Manhattan runway. Sloan swallowed hard, instantly wanting Michael's mouth on her again.

"Wow," Dell blurted.

Sloan cut her a look.

"Hello, Dell," Michael said. "Everything all right?"

"Fine."

Sandy ambled in wearing one of Dell's T-shirts and something under it that wasn't immediately visible. She went directly to Dell, took the open beer bottle from her hand, and said, "Stop drooling over Michael."

"I'm not!" Dell exclaimed.

"Uh-huh." Sandy settled her butt into Dell's crotch and sipped the beer. Dell wrapped an arm around her middle. "You look awesome. Both of you."

Michael smiled. "Thanks. I almost feel like we're going out on a date."

Inwardly, Sloan grimaced. Nothing could be further from the truth. She was supposed to be watching Kratos Zamora, trying to find out who his upper-echelon political associates might be. And she was going to be busy keeping Michael far away from him. She was not looking forward to the evening.

"I want to stop downstairs for a second," she told Michael. "I've got a program running I need to check. Give me five minutes, okay?"

Michael stroked her cheek. "Promise you won't get distracted?"

Sloan caught her wrist and kissed her fingers. "Promise."

"Go ahead, then," Michael whispered.

Sloan nodded to Dell and Sandy and took the stairs down to the third floor. She had set several programs to launch in an attempt to trace probes being sent out against her system. She wanted to see if they'd been activated. As soon as she caught sight of her main screen, she knew there was a problem. Images flickered across the surface, where there should be only data.

As she drew closer and could make out details, a red haze of fury clouded her vision at the same time as her stomach turned to cold, hard stone. She stared at photos of Michael. Michael stepping out of the building. Michael at the wheel of her car. Michael talking to several colleagues in the lobby of her building. And one final photo that seared into her brain.

Michael seated at a window table in a restaurant with Kratos Zamora.

CHAPTER EIGHTEEN

"Sloan?" Michael reached across the space between them and put her hand on Sloan's thigh. "What's wrong?"

Sloan hit the gas and whipped the Porsche around one of the many horse-drawn carriages that shared the roads in Old City, providing tours of the myriad historic sites. She didn't trust herself to speak. She wasn't certain what she was going to do when she was actually in the same room as Kratos Zamora. She could still see him leaning slightly across the restaurant table toward Michael, his expression intent, as if he were riveted to every word Michael might say. Michael had been laughing, and she was so damned beautiful. Beautiful and innocent. Innocent of the kinds of games that men like Zamora played. Innocent of the world he lived in and that Sloan had lived in not so long ago. There were no dark places in Michael's heart, no monsters buried in her past. Michael was everything good and pure in Sloan's life, and she would kill to prevent anyone from changing that.

"You know how much I hate these things." She kept a grip on the wheel, afraid Michael would see her hands shaking. Her head pounded with rage.

Michael always knew when Sloan was holding something in, forcing something down, containing her anger. She rubbed her hand up and down Sloan's thigh. The muscles were hard as iron, and even in the low light of the car, the set of Sloan's jaw was unmistakable. She was oh so very good at holding on to her control. Except the price for that remarkable control was distance, the one thing Michael could not bear.

"I've only had you for a few minutes tonight," Michael whispered. "Please don't go away so soon."

The pain in her voice cut through the wall of Sloan's fury like nothing else could. She dropped her hand from the wheel and covered Michael's, lacing their fingers together. "I'm sorry. I'm…a little preoccupied with the investigation." Forcing a smile, she lifted Michael's hand to her lips. "And I really do hate these fancy parties."

"For someone who looks so good in a tux, that's a shame." Michael withdrew her hand and moved it to the back of Sloan's neck. She toyed with the wavy black strands that curled over the stiff collar of Sloan's shirt. "You know I don't resent your work, don't you?"

Sloan nodded.

"What's hard for me is losing you to it."

"You don't," Sloan said hoarsely. She glanced at Michael, then back at the road. "You're always in my heart. I'm sorry if I—"

"Pull over."

Wordlessly, Sloan obeyed. As soon as she slid the transmission into Park, the powerful engine still idling, Michael leaned over for a kiss. With a soft groan, Sloan gave herself over to the silky heat of Michael's mouth. She wished she could take her home, away from the evil and depravity, and let Michael exorcize her fear and anger. But Michael was a woman with her own needs, her own life, and Sloan could not protect her from everything that might hurt her.

"Does this mean you forgive me?" Sloan asked when she drew back for a breath.

Michael smiled and skimmed her fingertip over Sloan's mouth. "Nothing to forgive. That was me telling you I love you exactly the way you are."

Sloan lowered her head. If Michael knew everything about her, she might not say that. She whispered, "I love you so much."

"You love me exactly the right way." Michael stroked Sloan's hair. "Someday, my darling Sloan, I want you to help me do the same."

"You do," Sloan exclaimed.

"Only as much as you let me." Michael smiled a little sadly. "Now we need to go."

Sloan let out a long breath and put the car in gear. "Let's do this thing."

❖

"You can leave your dick in the drawer," Sandy said, crossing her arms beneath her small breasts. "Because Mitch isn't going anywhere tonight."

Dell pulled on her clean T-shirt and stared at Sandy. "What the fuck, San?"

Perched on the edge of the bed, still in her T-shirt and panties, Sandy said, "I heard Sloan say you don't have any backup tonight. So you can't work."

"What else did you hear?" Dell grabbed a clean pair of black jeans from the pile of clothes Sandy had brought from her apartment. She didn't exactly mean to keep secrets from Sandy, but she hated for her to get worked up about things that *might* happen. Or might not. And she definitely didn't want her getting worked up over Irina. Like that was ever gonna happen. "Thanks for bringing clothes for me."

"Let's see. You were saying…" Sandy put a finger on her chin as if she were thinking. "Oh, right. You've also got a hard-on for Jasmine."

"I do not!" Dell stuffed her T-shirt into her jeans and bent over to strap on her ankle holster before pulling on her motorcycle boots. "I just said she was hot. Merely an observation."

"Oh yeah. Like a guy says a girl has great tits, but he's not *really* thinking about getting his hands on them or anything."

"I didn't say she has great tits. Actually, I think she has a great mouth." Dell ducked, laughing as Sandy grabbed the pillow from behind her and flung it.

"You blockhead." Sandy flung the other pillow. "There's no way Jasmine could ever give you the kind of blow job I can. I don't care how pretty her mouth looks."

Dell dropped to her knees in front of Sandy and wrapped her arms around Sandy's waist. She pulled her to the edge of the bed until she could pillow her face against her breasts, then she nuzzled Sandy's nipple through the thin cotton T-shirt. "Babe, nobody can do anything to me the way you can." She tilted her head back and kissed Sandy's chin. "How come you're so grumpy?"

"Maybe because my girlfriend is spending every night with a girl who wants to get into her pants." Sandy tugged a fistful of Dell's hair, and her expression darkened. "Maybe because you're coming home so wound up I'm afraid you're going to get hurt out there."

"Babe." Dell stroked Sandy's cheek. "I'm being careful. I promise. And I'm going to be back early tonight. It's just a quick check, okay?"

Sandy ran her fingertips over Dell's eyebrows, then kissed her. "Do what you have to. Just keep your dick on ice. 'Kay?"

"I will." Dell stood and grabbed her motorcycle jacket. "I'll be back really soon."

Sandy waited until she heard the elevator go down, then headed for the shower. It was Saturday night, and she had things to do too.

❖

Rebecca angled through the crowd toward Sloan, who stood next to the bar set up against one wall, cradling a glass of liquor in her hand. The city's wealthy and influential occupied most of the linen-covered tables filling the banquet hall. At the front of the room, a dais stood in the center of an elevated stage, flanked by two tables. Catherine and several board members from city and charitable organizations sat at one table. Michael sat at the other, between the mayor and Kratos Zamora, directly on her left. The police commissioner occupied the end seat next to Zamora.

After the obligatory mingling over hors d'oeuvres and drinks, dinner had been served and now the real work of the evening began. Speakers took the stage in turns praising the mayor's efforts to support the city's poor and disenfranchised and strengthen the local economy. Pleas were made for more donations and pledges of support for the mayor's reelection campaign.

"Looks like the mayor's got some important people on his side," Rebecca murmured. "Including our friend."

"We pretty much already knew that," Sloan said, clenching the glass in her hand as Zamora leaned close and said something that made Michael smile, even as she kept her eyes on the current speaker.

"Did you say anything to Michael about our interest in him?" Rebecca asked.

"No."

"His attention to her is just coincidental, then." Rebecca watched Sloan carefully. From the moment she and Michael had arrived, she'd looked ready to explode. Anyone who didn't know her as well as Rebecca did probably would have missed the signs. Her usual feline grace was absent. She moved instead with the wary precision of a trained martial artist on the verge of launching a killing blow. Coiled muscles and singular focus. And her prey was very obviously Kratos Zamora. She hadn't taken her eyes off him the entire evening. If he'd noticed, he gave no indication of it, but Rebecca had seen his bodyguards scanning the crowds. Their eyes continually returned to Sloan.

"His muscle has picked up on you," Rebecca said.

"Fine."

"You need to go outside. Take a walk around. Get some air."

"I'm not going anywhere."

"You might as well be waving a banner with his name on it, saying 'I'm after you.'"

Sloan slugged down her scotch. "You think they don't know."

"Probably they do. But we don't need to take out an ad."

"Fuck them." Sloan finally took her eyes off Michael and focused on Rebecca. "Doesn't it bother you? That they flaunt their invincibility? That they spit on us while cozying up to the mayor and the police commissioner? When we know he's dirty?"

"It doesn't matter what we know. It matters what we can prove."

"No," Sloan said. "It matters what *you* can prove."

"Times have changed. Men like him have become politicians."

"What does that make men like the commissioner, then? Front men for felons?"

"I haven't had dealings with the commissioner. He didn't come up the ranks. It's an elected position."

Sloan held out a glass to the bartender for a refill. "And money buys votes."

"You don't need that drink," Rebecca said. "But you need to tell me what lit your fuse."

Sloan narrowed her eyes, challenging Rebecca. Rebecca was the team leader, but she wasn't technically Sloan's boss. Sloan still hadn't decided whether to tell her about the surprise slide show. She trusted Rebecca, but she didn't trust anyone else and she didn't have any idea where the images were coming from. All she knew was that Zamora had gotten close to Michael. And someone was playing with her. She needed to know what they wanted, and why they were willing to use Michael to send a message. Until she knew, she wasn't telling anyone who might further endanger Michael, willingly or unwillingly. Including Rebecca. She cared about the investigation, she cared about justice. But she cared about Michael more.

Rebecca held her gaze, her blue eyes cool and steady. Silence stretched between them, heavy and thick, as the seconds ticked by. Sloan took a shuddering breath and carefully placed her untouched drink on the bar behind her. She needed to convince Rebecca nothing was going on.

"Sorry. He's sitting next to Michael. It's driving me crazy."

"She's safe here."

"I want to send her out of town."

"I don't blame you. Maybe Catherine will go with her."

Sloan laughed shakily. "Yeah, right."

"There's no reason to think she's in danger. He's an influential businessman. She's the head of a multimillion-dollar corporation. They swim in the same waters. It makes sense that he's friendly."

"Yeah," Sloan said dryly. "Friendly."

With a hand on Sloan's back, Rebecca steered her away from the bar and the occasional attendee who came for a refill. She didn't want to spend too much more time talking to her, not with Zamora's men watching, and Sloan seemed calmer now. "We'll compare notes tomorrow as to who else he's friendly with. I've got Watts on camera duty."

Sloan rubbed her eyes. "Look. Sorry. I'm okay. I hate these goddamned things anyhow."

"Me too. But we can tell Clark and the captain we've done our duty." Rebecca squeezed Sloan's shoulder. "And we've got a good look at his muscle. That might come in handy."

"Yeah," Sloan said, planning to search the security tapes at Michael's office building for those same faces. "It might."

❖

Talia waited until the tall, sharp-eyed blonde moved away from Sloan. That would be the detective Kratos had told her about. Frye. A very capable-looking woman. Very intense. Very focused. Very cool. Talia preferred her women hotter, although she knew the ones who seemed cool on the surface very often boiled over if you knew how to stoke their fires. She wondered what it would take to fire up the detective. She didn't have to wonder about Sloan. It was written all over her face every time she looked at the woman next to Kratos. The woman Kratos had met for an impromptu business discussion the day before.

Talia picked up a glass of Burgundy from a passing waiter and gravitated toward Sloan. "I hate these things, don't you?"

Sloan glanced at her and smiled politely. "I don't think we're supposed to admit that."

"I'll keep it a secret if you will." Talia sipped her wine. It was better than average for affairs of this type. And Sloan was far more attractive in person than in her photos. Her body appeared to be solid muscle, and her eyes were the most startling shade of indigo-violet. With her dark hair and square jaw she exuded raw sexuality. Talia registered a spike of pleasure and struggled against the urge to touch her, but she let her interest show in her voice. "I'm quite good at keeping secrets."

"That's a rare skill." Sloan watched the stage as Zamora moved to the lectern. She stiffened as his left hand drifted over Michael's shoulder in passing.

"He's quite charismatic, isn't he?" Talia observed, leaning lightly against Sloan's arm. She wanted to set her off. Women like her could be thrillingly unpredictable when ignited.

"Not my type," Sloan said through gritted teeth.

"No," Talia said with a laugh. Her breast brushed Sloan's arm and her nipple tightened so quickly she almost gasped. "I don't imagine he is."

"Friend of yours?" Sloan asked.

"Not precisely." Talia smiled as the woman onstage looked over at Sloan, then took Talia in with a curious expression. Curiosity. Not jealousy. That was interesting. "But *she's* a friend of yours."

Sloan finally focused on Talia, her expression moving from distant politeness to intense scrutiny. "More than a friend. But you knew that, didn't you?"

Talia sipped her wine to hide her smile. Oh, this woman was very good. Very very good and very very exciting. She would have to be careful. "I made a calculated deduction. You've been watching her all night."

"Does that mean you've been watching me all night?"

"Oh my. Am I that obvious?"

"No. Not at all."

Talia looked toward the stage, breaking eye contact. She wasn't usually concerned with what others could read in her expression, but she feared Sloan might see more than she intended. She was painfully aroused and she did not want Sloan to realize she had an advantage.

"He seems quite taken with her," Talia said, then continued as if she didn't hear the sharp breath Sloan sucked in. "But then, that's understandable. She's quite beautiful."

"You can give him a message for me," Sloan said. "Tell him it would be dangerous for him to even think about her, let alone touch her again."

"If I knew him that well, I would surely give him your message." Talia slid her fingers around Sloan's forearm. "But I do know him well enough to know that he always gets what he wants."

"Not this time."

Her fingers shifted to Sloan's hip, and down. She slipped her card deep into the left front pocket of Sloan's tuxedo pants, her fingers gliding inward, stopping just short of the point of flagrant groping. "If he gets to be a nuisance, call me. Maybe I can help." When she withdrew her hand, she let her fingers drift upward over Sloan's abdomen. "Of course, you can call me anytime."

"I didn't get your name," Sloan said.

Talia reluctantly stepped back, finished her wine, and set her glass aside. "It's Talia. You have my number. I'll look forward to your call."

❖

"Is she all right?" Catherine slipped her arm through Rebecca's and tilted her head toward Sloan.

"I don't know." Rebecca frowned, studying Sloan from across the room. The crowd was breaking up, a few people lingering in small clusters, trying for one last connection, one last vote, one last dollar. Sloan was headed straight through the throng for Michael. "She's strung pretty tight. I thought she was just worried about Michael's health."

"But now you're not sure?"

Rebecca shook her head. "I can't read her, which means she doesn't want me to." She clasped Catherine's hand. "What do you think?"

"I think everyone is under a great deal of pressure. I saw Sloan at the hospital when Michael was injured. She was very badly shaken. She's understandably frightened and trying not to be." Catherine sighed. "She's not all that different than you. She doesn't know she doesn't have to be strong all the time."

"Every cop is like that. And she's a cop, even if she doesn't want to admit it."

"I know." Catherine turned aside for a few seconds to say good night to the deputy mayor, then she placed a hand on Rebecca's arm. "Are you coming home with me?"

"I think we're done here for the night." Rebecca watched Zamora move toward the exit, followed by his entourage of bodyguards masquerading as business associates. He stopped every few feet to speak with some highly placed official. The deputy mayor. The district attorney. The head of one of the local political parties. "We've seen what we came to see."

"Then I'm going to take advantage of the few hours when you're not working and I'm actually awake. Let's go."

Rebecca raised an eyebrow. "Does that include taking advantage of me?"

Catherine laughed. "Most definitely, my darling."

CHAPTER NINETEEN

D ell was always relieved to find that Irina hadn't taken off. But then, where would she go?

"Sorry I didn't think of this sooner," Dell said, setting a large cardboard box down by the foot of the mattress. She noticed a neat stack of magazines and newspapers nearby. Some in English, some in Russian. She knelt down and started opening the box. "You read English?"

"Yes."

"I guess that's a dumb question. You speak English." Dell shook her head. "Sorry."

"It is all right." Irina walked to the refrigerator. "There is beer. Do you want one?"

Dell glanced over her shoulder, surprised when she saw Irina holding up a bottle of the brand she drank. Irina wore navy slacks that hugged her legs like skin and a pink V-neck tee with little sequins along the neck. The shirt ended an inch or so above her waistband. Jewelry of some kind winked in a navel piercing. She wasn't wearing a bra. She usually didn't. Her breasts were a lot bigger than Sandy's. Dell looked away. "Beer would be great. Thanks. Did you have enough to eat?"

"I am fine here." Irina placed the bottle on the floor next to Dell and curled up on the mattress nearby. She popped her head on her elbow and watched Dell work. "You brought a television?"

"I thought you might be bored."

"We are not going out tonight?"

"I thought after last night we should lay low for a little bit." Dell sat back on her heels. "Did anything happen today? Did anyone call? This guy Olik, he has your cell number, right?"

"Yes, although before he would not call me. He would call Yuri. When he wanted the girls for something special."

Dell tried not to let her disgust show. "When he wanted them for what? You took care of scheduling them at the club—to dance, right?"

Irina reached for Dell's beer and took a swallow, then put it back on the floor. "A van would come and bring the girls to Ziggie's and home again after. They were always guarded. That was usual. But sometimes he would want them for parties. Or to make a movie."

"What did you tell them? How did you get them to do this?"

"I told them the truth," Irina said. "That if they did not obey they would never have a chance to be free."

"So why hasn't he called you?" Dell carried the television across the room, placed it on the kitchen counter, and plugged it in. "Why hasn't he come after you?"

"With men like this, it is all about games in the mind," Irina said. "He will not want me to think I am important. He will want me back, but he will make sure I understand it is because I belong to him, like his car or his dogs. Maybe he thinks I am going hungry, maybe he thinks I will be frightened alone. Maybe he wonders about my new boyfriend."

"You think he knows about us?" Dell leaned against the counter and crossed her ankles, her arms braced on either side.

Irina smiled. "He does after last night. I have fucked boys for the job, but I have never had a boyfriend before. He will be suspicious."

"The bartender has seen us together before. He knows I was trying to get with you."

"Yes." Irina seemed to focus on Dell's crotch. "They know I was playing with Mitch."

"That's good, then," Dell said, acutely aware of not packing. She felt naked even with her clothes on.

"Very good." Irina's gaze drifted back up to Dell's face. "When will we go out again?"

"Tomorrow or the next night. Unless something happens before then." Dell thought it was time to bring up the other items they had to deal with. "We want you to talk to someone—a doctor—about these men, about how you lived. What they did. Where you went with them."

Irina's expression went blank. "A prison doctor?"

"No. Just a doctor to talk to. A therapist."

"No drugs."

"No," Dell said quickly. "No. Only talking. About the girls. About you. About things that have happened. It might help us figure out where to look for them, and for the other girls. And your sister."

"Where is this doctor? I won't go to the police."

"I'll take you to see her. At her office, okay?"

"Her?"

Dell nodded. "It's okay. You can trust her. I promise."

Irina studied her for a long time. "You will be there?"

"If you want."

"When?"

"Monday."

"Will I see you before then?"

"Sure," Dell said. "I'll come by tomorrow sometime."

"Then I will talk to your doctor."

❖

"Hello?" Sandy took a cell phone call as she climbed out of a cab at the corner of Vine and Delaware Avenue. She handed the driver ten dollars and motioned with her fingers for him to give her back three.

"Lily said you were looking for some extra action," a female voice said.

"Darla?" Sandy thought she recognized the soft Southern accent of a black girl about her age. She didn't know her very well, only that she had a story like all their stories. A home she didn't want to talk about, a family that didn't miss her, and the new family she'd made with other girls like her, living in squats or four to a room in crowded walk-up apartments. But they were making it. And they were proud of that.

"Sandy? Yeah, it's me. I wasn't sure I had the right number at first."

"Where are you, honey? The Blue D?" Sandy skirted through traffic and crossed to the far side of Delaware and hurried north.

"Nuh-uh. The Iron Fist."

"Alone?" The Fist was a biker bar, and the clientele was into heavy-duty action. Sandy tried to stay away from there, even when she'd been working regular. She disliked sweating men mauling her and demanding she do things they'd be embarrassed to ask their regular girlfriends for. Somehow, giving blow jobs to some anxious accountant whose wife was too uptight to put her mouth on his cock was a lot different than having a drunken pig piss on her.

"A trick dropped me off in the parking lot," Darla said. "I just ran in to use the phone, and I bumped into one of the guys as they were leaving. They said there's a party tonight and they'd pick me up on the corner of Spring Garden and Second in ten minutes. Wanna come?"

"Which guys are these again?" Sandy asked, crossing back over Delaware. She was only a few blocks from Spring Garden. She wondered if she could reach Dell, and if Dell would even have time to get here before the guys showed up.

"I don't know their names," Darla said. "Foreign guys. Russians, I guess. They've got money. They promised me five large just to hang around this party."

"Hang around?"

Darla laughed. "Well. You know. I figure that means put out a little bit."

"Who else you got lined up?"

"No one yet. You're the only one I could reach."

Sandy couldn't let Darla go alone. She could be walking into something she couldn't handle. Even if Sandy didn't want to get information for Frye, she couldn't let any girl, even one she didn't know that well, do something like this alone. Shit, Dell was going to be pissed. "I'm five minutes away. Don't go without me."

"Don't worry, sugar. I'll tell them someone extra special is on the way."

❖

Dell tucked her phone between her ear and shoulder while she looked under the sink for a place to stash her empty. "You sound short of breath or something. Where are you?" She got a sudden cramp in her stomach followed by a very bad feeling. "San?"

Across the room, Irina sat up, watching her intently.

"I'm on Spring Garden. I'm meeting up with a girl who's going to a party with some Russian guys."

"No!" Dell exploded. "Do not go. You hear me? *Do not go.*"

"It's just a party, baby. I won't do anything, I promise."

"I'm not talking about that. It's not about that. God damn it, Sandy. It's not safe."

"I've been to a hundred of these things, baby. I know how to handle myself with party boys."

"These are not just good-time guys. These are—"

"I can't let her go alone."

"Yes, you can! Yes, you fucking can! She's not your responsibility." Dell turned in a fast hard circle. She didn't know what to do. She didn't know if she should run out the door and jump on her bike or if she should call Frye. What she wanted to do was crawl through the phone and shake Sandy until her teeth rattled.

"I'll call you when I get there, okay? I'll go to the bathroom or something and call you. I'll be okay."

"Sandy, please don't do this. San—"

"I'll call you, baby."

Dell was left staring at the silent phone. The helpless feeling was so overwhelming she almost threw it across the room. For a second, she didn't know what to do. "Jesus. Jesus Jesus Jesus."

"Tell me what she said."

Dell focused on Irina and her training kicked in. She held up a hand and punched in Frye's number on her speed dial. Then she held her breath and counted. One ring. Two rings. Three rings. Four ri—

"Frye." The lieutenant sounded hoarse and a little breathless, as if she were out running. Maybe she was.

"It's Mitchell. Sandy's gone off to a party with some Russians."

"When?"

"Now. She just called me from Spring Garden."

"Where on Spring Garden?"

Dell closed her eyes, wondering what the fuck kind of cop she was anyhow. "I don't know. Jesus, I—"

"Tell me exactly what she said."

Frye's voice was calm and steady and Dell felt herself settle. She relayed the conversation, what little there had been of it.

"Where are you now?"

"In Queen Village. At Mitch's apartment with Irina." Dell checked her watch. Half past midnight. "Should I call her back?"

"No. She might already be with them. I'll raise Watts and we'll pick you up. If she calls in the meantime, find out where she is and call me back."

"Okay." Dell took a full breath, the first one in what felt like a long time, and her brain seemed to click into gear. "Maybe Irina knows something that can help us."

"Good idea. Stay put. I'll be right there."

"Yes ma'am. Thank you, ma'am." Dell disconnected and shoved the phone back into her jacket pocket. "Do you know where they take the girls to party?"

"There are a few places. Hotels, usually."

"Names. Can you tell me names?" Dell searched through her jacket and came up with a takeout receipt. "Pencil? Pen?"

Irina found her bag, fumbled in it for a few seconds, and handed Dell a ballpoint pen. "I am not sure of all the names. I had no reason to look at them. This is your girlfriend?"

Dell clenched her jaw and nodded. "Just tell me anything you can remember."

"They are not going to hurt her, Mitch. They don't hurt the girls. They need them. As long as they think she is just there for them to use, she will be fine."

"Fine." The word felt like ashes on Dell's tongue. As long as Sandy let them use her, she would be fine. But Dell knew Sandy, and even when she was still hooking to survive, Sandy never let anyone use her. Christ, she had to find her. "Whatever you can remember."

"I'm sorry about this," Rebecca said, pulling on a pair of jeans.

"It's all right. Is Sandy in trouble?" Catherine got out of bed and found a pair of silk pajamas. She handed Rebecca a black pullover that Rebecca shrugged on without even looking at it.

"Hopefully not. She could be with some college guys who are just looking for a few girls to liven up their weekend in town. I don't have much information." Rebecca opened the bedside drawer and pulled out her weapon and shoulder harness. "God damn it. What the hell was she thinking?"

"I imagine she's thinking that she's doing her job."

Rebecca stopped moving. "Her job?"

"She is your CI still, isn't she? You pay her to find out things. To talk to people who won't talk to anyone else. To go places no one else can go."

"I don't pay her to put herself in danger." Rebecca realized as soon as she spoke that it was bullshit. Every time she asked Sandy to pump her sources for information, she was asking her to take a risk. If someone got suspicious and made her as an informant, Sandy wouldn't live long. "Ah, hell. You think I'm wrong, don't you, for using her."

Catherine sighed. "Rebecca, I wish many things in this world were different. I wish Sandy had never had to sell her body to survive. I wish there weren't men who use the misfortune of girls like her for their own pleasure. I wish you didn't have to put the people you care about in danger to stop evil. We live with what we must, and you do what you must. You are not using her. Sandy is far too strong for that. Remember, she's very resourceful. And very, very bright."

Rebecca sat down on the bed next to Catherine and took her hand. "You help me see things in ways I never have before. You don't excuse me, and that's okay. But you understand me, and that…that means everything to me."

Catherine took Rebecca's face in her hands and kissed her. "I love you. If you didn't see the world the way you do, you wouldn't be so good at your job. And you need to be good at your job to keep yourself and the others safe. And to do what's right." She brushed her fingers through Rebecca's hair. "Go now. Be careful."

"I'll be back as soon as I can." Rebecca kissed her swiftly and disappeared into the night, again.

❖

Sandy made it to the corner of Spring Garden and Vine just as a Lincoln Navigator with blacked-out windows veered out of traffic and shot to the curb where Darla leaned against a signpost. Like Sandy, she wore a miniskirt that hit just below the crease of her ass, although her skirt was shiny red vinyl and Sandy's was a black stretchy material. They both wore cheap, skimpy jackets with oversized zippers and not much else underneath.

Darla waved to Sandy, relief showing on her face in the light of the street lamp just above them. The back door of the Navigator swung open and a man stepped out. He wore dark slacks, a black leather jacket, and sunglasses, which was weird, because it was the middle of the night. He didn't look like a college boy. He looked exactly like what Sandy figured he was. A thug, probably a pimp. Not the ordinary kind of pimp who provided girls shelter and protection, ha ha, in exchange for the money they earned on their knees and their backs. No, this guy looked like he worked for some man who didn't want to get his hands dirty, so he sent his men out to get what he wanted. And apparently, he wanted pussy.

"Hi," Sandy said, swinging her ass as she hurried toward Darla. She hooked her arm through Darla's and kissed her cheek. Then she tossed her head and smiled at the man who stood watching them. "Are these our dates, honey?"

"I guess," Darla said, looking a little uncertain.

Sandy figured this wasn't the guy Darla had talked to in the parking lot at the Fist. Guys like the ones in the Navigator didn't troll the streets for what they wanted. They had someone else do it. She tried to get a look at the rear of the car as she and Darla walked over, but she couldn't see the license plate.

"Who's your friend," the man said to Darla in crisp English. He had an accent, but his speech was polished.

"This is—"

"Samantha," Sandy said quickly, cocking her hips to give him a good look at her legs as the skirt pulled up almost to her crotch. "But everyone calls me Sam. Darla says we're going to a party. I can't wait. I love parties."

He looked them over for a long minute, then stepped aside and gestured to the rear of the SUV. Sandy looked down the street, but she didn't see Dell's motorcycle or anything resembling a cop car. Used to be Frye showed up in her Corvette, but lately she'd been in a standard issue. There was no sign of an unmarked. Which meant no one was going to know where they went. She took Darla's hand. "Well, come on, honey. Let's party!"

Sandy slid into the backseat where another man waited on the far side and Darla crowded next to her, as if seeking shelter. Then the door closed and the Navigator pulled out and headed north. Sandy tried to get a look out the window around the big guy sitting next to her, but all she could see was the sign pointing to the on-ramp to 95 North.

They could be anywhere from Trenton to New York City in an hour.

❖

Michael reached out in the dark and switched on the bedside light when she felt Sloan get out of bed. Sitting up, she let the sheet fall to her waist. Sloan stood just inside the bedroom door, pulling on a T-shirt over her boxers. "Can't sleep?"

"Hey," Sloan whispered. "Sorry. I thought you were asleep."

"Drifting. I didn't drink because I was afraid it might give me a headache, so I didn't have anything to dull the pain of the evening."

Sloan laughed. "You too, huh?"

"It did seem endless. I'd forgotten how much I dislike these functions, even if they are for a good cause." Michael shrugged. "I'm not altogether certain about this particular cause."

Sloan sat on the edge of the bed. "Don't like the mayor?"

"I don't know. I don't know him, but I'm not entirely certain that he's really the one making the decisions." She frowned. "There was a very interesting assortment of people there tonight."

"Some pretty high-powered ones," Sloan said carefully, not wanting to alarm her unnecessarily. Even though Michael said she was feeling better, she'd only begun to put in regular workdays and she still seemed pale and fragile. The last thing she needed was to worry about things that might not even involve her. Not when Sloan had a feeling *she* was the one who really interested Zamora. If he didn't want her attention, why send those photos to her computer? They had to be a warning. And if they were, then it was Sloan they wanted, not Michael. "Your neighbor tonight—Zamora. I understand he's pretty influential."

"Mmm," Michael said absently. "He owns a great deal of real estate along both sides of the river, as well as major shares in several investment companies." She reached for the cup of tea she'd left on her bedside table, and sipped it. "It's funny you should mention him. He contacted me yesterday about a business proposal."

"For Innova?" Sloan asked. Michael's design company had an international reputation, and Michael was often approached with investment opportunities. She didn't believe for a second that was Zamora's true intention, but Michael had no reason to suspect him of anything out of the ordinary, so Sloan forced herself to sound casual. "What did you tell him?"

Michael leaned back against the pillows and stroked Sloan's forearm. "Oh, I told him I'd keep him in mind." She smiled. "But that right now, I wasn't looking for partners."

"He seemed pretty friendly at dinner tonight."

"With men like that, charm comes naturally. He reminds me of Nicholas."

Sloan wanted to say that Michael's ex-husband Nicholas, a low-life cheating embezzler, was a choirboy compared to Kratos Zamora. "Impressed with himself, huh?"

Michael smiled. "He's certainly self-assured." She threaded her fingers through Sloan's and gave her hand a little shake. "I noticed you getting some attention yourself."

Sloan frowned. "I don't—"

"The redhead in the very revealing dress."

"Oh. Her." Sloan thought about the business card with a telephone number scrawled on the back she'd slid from the front pocket of her pants and stowed in the glove compartment of her car when Michael wasn't looking. She thought about the fingers grazing the inside of her thigh, drifting over her stomach. "She was just making idle chat."

"I've never seen her before. Who is she?"

"I don't know. Probably another Society Hill heiress with more money than she knows what to do with. Isn't that one of the primary requirements for an invitation to fund-raisers like this?"

"Well, the money part certainly is." Michael sighed. "Will you try to come back to bed tonight?"

Sloan leaned over and kissed her. "I just want to check a few things. I won't be long."

Michael cupped the back of Sloan's neck and held her close for another long kiss. "Wake me when you come to bed."

❖

"That's our second pass through here," Rebecca said. "I don't see her."

Dell leaned forward from the back seat of the unmarked, craning her neck to see around Watts. This section of Spring Garden was crowded with bars, and foot traffic was heavy. They were almost to Delaware Avenue, and they still hadn't seen Sandy.

"Maybe she walked up a few blocks. Let's go around again," Dell urged.

"Hey, kid, you're breathing down my neck," Watts said. "Take it easy. We'll find her."

"How?" Dell snapped. "She's gone already. She could be anywhere."

Rebecca pulled into the darkened parking lot of a restaurant that had gone out of business and turned off the engine. "We wait for her to call us."

"I'm going to check the clubs," Dell said, pushing open the back door. "Someone may have talked to these guys tonight. They might know where the party is."

"Yo," Watts yelled, reaching for his door.

"I'll handle it," Rebecca said quietly. She slid out of the car and closed her door. "Mitchell. Wait."

Dell took another few steps, then stopped just short of the street. Rebecca walked unhurriedly over to her. "Step back from the light."

Together, they moved into the shadows of the boarded-up building.

"Why is it a bad idea for you to start asking around about Sandy in the clubs?"

Dell balled up her fists, her arms rigid at her sides, and looked past Rebecca at the cars streaming by on the street. She didn't want to answer the question. She didn't want to think about why she couldn't do what she needed to do to find Sandy. To look after her. She didn't want to have to choose anything over the woman she loved, ever again. "I can't do this."

"Can't do what?"

"I can't be a cop if it means I have to put everything else in front of her." She stared at Rebecca, her eyes hot with tears she refused to shed. "I'm sorry, Lieutenant."

"What do you think is going to change if you're not a cop

anymore?" Rebecca leaned against the building as if they had all the time in the world to talk.

"I could…"

"What? Spend your time following her around? Checking out her friends? Making sure she doesn't go anywhere she could get hurt?" Rebecca laughed. "Sandy would hand you your ass in under a week."

"I could look for her right now. I wouldn't have to worry about blowing my cover. That's what you're talking about, isn't it? I'm supposed to be with Irina now. So I can't go running around trying to find out if Sandy talked to some Russians tonight."

"It wouldn't be a very good idea, no. And chances are slim to none you'd find out anything anyhow."

"But what if it *did* make a difference," Dell insisted. "What if I found one of her friends who knew these guys, too, and they could tell me where the party was."

"What would you do? Crash it? All that would do is probably get both of you beaten up." Rebecca straightened. "You've had a lot thrown at you in a short time. You're undercover, and that's always a tough assignment. Sandy is right in the thick of things, and I know it's hard. Hard and…scary."

"I let the Army take everything from me," Dell said hoarsely. "Everything I thought I was, everything I thought I believed in. The woman I thought loved me. I couldn't do a damn thing to change it."

"You're not alone now. You've got help. That's why we're here." Rebecca gestured toward the car. "Now we've got a lot of work to do and it's gonna be a long night. I suggest you sit your ass down and wait for her to call. She'll call."

"I'm sorry I'm not…" Dell pushed her hand through her hair. "Fuck, I'm sorry if I let you down."

Rebecca clasped the back of Dell's neck and rubbed the tight muscles for a few seconds. "You haven't let anybody down. And you won't. Not me. Not Sandy. Come on, let's go."

Rebecca dropped her hand and walked away, and after a second's hesitation, Dell followed. As she walked across the cold dark parking lot, she felt the warmth in the back of her neck where Rebecca had touched her. She didn't understand it, but she wished for that touch to return.

CHAPTER TWENTY

Well, Sandy thought, she was right about one thing. They were in Trenton. She caught a quick glimpse of a sign as they pulled off I-95. She couldn't see much else with the silent giant next to her blocking most of the window. He hadn't said anything. He hadn't touched her, for which she was thankful. Darla had been silent for the entire forty-minute trip too.

"So where is this place?" Sandy asked brightly. She'd tried getting information from the Russian a couple of times, but every question she asked was greeted with a grunt or nothing at all. "Don't they have hotels in Philly? We have to come all the way up here for a party?" She leaned forward and turned sideways on the seat so she could peer into the man's face. "Hey. You're not sleeping, are you? We're gonna party tonight, remember?"

"I am not sleeping," he said roughly.

"So where are we going?"

"We will be there soon."

Sandy debated pushing him a little bit further, but she didn't think he was going to talk and she was pretty certain if she pushed him too far, she'd find herself on the side of the road. Maybe walking, maybe not moving at all. She settled back down on the seat.

"Is there anything to drink?"

"There will be drinks at the party. But you should not drink."

"Why not?"

"Because men do not like drunken girls."

"These guys. They're your friends? Germans, like you?"

"I am Russian, not German," he growled, confirming her guesswork.

"Oh, cool." Sandy felt the car slow and slid her hand into the front pocket of her jacket. Her fingers closed over her cell phone. "Hey, we're here. Cool."

A few seconds later, the rear door opened and the first man reached in and grasped Darla's hand. He guided her out, not roughly, but he kept a grip on her, as if she might suddenly run away. When Sandy climbed out, the other guy was right behind her. She glanced around quickly. They were in the turnaround at the side entrance to a hotel, and she couldn't see the main sign from where they were. She could make out letters on the glass door of the entrance opposite where they parked. A hand closed around her left arm, marching her quickly toward the hotel. She slid the cell phone from her pocket and held it down by her leg, pushing buttons from memory. When they got almost up to the door, she took a picture, hoping she got the name. Then she carefully slid it back into her jacket. She had a lot more pictures to take.

She stepped into the hotel and put on a bright smile as they waited for an elevator. "This is going to be fun."

Twenty-second floor, room 2208. She repeated the numbers to herself. She and Darla were sandwiched between the two big men in front of a room at the end of the hall. When the door opened, she felt a hand on the small of her back directing her forward. The suite was huge, with two seating areas joined by open double pocket doors. She counted eight men at first glance and three or four girls about her age. The men all wore shirts and trousers, as if they had just recently come from a business meeting. The girls didn't wear much of anything at all. Short skirts, thin cotton tops, high heels or thigh-high boots. A couple looked young. Really young. Fifteen, maybe. She knew, because she'd been fifteen when she'd started. But she hadn't started off in places like this. The first trick she'd ever turned was in a bus station. She'd blown a guy for the price of a ticket to somewhere, anywhere, except where she was.

The night she'd met Dell she'd been giving a routine hand job in an alley when the john decided to get rough. If Dell hadn't stepped in, she probably would have been able to handle him, but she'd have worn the bruises on her face and body for a long time. Sandy pushed that memory away. She wasn't that girl anymore. She wasn't a girl at all.

Next to her, she sensed Darla getting skittish. She had probably expected a fraternity party, with boys and beer and a couple of blow jobs in the bathroom. These were not boys. These were men, and the way the men looked at them made it clear they considered the girls on a par with the trays of hors d'oeuvres sitting around the room. She was surprised that most of them were speaking English. For some reason, she'd expected them to be foreign, like the guys who brought them, but they weren't.

Sandy took Darla's arm and tugged her toward the wet bar along one side of the room. The surface was covered with ice buckets, open bottles of liquor and champagne, and stacks of glasses. "Let's get a drink, honey," she said loudly, "and then we can get acquainted with these handsome men."

"This place is creeping me out," Darla whispered. "Who are these guys?"

As they reached the bar, Sandy lowered her voice. No one was really paying all that much attention to them, and she slid her camera from her pocket again. "High rollers. If you hear a name, try to remember it. Mix us a couple of drinks. Make them weak—mostly water and ice. You want them to think you're partying, but you need to keep your head on straight, okay?"

"Can't we just get out of here?" Darla pleaded. "I've got enough money for us to get home on the bus."

"Once you tell these guys you're in, you're in for the whole ride. It's the safest way to play it." Sandy leaned on the bar, her phone propped between a couple of glasses. She shielded her cell with her hands, hoping there was enough space between the glasses to get some shots of the guys sitting around the room.

"Should I offer to do them or anything?" Darla dumped ice cubes into a couple of short glasses and dashed a little scotch into each one.

"Just sit down next to one of them with your drink and wait until someone talks to you. They'll let you know what they want. Try not to go into a room alone with any of them. After they've had a few drinks, they'll probably do it right out here."

"Don't leave me, okay?" Darla said, her voice trembling.

"I won't. I gotta pee right now, but I won't go anywhere. Promise."

❖

Watts shifted in the front seat and the car rocked slightly. "There's a Stop and Rob around the corner. I could use some coffee. Anyone else?"

"Not me," Rebecca said.

"I'm okay." Dell checked her watch again. 1:30. Jesus. "Don't take too long, huh?"

"You need me, you know where I am." Watts heaved himself out of the vehicle and slammed the door.

Dell leaned her head back against the seat and stared at the ceiling. "I shouldn't have left her alone. I went over to check on Irina. I should've stayed home."

"It's Saturday night," Rebecca said. "Sandy is usually out and about for a while."

"Yeah, I guess." Dell sighed. "Sorry. Guess I messed up your night. Watts's too."

"It's not a big deal, Mitchell. I wasn't asleep yet, and Watts was just heading out for a late date when I called him."

Dell rocked forward. "A date? Watts?"

"Apparently with a certain Port Authority captain." Rebecca chuckled. "Anyhow, this is the job. And it's Sandy."

"Man, I—" Dell's cell rang and she jerked, fumbling at her belt. She yanked it off. "Mitchell."

"Baby, it's—"

"Sandy," Dell said, forcing herself to be calm. "Tell me where you are."

"I don't know exactly. Somewhere in Trenton."

Sandy spoke so softly Dell had to close her eyes and concentrate as hard as she could to hear her over the pounding of her own heart. Some kind of rushing noise in the background. Water running? "Are you in a house somewhere? Did you see any street signs?"

"No, a hotel. Wait a minute. Let me see. I took a picture."

Dell's stomach twisted into a chain of knots. "Can you leave? Sandy, can you leave right now?"

"I don't think so. Darla's with me. I don't think they're going to let us just walk out." Silence. "There. Sheraton."

"Which one? Does it say?"

"I'm not sure. Close to 95."

"We'll be ther—"

"I gotta go, baby. I'll try to call you when we're leaving. It might not be until morning."

"Jesus, Sandy," Dell yelled, finally losing her cool. "I want you to get out of there. You—"

"I'll be okay. I love you."

Dell was left listening to dead air again. "Jesus Christ!"

"Where is she?" Rebecca said, starting the engine.

"Trenton. Fucking Trenton!"

Rebecca pulled out onto Spring Garden and headed east, cruising around the corner toward the all-night food mart. Watts was just walking up the street with his coffee. She eased up to the curb next to him. "We'll head up there. But chances are whoever took her will transport her right back down here. They're not likely to hurt these girls, Mitchell, as long as they don't find out what Sandy's doing there. And Sandy's smart."

"If she was that smart, she wouldn't be there."

"No. If she weren't as brave and ballsy, she wouldn't be there."

Mitchell rubbed her face. "I could use some of those balls right now."

"What's this about your balls?" Watts said, sliding into his seat. "You having equipment problems, kid?"

"Not now, Watts," Rebecca said softly.

"No," Dell said gruffly. "Woman problems."

Watts blew on his coffee. "Join the rest of us, kid."

❖

Sandy didn't think she'd been gone more than a few minutes, but when she returned, someone had turned the lights down so that she almost stumbled over an end table. Darla was on the sofa next to a thin man in a white shirt and dark pants. He'd removed his jacket and tie and had his arm draped over her shoulders, his hand on her breast.

Sandy scanned the room. The Russian who'd been in the backseat with her leaned against the wall next to the hallway door. His gaze flicked over her as if she weren't there, but she had no doubt he knew exactly where she was. Since no one seemed to be paying her any particular attention, she sauntered over to Darla and plopped down next to her. She leaned close, and to anyone looking, it would almost seem as if she had kissed her neck. She knew from experience that at these kinds of parties, guys got off on seeing girls getting it on together. Most of her friends in the life were totally comfortable having sex with each other, and most of the time, would prefer it to the anonymous johns. So they always tried distracting the men with a little girl-on-girl action at parties like this. If they got really lucky, sometimes that was enough.

"Everything okay?" Sandy whispered.

Darla clamped onto her thigh with one hand as if to anchor her to the couch. Then she turned and kissed Sandy full on the mouth. "Missed you, baby."

Sandy snuggled close, checking to see who might be watching them out of the corner of her eye. A girl knelt on the floor in front of the adjacent chair, giving a man a blow job while he talked on the phone. On the opposite sofa, a big man with hands the size of baseball gloves mauled another girl's breasts, which he had exposed by pulling her top down and scooping them out like treats from a candy sack. Sandy hadn't done anything like this in weeks, longer really, since she'd started falling in love with Dell, and she was sickened in a way she never had been before. She had been numb for a very long time, but she wasn't anymore. Now she was even more determined to stop these men. All of these men.

"Well, I'm back now and I promise not to leave your side for the whole night. Who's your friend?"

"Oh, this is..." Darla, despite being a little freaked by her surroundings, was no neophyte. She read Sandy's message loud and clear. Dropping her free hand into the thin man's crotch, she squeezed fleetingly, making him grunt in surprise. "What did you say your name was, honey?"

"I didn't." He looked past Darla to Sandy. "Who are you?"

"I'm Sam," Sandy said, putting a purr in her voice. "I guess my girlfriend got the lucky seat first."

"You two together?"

"Uh-huh," Darla and Sandy answered in unison.

Sandy saw his pants tent under Darla's hand. Bingo. He liked to watch, and watching was the safest thing for them. If they were really lucky, they could string him along until all the other guys were occupied.

"You don't mind if I join in, do you?" Sandy slid her arm around Darla's waist and nuzzled her throat.

"Kiss her," he said, covering Darla's hand with his and curling her fingers around the ridge in his pants.

Darla had had practice at this, and they made it look and sound like they were really into each other, showing a lot of tongue more than really kissing. Giving the guy what he expected. Sandy almost never kissed her johns, and hadn't kissed another woman since Dell. The touch of Darla's mouth felt strange. Too soft, too casual. When Dell kissed her, she always felt Dell's need. Dell's hunger for her. Dell's kisses could be gentle, but they were always demanding. This was an act, and that was cool with her, especially if it kept her mouth off some guy's cock.

"Go slow on him," Sandy whispered in Darla's ear when they broke for breath. "Don't let him come right away until everyone else gets busy."

They went back to fondling and making out while Darla massaged him through his pants. After a while, he unzipped and pulled himself out, but Darla knew how to stretch a hand job into a marathon. By the time he came, everyone else in the room was busy. No one bothered Sandy and Darla as they curled up together in the corner of the couch. After a while the thin man tucked his flaccid penis back in his pants and sat with his eyes closed, drinking his drink.

❖

"What about letting me check out the lobby." Dell stared at the hotel, her skin itching like fire ants were crawling inside her clothes. Sandy was in there somewhere. With men who would dispose of her like so much trash if they discovered why she was there. Even if they didn't hurt her, they were using her. Dell knew what Sandy had done to survive. She didn't care what Sandy might have to do tonight to stay safe, as long as doing it didn't hurt Sandy.

"Can't," Rebecca said. "You can bet there's someone in the lobby. They'll have someone watching the ground-floor elevators, the stairwells, and outside in the hall by the room. No one is going to get close to the men in there."

"I can get a look at the guy."

"And he might look at you. We can't risk it." Rebecca turned sideways and stared at Dell in the faint glow of the hotel marquee. "You're going to get up close and personal with these guys. But when you do, it's going to be because Irina introduces you."

"I'll take a walk around the block," Watts said. "They're going to have a car, maybe two, near an exit. I'll get the license plates."

"Make sure your cell is on," Rebecca said. He waved a hand as he closed the door.

"What good is it to her with us out here," Dell griped.

"This is surveillance, Mitchell. You know how it works. We watch." Rebecca moved her seat back to give herself more legroom and rubbed the back of her neck.

"You okay?" Dell asked quietly.

"Yes. Little headache. It's nothing."

"I'm sorry. I keep thinking I should've seen this coming."

Rebecca laughed softly. "If you ever get to the point where you know what Sandy's going to do before she does it, let me know. I'll promote you."

"Irina agreed to talk to Dr. Rawlings."

Rebecca turned her head. "Really? Nice work."

"I think if we could get Witsec for her, she'll come around about her sister too."

"I'll talk to Clark on Monday." Rebecca grunted. "Hell. Why should he have a day off. I'll call him later on today."

"I want to be at the next one of these parties," Dell said.

"Good. Because that's the plan."

❖

By sometime around 4:00 a.m., the only sounds in the suite were a few intermittent moans. Several of the girls were curled up asleep on the floor or draped over slumbering men. A few men, still awake, sat drinking and talking. Another was being serviced by two girls, one with her mouth on his cock, the other offering him her breasts to bite.

"I'll be right back. Don't move," Sandy whispered.

She slid from the couch and carefully slipped into the shadows, making her way down the hall. Earlier when she'd gone to the bathroom to call Dell, she'd seen an open door with coats on a bed. After checking that the hall was clear, she darted into that bedroom and closed the door almost completely. A wall sconce gave her just enough light to maneuver by. She pulled her camera out one more time and rummaged through the coats. She knew where to look and quickly found several wallets. Holding the billfolds open to the light, she shot pictures of the driver's licenses behind their clear plastic coverings. She had no idea if her cell phone camera would be good enough for what she needed, so she committed the names to memory. But she knew her word would never be enough. She needed proof.

She'd just opened the third wallet when a muffled curse and the sound of stumbling footsteps alerted her that someone was approaching. Her options were limited. The bed was too close to the floor to crawl under. She didn't want to hide in the closet in case someone had left their coat in there and was coming to retrieve it. Behind the bedroom door. No. If someone came in and closed the door, she would be instantly exposed. She shoved the wallets back into the coats, praying she had them in the right order, and bolted over the bed and onto the floor on the far side, rolling as close to the bed as possible. The bedroom door opened wide and a shaft of dim light, seeming as bright as a searchlight beam, cut across the room. Sandy held her breath, afraid her panting would give her away. Heavy footsteps approached. The bed sagged as someone sat on the far side, then she heard a few mumbled words in a language she couldn't understand. It must be one of the Russians.

The unmistakable sound of a zipper sliding down, a grunt, then the liquid sounds of someone sucking. He was collecting a little bonus pay before leaving, which meant that the party was probably going to break up soon. Within minutes he was breathing heavily, and Sandy prayed he would pop quickly before other men began rousing to leave. His grunting increased and the sucking turned to gagging chokes. The bastard wasn't letting her breathe, and it was all Sandy could do not to vault over the bed and smash him in the face. She squeezed her eyes tightly shut, closed her hands until her nails dug into her palms, and told herself she would only make matters worse if she were discovered. He gave a hoarse cry and she slowly let out her breath. It was over, and within seconds, they were gone. Trembling, she got to her knees, checked that the room was empty, and hurried to the door. The hall was clear.

The lights in the main rooms were still turned down low, but as soon as she angled toward the couch she realized something was wrong. Darla wasn't there. Quickly, she hurried back down the hall the way she had come. Beyond the room where the coats were stored was another room, and she could hear the wet slap of flesh on flesh. She could also hear Darla crying no.

Bastards. Sandy shoved open the door and stormed across the room all in one motion, yelling, "Hey! That's my girl."

A heavy man with his pants down around his thighs had Darla pinned to the bed, one hand on her throat, the other on his cock, which he was trying to shove between her legs. Even in the half light, Sandy could see Darla's eyes bulging. He was choking her for real. Sandy shoved his shoulder with both hands as hard as she could, catching him unawares and forcing him to release Darla as he stumbled. He was too quick for her to avoid the slashing backhand blow that caught her across the face and knocked her onto the floor. She felt her lip split and managed to roll partially onto her side so that the kick caught her on the back, and not in the face. The force of the blow knocked the air from her lungs, and a buzzing filled her head as another kick skidded off her temple. She gagged, gasping for air, and dimly heard Darla screaming. Then angry shouts in English, then Russian. Someone lifted her onto the bed next to Darla, who gathered her into her arms.

"Leave her alone," Darla shouted. "That bastard was choking me."

"Let it go," Sandy mumbled, still dizzy and sick. "Don't fight them."

Darla pressed her face to the top of Sandy's head. "I'm sorry. I'm sorry. You told me not to go anywhere with anyone. But he said to come with him and I—"

"S'okay. S'okay."

"We go now," one of the Russians who had brought them said impatiently. He grabbed them by their arms and yanked them up. "Now."

Sandy's right arm was numb, but her shoulder was in agony, and when he jerked her up, her knees gave way. "Wait. Just a minute. Please."

"No," he said fiercely and dragged her down the hall toward the door.

Her vision swam and she was only dimly aware of the elevator, the bright lights of the lobby, the cold night air. "Darla?"

"I'm here, honey," Darla whispered.

Baby, Sandy thought as the doors to the Navigator opened and the big man pushed her inside. *Dell, baby, I'm so sorry.*

Chapter Twenty-one

S loan swirled the melting ice cubes absently in her glass, then swallowed the rest of the vodka while keying in a new diagnostic with one hand. She was close. Very close. There was a ghost in her machine, and she intended to find it and follow it.

"You're not quite as good as you think, are you," she murmured.

She thought of the men she'd seen earlier that night with Kratos Zamora. Somehow, none of them struck her as likely candidates to be her hacker, but appearances really meant nothing. Still, they all looked like handlers or enforcers. Maybe Gregor, the brother, was more than just a figurehead. Maybe he was the brains after all.

While the program ran, she wandered back to the small kitchen to replenish her drink. It was almost dawn. She'd told Michael she wouldn't be long. That was hours ago, and Michael would be asleep, which was what she really needed, not Sloan's restless anger. Sloan poured an inch into her glass, not bothering with ice, and leaned against the counter as she sipped it. Her nervous system twanged as if a continuous current ran through it, keeping her edgy. The vodka stirred a fire in the pit of her stomach and with her ass pressed into the counter, she thought of Michael kneeling in front of her in the bathroom earlier, taking her into her mouth, soothing her even as she burned away her unrest.

She sighed and put her glass in the sink. When she returned to her desk, code scrolled rapidly down her screen. It might be a while. She clasped her hands between her knees and fought not to think about the images of Michael and Zamora that had covered her screen earlier. Mocking her. With an oath, she shot upright and her chair spun away.

She covered the distance to the stairs in a few rapid strides and was in the loft seconds later. She only slowed as she reached the corridor leading to their bedroom. She did not want to frighten Michael. She undressed in the semidarkness and slid into bed, nude. Carefully, she pressed against Michael's back, sliding her arm around Michael's waist.

Michael murmured and rolled over, drawing Sloan's hand to her breast. "Sloan?"

"It's me, baby."

"Is it late?"

"Yes." Sloan kissed Michael's forehead. Her skin was smooth, warm, her breasts soft against Sloan's chest. She rubbed her hand up and down Michael's back, feeling calmed by the caress.

"Are you all right?" Michael asked.

"I just needed to be with you."

Michael ran her fingers through Sloan's hair. "Do you need to make love?"

"No." Sloan pillowed her head on Michael's breast, realizing that the beat of Michael's heart, the scent of her skin, the touch of her hand was enough. For now, in this moment, she had everything she needed. "I just need this."

"Go to sleep, darling. Can you do that for me?" Michael murmured.

"Yes."

"And will you be here when I wake up, so I can have you? I need you."

"I'll be here."

❖

Watts pulled open the passenger door and slid into the front seat. Puffing slightly, he snapped, "Head down to the corner and turn right. They're moving and we've got trouble."

"Got it." Rebecca started the sedan and took off in the direction Watts indicated.

Dell rocketed forward from the backseat. "What's going on?"

"Three guys just came out a side entrance—right around the corner in that narrow service alley we passed—with Sandy and the black girl.

Darla." Watts glanced over his shoulder. "One guy was holding Sandy up. She wasn't walking any too steady. Drunk maybe. Or high."

"No," Dell said instantly. "She wouldn't be. She doesn't use, and even if she has to take a hit of something to keep her cover, she's careful to keep her head on straight."

"There." Watts pointed through the windshield. "Four cars up. The Navigator."

"I see it," Rebecca said calmly. "What's your read, Watts?"

"I couldn't tell for sure, but if Sandy's not high, she's hurt."

"Fuck," Dell exclaimed. "Fuck! We have to get her out of there."

Rebecca dropped back when one of the cars in front of them turned off, leaving them too close to the Navigator. Without another backup car to work with them, they couldn't leapfrog, making it more likely the driver of the SUV would pick up on their presence. She had to think looking for a tail would be SOP for those guys. "They're heading for 95."

"There's a two-block stretch that's pretty deserted right before the on-ramp," Watts commented casually. "We could probably take them there. They're sure to have firepower. If they use it, it could turn into a clusterfuck to end all clusterfucks."

Rebecca glanced back at Dell, then at the road. "Detective, you make the call."

Detective, you make the call. Just like that, everything inside Dell went still. Sandy was in the SUV ahead of them. Maybe seriously hurt. An innocent civilian was with her. And her partners, her fellow cops, were in this car waiting for *her* to decide what they would all do next, putting their lives in her hands. What was happening was bigger than her fear, bigger than her anger. If she traded Sandy for any one of the others—the lieutenant, Watts, Sandy's friend—Sandy would never forgive her, and she would have failed in her duty. She'd been trained to lead soldiers in battle. To make the necessary sacrifices. And to never, ever, leave one of her own behind. She had never feared for her own life, and she had been honored to be responsible for the lives of her fellow soldiers.

"Here's the plan," Dell said, her voice steady and strong.

❖

Sandy bit her lip to keep from crying out every time the heavy vehicle hit a rough spot in the road. Her chest hurt and she couldn't take a deep breath without causing a sharp pain to shoot down her side. She leaned against Darla, who steadied her with an arm around her waist.

The Russian next to her grunted what sounded like a curse as a flashing red light shot through the back window. Sandy pushed herself upright, despite the pain. The man sitting next to the driver turned around, the craggy black and red shadows shifting across his face making him look like Hellboy. Only not as hot.

"You do not talk," he said.

The man next to Sandy drew an automatic from under his jacket and placed it on the seat between his leg and Sandy's, his hand on the grip, his finger on the trigger. She glimpsed movement in the front seat and realized both men had their weapons out. The road was almost deserted, with only an occasional vehicle passing. The night was dark. Perfect spot for an ambush. *Oh my God, Dell,* Sandy thought. *Don't be a hero. Please, baby.*

"We won't be starting any conversations," Sandy snorted. "We don't want nothing to do with the fucking cops." Even though every movement felt as if her chest were tearing apart, she shifted closer to the man beside her, ignoring the gun on the seat, and leaned her head against his upper arm. "I'm just sitting back here with my man and my girlfriend. Fuck them if they don't like it."

"Good," the man in the front said, facing forward again as the strobing red light was replaced by a harsh white glare from the cruiser's spotlight.

Sandy tensed as the driver rolled down his window. *God, please don't let them shoot anyone. Please.*

"Good evening, sir," Sandy heard a man say. Not Dell. Not Dell. It didn't sound like Watts, either. "You appear to have a short in your right rear taillight. It keeps blinking on and off."

"I will repair it right away," the driver said.

"Are you sure your electrical system is okay?"

Sandy saw a shadow cross the driver's face as the officer outside the vehicle leaned down and looked in the window.

"Looks like you've got a full house here," the state police officer said. "You don't want to break down out here this time of night. The next service station is a good twenty miles away." He nodded at Sandy.

"I don't imagine the young ladies would enjoy sitting out here in the cold for a few hours."

"Everything looks fine," the driver said, his tone friendly. He gestured to the dashboard. "No warning lights. It must be a loose connection. I will have it repaired immediately."

"All right then. I'll follow you for a few miles to make sure there's no problem." He touched the brim of his hat. "Ladies."

And then he was gone and Sandy could breathe again. The man beside her relaxed infinitesimally, placing his gun back inside his jacket. Sandy slumped, the effort of having held herself upright leaving her sick and dizzy. Awash in sweat, she felt cold and shaky and a little bit like she might throw up. Darla circled Sandy's waist and gently eased her down until her head was pillowed in Darla's lap.

"Close your eyes, honey," Darla said. "We'll be home soon."

Home. Sandy closed her eyes. She really wanted to be home. She wanted Dell.

❖

Rebecca's phone rang and everyone in the car tensed. She found the speaker button and held the phone up for Mitchell and Watts to hear. "Frye."

"Three men, just like you said. Two in front, one in the left rear. Two young females—also in the rear—one Caucasian, one African-American. Both conscious. Looked okay as far as I could tell."

"Did the men seem suspicious?"

"Let's just say I'm glad I'm wearing Kevlar. They didn't look jumpy. They looked cool. Very cool. Professionals."

"You can pull off their tail in another mile. They know you can place them with those two girls. They're not going to do anything that might jog your memory."

"I thought if I asked for IDs I'd be pushing it," the Statie said.

"Agreed. They know you'll have their plates. Better for them to think it was a courtesy stop. Nice work. We owe you one."

"Don't worry." He laughed. "We'll collect."

Frye disconnected and rested her phone in her lap. "That should give Sandy and Darla a little bit of a safety net. Those guys won't want their bosses to know they were stopped, and they're not going to want Sandy and Darla's pictures circulating around the law enforcement channels." She took a quick look at Mitchell. "Good thinking, Detective."

Dell wasn't convinced it was enough. What if the guys operated so far off the grid they wouldn't care if the state police were looking for them? Maybe they'd dump Sandy and Darla's bodies in the river and take their chances. She just hadn't been able to think of any other way to force the men *not* to hurt the girls without the possibility of a gun battle. But what if she'd been wrong? She was so agitated she thought she might puke.

"We'll be back in Center City in twenty minutes," Rebecca said as she punched in a series of numbers with her thumb. "Hey, it's me."

"Are you all right?" Catherine asked instantly.

"I'm fine." Even though she spoke with calm confidence, Rebecca knew Catherine wouldn't really believe it until she saw her. "But we might have a casualty. Sandy. Can you get dressed in case we need you at the hospital?"

Dell concentrated on staying strong for Sandy through whatever was coming, but she had to convince Sandy to quit risking her life for Frye. She just had to, because she wouldn't make it without Sandy.

❖

Sandy heard the crunch of gravel as the Navigator slowed. She opened her eyes and for a few seconds couldn't remember where she was. Then the pain returned. The light inside the SUV had turned gray, the sickly pallor of a rainy winter morning. The driver slammed to a halt and she rolled partially forward, swallowing a moan as Darla clutched her to keep her from falling to the floor.

The rear door opened and the handsome Russian in the sunglasses said, "Get out."

"What about our money?" Sandy slid to the edge of the seat but did not get out. She looked up at him as he stared down at her, his face impassive. She held his gaze. Finally, he laughed shortly, reached into his pocket, and came out with a folded wad of bills. He waved them in the air before turning and walking a few yards away from the Navigator. She followed him, motioning for Darla to wait nearby.

"Okay," Sandy said, holding out her hand. "Give."

With a thin smile, he leaned forward, cupped her right breast in his huge hand, and squeezed as he slid the money inside her blouse.

"You're lucky you and your girlfriend look good together," he said. "The client liked your little show." He pulled on her breast, dragging her closer, and she felt the ridge of his cock against her stomach. His fingers closed around her nipple, twisting until it burned. "Next time, don't interfere. They pay to fuck you any way they want."

"Next time," Sandy said, trying not to gasp as her head swam. "Tell them not to rough us up. Because no one will want to party with you."

"Who says?" He grabbed her hand and squeezed it around his cock. It felt like he had an iron bar in his pants.

Sandy tilted her head back and smiled. "I do. And if you want me to make that rocket blast off the next time I see you, it's going to cost you five bills." She tightened her grip until she knew the pressure bordered between pleasure and pain. For men like him, it was often the same thing.

His voice came out tight, the corners of his mouth white with strain. "What makes you think we'll meet again?"

"Because I know what you want." She twisted her wrist until his breath grew shallow. "And you know it."

He looked toward the car and lowered his voice. "Give me your number."

Sandy told him, squeezing one last time before she yanked her hand out from under his. She wasn't going to let him come for free. She needed him to be thinking about how good it would feel when she finally did him for real.

"We'll want your girlfriend too."

"So call me." Sandy stepped back hoping he couldn't see how badly she was shaking.

He turned and strode to the Navigator, his back rigid. Gravel spewed as the SUV careened out of the lot.

Sandy reached out for Darla, her legs suddenly numb. Distantly she heard Darla call her name as she sank to her knees, then crumpled to the ground. Pinpoints of pain shot into her cheek. Stones. But she could move her head. She heard the roar of the engine again, but she knew she couldn't get up. No matter what they were going to do to her, she couldn't fight anymore. She tried to tell Darla to run, but she couldn't form the words.

A gentle hand slid behind her neck, a strong arm lifted beneath her knees. Then she was cradled against a lean, firm chest. "Dell?"

"Right here, babe."

"'Bout time." Sandy closed her eyes and let herself drift. Safe now.

CHAPTER TWENTY-TWO

I can walk," Sandy said, sounding irritated.

"Well, that's very good news." Catherine ducked lower to reach into the back of the car and brushed a few strands of blond hair off Sandy's cheek. She could only see the part of her face that wasn't cradled against Dell's chest, but even in the poor light, she could see that her mouth was swollen and a streak of blood trailed down her neck. Anger welled within her and she struggled to find the calm that Sandy needed. That Dell needed. "We have rules, you know, even if they don't always make sense. So rather than get me into trouble, why don't you just stay here a few more minutes and then let us give you a ride inside."

"Don't fight it, babe." Dell cradled Sandy in her arms. In the dim light, Dell's pale face looked bloodless, her eyes dark pits of fathomless sorrow. Stroking Sandy's back, she said, "You won't win this one."

"'Kay," Sandy muttered.

Catherine smiled, nodded to Watts, who emerged out of the passenger side like a dark behemoth out of the sea, and squeezed Dell's shoulder. "Just another minute."

When she straightened and turned, she saw Rebecca emerging from the emergency room pushing a stretcher. Her emotions warred in the familiar battle between relief that Rebecca was unhurt and guilt over her happiness, because someone else *was* injured. Sandy. God, Sandy. Barely more than a child and already with a lifetime of pain, and now possibly more. Why was life so unfair? She knew better than most not to ask those questions, but sometimes in the dark hours of the night when she was weary, she couldn't help but ask herself.

She hurried forward. "Let me do that. Are you all right?"

Rebecca stopped the gurney with one hand and cupped Catherine's jaw with the other. She kissed her fleetingly. "I'm okay. This is a mess, though."

"We'll take care of it. Can you see about getting her inside? I'll find Ali." Catherine wanted to tell Rebecca to go inside and sit down. She looked exhausted. But she knew that would be pointless. Rebecca would not rest until Sandy was cared for, and probably not even then. Whatever had happened tonight would demand her attention. They would not, none of them, stand for one of their own being hurt this way.

As Catherine hurried away, she heard Rebecca tell Watts to get Darla's statement. Darla, she assumed, was the frightened young African-American she'd seen getting out of the car. She blinked as the harsh lights assaulted her eyes, and she blamed the sudden tears on that rather than the ache in her heart at the thought of yet more young victims.

Dell couldn't seem to move. She feared once Sandy was inside the hospital she would lose her, even though rationally she knew that wasn't true. Still, how could she protect her if she let her go?

Rebecca leaned into the vehicle and held out her arms. "Give her to me, Mitchell. It's okay."

"I can't," Dell whispered, sheltering Sandy in the curve of her body.

"Yes, you can. You'll be right beside her. You know I won't let anyone hurt her." Rebecca slid her arms around Sandy's shoulders and under her knees, alongside Dell's. "Trust me."

Rebecca's eyes held hers steadily, utterly sure, unwaveringly strong. Dell eased her grip on Sandy, who murmured something she couldn't understand.

"What?" Dell asked hoarsely. "Babe?"

"Everything is all right, baby," Sandy whispered. She opened her eyes and tried to smile. "Stop stressing."

Dell clamped her lower lip between her teeth so tightly she tasted blood. Desperate to believe, she let Rebecca take Sandy from her and settle her onto the stretcher. She felt dizzy as she climbed out of the car, and grabbed the metal railing on the stretcher as much to steady herself as to stay connected to Sandy. "Don't worry. I'm solid."

Sandy closed her eyes. "I know."

Rebecca pulled the stretcher toward the double ER doors. A willowy brunette nurse in navy blue scrubs and a stethoscope dancing around her neck hurried outside and grasped the stretcher opposite Rebecca.

"Dr. Rawlings said you had a patient for us. Trauma two is open. Right down the hall on the left."

"Thanks," Rebecca said. The nurse smiled at her.

"You're Dr. Rawlings's detective."

Rebecca smiled back. "I am."

"This light might bother your eyes, honey. I'm sorry." Ali flicked her penlight quickly between Sandy's left and right eyes, watching the pupils constrict. "Everything looks good here." She clipped the light to the pocket of her scrub shirt and put her hands on her hips. "You didn't lose consciousness?"

"No." Sandy glanced toward the end of the stretcher where Dell stood, her hands still clenched around the metal railing. "I wasn't out. I know what that feels like."

Ali shifted her gaze to Dell. "You might want to wait outside, Dell."

"No. I'm staying."

"Go ahead, baby," Sandy murmured. "This is just routine."

"No."

"Sandy, do you want Dr. Rawlings to come in?"

"No, just go ahead, Doc."

Ali covered Sandy's hand with hers. "Were you sexually assaulted?"

"No one touched me." Sandy's eyes flickered to Dell again. "No one."

"I only care about you being okay," Dell said gruffly.

"You're sure nothing else hurts?" Ali asked.

Sandy started to laugh, but then caught her breath when her ribs screamed in protest. "That's it."

"Once we finish the x-rays, we'll move you upstairs—"

"I want to go home," Sandy said immediately.

Ali blew out an exasperated breath. "Now why doesn't that surprise me?"

"You should stay here, San, if that's what the doctor wants," Dell said.

Sandy frowned. "Oh. Look who's talking. Macho cop who doesn't want to stay in the hospital even after she's been stabbed."

"Ah, Jesus. Save me from the whole bunch of you." Ali pointed at Dell. "See that she stays in bed." She fixed Sandy with a lethal stare. "You take the medications I prescribe and get your butt back here if you develop any problems. All of which I will write down for you." She started toward the curtain that enclosed the cubicle, then looked over her shoulder. "And I really don't want to see any of your team back here again. I'm sick of you all."

Sandy smiled as much as her swollen lip would allow her. "We all love you too."

"Yeah yeah," Ali muttered as the curtain swung closed behind her.

"How is she?" Rebecca asked as soon as she came through the door.

"She's stable, and all things considered, lucky." Ali shook her head. "Scrapes and contusions, probably several cracked ribs. Her face is bruised, but the abrasion on her lip doesn't require sutures. If she weren't eighteen, I'd say she'd be too sore to get out of bed for a few days. But, knowing her, anything is possible." Ali grinned ruefully. "She wants to go home, and there's nothing more we're going to do for her here. I'm inclined to let her go." She glanced at Rebecca. "She needs to stay off the streets for a few days. Until she can move enough to protect herself."

"I'll see to it."

"Isn't there some way you can get these pricks?" Ali gestured toward the hall and the cubicles beyond. "These girls, the streets are eating them alive."

"If I could take her place in there right now, I would."

"Hell. I know. I'm sorry." Ali let out a weary breath and rubbed her forehead. "I'm just tired. Tired of seeing them come in like this." She met Rebecca's gaze. "So take care of it, will you?"

Rebecca smiled wryly. "I'm working on it."

❖

"Look, rookie," Sandy said, "I know Rebecca wants you downstairs with the rest of the team. So go."

"They're just finishing up reports and filling in Sloan and Jason." Dell hovered inside the door of the bedroom in Sloan and Michael's loft. "They don't need me."

"Neither do I. So just go do your job." Sandy couldn't find a comfortable position to lie in. She usually slept on her stomach unless she was with Dell, and then she slept with her leg over Dell's and her head on Dell's shoulder. She wanted Dell in bed with her, but she didn't want Dell thinking she had to babysit her.

"I'll get you some water in case you need to take some more pills."

"I don't want any pills. I don't want any water. I just want you to take off."

Dell shoved her hands in the pockets of her jeans, staring at the floor. "I'm sorry about last night."

"Oh Jesus." Sandy stretched out her arm. "Come here."

"That's okay. I'll just—"

"Now, Dell."

Dell crossed the room in three big strides and knelt by the side of the bed. She grasped Sandy's hand in both of hers and lowered her head until her forehead touched the back of Sandy's hand. After a few seconds, Sandy felt tears on her skin and her heart did the tighten and roll thing that only Dell had ever made it do.

"Baby," Sandy murmured. "Everything is all right, baby."

"I was so freaking scared," Dell whispered without looking up.

"I wasn't. Because I knew you were there. I knew you would find us. And you did."

Dell's head snapped up. "I fucked up. I left you here to go buy Irina a fucking television."

Sandy narrowed her eyes. "You bought her a television?"

"I figured she needed something to do. And the more time she spends inside, the safer she is."

"Yeah well, as long as it isn't flowers. No flowers, right?"

Dell shook her head, grinning weakly.

Sandy stroked her face, brushing away the tears. "You know I still would've gone out whether you were here or not."

"I wouldn't have let you go with those guys."

Sandy sighed. "And what? We let Darla go by herself? She almost got raped, Dell."

"I'm going to fucking kill them."

"No, you're not. You're going to do exactly what Frye tells you to do, because that's who you are. That's your job." When Dell tried to look away, Sandy grabbed her T-shirt and tugged her closer, ignoring the pain that reared up in her chest. "Look at me. Look at me, rookie."

Dell finally met her eyes.

"Promise me. Right now. Promise me you won't do anything crazy. You're a cop, Dell. That's important. It's important to you. It's important to me."

"Oh fuck," Dell whispered. She started to shake and lowered her head again.

"Baby?" Sandy asked gently.

Dell took several long, deep breaths, then raised her head and smiled crookedly. "I'm okay. Long night, you know?"

Sandy laughed. "Yeah. I noticed."

"So I was thinking, after I finish with the meeting downstairs, I could maybe sleep in here. Grab some blankets and a pillow. You know, sleep next to the bed so I wouldn't bother—"

"When you're done, you get in bed with me." Sandy stroked Dell's arm. "I'll sleep better if you're here. You make me feel safe, baby."

Dell swallowed hard. "Okay then. I won't be long." She leaned over and kissed Sandy's forehead. "I love you lots."

"Same here. Go do your cop thing now, baby." Sandy waited until Dell left to try to get comfortable again. She moaned as a hot flash of pain raced around her rib cage.

From the doorway, Michael said, "Can I get you anything?"

"There's some pills on the table next to me," Sandy said, trying to breathe evenly so the pain wouldn't get worse. "I think I might need another one."

"I'll get some water and be right back." A minute later Michael returned. She opened the medication, removed a pill, and handed it to Sandy. Then she sat on the side of the bed and gently slid her arm behind Sandy's shoulders, helping her to sit up so she could sip the water. "I heard about what happened. How are you feeling?"

Sandy leaned against her. "Pretty crappy. Don't tell Dell, though."

"I won't." Michael eased her back onto the pillows. "How are you doing besides the pain?"

"It was scary there for a while." Sandy held Michael's hand. "But I think I'm okay."

"Good. If you need to talk, I'm here. Or Catherine."

"They didn't hurt me. I mean, not the way you're worried about."

Michael sighed. "I don't know what to be worried about first anymore. Or who." She stroked Sandy's hair with her free hand. "So just don't frighten me like this again, okay?"

"Top of my list."

"You should get some sleep."

"Are you okay? You look pretty tired."

Michael smiled a little. "I am tired. Good tired, though."

Sandy grinned. "Oh. Sloan gave you a nice wake-up call."

"No," Michael said playfully. "I gave *her* a nice wake-up call." She rose carefully and tucked in the blankets around Sandy. "I understand you're supposed to stay in bed all day today. I'll check on you later."

"Hey," Sandy called as Michael started toward the door. When Michael looked back, Sandy said shyly, "Thanks."

"You're welcome, sweetie. And remember, I'm here if you need anything."

Sandy closed her eyes. Dell would be back soon. And she was among friends. She didn't need anything else.

CHAPTER TWENTY-THREE

Rebecca nodded to Mitchell, who came into the conference room after everyone else, dressed in the same clothes she'd worn the night before. She looked tired, but steady. "Grab a cup of coffee, Detective."

"I'm okay, Lieutenant." Dell sank into the chair on the far side of Watts. "Sorry I'm late."

"Understood. How's Sandy?"

"Crabby."

"Doing all right, then," Rebecca said with a flicker of a smile before glancing down at her notes. "Okay. Last night confirms what we've suspected all along. The Russians are part of a high-level prostitution game, but they're not likely to be the ones pulling the strings. They're doing a lot of the ground-level work—procuring and delivering the girls. Providing security." She looked at Jason, who was rapidly keying data into the laptop in front of him. "You have those images for us yet?"

"Coming…now." Jason hit a few more keys and images appeared on a screen built into the wall at the end of the conference room.

Rebecca squinted. The images were murky, the resolution poor. "Can you clean those up at all?"

Jason raised a brow.

"Sorry," Rebecca said dryly. "Foolish question."

"Give me a minute," Jason said, working away. "When I get these into my other program I'll be able to do better for you."

"There—that's good for now. Thanks." Rebecca waited while the entire series of images Sandy had taken flicked across the screen. "We got three names from the license photos Sandy shot. Two businessmen with strong ties to local government and a city comptroller. I recognize at least one of the others. A state senator."

Sloan said, "There's no way men like that would do business directly with the Russian mob."

"No," Rebecca said. "They wouldn't. They would only trust someone who moved in their circles. Someone they considered one of them."

"The Zamoras?" Watts said skeptically. "Why would these guys trust them?"

"Not *them*, necessarily," Rebecca said. "But Kratos. Remember, he's kept himself apart from the family business, at least on the surface. The good brother. He's just a businessman."

"Yeah." Watts pulled a face. "And I'm the next chief of detectives too."

"Sandy got us the kind of intel it might've taken us months to get. These guys." Rebecca waved a hand at the screen where Jason had arranged the images in a series of headshots. "One of them will talk."

"Maybe," Sloan said. "If Clark doesn't get to them first."

"Clark doesn't know we have this information. And for now, that's exactly the way it's going to stay."

"That's not gonna win you points for interagency cooperation, Loo," Watts said. "Could put you in a tight spot, especially since the brass told us to play nice with the feds."

Rebecca rolled her shoulders, fighting a headache that had beat at the back of her skull for the last two hours. "If anyone in the PPD thinks this unit is going to lay down so Clark can fuck us over again, then they haven't been paying attention."

Watts grinned. Sloan stared at the table, her expression remote.

"So what does that mean for Mitch's part of the operation? Him and Irina?" Watts asked. "Maybe Sandy got us everything we need."

"Sandy only got us a piece," Dell said before Rebecca could answer. "Those pictures don't tell us who's putting the clients and the Russians together. We need the connection, hopefully someone close to Zamora, and Irina knows the men who know *them*. Those are the guys we want. Irina can get me close to the key players. And then we can put on some real pressure."

"I agree," Rebecca said. "We've got verification of one piece of the puzzle. But we need someone higher up than street-level soldiers like the men who picked Sandy up last night." She nodded at Dell. "We still need Irina, and I imagine the Russians want her brought back in. They know she's alive. And they know how much she knows. I think it will be safer and smarter if she initiates contact now. A show of good faith on her part."

"What if she can't bring me in with her?" Dell glanced round the table uncomfortably. "You said it yourself. She knows a lot. They could decide she knows too much, especially since the house she lived in was raided."

"If it looks like she's in trouble, we'll pull her out and try to get Sandy back in again. That's probably a good idea anyhow. We know these guys are interested in—"

Dell shot to her feet. "No!"

Watts coughed into his hand and muttered, "Sit down, kid."

Rebecca stared down the length of the table at Mitchell, watching the young detective struggle with her emotions. After a few seconds she said to the room in general, "Would everyone take a break, please. Except for Detective Mitchell." After the door closed behind their colleagues, she said, "You have an objection you would like to make, Detective?"

Dell automatically stepped to attention. "Yes ma'am, I do. If I might speak freely."

"Go ahead."

"Sandy's hurt. They could have killed her last night. She's not trained to do this."

"Do what, Detective?"

"Work undercover," Dell shot back. "She doesn't know how to fight. She doesn't carry a gun. She doesn't have any goddamn backup."

"And you conclude from this?" Rebecca asked. "As a cop, Mitchell, not as her lover."

Dell sucked in a breath. "The risk of sending her back in again is unacceptable."

Rebecca scanned the faces of the men in the images splayed across the wall, a silent gallery of users and abusers. She wondered fleetingly what separated her from them, and if the shield of justice was after all only a façade to hide the crimes of those sworn to uphold the law.

"I won't argue, although I don't completely agree." Rebecca spoke quietly, trying to separate the cop in her from the woman and the friend. After a few seconds, she stopped trying because she could only be who she was. "But I will point out this. Sandy *is* trained. More than you for the work you're doing with Irina." When Dell started to protest, Rebecca cut her off. "She has street training. Real-life experience. She handled herself perfectly last night. Probably better than you would have. Or me."

Rebecca sighed. "She got into trouble not because of the situation, but because she did what she would've done if she'd been in a bar on Delaware or a street corner on Arch. She defended one of her own. It had nothing to do with her being at that party because of this investigation."

"You're saying it's her fault," Dell said flatly.

Rebecca shrugged. "Probably as much as it's your fault you got stabbed or my fault that I got shot. We do what we do because we can't do anything else. Neither can she." Rebecca put her hands flat on the table and leaned forward. "I guarantee you this, Mitchell. If we tell her to stop, she's going to laugh in our faces and go out there on her own. And I for one would rather know where she is and what she's doing. I'd rather be sitting in a car on the street in front of that hotel than sixty miles away."

Dell looked down at the floor. When she spoke, her voice was low and rough. "You know her better than I do. You'd probably be better for her than me."

"Well, that's fucked-up logic on many levels." Rebecca laughed. "Forgetting Catherine, which is impossible, I don't love Sandy the way you do. Not with my last breath. So unless there's something else you want to say to me, I think we should let that topic rest."

"Noted."

"Look, Mitchell. It's been a hard night. We're all tired. And before you and I decide what's best for Sandy, we'd better check with her."

Dell finally smiled. "Oh yeah. Not a bad idea."

"That's why I'm the lieutenant." Rebecca walked around the table and dropped her hand on Dell's shoulder. "If she goes out again, I promise you she'll have backup. They didn't check the girls last night.

They don't think of these girls as a threat. That's to our advantage. We'll wire her somehow."

"Okay." Dell colored. "I'm sorry for the outburst, Lieutenant."

"Forget it. I'd have done the same." Rebecca thumped Dell lightly on the arm. "In fact, I have. Now let's get the team back in here and work out a plan to put these guys out of business."

❖

"Okay. Jason." Rebecca pointed. "Your job is to ID the rest of the clients. DMV, Armed Forces databases, newspaper archives. You know the drill. They're too high profile to be hidden. Run the SUV plates... maybe we'll get lucky there and turn a name that isn't fake."

"On it." Jason closed his laptop, tucked it under his arm, and headed out into the main office.

"Mitchell. Get some sleep. Then I want you to show Irina copies of these photos. See if she can ID the Russians or any of the clients."

"I'll see her tonight," Dell said.

"Right. Good." Rebecca turned to Watts. "I'm going to pay Clark a visit later. You stay close in case Mitchell needs backup. Mitchell... Watts is your first call if you so much as go out for pizza with Irina."

"Make sure you call me, kid." Watts shrugged into his raincoat. "I thought I'd check to see if we've turned up anything on the computer forensics at the pier too."

Rebecca grinned. "Do that."

With the room emptying, Rebecca faced Sloan, who closed the door behind Watts and leaned against it. She'd been wondering if this moment would come. "Okay. Let's hear it."

Sloan hooked her thumb over the waistband of her jeans. "Hear what?"

"Whatever it is you've been chewing on the last couple of days. Trying to decide whether to handle it on your own or not."

"What makes you think that?" Sloan held Rebecca's gaze without blinking, her eyes a cold, flat indigo. Storm clouds at sunset on a winter night. When Rebecca said nothing Sloan grinned wryly. "Okay. You know how we've been thinking Clark's ultimate goal is to use us to turn someone in Zamora's organization?"

"SOP for the feds. They make most of their cases by squeezing the guys they're trying to put away until somebody cracks and makes a deal. This time we're the nutcracker."

Sloan nodded. "So I think someone on the other side is looking for the same thing."

Everything in Rebecca went completely still. Fury ate at the edges of her control. She would not tolerate an assault on her team. Not on the streets. Not in secret. Not anywhere. "Who?"

"Me."

"Michael?" Rebecca couldn't think of any other threat that would be powerful enough to tempt Sloan to cross a line. And she knew with absolute certainty that Sloan had been considering it for the last two days. The question was, what line. Rebecca could not imagine Sloan betraying the team, which left only one option. "How did they get to you?"

Sloan gestured to her laptop and pulled a jump drive from her pocket. "Sit down. I'll show you."

Rebecca yanked out a chair at the conference table and Sloan slid the laptop in front of her. Rebecca watched the images of Michael with Kratos Zamora flash by, one after the other. "Son of a bitch."

"Yes." Sloan removed the jump drive and slipped it back into her pocket.

"Have a seat." When Sloan hesitated, Rebecca said, "Don't fight me on this, Sloan."

Wordlessly, Sloan sat across from Rebecca.

"Have they approached you with an offer?"

"No."

Rebecca frowned. "Then what the hell have you been trying to work out for the last few days?"

Sloan shrugged. "Whether I was going to take out Zamora. And if I did whether that would neutralize the threat."

"Oh for Christ's sake. Who else knows about this?"

"No one."

"Michael?"

Sloan shook her head.

"Jesus." Rebecca wanted to climb over the table and knock Sloan on her ass. The problem was, she understood. And she also understood that Sloan could not be contained by the ordinary rules of engagement.

She had not been trained that way and she didn't have the temperament for it. She was as close to rogue as a member of a team could be and still be trustworthy. But Rebecca trusted her. She trusted her because Sloan was sitting across from her right now telling her she'd been considering her own brand of justice. "Can we prove who sent the pictures?"

"No, and we never will be able to. I can tell you where they came from." Sloan shrugged. "Well. Not just yet, but soon. But that doesn't prove who entered the data. And, unless an overt threat is made, they're just pictures. Michael was at a business meeting. Zamora moves in the same circles. No crime in that."

"But you think you can get a name."

"I guarantee it."

"I don't want you to take a single breath between the time you know the name and the time you call me with it. Are we clear?" Rebecca watched Sloan's eyes, because the answer would determine the future of their team and their friendship.

Not a muscle flickered in Sloan's face until she said, "Crystal, Lieutenant."

Rebecca shoved to her feet, suddenly very tired. "I'm going to grab a few hours' sleep. Then talk to Clark."

"What are you going to tell him about this?"

"I'm not going to tell him anything. If he knew, he'd bury you so deep you wouldn't see daylight for a year."

"He could try."

"He could do it." Rebecca stopped with her hand on the doorknob. "I want you on this team. I need you on this team. And Michael needs you with her. You're not alone anymore, Sloan." She opened the door, then looked back. "And if anyone kicks your ass, it will be me."

❖

Michael stood by the windows and looked out at the river. Sloan was somewhere behind her. The loft was dark, the only light coming from the fireplace. The reddish glow reflected off the walls of glass as if the world were on fire. For a few terrifying moments, Michael felt as if her life was crumbling to ashes. She'd listened to what Sloan told her, trying to take it in. She'd understood the facts, but she had no context for the actions. She had no reference point in her life for such events.

She wasn't frightened by what Sloan told her, but she was terrified by the fact that Sloan had not told her until now.

"What did Rebecca say?"

Sloan stood a few feet away, afraid to cross the gap between them. Michael's hair shimmered like red gold, and her slender frame looked fragile and so far away. Sloan's chest constricted with the sudden fear that Michael would somehow slip into the night and she would lose her. "Something along the lines that I'm an ass. That if I didn't do exactly what she said she'd kick mine."

Michael turned, hugging herself. "She's right. On both counts. Except she might have to get in line for the ass kicking part. Behind me."

"I'm sorry."

"Not good enough." Michael crossed the few feet between them and slapped her palm against Sloan's chest. "You think so little of me that you don't trust me to handle a problem? How do you think that makes me feel?"

"Michael, I—"

"Am I your partner, Sloan? Or just the woman who keeps your bed warm?"

Sloan jerked back. "God, Michael! I love you. I love you with all my heart. You're the only thing in my life that really matters to me."

Michael cupped Sloan's face in both hands and kissed her softly on the mouth. Then she drew back and stared into her eyes. "Then treat me that way, Sloan. Not like I might break. Not like I might leave you because I'm angry or because things are dangerous or difficult. Treat me like I'm the woman you want to stand by your side. Forever."

Sloan started to shake and looked away, but not before Michael saw the glitter of tears on her cheeks. Her anger evaporated, replaced by an enormous, aching need to take away her pain. "Oh, baby." She pulled Sloan into her arms and stroked the back of her head. "I love you. I love you even when you're an ass."

"I'm sorry," Sloan whispered, burying her face in Michael's neck.

"I know. And later," Michael said, pulling Sloan's T-shirt from her jeans, "I'm going to want to know everything that Rebecca said." She slid her hands up Sloan's back, then down the tight muscles on either side of her spine. She kissed Sloan's neck and dug her fingers into

Sloan's tight butt, dragging Sloan against her body. "And everything that you're going to do about it." She sucked Sloan's earlobe, then bit down until Sloan groaned. "But first, I want to go into the bedroom."

She insinuated one hand between their bodies and cupped Sloan's crotch, squeezing the soft denim in her palm. "I want you to make love to me." She caught Sloan's lower lip between her teeth and tugged, then slipped her tongue into Sloan's mouth. She toyed with Sloan's tongue, teasing and taunting until she was breathless and Sloan's hands were on her breasts, inflaming her. "What do you say, Sloan?"

"Yes," Sloan gasped. "I say yes."

"Why offer her Witsec when we can get what we need without it?" Clark drained the glass of bourbon and gestured to the hotel bartender for a refill.

Rebecca sipped her coffee, wondering if Clark actually had a house or if he just moved from one hotel to another. She thought about going home to Catherine that morning, of crawling into bed and having Catherine join her. Falling asleep with Catherine's arms around her, just holding her. Just being there. For a fraction of a millisecond she almost felt sorry for Clark. And then she thought about Irina and the other girls who were nothing but pawns to him. Players on a game board. She realized in that instant that appealing to his better instincts was pointless. She knew how he saw the world. His was the righteous path, and the end always justified any means. Collateral losses were simply the cost of doing business.

"She has a picture of her sister, but she won't give it up to us because she doesn't trust us. If we find the sister, we'll have more leverage on Irina and we'll also have another girl on the inside." Rebecca drank more coffee but it tasted like acid as she said what she knew she needed to say. "New identities and protection for both of them. The cost is nothing compared to how big this will be if we make the case against the Russians. And if we connect them to someone bigger." Rebecca shrugged. She didn't need to tell Clark it was a career-making case.

"All right. I'll see what I can do."

"I'll need to have her meet with the federal marshals to convince her." Rebecca pushed the coffee away. "She's not your biggest fan."

Clark snorted. "You're breaking my heart." He finished off his bourbon. "I'll set it up."

"Thanks." Rebecca walked out of the bar, the scent of bourbon lingering in her consciousness. She opened her phone and punched in a number. "I'll be home in twenty minutes. Can you throw some things in a bag—enough for overnight."

"Where are we going?" Catherine asked.

"I don't know. Somewhere not here. Just us."

"That's just what I need."

"Yeah. Me too." Rebecca closed the phone and took a deep breath of the chill night air. "Me too."

CHAPTER TWENTY-FOUR

Dell put the pizza box on the counter next to the six-pack of beer she'd picked up at the corner deli. The television was turned to a nature show. Irina sat cross-legged on the bed, barefoot in black tights and a cobalt blue sweater. Without makeup and with her dark, wavy hair loose around her shoulders, she looked much younger than Dell had previously thought.

"How old are you?" she asked.

"Twenty-three."

Dell slid a piece of cheese pizza on a paper plate and carried it to Irina, then went back to get extra napkins and a piece for herself. Irina shifted over on the mattress, which she'd covered with a floral print sheet and lime green blanket, and Dell sat on the corner of the bed, her booted feet stretched out in front of her.

"If you had called me, I would have cooked you something to eat," Irina said.

"You don't need to do that. But thanks." Dell took a bite of her pizza as she framed her next question. The topic was sensitive and she didn't want Irina to close down. "Your sister's younger, isn't she?"

"She will be seventeen next month." Irina crumpled the napkin she was holding.

"Fuck," Dell muttered, but before she could ask her next question a hand slid along the inside of her thigh and Irina changed the subject.

"You aren't dressed to go out tonight."

"No." Dell methodically chewed her pizza and ignored Irina's hand. Maybe if she didn't make a big deal out of it, Irina wouldn't either. "My lieutenant thinks it's a good idea for you to contact Olik, though. Call him and tell him you feel safer now, as long as you have Mitch, and you want to come back in." Dell glanced at Irina. "It's important that I go with you. Olik isn't going to hurt you with a witness there, Irina."

The assurance sounded more confident than realistic. Dell was pretty sure Olik wouldn't want a boyfriend hanging around, seeing too much. He'd have to convince Olik he could be useful.

Irina's fingers drifted higher, skimming Dell's crotch. "If I bring Mitch, Olik will be angry."

"What will he do?" Dell covered Irina's hand and placed it on the bed between them.

"I don't know. He will test us."

Dell thought of the undercover narco detectives who were forced to sample drugs during drug buys to prove they weren't cops. Some of them developed a taste for the product they were trying to eradicate. She wasn't exactly certain what Olik might want, but she couldn't worry about that. "That's okay. We'll be fine."

"So you say, new boy," Irina said softly.

Dell pulled the envelope from the inside pocket of her jacket and showed Irina the images Jason had printed. "Do you know any of these men?"

Frowning, Irina took the photos and sorted through them. Once or twice she slowed and Dell noticed her hands trembling.

"What? You recognize someone?" Dell probed.

Irina's mouth tightened. "I know the big man, Sergei. He is one of Olik's men."

"What does he do, exactly?" Dell's heart raced. This was the kind of information they needed.

"He…" Irina hesitated, as if searching for words. "He makes sure that the girls get to the parties or the movie set or wherever Olik wants them to go. Then he stays to make sure no one bothers them. That the girls behave. That the customers are satisfied."

"He's an enforcer—like the guy in the club the other night?"

Irina shook her head. "No. He is more like an officer. Not a regular soldier." She looked frustrated. "I'm sorry. I don't know how to explain."

"No, I get it. He's one of Olik's lieutenants. How high up is Olik?"

"I don't know for sure."

Dell thought for a second. "You've been to these parties. These movie shoots. That Olik arranges, right?"

Irina nodded.

"Where? Where were they?"

"All over. Here. New York City. Washington, once."

Dell wanted to shout. The Mid-Atlantic corridor. Moving women, girls, between states for the purpose of prostitution was going to buy someone a lot of years in federal prison. "That's good. You're doing great."

Irina smiled. "I made a mistake, believing men like Olik back in Russia. I have been paying for that ever since."

"You did what you had to do." Dell squeezed Irina's hand. "And you're doing the right thing now."

"I will leave a message at Ziggie's. Olik usually comes around on Wednesday nights. To check on the girls. Collect money, I think. I'll say I want to meet him."

"Okay," Dell said. "Mitch and you. Ziggie's. Wednesday night."

❖

"Rebecca, darling," Catherine murmured, stroking Rebecca's face, "it's time to get up."

The night before they'd driven an hour outside the city to a small bed and breakfast in the mountains. After an unhurried, intimate dinner, they'd gone to bed early with a fire burning in the fireplace in their room. Rebecca had fallen asleep in her arms, and Catherine hated to wake her. She studied her lover's face in the predawn light. The bruises hadn't completely faded yet and now smudges of fatigue were visible beneath her eyes. If she had her wish, they would stay here for a week, to heal in body and soul. But that was not to be.

"Rebecca," Catherine whispered.

Usually, even when completely exhausted, Rebecca would awaken at full alert, but not this morning. She murmured something unintelligible and rolled closer, pressing her face to Catherine's breast.

Catherine felt her nipples tighten and the familiar stirring in the pit of her stomach, and even though she knew they needed to get up soon if they were going to beat the rush-hour traffic back to the city, she responded to an even greater need. Not for the sex, but for something far more important. Sliding her fingers through the short thick hair at the base of Rebecca's neck, she cradled Rebecca's head and guided her nipple into Rebecca's mouth. She gasped in surprise at the swift tug of teeth against her already turgid flesh.

"You're awake, you faker."

Rebecca shifted her hips and pushed her leg between Catherine's, forcing her onto her back and following her over. "I wanted to see if you were really worried about the traffic."

"I think you have your answer," Catherine said, knowing Rebecca must feel the rush of wetness where her thigh was pressed to Catherine's center. "I do have appointments, though."

"Don't worry," Rebecca murmured, kissing her way down Catherine's body. "I'll use the siren."

❖

Six hours later, Catherine leaned back in her office chair and closed her eyes, allowing herself a few minutes to relive the earlier moments of pleasure. The sex had been wonderful, but what lingered with her now was the unique feeling of connection to Rebecca that she shared with no one else in her life. Between clients, she thought about calling her just to hear her voice, but then she remembered that Rebecca had said she would be in court that morning and unavailable. Because the HPCU functioned outside the normal hierarchy of the department, Catherine often forgot that Rebecca still had to perform the routine duties of any other detective. The phone call would have to wait until the afternoon.

Just as she reached for a stack of insurance forms, her secretary rang.

"The special appointment you're expecting has arrived," Joyce said with a hint of disapproval. She'd informed Catherine in no uncertain terms earlier that morning that there was no time in her schedule to squeeze in another patient. She'd been very unhappy when Catherine told her she would work through her lunch hour.

"Thank you. Detective Mitchell is with her?"

"Yes."

"Send them both in, please."

"You have clinic at one," Joyce said curtly.

"I know. Thank you."

"Do you want me to get you a salad to take with you?" Joyce asked in a conciliatory tone.

"That would be wonderful. You're a dream."

"I know."

Catherine smiled to herself as she waited for Joyce to bring Dellon and Irina back. When the door opened, she walked around her desk to greet them. The beautiful young woman with Dellon was not what she'd expected. In Catherine's experience, criminals tended to be either extremely guarded, hostile, or psychopathically charming. This woman appeared to be confident and without subterfuge. Her gaze was clear eyed and direct, and she regarded Catherine with a mixture of curiosity and suspicion.

Adjusting her expectations for the interview, Catherine shook hands with her as the introductions were made, then asked, "Do you know why we asked you to come in to talk to me?"

Irina sat on the edge of the armchair as though poised to flee at the first opportunity. "Mitch said if we talked, it might help the police."

"Ordinarily, I don't discuss with the police the things I talk about with my clients," Catherine said, settling back into the chair behind her desk. "Are you comfortable with Mitch being here? Because you do know Mitch is a police officer."

Irina smiled. "I know who he is. He can hear what we say."

"Detective Mitchell?" Catherine said. "If at any point Irina wishes you to leave, I'll ask you to do that and what we discuss after that time will be confidential."

"I understand, ma'am."

"Before we talk about what's happened to you since you arrived here," Catherine said, "I wonder if you could tell me a little bit about your life before. Where you grew up. Detective Mitchell said you have a sister. What about the rest of your family?"

"My sister is my only family," Irina said. After a slight pause, she told them in a dispassionate voice of the small Russian village where she grew up. Of her father who died in an accident when she was too young to remember him. Of her mother, uneducated and unskilled, who had barely been able to provide for them. Of the men who offered young girls a way out of poverty, a chance to realize their dreams in a bright and shiny new world.

For the first time, her voice faltered and she looked down at her hands. "I brought my sister here and now I cannot protect her." Tears glittered on her lashes and she turned to Mitch, reaching out a hand. "Even if we find her, how can I get her away from these men?"

Dell clasped Irina's hand. "There might be something we can do about that. I didn't tell you before, because it's not totally set up yet, but my lieutenant called me this morning. She's arranging for you and your sister to go into the witness protection plan. When we find her."

"Protection?" Irina looked uncertain. "We will have to go away?"

"Yes." Dell explained the plan, trying to make the legal process sound more straightforward than it really was. "You'll be sent somewhere secret where you can start fresh. You'll have people to help you. And you'll be safe."

"What if we do not want this? To go away?"

"Irina," Catherine said gently. "You don't have to decide that right now. You'll be able to talk to the federal marshals who are in charge of the program. Then you can decide. But Mitch and the other police officers want to help you and your sister."

"Not the man who put me in jail," Irina said. "He does not want to help me."

"Ah," Catherine said. "Forgive me. I was speaking of the officers who work with Mitch. You can trust them."

Irina threaded her fingers through the detective's. "I trust Mitch."

Catherine understood the message. Irina believed Mitch and probably no one else. "Tell me about your sister."

Irina picked up the purse she had placed by her feet. She rummaged in it for a few seconds, then withdrew a photograph and handed it to Catherine. "This is her. She was only thirteen in this picture." She smiled sadly. "She looks different now."

"We can have our artist work with the image," Dell said. "Change it until it looks more like her now."

"You will not need to," Irina said. "You already have a better picture of her."

Dell frowned. "I don't understand."

"You showed it to me last night."

❖

"We finally got a bit of a break," Rebecca told Sloan and Jason when she arrived at the HPCU headquarters. "One of the girls Sandy got a shot of at the party the other night is Irina's sister."

"Which one?" Jason said, pulling up the images.

"Give me the full-room shot." Rebecca leaned down and pointed to one of two girls flanking a distinguished-looking man in his sixties. He was fondling one girl's breasts while the other girl worked the erection that jutted through his open fly. She pointed to the girl with her hand on his penis. "That's her."

"And that's the Most Reverend Joseph Thomas," Jason announced. "He's that bishop who's been getting all the press for wanting to root out gay priests, even if they're celibate."

"Shit," Rebecca muttered. If politics weren't bad enough, now she had a high-ranking cleric in the middle of her case. "This has the makings of a real media nightmare."

"You know," Sloan said, "as soon as Clark gets wind of this, that's the guy he's going to go after. The church will want the priest to cooperate and turn state's evidence. The other guys in this photo—they might get fancy lawyers to keep their names out of the paper, protect their interests. But with a priest, nothing has to be made public and he's still completely fucked if they ship him off to some backwater parish. His political power and influence within the church will go up in smoke."

"And once Clark gets his witness," Jason added, "he's not going to care about anything else. He might even convince the brass to pull the plug on our end of things."

"Which leaves us with nothing," Rebecca said, thinking about the men who would still be left to take advantage of girls like Sandy. "Jason, print me out a copy of Bishop Thomas and his friends. I feel the need for a little salvation coming on."

❖

Rebecca knocked on the door to Sandy's room. "You decent?"

"No. Come on in."

Laughing, Rebecca pushed the door open. Sandy, wearing a PPD T-shirt, sat up in bed, the covers pooled around her waist. She had an open magazine in her lap. The left side of her face was swollen and when she tossed the magazine aside, she moved carefully.

"Mind a visitor for a few minutes?"

"No, I wanted to talk to you anyhow." Sandy patted the space beside her. "You can sit here. I'm too sore to jump your bones."

There was no chair in the room, so Rebecca sat where Sandy indicated and clasped her hands around her bent knee. "How are the ribs?"

"They're okay as long as I don't move too fast or poke them."

"I'm sorry about the other night."

Sandy narrowed her eyes. "Why? You didn't hit me."

"You shouldn't have been out without backup. Not on this operation." Rebecca shook her head. "We should have placed an undercover cop with you. Someone from vice, maybe."

"No way," Sandy said dismissively. "You know these guys can smell a cop in the next state. Plus, you're not going to have anyone young enough. These guys, they like them young. I'm surprised I made the cut."

"You look young, Sandy." Rebecca took a deep breath. "I don't want you going out again."

Sandy sat up straighter, then grimaced. "Fuck."

Rebecca put her hand on Sandy's arm. "Hey. Take it easy. I didn't come here to upset you."

"Then stop acting like you get a say in my life."

"I get a say in what you do for me. And I say—"

"Look, I feel like shit. I don't want to fight with you, okay?" Sandy covered Rebecca's hand.

The contact was so out of character that Rebecca took a few seconds to react. "I'm sorry. I shouldn't have brought it up right now. I just wanted to make sure you were okay."

"I will be." Sandy withdrew her hand. "But I'm glad you came by. There's something I need to talk to you about. Something I don't want you to tell Dell."

"Sandy." Rebecca shook her head. "She's my officer. Hell. And you're my CI. I knew this was a bad idea."

Sandy laughed and then caught herself, rubbing her side. "Just listen. Okay? You think you can do that?"

"I'll try, but it's not my strong suit."

"Yeah, no kidding." Sandy hitched up the oversized T-shirt that had fallen down over her shoulder. "Here's the deal."

When she finished, Rebecca studied her for a long moment. Sandy held her gaze, looking years older than her age.

"You sure?"

"Yeah. I really am."

"Okay then."

Sandy's eyes flashed. "You mean it?"

"Yes. I mean it." Rebecca squeezed Sandy's knee. "But you have to deal with Mitchell. And soon."

"Okay," Sandy said with a sigh. "I will."

Chapter Twenty-Five

A lone in the office, Sloan stared at the screen. A lot more than a minute had passed since she'd traced the IP address for the computer where the images of Michael and Zamora had originated and pulled up a name and address for the account. Frye expected her to provide the details as soon as she was certain, preferably within sixty seconds. *Before* she took action. That was the part Sloan struggled with, because as soon as she turned over the information, what happened next would be out of her hands. And Michael's safety was at risk.

She tilted her head back and closed her eyes, trying to sort through the labyrinth of choices, some of which would take her well outside the law.

"What's the matter?" Michael said from behind her.

"I'm pretty sure if I open my eyes," Sloan said, not moving, "I'm going to see the Sword of Damocles right above my head."

"So if I've got this right," Michael began to knead the bunched muscles in Sloan's shoulders, "you know something you're not certain you want to know. That's not like you."

"I know." Sloan opened her eyes, swiveled her chair around, and tugged Michael onto her lap. Kissing her neck, she said, "I think I'm losing my edge."

"No, you're not. You're finding a different edge." Michael rested her cheek against the top of Sloan's head. "Tell me."

Sloan hesitated. Involving Michael went against every instinct she had. Her need for secrecy, her need to protect, her need to mete out justice according to her own rules. She'd lived by those tenets all her life, and the one time she'd broken her own rules, she'd paid with her career and a huge piece of her heart. But all that had transpired before Michael. And now everything had changed.

She took a breath, and before she could question where this new path would take her, she said, "I know who sent the pictures of you and Zamora. I'm supposed to tell Frye." She looked at her watch. "Twenty-two minutes ago."

"Why haven't you?"

"Why aren't you asking me who it is?"

Michael caressed the side of Sloan's neck. "Because I care about you more than I care about them."

"If I tell Rebecca, then what happens will be beyond my control."

"What do you want to do that Rebecca would stop you from doing?" Michael asked as calmly as she could, but her heart was racing and she felt slightly sick to her stomach. She didn't fear what Sloan was capable of, only what Sloan might suffer as a consequence of her actions. She felt as if she were walking through a minefield, but *she* would not be the victim of a misstep. Sloan would. Michael was certain of only one thing. All that mattered was helping Sloan find her way to a decision that would not destroy her. "Baby?"

"I want to pay her a visit."

Michael stiffened. "Her?"

"Yes. The redhead you saw talking to me at the fund-raiser the other night." Sloan laughed shortly. "I guess that wasn't a coincidence."

"Apparently not," Michael said coolly. "What kind of game do you think she's playing?"

"I imagine they're hoping to buy my cooperation with a threat to you."

"So why would she reveal herself to you at all? Why not a phone call? A message on your computer?" Michael walked a few paces away, then spun around. "She might be in league with Zamora, or someone like that. But she's got her own agenda." Michael pointed a finger at Sloan. "And you are on the menu."

Sloan's eyebrows rose. "Me?"

"Darling, you are so clueless sometimes." Michael walked back and leaned down, gripping the chair arms on either side of Sloan's body.

"I thought at one point the other night, when I noticed the two of you together, that she was flirting with you, but I told myself it was just my imagination. Obviously it wasn't. She has designs on you."

"Designs?" Sloan thought back to the business card and the phone number. "She gave me her card. With her home number on it."

"Did she?" Michael studied Sloan through narrowed eyes. "Does that happen to you often? Women you've just met giving you their number?"

"Not anymore." Sloan held up her left hand, where she wore a platinum band that matched the one on Michael's finger. "But I knew something was off, that's why I kept it."

Sloan lifted Michael's arms away from the chair and kissed her soundly as she stood up. Talia Ballenger had made a mistake by revealing herself. She'd misjudged just how meaningless Sloan found the attentions of any other woman except Michael.

"Not so fast." Michael grabbed the back of Sloan's shirt when she would have hurried away. "What are you going to do?"

"Why, I'm going to call Rebecca, of course." Sloan pulled Michael close and kissed her once again. "What else?"

❖

"Thank you for seeing me on such short notice, Bishop Thomas," Rebecca said, taking the chair he indicated across from his desk.

The Most Reverend Joseph Thomas was even more distinguished looking in person than the poor-resolution photograph had conveyed. He wore a black suit and dark shirt with a clerical collar. His steel gray hair was thick and expertly cut, his body fit, and his face tanned and healthy. His blue eyes regarded her with speculation.

"How can I help you, Officer?"

"Lieutenant." Rebecca crossed her legs and regarded him silently for a moment, letting him look her over. She waited until his gaze flicked away. "I wonder if you could account for your whereabouts Saturday evening from, say, ten p.m. until three a.m.?"

"I can't think why you would need to know that," he said with casual confidence.

"I imagine if you gave it a little time, you would." Rebecca smiled.

"Since it was only a few days ago, I suspect you remember. So perhaps you would just indulge me so that I won't have to take up any more of your time. I'm sure you're busy."

Bishop Thomas's eyes became glacial. "Do I need to consult an attorney, Lieutenant?"

"I don't know." Rebecca withdrew the photo from her inside pocket. She'd had Jason print it on photo paper, highlighting the date and time stamp. She slid it across the desk to him. "What do you think?"

He looked at the photo for a long moment without picking it up. Then he pushed it back to her, obviously knowing that other copies existed and that keeping that one would not protect him. Rebecca was impressed with his control. He was faced with potentially ruinous exposure, and if they could find the girls in the photograph and prove their ages, he could be prosecuted for rape and would undoubtedly go to prison. Still, by all outward appearances, he was unruffled.

"The fact that you're here and haven't gone to my superiors or," he laughed humorlessly, "simply arrested me, tells me there's something that you want."

"There are a lot of things that I want," Rebecca said softly. "I would be happy just to see you in prison, and if that's all I can get out of this, that will be enough."

"But?" He steepled his fingers under his chin, as if waiting patiently for *her* to confess so that he could absolve her of her sins.

For a few seconds, Rebecca wondered if he really believed he was above the law. "Arresting you would make my day. But I'd rather make my week or even a whole month. I want the men who organized this little soirée." She held up her hand before he could speak. "And you know who they are. If you want to plead ignorance, you certainly may. But then I'm going to walk you out of this building in handcuffs and let the lawyers fight it out. And I guarantee you'll spend time in a cell while they do."

The bishop nodded. "I don't suppose you'd care that I have some very important friends who might be unhappy if you did that."

"Not a bit."

"No, I didn't think so. What do you want?"

"I want to know how it works. Who you call when you want… What? A date?"

He winced. "A companion."

Rebecca thought of the young girl with her hand on the man's penis, and the fact that he could sit across from her as if it hadn't happened. She had to struggle not to cuff him on the spot. "I want to know who you call. Who gives instructions as to where to go. Who do you pay? I want to know how it works."

"And then?"

"And then I want you to request an evening's companionship."

❖

"You're overstepping on this, Lieutenant," ADA Eva Dunbar snapped when Rebecca laid out the plan for her.

After she'd left the Bishop Thomas, Rebecca had called the thirty-five-year-old African-American prosecutor and asked her to meet in a coffee bar near City Hall. She'd chosen Dunbar because she'd worked with her a few times before and knew she had a sense of the big picture. Dunbar wasn't about a quick and easy win if there was a bigger prize to be had, even if there was some risk involved.

"If you're not interested, I'm sure the feds will be."

Eva Dunbar wore a deep red Armani suit with a thin black shell and heels. She and Rebecca were nearly the same height, but Dunbar's body was fuller than Rebecca's. When she leaned across the table, her dark eyes sparked with irritation. "I'm not a rookie, Rebecca."

"I know," Rebecca said with a slight smile. "That's why I picked you."

"If you trusted the feds, you would've gone to them first."

"You might be right." Rebecca shrugged. "But I favor the home team. So I thought you'd want a shot."

"What I want," Dunbar said, "is to make my own deals. What did you promise him for his cooperation?"

"Not a thing. Only that his cooperation would be given serious consideration."

"I want to nail his ass to his own cross," Dunbar said vehemently.

"Perhaps you could keep that sentiment to yourself until I get the one I'm after."

Dunbar leaned back in her seat. "You really think you're going to get Zamora?"

"I think I'm going to get someone high enough up the ladder to give him to me."

"Wouldn't that be pretty."

When Dunbar smiled, Rebecca had the sense of a powerful predator savoring the coming kill. "So do we have a deal?"

"You'll still owe me for not coming to me first with this."

"Consider me in your debt."

❖

"Hey, babe," Dell called, walking into the bedroom at Sloan and Michael's. "Your sexy cop is home."

"Good. Because I want to shower and I need you to wash my hair."

Dell frowned. "Are you sure you feel up to it?"

"I'm sure if you don't give me a hand, you're going to be one dead sexy cop."

"Okay. Okay. I'm on it." Dell kicked off her boots and shed her shirt and jeans in record time. Naked, she walked to the bed and pulled down the covers. Holding out her hand, she said, "Ready?"

Sandy surveyed her, taking her time, looking over Dell's wiry muscular frame, her small neat breasts, her tight ass. She licked her lips. "Man, do I want a piece of you."

Watching Sandy's tongue skate across her soft, full lips, Dell got hot all over and her clit went wild. "You just gave me a full-on hard-on, babe."

"Yeah?" Sandy smiled in satisfaction. "That's nice."

Dell groaned and ran the flat of her hand down her stomach, brushing lightly through the crisp hair at the apex of her thighs. "It would be except you're in no shape to take care of it."

"So?" Sandy patted the bed next to her. "You've got a hand. Get your butt down here and kiss me while you do the job."

"You sure?" Dell was already having trouble catching her breath.

"Move, rookie." Sandy eased back on the pillows and turned onto her good side. When Dell stretched out beside her, she skimmed her fingers over Dell's chest, lightly brushing her nipples. "Come here, baby."

Dell almost forgot about the pressure in her clit because Sandy's tongue teasing inside her mouth, playing over her lips, sucking and nibbling, felt so good she got lost in the kissing. When Sandy scratched her nails down the center of Dell's belly, her clit jerked and she remembered it in a big way. Dell groaned and cupped her crotch in the palm of her hand.

"Need to come, baby?" Sandy whispered, flicking the tip of her tongue rapidly over Dell's.

"Yeah," Dell gasped roughly. "You get me so hot."

"Let me watch you jerk off." Sandy covered Dell's hand and pushed her fingers down on her clit. "Keep your eyes open while you do it."

Sandy started kissing her again and Dell didn't have to think about the rest of it. She just stroked and squeezed, drifting in the blue of Sandy's eyes until the tension deep in her belly started to uncoil and lick at the edges of her consciousness like flames flaring from embers.

"I'm gonna come, babe," Dell murmured against Sandy's mouth. "You feel so good."

"I love you, Dell," Sandy said, sweeping her hand down Dell's back to massage her ass. "Oh yeah. That's it, baby."

Dell whimpered, clenching her ass as she pumped into Sandy's hand, coming in long, hard pulses while Sandy kissed her. Finally she closed her eyes and let her head fall onto Sandy's breast. "You kill me."

"Good." Sandy slapped her butt. "Don't fall asleep, rookie. I want my shower."

"Man, I can't move." Dell flopped over onto her back, grinning. "It never feels that good when I do it by myself."

Sandy rolled her eyes. "You're such a dog. Get up."

Dell had a better idea. "I could, you know, make you come really easy so you wouldn't move too much."

"Oh yeah? Since when." Sandy eased her legs to the floor and grabbed Dell's arm to steady herself as she stood. "I'm horny, but I'd rather wait until I don't have to worry about breaking anything when I come." She looped her arm around Dell's waist. "Tomorrow, maybe."

"Okay, babe." Dell led her into the adjoining bathroom. "Sit down while I get the shower ready." When the water felt warm enough, she helped Sandy up and joined her in the shower. "Stand still. I'll do everything."

"Deal."

Dell squirted shampoo into her palm and lathered Sandy's hair.

"Did everything go okay today?" Sandy asked.

"Yeah. Irina told us that you got a shot of her sister at that deal the other night." Dell cupped Sandy's chin and looked into her eyes. "You did a really good job, San."

"About that," Sandy said quietly.

"Look, I know you want to help. I get that. But—"

"I talked to Frye today, Dell."

Dell tensed. "Yeah?"

Sandy punched her shoulder. "Don't get all bristly right away."

"You told her you want to go back out again."

"Well, yeah," Sandy said as if Dell were being dumb. "But I talked to her about something else too."

Dell frowned. "What do you mean?"

"I'm not gonna go to work for Michael." Sandy cradled Dell's face and kissed her. "I'm going to be a cop."

CHAPTER TWENTY-SIX

S loan pulled her Harley Super Glide into an empty parking space across from Talia Ballenger's address on the Benjamin Franklin Parkway. She swung her leg over the big machine, clipped her helmet onto the back, and slid her hands into the pockets of her black motorcycle jacket while she sauntered across the street. Casually dodging the cars as she cut across six lanes of traffic streaming along either side of the Parkway, she checked out the building, recognizing it as one of the most exclusive in the city, gated and guarded, with a waiting list that was more for form than function. No one got one of the luxurious apartments unless someone died and willed it to them, or they knew some very important people in very high places.

A security guard behind the desk in the lobby was dressed in an elaborate uniform that was supposed to make him look like a doorman. It didn't. He regarded her as if she were lost. "May I help you, madam?"

Sloan smiled. "I'm here to see Ms. Ballenger. The penthouse, right?"

"Are you expected?" he said with just a little more warmth.

Sloan tilted her head from side to side. "Expected. In a manner of speaking. Yes."

His brows knit as if he didn't understand the language. "Madam?"

Sighing, Sloan leaned her elbow on the ornate, carved wood counter. "Call her up and tell her it's Sloan."

"Of course. She usually lets me know if she's expecting a visitor," he said apologetically. Apparently, it wasn't so unusual for Talia to receive female visitors. Even ones who didn't look like they belonged in her social circle.

"I'm sure she's been busy."

His face flushed, but he said nothing. After pushing a number on a portable phone, he muttered a few words, then set the handset down briskly. Coming around the side of the counter, he removed a small key from his belt. "Right this way, please."

Sloan followed and waited while he keyed the private elevator. "Hers is the only residence on the top floor. Have a nice evening."

"Thanks. I'm planning on it." As the doors slid closed, she saw him flush once again.

The ride up was swift and silent, and when the doors glided open she stepped out into a foyer as large and well appointed as some people's living rooms. Thick wool carpets, a crystal chandelier, paintings on three walls above dark wood wainscoting, and a solid wood door worthy of an English mansion. A buzzer was discreetly inset into the wide, carved molding, but before Sloan had a chance to push it, the door opened.

"This is a nice surprise," Talia said in a voice like warm honey. She wore a dressing gown—not quite a robe, but not a dress, either. The maroon silk dipped sharply into the cleavage between her obviously unfettered breasts, and the belt tied loosely at her waist was more an invitation to be opened than anything else. Her legs were bare below the knee-length hem, her feet ensconced in backless sandals.

Sloan leaned her shoulder against the open door. "I assumed I was invited. You did give me your card."

"Yes, but my address wasn't on it." Talia stepped aside so Sloan could enter. "I just opened a bottle of Romanée-Conti. Won't you join me."

"Not the '78, I hope," Sloan said, referencing one of the costliest red Burgundy vintages ever produced by the fabled vineyard.

Talia smiled slowly and surveyed Sloan from head to toe. "Why not? I'm sure you're worth it."

"I appreciate your confidence in me." Sloan followed her through the high-ceilinged living room, noting a dining room off to one side beyond a set of double French doors, and a hallway that she presumed led to the bedrooms.

They passed through an archway into a formal library where a fire burned in a marble fireplace. A laptop occupied the center of a huge desk positioned in front of floor-to-ceiling windows with a million-dollar view of the city. Several books rested on an antique cigarette table next to one of the chairs facing the fireplace. An open bottle of wine and a single glass sat on a silver tray on a low table between the two empty chairs.

"Please." Talia gestured toward one of the chairs. She retrieved another wineglass from a sideboard near the fireplace and poured two glasses of wine. Handing one to Sloan, who had remained standing, she said, "Let me take your jacket."

Sloan placed the wine on the low table and shrugged out of her jacket, aware that Talia was watching her intently. She wore a black T-shirt with her jeans. She tossed the jacket on the floor next to her chair and sat down, retrieving her wineglass. "No need to bother hanging it up."

Talia settled into the opposite chair, one leg tucked beneath her. Her gown clung to her thighs, opening enough to show a triangle of tanned flesh from her knee to the top of her leg. Sloan glanced down briefly, then looked up into her eyes, waiting.

"How did you find me?" Talia asked, cradling the wineglass in her palm.

"Phonebook?"

Talia laughed. "I don't think so." She sipped her wine and regarded Sloan over the top of the glass. "Unlisted."

"Of course." Sloan grinned. "This is an excellent red."

"A modern classic." Talia leaned forward to replace her wineglass on the table between them. The folds of her gown shimmered, affording a tantalizing glimpse of the inner curve of her breast. When she settled back, she ran her fingers casually from the base of her throat down the center of her chest and back up again. "I believe it's your move."

Sloan positioned her wineglass next to Talia's and bent down to reach into the inner pocket of her jacket. She withdrew an envelope and passed it wordlessly to Talia. Their fingers touched briefly as Talia accepted it. Talia's long, tapered fingers were warm and soft. The only sound in the room as Talia looked through the prints, one after the other, was the crackling of the wood in the fireplace. At length, she replaced the photos in the envelope and handed it back.

"You're better than I expected," Talia said.

"You weren't easy to track," Sloan replied. "Cost me a few sleepless nights."

Talia smiled wryly. "I suppose that's some comfort." She gestured toward the envelope that Sloan had dropped onto her jacket. "She's very beautiful."

"Yes, she is."

"Zamora is quite taken with her."

"If he touches her, I'll kill him."

Talia regarded Sloan intently. "Is that why you came? So that I could give him a message?"

"No. If he doesn't already know that, he's a fool. And I don't think he is."

"Then why expose yourself to me?"

Sloan chuckled. "Have I? You already know who I am." Her smile disappeared and her voice dropped. "And you know what matters to me. What else is there?"

"Yes, but now I know that you know who I am. So you've lost the advantage."

Sloan spread her legs, draped her arms over the sides of the antique chair, and watched the fire eat away at the substance of the wood. "On the surface it looks like a stalemate." She glanced over at Talia. "But I have one more move to make."

"What would that be?" Talia refilled their wineglasses. "You can't prove I sent those images. I often have visitors. My computer is readily accessible."

"I doubt any of them have the skill to infiltrate a highly protected computer network at Port Authority, intercept and reroute dozens of shipping containers, and alter the security programs set to track them." Sloan was impressed with Talia's nerves. Her expression didn't waver. She gave no sign of being shocked or anxious. "But you do. And given time, I'll be able to prove it."

Talia crossed her legs and folded her hands in her lap. "An ambitious undertaking."

"Do you want to bet against me?"

The silence stretched for several minutes until Talia sighed. "No. I don't think so."

Secretly, Sloan was relieved. Talia was good. Very good. And the odds were probably sixty-forty that Sloan would actually be able to prove her complicity in the human trafficking operation at the port. She had wagered that like her, Talia would bet the odds. And when losing meant decades in a federal prison, a smart woman would not risk coming up short.

"I should tell you," Talia said, "that I am not in his employ. I'm a freelancer. I don't have any information of value."

Sloan and Rebecca had discussed the merits of arresting Talia and trying to force her into testifying against Kratos Zamora. They'd agreed that the evidence supporting her involvement in anything illegal was thin, and cyberevidence was often the least convincing to a jury because they didn't understand it. Any good attorney would know that and advise Talia not to deal.

"I would imagine that your freelance enterprises must be very interesting. I'd really like to get a look at them one of these days." Sloan spoke casually, but she knew that Talia would get the message. Sloan had the skill to chase her through cyberspace for as long as she wanted, monitoring her activities and making it very difficult for her to do business. Eventually, Talia would slip up, and when she did, Sloan would be there. She was not only a threat to Talia's business, but her freedom.

"While I think you're terribly attractive," Talia said, "and I admit I had hoped we would have the opportunity to share some of our skills privately, I'm not interested in a long-term relationship."

"No promises if your name surfaces in the future," Sloan said, "but at the moment, neither am I."

"Then what is it you want?"

"Nothing very complicated. I just want you to send your... client...a report with a little something extra from me."

"You understand that if he discovers I've compromised him, he'll kill me."

"Fortunately for you, there are only a few of us good enough to prove it." Sloan grabbed her jacket and stood up. She removed a jump drive from the front pocket and held it out to Talia. "I think you know what to do with this."

Talia rose and closed her fingers around Sloan's. She stepped so close their bodies touched. Skimming her palm over Sloan's chest, she said, "It's not too late for that private conversation. After all, we've already started, there's still half a bottle of wine, and we both know it would be good."

Sloan extracted her fingers and dropped the jump drive into Talia's open palm. "You were quite a challenge, and I enjoyed the hunt. But make no mistake. If any harm comes to Michael, I'll come for you too. And I'll never stop."

"I envy her," Talia said.

Sloan shrugged into her jacket and started toward the door, Talia beside her. "Thanks for the wine."

"You're welcome. I'm only sorry I couldn't offer you more than that." Talia kissed her on the mouth, then opened the door. "Good night."

❖

As soon as Sloan turned the corner, she saw Rebecca's Corvette parked across the street from their headquarters. She rolled into the garage, parked, and rode the elevator to the third floor.

"That was fast," Rebecca said. Rebecca was alone in the conference room. "Should we have gone in wired?"

Sloan kicked out a chair and dropped into it. "No. She's careful. We wouldn't have gotten anything."

"Did we get *something*?"

"Nothing you want to know about." Grinning, Sloan checked her watch. By morning she expected to be walking around in Kratos Zamora's virtual office. She'd be able to see who he e-mailed, his financial statements, his business plans, his real estate holdings, and anything else he did with his computer. The cybertap didn't precisely fall under the investigative parameters the team was officially bound by, but then the laws regarding cyberinvestigation were still murky. "To be safe, we'll need to corroborate anything we eventually want to bring to court, but we're finally getting ahead in this game."

Rebecca nodded, thinking of Jeff and Jimmy, and the men who had taken their fists to Sandy. "Work it."

"That's my plan." Sloan started for the door, then turned back. "I, uh…I want to thank you for trusting me on this. I know I screwed up not telling you sooner."

"Yeah, you did." Rebecca rubbed both hands over her face. "But I never doubted which side of the line you stood on."

"Thanks." Sloan shrugged. "I suppose you know you look like shit. Maybe you should call it a night."

"I'm going to. I just need to check in with Mitchell."

"Okay then." Sloan left her there, hoping she'd get some rest, because she had a feeling things were going to move quickly now.

Upstairs, Michael was waiting on the sofa in the living room, curled up in the corner, reading. Sloan pulled off her jacket, tossed it on the adjoining chair, and kissed her.

"She gave you wine?" Michael grabbed Sloan's arm and pulled her down next to her.

"A very nice red Burgundy."

Michael raised her eyebrows. "Friendly of her."

"We parted on friendly terms."

"You got what you needed?"

Sloan nodded. "Yes."

"I gather she didn't."

Laughing, Sloan kissed her again. "You'd have to ask her, but I don't think so."

"No need." Michael cupped the back of Sloan's neck and pulled her closer. The lingering taste of wine and the heat of Sloan's mouth were intoxicating. "I'm just feeling a little territorial."

"I've got a few hours before I need to get to work."

Michael reached behind her and blindly dropped the book onto the end table. "Then let's not waste any time."

❖

Dell knocked on the open conference room door. "You want to see me, Lieutenant?"

Rebecca was leaning back in her chair, her eyes closed. "Come on in. Have a seat, Detective." She straightened. "Any word from Irina?"

"Yes ma'am. I was on my way back from seeing her when you called." Dell pulled out the chair opposite Rebecca. "Olik left a message at the club. He wants to see her Wednesday night."

"She's still at the apartment?"

"Yes. I'm going to meet her there and we'll go over to Ziggie's together."

"I don't think we can risk wiring you. Not for the first meet with Olik. He's going to be suspicious."

"I agree. But at least we'll be at the club. That's probably safer than meeting him anywhere else."

Rebecca nodded. "I'm going to put Jasmine inside again."

Dell nodded. "Jasmine will need an escort. One of the Kings, maybe."

"How much do you trust them? I don't want to bring them in on the whole investigation, but they need to know there's some risk."

"I think they've got a pretty good idea what's going on. I trust them." Dell considered the guys. "Phil has a bit of a thing for Irina. He'd be willing to help."

"We'll have Jasmine talk to them."

"Okay." Dell hesitated. "Do we have anything from Bishop Thomas yet?"

"He was instructed to put a message out that he wants in on the next big party. We're waiting for someone to contact him. Hopefully Irina will get some idea as to when and where that will be in time for us to set up the takedown. I want her to be there."

"And Sandy?"

"We'll play that as it comes." Rebecca watched Dell, waiting.

"She told me what she wants to do. About applying to the academy. That you'll back her application."

"She's a natural. And she wants it." Rebecca grinned. "She's a lot like you that way."

"I just want you know," Dell said as she stood, "that I'm glad she's got you to help her."

"She's got something she needs even more than that. She's got you, Mitchell. Don't ever let her forget that."

"No ma'am. I won't."

CHAPTER TWENTY-SEVEN

"Darling, your brother is here," Sofia Zamora said from the doorway of Kratos's den.

Kratos smiled at his wife and motioned her in as he placed the report he was reading next to his coffee cup on the table where he was enjoying a late breakfast. The small dining alcove adjacent to his den overlooked the gardens in the rear of their home. "Tell him to come back. And would you have Marianna bring in more coffee and food."

"Of course." She leaned down and kissed him. "You won't forget that we have tickets to the symphony on Friday."

"I'm looking forward to it." He caught her hand and brushed his lips over her knuckles. She smelled of roses, the delicate scent reminding him of her deceptive strength. Her small-boned figure, luminous dark eyes, and pale skin made her appear fragile, but he knew that, like the rose, she was not only beautiful but also dangerous. She guarded her territory—her family—as fiercely as he guarded his business. They were well matched.

"And tell Jacqueline," his wife said, referring to his private secretary, "to schedule you for a haircut too." She ran her fingers through the hair just above his collar. "You're looking a little uncivilized."

He laughed and pulled out his PDA to send a message. "Done."

"Thank you, darling." Sofia skimmed his mouth with hers. "I'll see you tonight."

Kratos watched her depart, feeling a pull in his groin. Even after two children she was still striking, and he knew he was the envy of other men. He had chosen well. He stretched out his legs, pleased with his life. Gregor entered followed by the maid, who pushed a cart laden with more coffee and pastries. She arranged these on the table and quickly left without making eye contact with either man.

"You're up early," Kratos said. Much of Gregor's part of the business involved meetings with men who spent their nights in bars or private clubs and didn't go to bed until after sunrise. Ordinarily, his brother's day began at three in the afternoon.

"I felt the need for confession this morning," Gregor said, helping himself to coffee.

"And now you feel closer to God?" Kratos laughed.

"God's money, definitely."

"I take it our religious friend enjoyed his evening out."

"Not only the evening, but the company." Gregor tilted back in his chair with a smirk. "Apparently one of the girls twists his crank in just the right direction. He wants her again."

"How soon?"

"Whatever she did to him, he's addicted. As soon as we can set something up."

Kratos frowned. The interruption in their supply lines from the port, coupled with a lapse in security at one of the Russian safe houses, had strained their escort business. If all their girls were out on private calls, it was difficult to set up a group gathering quickly. "Will he solo?"

"No. He thinks he's more anonymous if he's with the others." Gregor laughed. "Who knows. Maybe he's secretly a homo, and he gets off watching the other guys get their pipes cleaned."

"Can we accommodate him?"

"We've got a couple other clients who are hot for an instant replay. That makes it worth setting up something soon. Maybe the weekend."

"What about the girl he wants?"

Gregor shrugged. "She's one of the Russians. They can't seem to keep track of their merchandise. Hopefully they haven't lost her." He finished his cheese Danish and brushed off his hands. "I'll tell them to bring the same group as the last time. A few others want the same girls too. Jesus, you'd think when you were paying for it, all you'd care about was the pussy, not who it belonged to."

"These are discerning men," Kratos said dryly.

"Yeah, right." Gregor squeezed his crotch and shook his head.

"Set it up. Let me know if you have any problems."

"I'll put a call in to Olik."

"Good." Kratos checked his watch. "I've got a meeting with the board in an hour. Anything else?"

"Yeah. The Russians are grumbling. They want to know when they can start bringing girls in again. They're running short in the clubs too."

Kratos lifted the report he'd been reading and smiled. "I got an update this morning from Talia. She's not only beautiful, she's good."

"Have you had a piece of that yet?"

Kratos had a quick flash of Talia's smile as she denied him, and his temper spiked along with his erection. Determined not to give his brother the satisfaction of seeing his frustration, he ignored the uncomfortable throbbing in his groin. He'd have her soon enough. He could tell she was enjoying the game, but she was as ready as he was for it to end. "She's been able to hack into the HPCU databases. They're pulling back surveillance at the port."

"Ha. Why?"

"Lack of manpower. And they couldn't trace anything in the computers." Kratos smiled with satisfaction. "Security will be tightened temporarily, but it shouldn't take long to loosen up. It's a big port and it costs money to keep a big security force."

"What can I tell the Russians about resuming business as usual?"

"Tell them soon."

"What else do they have?" Gregor asked, indicating the papers resting under Kratos's hand.

"They're focusing their investigation on the Russians, but thus far they've only identified a few street-level numbers runners. Nothing in our line of work."

"Nothing to worry about, then."

"No," Kratos murmured, reaching down to adjust himself, letting his hand linger for a few seconds on the turgid reminder of his own power and prowess. "Nothing to worry about at all."

❖

Bishop Thomas opened the door to his study and motioned Rebecca inside, checking up and down the hall as if to be certain they were alone. Before the door had even closed behind her, he said sharply, "I hope this is the last time."

"Problem?" Rebecca reached for the credit card–sized recorder he passed to her over his desk. The thin wires leading to a microphone the size of a shirt button were barely visible to the naked eye.

"No." He sat down behind his desk, his expression registering distaste. "He has no reason to be suspicious."

"Good."

"I can't carry that to the meeting."

Rebecca smiled thinly. "Meeting. Is that what you call it?"

He clenched his jaw and didn't answer.

"Why not? Do they search you?"

He looked affronted. "Of course not. We're paying them to see that we are protected. Just the same, it would be too easy for one of the women to find it."

"The girls, you mean. The underage girls providing you with sexual services." Rebecca remembered the pictures of the teenagers servicing him. He should be behind bars, and in all likelihood, the worst that would happen to him was that he would be transferred to another prestigious diocese in another city. She wondered if letting Talia Ballenger walk away was as difficult for Sloan as allowing this man go practically unpunished was for her.

"You have no right to put my life at risk."

Rebecca shot up so quickly he flinched back in his chair. She leaned over his desk, her arms braced on either side of his expensive leather blotter. "The minute you put your hands on one of those girls you gave me the right to do whatever I want."

"I've paid you back."

"Not enough," Rebecca whispered. "Not nearly enough."

❖

Rebecca placed the recorder in the center of the conference table. "Jason, it's all yours. Another link in the chain. I want a copy secured off-site. Nothing about this goes into the central records system."

"Our network is completely separate from anything at One Police Plaza." Sloan grinned. "And about a thousand times better."

"I hope so," Rebecca said.

Jason, seated next to Sloan, picked up the small device. "Have you listened to it?"

"No. I didn't trust myself not to ram it up his ass," Rebecca said tightly.

"What about Irina's sister?" Mitchell asked. "Did he say anything about her?"

"He was instructed to ask for the same girls as last time. He's smart enough to do as he's told at this point."

Watts grunted. "He's not as smart as he thinks. We're going to bust him with the rest of those pervs, right, Loo?"

"We are." Rebecca sighed. "But he's probably going to get a walk on most of the charges. And no official record of any of them. But his superiors will be informed. That's nonnegotiable."

"It's not right," Mitchell muttered.

Rebecca swung around in her chair. "You're right. It isn't. But we trade up, or we get nothing."

"I know." Mitchell stared at the table, a muscle quivering along the edge of her jaw. "But it blows."

Watts laughed. "You keep getting pissed off about pricks like this getting a deal, kid. It'll keep your edge."

"Sloan?" Rebecca asked. "Something for me?"

"Zamora got the package from Talia. It's going to take Jason and me a few days to comb through his system, but he downloaded her report with what she supposedly found in our records. And left a little present behind."

"So he thinks we're getting nowhere at the port, correct?" Rebecca confirmed.

"Yes. By the time they start up their operations again, we should have traps in place to detect when they start manipulating the records of the containers coming in and their positions on the docks. We'll be able to track them."

"Even if Ballenger is behind it?"

"She won't be," Sloan said with certainty. "She's too smart not to know when she's out of the game."

"Won't Zamora be suspicious if she pulls out?" Mitchell asked.

"As far as he'll know, thanks to the disinformation we're feeding him," Sloan said, "it's safe to keep using the same system they had." She shrugged. "By the time they find out otherwise, I imagine she'll be long gone."

"So," Rebecca said, surveying the team. "We're just waiting for the last link in the chain. This tape ties Gregor to the girls, and when we have him, we'll get his brother." Everyone looked at Mitchell. "Now we need the Russians to make a clean sweep of all the garbage."

"I guess I'm up tomorrow night," Mitchell said.

"You're ready." Rebecca stood. "That's it, then. Game's on."

CHAPTER TWENTY-EIGHT

S andy checked her makeup in the bathroom mirror. The bruise along her jaw was still visible, but that wasn't anything unusual for girls in her line of work. Her lip was puffy, but it didn't hurt anymore. She cupped her breasts and jiggled them a little inside the tight white lycra top to get as much bang out of her minimal cleavage as she could. Then she shimmied into her miniskirt and pulled on knee-high white vinyl boots with three-inch heels.

"You look like such a whore," she said to her reflection, laughing as she gelled her hair into short blond spikes. For the first time in her life she felt like she was wearing a costume and not her work clothes.

"Do you have any underwear on?" Mitch said from the doorway.

She spun around and looked him over. He wasn't dressed in his usual T-shirt and jeans tonight, but a tight-fitting black shirt with the top two buttons open, black pants that hugged his thighs and stretched across the bulge in his crotch, a slick black leather belt with a small square silver buckle, and black shoes.

"Jesus, you look like a player." She stared pointedly at his crotch. "Are you wearing any underwear?"

"I asked you first."

Sandy thought about teasing him a little, but she knew he was still pissed off and they had serious work to do. "Yes. A thong. And no one is going to get close enough to find out. What about you?"

"You can see for yourself later. How do your ribs feel?"

"Baby," Sandy said, "I wouldn't have volunteered if I wasn't ready." She put her arms around his neck and kissed his ear. "Don't be mad."

Mitch held her stiffly, his hands on her waist. "I know you don't answer to anyone but the lieutenant, but I still wish you'd said something to me first."

"You know what? You're right. I should have." She skimmed his mouth with hers. "I wasn't even sure she'd go for it. But I still should have told you what I was thinking first."

Mitch let out a sigh and rested his forehead against hers. "I know it makes the most sense for you to go with Jasmine tonight. They know you at Ziggie's. I'm just worried."

"I know. But we're only going to be watching who's coming in and out. And keeping an eye on you and Irina."

"You haven't seen us together before, San."

Sandy gripped his shoulders and leaned back, pressing her pelvis into his. She could feel the hard ridge of his cock pressing against her stomach. She liked the way it felt. She imagined that Irina did too, and even if she didn't, she'd have to play like she did. "These guys are killers, Mitch. You think I'm going to care if you have to feel her up or she grabs your dick to prove to these guys that the two of you are together?" She gave him a little bump with her hips. "I love you, and I know you love me. End of story."

Mitch grinned. "Just the same, I'd appreciate it—if you notice any of the dick grabbing—if you'd look the other way."

"What makes you think I wouldn't enjoy watching?"

"Ha ha."

"Okay. Maybe that's pushing it. Come on." Sandy took his hand. "The lieutenant wants to brief us, right?"

Mitch held her back. "Just trust me to do my job, okay? I know you know what you're doing, but I don't want you to get hurt."

Sandy stroked his cheek. "Right back at you, rookie."

❖

"Are you ready?" Mitch asked Irina as he opened the back door of Ziggie's.

"Yes," Irina said. "I'm tired of belonging to them."

The hallway was dimly lit by a few low-wattage bulbs, and clouds of cigarette smoke swirled indolently in the air. The atmosphere was close and hot, smelling faintly of urine and liquor and sex. As they neared the end of the tunnel-like passageway, the ever-present bump and grind music grew louder. Two girls performed onstage, hip-thrusting and pole-humping in a weary parody of ecstasy. Even at midweek, the swivel stools at the bar were half full and most of the booths were occupied. Sex for sale never went out of style.

"Have a good vacation?" the bartender asked snidely, eyeing Irina as he swiped a dirty rag over the surface of the bar.

"Vodka shot and a beer," Irina said, ignoring his remark.

"Olik's looking for you," he said, making no move to get the drinks.

Mitch straddled a stool with his back to the bartender and Irina snuggled in between his legs, leaning against the front of his body with her arms loosely draped around his waist. Her expression was bored.

"I am here now." She raised a brow. "Are you on vacation?"

He snorted and went off to get their drinks.

Irina ran her fingers through Mitch's hair and scanned the bar. She wore a wraparound emerald green blouse that left a generous expanse of her full breasts bare and a tight black skirt that came to mid-thigh. With her heels she was almost as tall as Mitch.

Mitch kissed her neck and murmured, "Any sign of our friends?"

She arched her back and thrust her breasts against his chest, exposing more of her neck to his mouth. "Two men, Olik's men… bodyguards, at the end of the bar. He must be here somewhere."

"What about the muscle we ran into the last time we were here?"

"I don't see him."

Mitch traced his tongue down the center of her throat. "Too bad."

Irina laughed and tugged his head back with her fist in his hair. "You are bad, new boy."

"Are you complaining?"

"No." Her eyes suddenly softened and the fingers in his hair slid down to caress his neck, catching Mitch off guard. Then her haughty expression returned. "Good boys bore me."

The bartender delivered their drinks. Irina handed the beer to Mitch, then picked up the shot of vodka and tossed it back.

Mitch checked out the rest of the room as he sipped the beer. Jasmine and Sandy sat at a small round table not far from the stage. He started in surprise when he noticed Phil with them. That hadn't been part of the plan, and he wondered if the King had arrived by himself. Looking for Irina, maybe. Sandy laughed at something Phil said and slid her chair closer to him, draping her arm around his neck. Phil grabbed her and pulled her into his lap. Sandy didn't even glance in Mitch's direction.

"So this is your new bodyguard," a deep male voice said from Mitch's right.

Mitch automatically shifted Irina in his arms, moving her away from the stranger who had walked up next to them. The man looked to be about forty, with broad shoulders and an irregular scar bisecting his left cheek that marred an otherwise coldly handsome face. His suit was expensive looking, and the watch on his left wrist appeared to be a Rolex. The tailored jacket nearly hid the weapon holstered on his right hip. He was not a street-level enforcer. Mitch smiled inwardly in satisfaction. Finally.

"Mitch takes good care of me," Irina said suggestively, rubbing his chest with her fingertips.

The man who must be Olik looked Mitch up and down, his gaze lingering between Mitch's legs. Then in a move so fast Mitch didn't have time to react, he shot his hand out and gripped Mitch's cock. Mitch sucked in a breath as pain bored into his pelvis from the pressure. He summoned all his willpower and said casually, "I don't want to embarrass you in front of your men, so I suggest you let go."

Olik started to laugh but stopped abruptly when Mitch flicked his right hand and a switchblade dropped into his palm. Mitch thrust his arm forward until the point of the six-inch blade was a millimeter from Olik's crotch. "Then again, I don't really care if you lose face. Or… anything else."

With a growl, Olik released Mitch and stepped back out of knife range. "You have balls after all."

Irina laughed and caressed Mitch's stomach, then let her fingers drift over the swell of his cock. "He has everything he needs."

"Come in the back."

❖

Sandy tensed when she saw the big man crowd Mitch, frustrated that she couldn't make out what was happening. The two men who'd been standing at the far end of the bar started toward Mitch and Irina. Three on one. She didn't like it. Irina seemed to be taunting the guy, fondling Mitch with a self-satisfied look on her face. Sandy hoped to hell she knew what she was doing, because if she got Mitch hurt, Sandy was going to send her back to Russia personally.

"I have to go to the bathroom," Sandy said abruptly, climbing off Phil's lap. She couldn't take it anymore. She needed a closer look.

"Oh, wait for me, honey." Jasmine gripped her arm. "But I want to finish my drink first."

When Sandy started to protest, she caught the look in Jasmine's eyes and checked the bar again. The big man had backed off, and Mitch and Irina were following him down the hall. The other two men were close behind them. Reluctantly, she settled back into Phil's lap. For now, all she could do was wait.

Phil circled her waist to steady her, but kept his hands to himself. "You and Mitch," he said, his voice pitched low. "You're not really done, are you?"

"You see me with him?" Sandy shot back.

"Nope." Phil grinned. "So does that mean you're going to give me a chance?"

Sandy patted Phil's chest. "I don't know, baby. I think you might be too much guy for me."

He laughed. "Yeah. That's what I thought. So, if you need anything." He tilted his head slightly in the direction Mitch and Irina had disappeared. "Say the word."

"Thanks, but we're cool." Sandy just hoped she wasn't lying.

❖

Olik's office was a converted storage room, with a plain desk, two file cabinets, a couple of straight-backed chairs, and an upholstered sofa that held the impression of a decade of asses pressed into the faded cushions. One of the two guards who'd followed them down the hallway stepped inside and closed the door. The other was probably outside in the hall making sure they weren't disturbed. Olik rested his hips against the front of the desk and gestured to the sofa.

"Sit down."

Mitch preferred to stay standing because he could fight better from that position, but he didn't want to get into anything with Irina in the room, so he let her tug him down beside her on the sofa. Spreading his legs, he leaned back and stretched one arm along the back. He slung the other around Irina's shoulders, pulling her close against his side. She crossed her legs, causing her skirt to ride up and expose a lot of creamy thigh. When she dropped her left hand casually onto the inside of his right leg, Olik's gaze followed her hand.

"The girls are getting out of hand. I want you to stay with them," he said gruffly.

"Until the police come for us like last time?" Irina scoffed. "I will stay where I am safe."

"You will stay where you are told."

"She stays with me," Mitch said softly.

"This is not your affair, boy."

"Irina is my business."

Olik gripped the desk on either side of his hips, his smile condescending. The outline of an erection was prominent beneath the expensive material of his trousers. "Maybe you should show me what you've got that Irina likes so much."

"That's private," Mitch said.

"Irina," Olik said, his voice low and dangerous. He drew back the edge of his jacket, exposing the automatic on his hip. "Explain to your boy who's in charge."

"It's all right, Mitch," Irina whispered. "I know what he wants."

Before Mitch could protest, Irina shifted until she straddled his thighs, her skirt pulled tight across the junction of her pelvis. He gripped her hips automatically.

"Irina, what—"

Then Irina's hands were in his hair and her tongue was in his mouth, and she was kissing him feverishly. For a second, he was too stunned to do anything but hold on to her while she rocked on his cock. He finally pulled out of the kiss and stared into her eyes. She was breathing fast and her lids drooped heavily.

"It's all right," she murmured again, sliding a hand down to his belt buckle. "I don't care if he sees."

She wasn't acting. She wanted him to fuck her. And suddenly

Mitch wasn't thinking about Sandy, or the job, or Olik, or what was right or what was wrong. He was thinking about Irina, a woman he cared for. He could feel her heat through his pants. He looked down and saw the ridge of his cock nestled between her thighs. Irina tugged at his belt. Oh fuck, she really was going to take him inside her, right here.

"Irina." Mitch brushed his thumb across her full lower lip, then cradled her hips in his palms. He tensed his thighs and lifted her off his body, rising to his feet all in one motion. He stared at Olik. "I know how to treat a woman right. That's why she prefers me."

Olik flicked his hand at the muscle by the door. "Show this boy how we treat disobedient dogs in our country."

The guy was twice Mitch's size, but Mitch had fought big men before. The cadets at West Point only came in two sizes. Big and bigger. With men like this, there was no choice but to hit hard and hit fast. He wouldn't get a second chance. With a leering smile, the Russian threw a looping haymaker and Mitch did exactly the opposite of what the guy expected. He stepped forward to the inside of the punch, blocked the big man's forearm with his own, and rabbit punched him with a straight hard shot to the larynx. The Russian's eyes bulged, he grabbed his throat with both hands, and sank to his knees. With a wet gurgling moan, he collapsed onto the dirty gray carpet.

Mitch sidestepped as he toppled. "His larynx is fractured. He'll drown on his own blood if someone doesn't take him to the hospital."

The man thrashed on the floor and the front of his pants turned dark as he urinated. Olik cursed in Russian and strode to the door, yanking it open so hard it ricocheted off the wall. He snapped out something else in Russian and the man in the hall rushed in, grabbed the prone man under the arms, and dragged him out. Olik kicked the door closed and spun around.

Mitch braced for the next round. Irina appeared beside him and put her arm around his waist. Olik stopped a few feet away, his face stony.

"The girls would feel safer with Mitch on security," Irina said. "He's good and he's not going to try to fuck them."

"You'll supervise them. Go with them on their jobs? Make sure they behave?" Olik asked.

"*Da,*" Irina said.

Olik regarded Mitch. "You provide security when they travel."

Trying to appear nonchalant although his heart was pounding, Mitch said, "When Irina's not working, she stays with me."

Olik nodded.

"Okay then," Mitch said. "When do we start?"

CHAPTER TWENTY-NINE

Mitch keyed in the security code so he could park his Ducati inside Sloan's building. When he turned around, Sandy stepped out of the alcove at the top of the stairs and headed his way.

"What are you doing out here alone?" Mitch asked. "It's the middle of the night and it's freezing."

"I was hoping I'd get lucky." Sandy linked her arm through his. "And I guess I did." She tugged him into the shadows and kissed him. "Everybody's here—upstairs rehashing tonight. I wanted to see you alone first."

Mitch rolled the bike in next to Sloan's Harley on the other side of the Porsche and closed the overhead doors. Then he unzipped his jacket and leaned back against his bike. Sandy took off her jacket and dropped it over the handlebars. When she kissed him again she tasted a little like liquor and smelled like fresh snow. Her skin was cold and her mouth was hot. Mitch tightened his grip and buried his face in the curve of her neck.

Sandy stroked his hair. "You okay, baby?"

"Yeah." He spoke without looking up. Olik had seemed satisfied with the agreement Irina had made to supervise the girls, but Mitch had taken Irina back to the apartment and waited for an hour to be sure she wouldn't have any unwanted company. They didn't talk about what had happened in the back room of Ziggie's. They'd both done what they'd had to do.

"Irina handle things?"

"She did fine."

"Was there trouble?" Sandy asked.

"Some. Olik needed a little convincing that Irina and I were a package deal." Mitch flexed his right hand and noticed for the first time that his knuckles were sore. Sandy caught the motion and grasped his wrist, drawing his hand up to the light.

"You broke some skin over your knuckles. Got any bruises anywhere else?" Sandy asked casually. She didn't want to fuss over him because she knew he needed to believe she had total faith in him. Her fears were hers to deal with, not to lay on him.

"He never touched me," Mitch said without much satisfaction. He'd thought he would feel better about taking one of these guys out, but he didn't really. He'd realized as he watched the Russian flail on the floor, choking to death, that all he wanted was to put the guy behind bars. He didn't need to deliver the punishment himself. "I hurt him pretty bad."

"Did he come after you?"

"Yeah."

Sandy framed Mitch's face so she could look into his eyes. "Then you did what you needed to do. Don't feel bad."

Mitch smiled wryly. "I don't. Not really." He brushed his fingertips through the soft, short hair at her temple. "I saw you had a new boyfriend tonight."

"Phil?" Sandy laughed. "He is so all talk."

"Glad to hear that." Mitch's smile disappeared. "You okay about everything?"

"Don't talk in code, rookie." Sandy poked his chest. "You mean am I having a fit about Irina—who happens to be very hot in the flesh, by the way—having her hands all over you?"

Mitch nodded.

"If I said I didn't mind, you'd know I was lying. But I'm not having a fit either." She leaned into him, her thighs against his thighs, her belly tight against his crotch. "When I was still working, you never told me not to. You made love to me when you thought I was still hooking. You loved me even when you thought I was giving my body away."

"Sandy," Mitch whispered.

Sandy pressed her fingers to his mouth. "If you keep doing what you're doing, and I guess you're going to since Frye thinks you're so good at it, you might have to do more than kiss a girl's neck some night.

Whether I see it, or I don't, it's about work. I don't need to know the details."

"Just so you know, it won't happen unless there's no other way. And…" Mitch sighed. "It won't mean anything to me."

"You sure you're okay?" Sandy ran her hands down his arms, then rubbed her palms over his chest inside his jacket. "You're pretty tight."

Mitch shook his head. "Maybe a little. How about we check in with the lieutenant and then you can find out if I'm wearing any underwear."

"I don't want to be distracted in front of Frye," Sandy whispered against Mitch's mouth while she worked the zipper down on his fly. Mitch stiffened as she slid her hand inside his briefs and gripped his cock. "One question answered."

"That's as far as you better go," Mitch said thickly. "Because we don't have time for the rest."

"Five minutes?"

Mitch laughed. "You know how to straighten out my head when I'm twisted around. No one else ever has."

Sandy licked his neck. "I know how to straighten something out. Got a safe in your wallet?"

"You know I do. But I'm still not going to fuck you right now." He gripped her hips and backed her off a few inches, then looked down at her hand inside his pants. "Jesus. You make me hot."

"That's more like it." She kissed him lightly on the mouth, rearranged his clothes, and zipped his fly. "Now, let's go to work."

❖

"Jesus Christ, Frye," Clark barked as he held his hotel room door open a few inches. He wore boxers and a white T-shirt, and he needed a shave. "It's five o'clock in the morning."

"Five twenty," Rebecca replied. "We need to talk."

"I'll be in the office by nine."

When Clark tried to close the door, Rebecca wedged her foot in the opening. "This can't wait."

Clark looked back into the darkened room. "I'll meet you downstairs in the coffee bar in fifteen minutes."

"Fine." Rebecca strolled back to the elevator, pleased that she had derailed his plans for morning wake-up sex. Since she hadn't been to bed yet, she figured that was an even trade. She ordered coffee and settled into a booth at the back of the nearly empty restaurant.

Twenty minutes later, Clark slid in opposite her. His hair was wet, his eyes bloodshot, and his rigid posture indicated he was not a happy man.

"Coffee," he snapped before the waitress had even reached their booth. She promptly spun around and disappeared. "What?"

"I'm getting warrants for Gregor Zamora, a priest, and half a dozen members of the Russian mob. When we make the sweep, we're going to pick up some high-profile public figures too." Rebecca smiled when Clark's eyes popped.

"Why am I just hearing this now?"

"I've been busy."

"I'll talk to the U.S. attorney. My people should make the arrests."

Rebecca shook her head. "You can have Zamora. You'll get him one way or the other. But the rest are mine." She pushed the coffee cup to one side. "The district attorney's office has already been informed."

"This isn't what we would call cooperation, Lieutenant."

"Sue me."

"What about the brother?" Clark asked.

"He's smart—doesn't get his hands dirty. But there's dirt on him just the same. Squeeze Gregor—you guys are good at that. Maybe he'll roll."

"Maybe isn't good enough."

"It's a lot more than you could have gotten on your own." Rebecca stood up. "We did all the work, and you'll get your chance to flip someone all the way at the top of the food chain. I'll let you know when we're ready to move, and you can send your agents for Zamora. Then we're done, Clark. All done."

"We'll see about that," he called after her.

Rebecca didn't bother to answer.

❖

Catherine met Rebecca at the front door and held out her hand for Rebecca's blazer. "You really need to wear an overcoat, darling."

"You know," Rebecca said, "that's exactly what I need to hear right now."

"Something ridiculously domestic?" Catherine hung the jacket in the closet, hooked her thumbs under the leather straps of Rebecca's holster, and lifted it off. "That sounds hopelessly unromantic."

Rebecca carried her weapon in one hand and circled Catherine's waist as they started toward the bedroom. "Believe me, it isn't. It's exactly what I need to come home to." She slowed just inside the bedroom. "I don't suppose you could come back to bed for a while."

"Only if you promise to go right to sleep."

"I promised you once I'd never lie to you," Rebecca murmured, drawing Catherine to the side of the bed. She unbuttoned her shirt and pulled it her from her trousers. "But despite my best intentions, I probably will fall asleep on you."

"That's all right. I like holding you while you're sleeping." Catherine worked Rebecca's belt loose from her trousers. "How did it go with the operation?"

"Mitchell's inside and we're close to the endgame," Rebecca said, shedding the rest of her clothes and climbing under the covers. The bed still held Catherine's warmth, and she felt as if she were slipping into a sanctuary. Catherine lay down beside her, and Rebecca settled into her arms with a sigh. "I'm sorry I didn't get here sooner."

"You're here now." Catherine kissed her. "Everything is all right with Mitch and Irina?"

"They made some heads-up plays tonight," Rebecca mumbled. "Why?"

"Irina is necessarily very dependent on him. He's her only chance for safety, and for having her sister returned to her. He's her lifeline."

"Meaning she's likely to get attached."

"Yes."

"Mitchell can handle it." Rebecca laughed quietly. "Mitchell's in for an interesting time. Sandy wants to be a cop."

"That makes perfect sense," Catherine said. "Do you approve?"

"Not for me to say. But, yeah. I do. She's got guts. And street smarts. And she'll understand what needs to be done in ways the rest of us never will."

"And you'll take care of her, won't you," Catherine said softly.

"You mind?"

Catherine kissed Rebecca's forehead. "No, darling. I don't mind."

"We know when the Russians are delivering girls to the next private party set up by the Zamoras. Mitch and Irina will be working the inside. We're going to hit them then."

"All I ask is that you don't take the door. You're not ready for that."

"Okay. I need to be there, but I'll let Watts take the lead. We'll have uniform backup for this too." Rebecca kissed Catherine's breast. "Don't worry. There's not going to be trouble."

"All right then." Catherine stroked Rebecca's face. "I still want to know when it's happening. Now, close your eyes. For the next few hours, you're just mine."

CHAPTER THIRTY

Mitch zipped his jacket and lingered by the bedroom door, watching Sandy pull on a fake fur coat that hit right in the middle of her pert, round ass, about three inches above the bottom of her skirt. Even though she was shorter than him, her legs looked like they went on forever, slender and shapely, her toned calves tightening with each step she took in her mile-high heels.

"I wish you'd wear shoes you could run in," he grumbled.

Sandy shot him a look. "Like no one would notice if I showed up in sneakers."

If he had his way, she wouldn't show up anywhere at all, but the lieutenant had called the shots. Business as usual tonight. Mitch knew it made sense not to change anything that might tip off the Russians that something was up. Even when that meant Sandy would be making the rounds at the clubs.

"Be sure to call Frye if they make contact," Mitch said for the fifth time.

"I will." Sandy picked up a tiny purse on a shiny silver chain and slung it around her neck. She had her cell phone, a spray container of mace, lipstick, and condoms. Work supplies. "You're the one who needs to be careful. You and Irina are gonna be right there when everything goes down. You don't need to be thinking about me. You don't need to be worrying about anything except keeping safe. You got it?"

"Don't go anywhere with them unless Frye knows."

Sandy rolled her eyes. "I know the drill. If I show up in Atlantic City tonight at this party, you don't worry about me. You just do your thing and I'll do mine."

Mitch cupped her cheek and brushed his thumb over her chin. "I love you. See you when this is over."

Sandy kissed him. "Just remember that."

❖

Sloan, in black jeans and a black T-shirt, settled the holster onto her right hip and shoved her federal credentials into her back pocket, aware that Michael was watching everything she did. She'd been in some tight spots in Southeast Asia, particularly when she'd been a field agent on the trail of some of the major drug smugglers in the region. She wasn't afraid of a fight, but things were different now. She had Michael to think about.

"It's just a precaution, and I'm not going to be anywhere near the action." She held out her hand. "Walk me out?"

"I'd rather see you spend twenty-four hours a day in front of the computer, than this," Michael said softly. "I don't know how Catherine stands it."

"There's really nothing to worry about. I promise." Sloan took her hand. "These are businessmen, not hardened criminals, and most of them are gonna have their pants around their ankles. They're not going to resist."

"What about the Russians who are with them?"

"Rebecca has the state police on standby. They'll go in first along with Watts. Once everyone is locked down, Rebecca and I will just coordinate the transfers. We don't trust Clark's men not to show up, and we're not losing our prisoners this time."

"I suppose this is going to sound selfish, but I don't really care if Clark makes off with a bunch of criminals or not." Michael stopped Sloan before she could call the elevator. "I just want you coming home in one piece."

Sloan kissed her. "It's not selfish. And at the first sign of trouble, I'll run."

"Sloan. You're such a bad liar." Michael laughed shakily and kissed her as the elevator doors opened. "Call me, darling. As soon as you can."

"I'll be late," Sloan said as the elevator doors slid closed. "Don't worry."

❖

"You know your sister is probably going to be there tonight," Mitch said, standing in the bathroom doorway.

Irina squinted into the small mirror above the bathroom sink and touched up her mascara. "I hope so. You said they would bring the same group as last week."

"The lieutenant will wait until the party is under way before making the arrests. You'll probably have to…you know, put your sister to work."

"Mitch," Irina said, turning in the tiny space to face him. "We don't think like you do. If she needs to fuck some man tonight, she will not care and neither will I. As long as later, we are free."

"I get that," he said. "I just…I don't know. I guess I didn't want you to be upset."

She smiled at him, her expression softening. Then in another one of those moves that always took him by surprise, she pressed close and whispered against his mouth, "This might be the last chance I get."

Then she kissed him in a way she never had before. Not urgent, not challenging, but softly, gently. Her fingers glided through his hair, her body undulated languidly against his, her hips rocked rhythmically into his. He responded before he had time to think about it, and then when he would have pulled away, she did.

"That was to say thank you," she said.

"You're welcome." Mitch stepped back from her so that their bodies no longer touched. "I think you're pretty special."

"But you already have a girl, don't you, new boy," she said quietly, her eyes searching his.

"I do."

She nodded and slipped past him. As she reached for the leather coat he'd bought her, her cell phone rang. She answered and spoke a few words in Russian.

"Olik is on his way with the girls," she said. "He wants to see for himself how we work."

Mitch grinned. "You ready?"

Irina took his hand and laced her fingers through his. *"Da."*

❖

Halfway up the block, a black stretch limo slid to the curb in front of Mitch's apartment. A burly, flat-faced man in a long black leather trench coat exited the front passenger side and walked around to the sidewalk. He pulled open the rear door, folded his arms, and stood there like a statue. A minute later, Mitch and Irina came down the steps and climbed into the limo. The man slammed the door, got back in front, and the car slid away.

"Here we go," Rebecca said, starting the engine. She waited until the limo had turned the corner heading east before following.

"Atlantic City, here we come," Watts muttered, slouched in the passenger seat of the unmarked.

Sloan leaned forward from the back to get a look out the windshield. "*New Jersey,* here we come," she said with satisfaction. "Taking those girls across the state line should make the federal charges nice and solid."

"Why don't we just drive right to the casino hotel," Watts said, "instead of following them around and risking them picking us up on their tail? That jerk-off Thomas already told us where this little fuckfest is going down."

Rebecca's gaze locked on the taillights of the limo five cars ahead of them. "Since Mitch isn't wired and there's no way he can call us if they change the location at the last minute. They could direct the johns to a new rendezvous spot, and we'd be sitting in front of the Boardwalk Hotel with our thumbs up our butts for the rest of the night."

Watts grunted. "Must be why you're the lieutenant."

"Of course, maybe you'd like Sloan's thumb up—"

"Hey!" Watts and Sloan objected at once.

Rebecca grinned fiercely, feeling the burn of anticipation in the pit of her stomach. Everything made sense now that she could finally see the big picture. Jimmy Hogan, a narcotics detective and one of Clark's agents, had gone undercover to get information on the Zamora organization. In the process, he'd stumbled onto the human trafficking operation at the pier being run by the Zamoras' new Russian associates. Needing help to investigate that, he'd arranged a rendezvous with Rebecca's partner Jeff in the Special Crimes Unit, but Jimmy's cover had been blown and he hadn't known it. He and Jeff had been executed, and Rebecca knew with every cop instinct she had that one of the

Russian enforcers had pulled the trigger. Tonight, she would have justice for her dead partner.

"I still can't believe the DA agreed to let that pervert priest walk," Watts said bitterly.

"We needed his cooperation and the church has a lot of power. We had to bargain." Rebecca had objected violently, but her arguments hadn't done any good. She'd been instructed to personally take charge of him during the bust and sequester him away from the other prisoners.

Thinking of the phone call she'd made just before she picked up Watts and Sloan, Rebecca turned onto the Atlantic City Expressway. "But you never know. Anything can happen."

❖

"You might want to work one of the other clubs tonight," Sandy said when Darla plunked down next to her at the bar at the Blue Diamond.

"How come?"

Sandy tilted her head toward the two men talking to a couple of girls across the room. "Our friends are back."

Darla followed her gaze and stiffened. "Oh man. Those nasty pricks—I was hoping I'd never see them again. You think they remember us?"

"Yeah." Sandy kept her eyes on the hard-eyed guy who'd gotten off manhandling her in the parking lot the week before. He smirked at her and adjusted his crotch. When he started toward them, she said quickly, "You don't want to be in on this tonight. Go out the back. Now."

"Are you going to be okay?" Darla didn't bother to wait for an answer. She just hopped down from the stool and hurriedly collected her purse and jacket.

Sandy held the Russian's gaze as he approached. She smiled at him, and she didn't have to fake it. She was really glad he'd found her, because now she'd have the chance to see him go down. "I'm gonna be just fine."

❖

Mitch leaned against the wall just inside the door of the penthouse suite at the Boardwalk Hotel and Casino and watched the party get under way. A Russian security guard occupied a similar spot on the opposite side of the door, looking bored. Irina directed the girls, speaking to them in Russian and moving them about the room like players on a stage. Placing one next to a portly sixty-year-old who immediately began to fondle her while gulping the drink Irina handed him. Instructing another to kneel between the spread legs of a thirtysomething in a business suit who unzipped his fly and tugged out his penis while sharing a joke with a man seated nearby. She'd chosen two of the youngest to sit on either side of Bishop Thomas on a wide leather couch.

Mitch recognized Thomas from the photograph Sandy had taken at the last party. He recognized Irina's sister, too, whom Irina had just delivered like a party favor to the priest. Nothing showed on Irina's face as she went about the business of seeing to the clients' needs, and her sister had been equally cool, only the faintest smile showing for a second when she'd first seen Irina. Mitch wondered if Irina struggled with the same blind rage that hammered at the edges of his control, or if she had long ago accepted the reality of what she must do to survive. He thought of her and Sandy, and ached for retribution for all the injustices they had endured.

Realizing his fists were clenched at his sides, he made a conscious effort to relax and put his personal feelings aside. He didn't know precisely when the lieutenant would greenlight the takedown, but when it happened, he needed to be completely focused.

When Irina finished distributing the girls, a few men were still without escorts, and one of them appeared to be having a heated conversation with Olik, who lounged on a stool at the wet bar on the far side of the room. The thin, agitated man stalked off and Olik pulled out his cell phone and made a call. The Russians didn't have enough girls of their own to cover the party, and Mitch knew what that meant. When a knock sounded at the door and the guard next to him exchanged words in Russian with someone outside in the hall, Mitch steeled himself for what was coming.

The guard pulled the door open and a man walked through with three more girls. Sandy didn't look at Mitch, and he gave her a cursory glance and then looked away. Even when Sandy and one of her girlfriends headed straight for the thin man who sat fidgeting on the love seat across the room, Mitch just stared straight ahead. He didn't flinch when the man said something to Sandy and pressed her hand over the bulge in his crotch. Sandy laughed and pulled her hand away before reaching for the girl beside her and deep-throating her. Mitch didn't mind the kiss as long as the guy wasn't touching her anymore. Sandy had a job to do, and so did he. The best way to keep her safe was to get between her and the Russians when the fireworks started. He would preserve his cover, but if he got the chance, he'd kick that slimy bastard's balls into his throat.

CHAPTER THIRTY-ONE

E veryone should be settled in by now," Rebecca said a few minutes after they watched Sandy climb out of a black SUV and go into the hotel with two men and a couple of other girls. She checked Watts and Sloan. "Ready?"

"Fucking A," Watts growled, releasing the strap on his holster before reaching for the door handle.

"Looking forward to it," Sloan said easily.

"I'll alert Clark to move on Zamora. Watts, radio when you rendezvous with the tactical team at the service elevators. We'll take the lobby and clear the stairwell. Wait on the door until we get there if you can."

"Roger, Loo." Watts slid out of the car and hurried away with a spring in his step.

Rebecca speed dialed Clark, snapped, "We're moving," and disconnected.

"The Russians will be armed," Rebecca reminded Sloan. "You stay at the rear and out of the line of fire."

"How about I just watch your back and we don't worry about where I'm standing."

"Fair enough. But Jesus, keep your head down." Rebecca grinned as she opened her car door. "I don't need Michael after me for getting you bruised."

Laughing, Sloan climbed out and joined Rebecca as they headed toward the front entrance. "I'm sorry Jason is missing this one."

"We need him back at headquarters monitoring Zamora, just in case he gets wind of this and starts dumping data." Rebecca slowed as her radio crackled and Watts relayed that the strike team was in position. "I copy. Give us thirty seconds. Then go."

Rebecca and Sloan sprinted into the lobby, jogged around guests and bellmen, and hurtled into the stairwell.

❖

Dell heard a muffled shout through the door and knocked the Russian guard next to her off balance as the door crashed open. Everyone in the room shouted at once as officers in riot gear stormed into the room. Girls cowered on the floor, men scattered while trying to zip and cover, and the Russians reached for weapons. Dell took advantage of the pandemonium and the momentary cover provided by the strike team to elbow the guard in the temple. The guy dropped like a stone.

Dell immediately checked for Sandy and saw her drag the girl with her behind the sofa. Across the room, Watts manhandled the other guard up against the wet bar and slammed his head down amidst the bottles and glasses. The lieutenant shoved the priest to the floor next to the sofa and cuffed him. The remaining johns jostled like spooked cattle, trying to get out the door past the police who were busy restraining them.

The situation seemed contained until Dell caught a glimpse of Olik yanking Irina by the arm toward the hallway that led to the rear of the penthouse. She wasn't certain of the layout, but she thought there might be another exit.

Shouldering her way through the melee, she raced down the hall. When she pushed through a partially open door, she found herself in another large sitting room with a wide foyer to her left and sofas and chairs grouped around an empty fireplace off to her right. In the foyer, Olik, one hand twisted in Irina's hair, jerked open the door to the hall. Dell couldn't let him take her. She yanked her backup piece from her ankle holster and leveled it at Olik's head. "Olik. Let her go!"

Seconds stretched into eternity as Olik thrust Irina in front of him and raised his automatic.

"Irina! Get down!" Dell shouted, desperately angling for a clear shot.

Then Irina lunged at Olik and the air erupted in gunfire.

❖

Rebecca dropped into a crouch in the doorway and scanned the sitting room. Mitchell knelt nearby, blood covering one side of her face and her gun hand wavering. Irina was sprawled in the center of the foyer, a widening patch of crimson soaking her blouse.

"Hallway," Mitchell gasped, staggering to her feet. "I'll cover you."

Sloan stormed by and yelled, "See to the girl! I'm with Frye."

Rebecca leapt for the door. "Go low."

"Got it," Sloan called.

They burst into the hall side by side. Rebecca pivoted against the wall and Sloan skidded to her knees on the far side, weapon extended. Olik was twenty feet away, almost at the stairwell doors.

"Police," Rebecca shouted. "Drop the weapon!"

Olik half turned in their direction and fired blindly while diving for the stairwell. Sloan and Rebecca opened fire.

❖

"Dell!" Sandy threw herself down next to Dell. "Dell. Oh, Jesus."

"I'm okay," Dell said, wiping her forearm across the side of her face. "Just nicked me. God, Irina."

Gunfire clattered in the hall outside.

"Go," Sandy yelled, flinging herself toward Irina. "I'll take care of her."

Dell rushed across the room and ducked into the hall. Sandy pulled up Irina's blouse and pressed the heel of her hand to the ragged two-inch hole below her left collarbone. Flecks of blood streaked Irina's lips, and her breath rattled with each shallow inhalation.

Irina's eyes fluttered open. "Mitch?"

"He's okay," Sandy muttered, pressing harder as the flow of blood picked up. "Don't talk, okay? Just lie still. You'll be okay."

"Mika," Irina whispered. "My sister. Someone take care…"

"Listen," Sandy snapped, leaning over so Irina could see her face. "Shut up. You're making the bleeding worse. You'll be fine. You can take care of your sister yourself. You got it?"

Irina smiled weakly. "Mitch's girl."

"You bet your ass. Now hush." Sandy's heart dropped when Irina's eyes rolled back and she went very still. When she heard pounding footsteps behind her, she prayed it wasn't one of the Russians.

"Fuck," Watts yelled. "Fuck. Fuck."

"Do something, will you?" Sandy screamed at him.

He already had his radio out and was shouting for EMTs. Then he disappeared into the hallway, too, leaving Sandy alone in the sudden stillness.

Chapter Thirty-two

R ebecca stepped over the pool of blood where Irina's body had lain. The bitter tang of blood and cordite hung in the air and coated her throat with frustration and fury. Uniformed officers strung yellow crime scene tape over the doorways, and a police photographer and the crime scene crew, talking in hushed whispers, processed the now empty rooms.

"I'll meet you at the car," Rebecca said to Sloan, stopping outside the bedroom door where she had posted one of the state police.

"You need help with this?" Sloan asked.

"No, but do me a favor? Call Catherine for me. Tell her…" Rebecca grimaced. "Tell her I'll be home as soon as I can."

"No problem."

The other johns had already been loaded into police vans and shipped off for booking. Her duty was to deliver the priest to a waiting squad car so he could be whisked away in anonymity. She nodded to the officer on the door. "Thanks. I'll take it from here."

The Most Reverend Joseph Thomas sat on the side of the bed, glaring at her, his hands cuffed behind his back. His unbuckled belt hung over his open fly, but he'd apparently had time to get his dick back in his pants. Too bad.

"Take these things off my wrists," he demanded. "They're very uncomfortable."

"Sorry, I can't do that until you've been transferred. Then you can complain to whoever will listen about anything that's bothering you." She grabbed him by the elbow. "Let's go."

She escorted her special prisoner down the hallway to the service elevator and then through a long, deserted basement tunnel to the delivery entrance.

"I certainly hope this isn't going to take the rest of the night," he complained.

"Not much longer now." Rebecca pushed the door open and, tightening her grip, pulled him out onto the loading dock.

Immediately, the harsh glare of television spotlights lasered in on them. A dozen voices shouted and as many arms thrust microphones toward the priest. When he tried to duck away, Rebecca forced him around toward the camera lenses.

"Is it true those girls were sex slaves?"

"How much did you pay them?"

"Were they all teenagers?"

"Does the church know of your involvement?"

"How long have you been using prostitutes?"

"Father..."

"Father..."

"Father..."

Satisfied, Rebecca dragged him through the crowd and pushed him into the rear seat of a waiting patrol car.

"You! You miserable bitch! You did this!" he screamed, his handsome face distorted with outrage and disbelief.

Rebecca braced her arm on top of the car and leaned in until they were eye to eye. "No, you did this. But you're finished now."

❖

Ninety miles away, Kratos Zamora reached over his wife in bed and picked up the phone. He listened for half a minute and said, "Call me back on the other line." Then he rose, careful not to wake her, and slipped out of the bedroom.

Once in his office, he took a Cuban cigar from the humidor on his desk, clipped the end, and lit it with a gold-plated lighter. Savoring the fragrant smoke, he waited for the call to come through on the disposable, and untraceable, cell.

"Where are they taking Gregor?" he asked. "Federal? Who do we have there?"

After he got the details he needed, he said, "I'll be in touch."

He disconnected and smoked in silence for a few moments. Then he called Talia Ballenger. When she didn't answer, he hung up, removed the cable connection from his personal computer, and pressed several keys to initiate the program that would wipe the hard drive clean. After he finished his cigar, he pushed the intercom to the guard's quarters.

"Vincent. Come around to the office, would you please."

He got up and poured himself a drink, mapping out his strategy for damage control. He had learned long ago that the most powerful weapon was often the unexpected.

❖

"Dell," Sandy said in a low soothing voice, rubbing the back of Dell's neck. "Baby, you gotta try to relax."

"I fucked up," Dell muttered for the tenth time, staring between her boots at the scuffed waiting room floor. "I should've known what he was going to do. I should've gone for Olik the second they came through the door. Man, I let him take her."

"You didn't *let* him do anything." Sandy resisted the urge to shake her because she knew her head must be hurting. The two-inch gouge on her cheek wasn't serious, but a bullet wound was a bullet wound, and it had to hurt. At least Sandy had been able to force her into letting one of the nurses in the emergency room clean it out and put some butterfly bandages on it. "You went after them. You stopped him from escaping with her. You know he would've killed her if he suspected she was involved. And you couldn't know she was going to go for his gun."

"After all this, what if she dies?" Dell searched Sandy's eyes, desperately seeking reassurance. "It's so fucking unfair."

Sandy smiled softly, loving that Dell still believed that life ought to be fair. "Baby. That girl is tough. She's not going to die. Besides, you and Watts got her flown here, didn't you? That was the best thing you could have done. 'Cause you know Ali kicks ass in the OR."

"That I do," Ali said, walking up to join them. "Your friend lost a lot of blood and I had to remove a little bit of her left upper lobe, but she's got plenty of lung tissue left. In fact, she's doing so well, we'll probably pull the breathing tube tonight."

Dell grabbed Sandy's hand. "She'll be okay?"

"You know the drill. Anything could happen, but yes. I think she'll be fine."

"Can I see her?" Dell asked.

"She's pretty out of it. And she won't be able to talk to you."

"That's okay. Just for a minute?" Dell looked at Sandy. "Okay, babe?"

"Sure, rookie. You go see her."

Sandy waited until Dell left with Ali, then she called Michael. "Hey. Sloan get home?...No, we're okay. We'll be here for a little while longer." She laughed, leaned back, and closed her eyes. "Nope. Haven't changed my mind. I'll need my GED to get into the academy, though. Now *that's* scary. You will? You'll help?"

She waited a few seconds until her voice was steady. "Yeah, I get it. That's what friends do."

❖

"Hey," Dell said softly, taking Irina's cool hand in hers. "I know you're probably sleeping…"

Irina's eyes opened and slowly focused on hers.

Dell swallowed hard. "I'll be back tomorrow, but I wanted to tell you that Mika is okay. She's in a safe house."

Irina squeezed her fingers with surprising force.

"She'll be there until you get out. I'll check on her. So don't worry, okay?"

Irina's lids fluttered and she seemed to make a huge effort to keep them open. Dell saw the question in them.

"Olik is still in the operating room. He's shot up pretty good. He might make it, but even if he does, he'll be in prison for a long long time. He's not going to hurt you anymore." Dell leaned over and kissed her forehead. "Go to sleep now. You're free."

❖

Catherine watched the report of the arrests on television and then fell asleep in the living room while reading through resident admission applications. She woke at the sound of the key in the front door and set the folders aside to make room on the sofa. When Rebecca settled next to her, Catherine took her hand and leaned over to kiss her.

"You looked good on camera."

Rebecca laughed. "Just as long as he did."

"Are you going to get in trouble for that? You were the one who tipped them off, weren't you?"

"The department is happy about the positive coverage, so for the moment, nobody's asking any questions."

"Good. Because you did the right thing." Catherine curled up in Rebecca's arms and rested her head on her shoulder. "I love you."

Rebecca rubbed her cheek against Catherine's hair. "I love you too."

"What about the rest of it?"

"Well, the politics still have to play out, but the Russian girls are with Immigration—they'll be okay after all the red tape is sorted. Clark has Gregor Zamora, and you never know what the feds might get out of him. We're still processing the Russians, but if we're lucky, we'll get more names. And I dragged Flanagan out of bed to run a ballistics test for me."

Hearing the tension in Rebecca's voice, Catherine tilted her head back to study her face. Her usual sharp profile was even more rigid than usual. "What? What did you find?"

"Olik's gun is a match for the one that killed Jimmy and Jeff."

Catherine caught her breath. "God, Rebecca. You got Jeff's killer."

Rebecca held Catherine tightly. "When I drive over to Shelley Cruz's tomorrow and tell her I caught her husband's killer, do you think it's going to make her pain any less?"

"I do," Catherine said firmly. "Maybe not today. Maybe not tomorrow. But at some point she'll be ready to face the rest of her life, and she'll be able to do that because she will know that justice has been done."

"It doesn't seem like enough sometimes."

"It's all that we have." Catherine placed her hand over Rebecca's heart. "That and what we hold in here for each other."

Rebecca kissed her. "Then I have everything I need."

EPILOGUE

One Week Later

H ey, kid." Watts clapped Dell on the shoulder as he reached for a doughnut from the box Sloan dropped into the center of the conference table. "I hear your squeeze is gonna be packing heat before long."

Dell stared at him. "Gimme a minute while I translate caveman-speak."

Watts laughed. "Sandy. The academy. Cop. Gun. Jesus, there'll be no stopping her then."

"Oh yeah," Dell said. "Like there ever was."

"True," Watts said around a mouthful of jelly. He leaned back, a happy smile on his face. "Man, it feels good to be on top once in a while."

Across from him, Jason sniggered.

"What?" Watts demanded.

"Nothing. Nothing at all."

Sloan cut Jason a look. "Don't tease the infirm."

"Aww, I never get to have any fun." Jason placed a Boston crème on a napkin next to his computer.

"It sounds like you've been having plenty of fun," Sloan said. "Don't you have a little something to share with us all?"

Jason turned red. "I guess Sarah called you, huh?"

"About time too," Sloan said.

"What?" Watts looked back and forth between Sloan and Jason.

"Sarah's pregnant," Jason said, referring to his partner.

After a second of silence, Dell gave a cheer.

"Nice work," Watts said, then frowned. "So if you're gonna be a daddy, what does that make Jasmine?"

Jason grinned. "You better ask her."

Watts's laughter broke off suddenly when Rebecca appeared in the doorway of the conference room. The look on her face had him sitting up straight in his chair. "Hey, Loo."

Rebecca walked to her customary spot at the end of the table but she didn't sit down. "I just got a call from Clark."

Everyone stared at her. The air in the room grew heavy and still.

"At five fifteen this morning, Gregor Zamora was shanked in the breakfast line. He's dead."

"Holy fuck," Watts whispered.

"At six thirty when Ali Torveau was making rounds, she found Olik with his throat cut in his bathroom."

Dell bolted upright. "Irina!"

"Irina and Mika are fine. I just talked to the federal marshals. They're en route to the safe house right now. Ali said Irina was okay to travel."

"Talia Ballenger?" Sloan asked.

"Status unknown." Rebecca shrugged. "The concierge at her building says she's out of the country. Maybe he's right. Apparently she has residences on several continents."

"What about the other Russian prisoners?" Dell asked, settling back into her seat.

"We've doubled the guards on them. They probably don't know enough to be a threat to anyone important." Rebecca pulled out a chair and sat down.

"Kratos Zamora's doing?" Sloan asked.

"That would be my guess, yes," Rebecca said.

"His own brother," Jason murmured.

"What do we do?" Dell asked.

"Nothing," Rebecca said. "The crimes will be investigated. Someone may even be found accountable. But as to who really gave the order? We'll never be able to prove it."

"What's the point, then?" Dell demanded angrily. "Everything we did. The people we put in danger. For what? Is this justice?"

"Justice is fleeting," Rebecca said quietly. "But we did our jobs.

That's what counts. Irina and her sister have new identities, a chance for a new life. The other girls aren't being abused anymore. We put a big hole in the Russian operation."

Dell stared at the table. "We're always one step behind because we have to play by the rules and they don't."

"You're absolutely right. We play by the rules, at least all the ones that matter, because if we don't, we're no different than them." Rebecca looked around the table. "Anybody want out? Because this is just the lull between innings."

Sloan looked at Jason, who nodded sharply.

"We're in," Sloan said.

"Fucking A," Watts said.

"Yes ma'am," Dell declared.

"Good. We got close to Zamora once, and we can do it again." Rebecca's eyes gleamed fiercely. "And I promise you this. When this game is over, we will be the winners."

About the Author

Radclyffe is a retired surgeon and full-time award-winning author-publisher with over thirty lesbian novels and anthologies in print. Five of her works have been Lambda Literary finalists including the Lambda Literary winners *Erotic Interludes 2: Stolen Moments* edited with Stacia Seaman and *Distant Shores, Silent Thunder*. She is the editor of *Best Lesbian Romance* 2009 and 2010 (Cleis Press), *Erotic Interludes* 2 through 5 and *Romantic Interludes 1: Discovery* with Stacia Seaman (BSB), and has selections in multiple anthologies including *Best Lesbian Erotica* 2006, 7, 8, and 9; *After Midnight*; *Caught Looking: Erotic Tales of Voyeurs and Exhibitionists*; *First-Timers*; *Ultimate Undies: Erotic Stories About Lingerie and Underwear*; *Hide and Seek*; *A is for Amour*; *H is for Hardcore*; *L is for Leather*; and *Rubber Sex*. She is the recipient of the 2003 and 2004 Alice B. Readers' award for her body of work and is also the president of Bold Strokes Books, one of the world's largest independent LGBT publishing companies.

Her latest release is an all-Radclyffe erotica anthology, *Radical Encounters* (Feb 2009), and her forthcoming 2009 romances include *Secrets in the Stone* and *Returning Tides*.

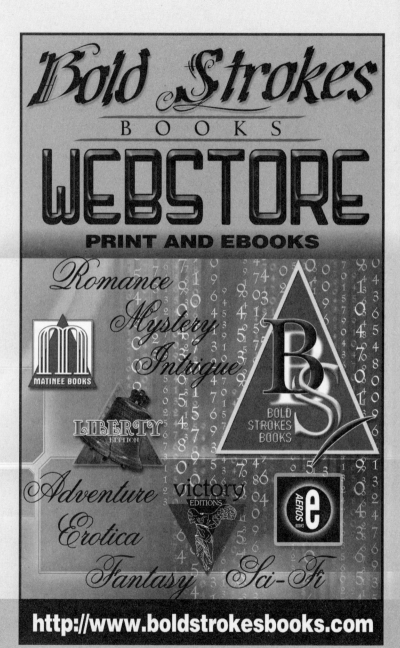